THE Newsstand

A Novel of Little Italy

J.J. Anselmo

First Edition printed in the United States of America at McNally Jackson Books, 52 Prince Street, New York, NY 10012. www.mcnallyjackson.com/product/newsstand

For the late Frank "Frankie" Toledo, a great pal from my days in New York's Little Italy; and for my late mother, Angie, who guided me throughout her long life and always encouraged me to be the best that I could be.

Acknowledgements

I would like to acknowledge my friend and former coworker, George Baker, for urging and encouraging me to write this book. I would also like to acknowledge Robin Rushfield for her research assistance and her help in designing the book's cover, which was artistically rendered and transformed by Suzanne Vidal. I would like to thank my daughter-in-law, Jaimee Taylor, my son, John, and my daughter, Diane, for their assistance and support throughout the writing process. Additionally, my wife, Mary, is deserving of a lot of credit for she converted my hand-written manuscript into a typed version – all 143,000 words of it – which was quite a task.

I am grateful for the guiding influence of Christine Zika during the early stages of the writing process, and to Gary Roebuck, my former high school classmate, who skillfully copy-edited the final draft of my manuscript.

Also, I owe a debt of gratitude to the following ophthalmologists for the medical knowledge, insight and advice that they provided, which was of immeasurable help to me in describing the complex ophthalmologic issues relating to one of the central characters in the book:

- Robert M. Sinskey, M.D., former Clinical Professor of Ophthalmology at the Jules Stein Institute at UCLA. He was an ophthalmic pioneer, inventing several instruments, including the widely-used Sinskey Hook. In the 1950s, his research of the Hiroshima bombing victims contributed to the body of medical knowledge of radiation-induced cataracts. He patiently conveyed to me a great deal of information regarding cataracts, and in particular, how cataract surgery was done in the 1930s.

- Anthony C. Castelbuono, M.D., Baltimore, Maryland, a distant cousin; a graduate of Harvard University with a medical degree from Johns Hopkins University, he is affiliated with Sinai of Baltimore.

Preface

Little Italy, New York: a place in my mind; a place in my heart. The Little Italy of which I have written is the Little Italy of the late '50s and early '60s—a true neighborhood, in contrast to its present-day form. The Little Italy of today is merely a façade, providing the backdrop for numerous Italian restaurants, shops and trendy boutiques because few Italian-American youths of my generation chose to remain in the neighborhood. Most fled the tenements for the promise of a better life in suburbia, typically upon getting married.

The Little Italy of the '50s and '60s was a predominantly Italian-American enclave bounded by East Houston Street to the north, The Bowery on the east side, Canal Street to the south, and Lafayette Street on the west side. It was, by most standards, a pretty tough neighborhood; a neighborhood that had numerous social clubs where young wannabe hoods would gather in hope of gaining favor with the various *capos* and "men of respect" whom they idolized; a neighborhood where most of the police officers and their superiors were "on the take," thereby allowing gambling, loan- sharking and other petty criminal activities to exist out in the open; and a neighborhood where having street smarts and being able to handle oneself in a fight equated to respect, while being a good student with an interest in academic pursuits was looked down upon by most of the neighborhood youths.

Numerous books have been written—both fictional and nonfictional—about the various mobsters who used Little Italy as their base of operations, beginning at the turn of the 19th Century, when hordes of Southern Italians left their beautiful country in search of a better life, and extending to the latter decades of the 20th Century. I have chosen not to follow that well-trodden path, with its predictable and formulaic plot lines. Instead, I have sought to present an insiders view of "the neighborhood"—as most residents referred to it—from the perspective of a rowdy, fun-loving, sometimes obnoxious and sometimes delinquent group of teenage boys who "hang out" at a neighborhood corner newsstand in the late 1950s and early 1960s. The proprietor of the newsstand, Joe, a middle-aged blind man, captivates the teenagers through his magnetic and complex personality, which could range from avuncular, to mischievous, to downright mean and nasty. Though his moral compass is somewhat skewed, he usually—but not always—points the youths in the right direction, as he lives vicariously through them, adding some joy to his dark and dull life.

The protagonist, John-John, is an intellectually gifted and studious teenager who is seeking to "fit in" with the neighborhood youths while steadfastly pursuing academics and ultimately, an Ivy League education. Fitting in wasn't easy on the "mean streets" of the neighborhood if one were a little different from the rest. (The label "mean streets" would later become the title of a Martin Scorsese movie about the very same neighborhood.) As hard as it may have been for John-John to fit in, fitting in was even harder for Zeke Daniels, a Tennessee "hillbilly," who settles in Little Italy soon after World War II to please his Neapolitan war bride—a woman who could never quite escape her prostitute past.

Since the story deals with teenagers coming of age, much of the story has sexual content. It relates to testosterone-charged teenage boys seeking their first conquests; but it is also a story about four Catholic high school girls who wrestle with their blossoming sexuality, and the morals and virtues inculcated upon them by their families and the Catholic Church. Parallel to the story of teenage love is the story of an adult love triangle, which plays a pivotal role in the plot.

As I grew up and began to meet people from all over the country, I came to realize that my childhood and adolescent experiences were remarkably different from theirs. Their neighborhoods didn't have storefronts that served as numbers drops, or places that sold hijacked goods *only* to neighborhood people; and they didn't have members of the Five Families conducting mob business on their corners. Initially, my intention was to write a memoir, but the work evolved into a novel. All characters are "composite characters," typically inspired by, or having the attributes of, a combination of various neighborhood individuals whom I have known. The names of the characters, including nicknames, are fictitious; however, nicknames used may, by coincidence, be common to other individuals from the old neighborhood. The newsstand that serves as the backdrop for the novel actually existed. It was demolished in 1974, but one can still see its footprint in the concrete sidewalk patch on the northeast corner of Spring and Lafayette Streets.

In writing this slice-of-life novel, I have endeavored to "recapture" the essence, fabric and ethos of that famous—or as some might say, *infamous*—Italian-American enclave that existed in Manhattan about a half-century ago.

Chapter 1: Boom!

Blood was oozing out of Joe Sorrentino's head as his slumping body was being propped up inside his newsstand by one of the many teenage boys who hung-out at the stand. Joe had heard the loud boom of the gunshot at almost the same instant that the bullet lodged near his right temple. He had not seen the bullet coming. How could he? The middle-aged man was blind.

About seven minutes after the shooting, the blaring siren of an ambulance could be heard in the distance, getting increasingly louder, overpowering the unusual quiet of the neighborhood— New York's Little Italy. It was the Saturday before the Christmas of 1963. The normal din of the neighborhood was tempered by the 15-degree frigidity of the noon hour. The ambulance, which was speeding south on Lafayette Street, came into view when it passed Prince Street with its red lights flashing. It soon came to a screeching stop alongside the newsstand. Two paramedics bolted out of the red-and-white Cadillac and did their best to usher away the concerned teenagers crowding the newsstand. They quickly bandaged the wounded man's head, noting that most of the blood was coming from a nasty gash on his forehead, which one of the teens told them he had suffered when he fell upon his nearby metal stool right after being shot.

The paramedics carefully placed Joe on the wheel-supported stretcher. He was lapsing in and out of consciousness, barely aware of the words of encouragement offered by several of the onlookers. He was a pitiful sight to behold. His baldpate was streaked with blood. His 5'-3" frame appeared to be even smaller in contrast to the lengthy stretcher. Two visibly shaken neighborhood women made the Sign of the Cross as the stretcher was locked into place in the cavernous rear of the hearse-like ambulance. One of those women, Serafina, a former Neapolitan prostitute, was already in a numbed state when she had come upon the scene because she was in the midst of the worst week of her life since her terrifying days in war-torn Naples.

The slamming of the ambulance's rear door spurred Joe back into full consciousness, at which point the attending paramedic heard him moan, "Why me, God? Why me? Haven't you given me a big enough cross to carry, already?"

His mind then flashed back to that fateful Sunday in May 1934 when his life had suddenly veered off course, moving from a life filled with happiness and joy towards a life filled with darkness and despair. Seconds later, he fell totally out of consciousness, becoming completely oblivious to the 100-decibel siren as the ambulance hurriedly wove through the holiday traffic en route to St. Vincent's Hospital in nearby Greenwich Village.

Chapter 2: The Bronx, 1934

Young Joe Sorrentino lay in bed shielding his eyes from the sunlight filtering through the shades. He squinted at the clock as he rubbed his gummy eyes, but he couldn't see the hands, even though the clock was within a foot of his face on the night table. He was extremely nearsighted. The world was a total blur to him without his "Coke bottle" eyeglasses.

"Where the fuck are my glasses," he mumbled.

After fumbling around the night table, he found his glasses and was surprised to see that it was already 9:30—an hour later than he would normally have awakened on a Sunday morning. But, he had needed the sleep, having gone to bed at about 2 a.m. after the biggest day of his life. He had "popped the question" to his lovely girlfriend of three years, Virginia Mancuso, on Saturday evening. Virginia, like Joe was nineteen years old. She had said "yes" to his proposal without any hesitation and was totally in love with the half-carat diamond engagement ring he had placed on her finger. May 19, 1934 would be a day forever engraved in their hearts.

After slipping on a pair of pants, he groggily made his way into the kitchen, where his mother was busily preparing Sunday's dinner, which would be served at two. His parents, who were both born in Naples, tried to maintain Italian traditions as much as possible, including having the main meal of the day—*il pranzo*—in the early afternoon. Although, doing so didn't fit into the American fifty-hour, six-day work schedule, there was no problem keeping that tradition on Sunday afternoons.

It was easy for Giuseppe and Costanza Sorrentino to retain their Italian identity in their adopted country because they had chosen to live right in the center of an Italian enclave. Their apartment on 2363 Arthur Avenue, at East 186th Street, was in the heart of New York City's *other* Little Italy. Although the city's more famous Little Italy was centered around Manhattan's Mulberry Street, the Little Italy of Arthur Avenue in the Bronx was every bit its equal, except in size. Arthur Avenue was sprinkled with Italian restaurants, bakeries, pastry shops, pork stores, and various shops that specialized in all kinds of Italian delicacies. On Arthur Avenue, one could get by without speaking English. Most of the neighborhood people were fluent in one of the southern Italian dialects. In the Sorrentino household, the Neapolitan dialect was the language of choice, although it would usually be punctuated with spurts of English.

Joe was glad to see the *New York Sunday News* lying on the kitchen counter because he loved to read the Sports Section. His father, an early riser, had gone down, as usual, to buy the newspaper before breakfast. As Joe's mother was frying a couple of eggs and toasting some Italian bread for him, he asked, "Where's Papa?"

"Oh, he just left. He's down at Carlo's Social Club, probably playing *briscola* with his friends."

Briscola is an old Italian card game that pits two teams of two players against each other. The players typically use pre-arranged signals and code words to assist each other in trying to beat the other team. Missed signals would usually lead to emotional outbursts by one or the other partner, which sometimes would result in cards being angrily thrown on the table, accompanied by some typically-Italian hand gestures. But, all would usually be forgotten after a couple of shots of Sambuca or Grappa. For Joe's father and his fellow *paisani*, the card game was just a Sunday morning pastime, since hardly any money would be wagered.

Joe picked up the main section of the newspaper and quickly thumbed his way to the Sports Section. He already knew that his Yankees had beaten the Detroit Tigers on Saturday by a score of 8 to 3, but he wanted to savor the details. He was happy to see that his favorite player, Tony Lazzeri, had belted a home run. Joe, despite having to wear very thick eyeglasses, was an excellent sandlot-level second baseman. It was only natural for him to idolize Lazzeri, the slick-fielding, solid-hitting, Yankee second baseman, because, for one, he was *the* Yankee second baseman—and perhaps more important— because he was an Italian-American.

He checked the standings. The Yankees were off to a great start, winning 18 of their first 26 games. They were in first place, holding a four-game lead over the second-place Tigers. He was optimistic that the Yankees were on their way to winning another World Series, although he wondered if 39-year-old Babe Ruth would be much of a force on this year's team.

As Joe ate his breakfast, he continued to peruse the sports pages because world events were of little interest to him. Occasionally, his mind would wander from what he was reading to thoughts of last evening's marriage proposal. He wanted to tell his mother the "good news" but he decided to stick to his original plan: to announce his engagement to his parents during *pranzo*, with Virginia at his side. Although neither of Joe's parents had had any inkling that their son—an only child—would be getting engaged, Virginia's parents had become aware of Joe's intentions a week earlier. Joe, in keeping with Italian tradition, had approached Signor Mancuso when Virginia was not at home, and he had asked him for his approval. After making Joe squirm for nearly a minute—an eternity in Joe's mind—Signor Mancuso nodded his head in approval, saying, "Joe, if Virginia will have you, I'll be happy to welcome you into the family as my son."

Joe was elated. Signor Mancuso was also elated because he really liked Joe, and—perhaps, more important—because the *eldest* of his four daughters would be the first one to the altar. He had always wanted a son, but after his fourth daughter was born, his wife, Jenny, had told him *basta*—enough—no more children! Signor Mancuso, who had known Joe's parents back in Naples, considered them to be *cugini*—cousins—even though they were not blood relatives. Since he had always been fond of Joe, he was more than pleased to welcome him into his family.

Joe donned his best Sunday outfit—a dark blue pinstriped woolen suit, a white-on-white dress shirt and a bright red-and-white tie. He completed the outfit with black wing-tip shoes. He gazed at himself in the mirror and was quite satisfied with his appearance. As he combed his wavy dark brown hair, he decided to forego wearing his fedora since the temperature was about 70 degrees. Besides, he liked the way he looked without a hat rather than with one. He felt that when he was sporting his fedora, his short stature was more obvious than when he went hatless. At only 5'-3", he was very self-conscious of his height. Since Virginia was barely 5 feet tall, she had to look up at him—which pleased his male ego.

He left his apartment at just before eleven. Within five minutes, he was standing in front of Virginia's building on the corner of the East 187th Street and Belmont Avenue — just three short blocks away from his building. After a short wait, Virginia exited from the hallway and greeted him with a kiss.

"How's the future Mrs. Sorrentino feelin' today?"

"Oh, Joe, I just gotta be the happiest girl in the neighborhood."

They then walked diagonally across the street to Our Lady of Mount Carmel Church—a formidable structure faced with light brown bricks, and the principal Roman Catholic church in the neighborhood.

They just managed to find a couple of seats in the last pew because the church was nearly filled with parishioners awaiting the start of the 11:15 mass. The priest's homily was somewhat hard to follow, but the organ music and choir were spiritually uplifting. Towards the end of the mass, both Joe and Virginia, dedicated Catholics, positioned themselves at the end of one of the lines and slowly walked down the central aisle to receive Holy Communion.

When the mass ended, Joe suggested, "Let's walk over to the Hughes Avenue park and hang out for a while. I wanna show the guys your engagement ring."

So, they strolled over to the site of the park that was being constructed between Hughes Avenue and Arthur Avenue, along East 188th Street. Joe knew that at around 12:30, many of his friends would begin playing a pickup game of baseball on the site of the future park. The park, which would be named Ciccarone Park, was about two months short of completion. It was not intended to be a baseball field, but at this stage of the construction, it could serve as a makeshift baseball field since it was mostly a dirt-covered level area with some stockpiled construction materials at several locations. It would have been more suitable in size for softball than hardball, but all the players had their minds set at playing hardball. Each and every player was a Yankees wannabe. They wanted to emulate the Yankees, who in less than an hour would be taking the field to play the Indians in Cleveland.

Joe and Virginia entered the field through an opening in the fence on Hughes Avenue as the players were taking batting practice. They walked along the chain-link construction fence to a point in foul territory, adjacent to first base. Soon, Joe's best friend, Nicky "Moon" sauntered over to the couple. Joe couldn't wait to give Nicky the good news. At Joe's prompting, Virginia proudly showed Nicky her engagement ring, which sparkled brilliantly in the afternoon sunshine.

"Congratulations to both of yous!"

"Nicky, I want you to be my best man. Whatta ya say?"

"Joe, how could I say 'no'? We been like brothers for as long as I can remember."

"Thanks, Nicky."

Joe and Virginia had their backs to the ball field while they were talking to Nicky, who was leaning up against the fence, occasionally glancing at the batter. A split-second after Joe had said "Thanks, Nicky," a line drive whistled towards the three.

"Look out!" yelled Nicky.

Unfortunately, before Joe could react, the whizzing baseball hit him squarely on the back of the head, making a loud but hollow sound—like that of a wooden mallet striking a dead tree limb. He instantly fell forward, forcefully hitting his forehead on a steel fence post; then, recoiling and spinning around, he fell hard upon the ground, first landing on his backside and then whipping his head upon a couple of bricks—miscellaneous construction debris. He lay unconscious, not moving a muscle. There was a great deal of commotion around his still body. Virginia and Nicky were frozen in a state of shock. Finally, one of the guys ran over to a nearby candy store to call for an ambulance. After being knocked out for three-to-four minutes, Joe slowly began to regain consciousness. By the time the ambulance arrived—ten minutes later—he was back on his feet, obviously dazed, but seemingly okay, despite some blood on the back of his head.

"How do you feel young man?" asked the medic.

"Not bad…but my head hurts a little."

The medic felt the bump on Joe's forehead and the one on the back of his head. The forehead bump was already quite evident, but the medic did not seem too concerned about it.

"Let me see you walk ten steps away from me, and then walk back."

Joe dutifully complied.

"Good…Now wave your arms for me and then move your head around in a circle."

"How'd I do?"

"You did good…One more thing, how's your vision?"

"Lousy…but it's always lousy without my eyeglasses…Virginia, where the hell are my glasses?"

"They fell off your head when you hit the ground…Here they are, Sweetheart."

When he put on his eyeglasses, he smiled at the medic and said, "Ah, I can see you clearly, now," adding, "By the way, I think you could stand to lose a few pounds."

Everyone laughed, including the overweight medic. Virginia was relieved. *Her Joe*, who was known to be quite a kidder, seemed to be back to his normal self.

"Well, you have two choices…We can take you to the hospital for observation, or you can go home, put a couple of ice bags on your head and take two aspirins every four hours."

"How long would I have to stay in the hospital?"

"They'll, probably, keep you overnight, and if all is well, they'll release you before noon, tomorrow."

After mulling over his options for about ten seconds, Joe replied, "Nah, I'd rather go home."

"Okay, but if you get dizzy or have problems movin' your arms or legs, go to the Emergency Room as soon as possible."

"Okay…and thanks for your help."

Charlie "Fish", who had hit the line drive, was quite relieved to see Joe walking away from the terrible incident. However, the horrible sound of the baseball hitting Joe's head would forever be etched in Charlie's memory.

Walking arm-in-arm, Joe and Virginia slowly walked the two-and-a-half blocks to his apartment building. He found the three-story climb to be a little taxing, but manageable. He entered the apartment with a forced smile on his face, but his mother quickly zeroed-in on the bump on his forehead.

"Oh God, what happened?"

"Mama, I was accidentally hit with a baseball in the back of the head…But I'm okay."

"Are you sure you're okay?"

"Yeah, just give me a couple of aspirins and let me put some ice on it."

"Let me have a look at your head," demanded his father.

After about twenty seconds of checking Joe's head for bumps and bruises, Giuseppe declared, "He'll be all right…Let's sit down in the parlor until it's time to eat."

At 2 o'clock, Costanza called everyone into the kitchen for *pranzo*. After grace was said, the plates of antipasto were passed around the table. As Giuseppe picked up a piece of provolone cheese with his fork, Joe announced that he had something important to tell his parents.

"What is it, Joe?" asked Costanza.

"I have asked Virginia to marry me, and she said 'yes'…Show them the engagement ring I gave you, Virginia."

Virginia stood up and first walked over to Costanza so that she could get a close-up view of the ring.

"*Bella…Auguri,*" which is to say, "Beautiful…Congratulations." Virginia smiled and replied, "*Grazie.*"

You know, Virginia, I spotted that ring as soon as you walked through the door, but I was so concerned about Joe, that I didn't ask you about it."

Giuseppe—a typical male—hadn't noticed the ring until it had been brought to his attention. He carefully examined it when Virginia placed her hand in front of him and he repeated, verbatim, what his wife had just said. Then he added, "My wife had always longed for a daughter, and now she will have a fine one. My son couldn't have found a better girl to marry if he had searched the entire world three times over! Welcome to the family! Raise your wine glasses…*Cin-Cin*…to a wonderful future together."

"Have you and Joe set a date for the weddin', Virginia?" "No, but I'm thinkin' we should get married in about a year." Joe added, "Yeah, maybe someday in next May would be good. I'll try to save up as much money as I can…You know I don't get paid much at the automobile battery shop where I work."

"Don't worry Joe, I know my father will pay for most of the weddin'."

"And we'll give yous a big weddin' gift. We're not rich, but we've been savin' money for this day a long time."

Although Joe's head ached throughout the rest of the day, he felt significantly better on Monday morning—at least, good enough to go to work. He realized that with marriage on the horizon, he couldn't afford to miss a day of work. He would need every penny he could possibly earn. He was even considering getting a second job, but he knew it would be hard to find one given the tough economic times of the day; after all, the nation was still in the midst of the Great Depression.

Chapter 3: A Life-Changer

No one reconditions automobile batteries anymore. In our present "throw-away" society, it would not be cost effective to do so; but back in the 1930's, it was standard practice. Typically, battery reconditioning would entail taking apart a battery's outer casing; carefully draining the sulfuric acid from the battery; removing and cleaning the interior lead plates; and scraping-off and removing up to a 1/2"-thick accumulation of reddish-gray lead oxide residue at the bottom of the battery case. This mushy, caustic residue, a byproduct of the lead plate and acid interaction, would short-out a battery if allowed to accumulate beyond a ½"-thickness.

Joe was at work at the AA Automobile Battery Repair Shop on Belmont Avenue. It was Monday morning, May 16th. He felt a little groggy from his lack of sleep the night before. His daughter, Anna, whose second birthday was just three days away, had kept him and his pregnant wife awake throughout much of the night as they tried to deal with her 103-degree fever. Fortunately, the little girl's temperature had broken in the morning. It appeared that Anna would be feeling fine on her birthday, which coincidentally, would be the same day that Joe and Virginia would be celebrating their third wedding anniversary. They had gotten married on Sunday, May 19, 1935, exactly one year after Joe's marriage proposal. The wedding had taken place at Our Lady of Mount Carmel Church and shortly after the ceremony, a reception was held at the local Knights of Columbus hall.

More than 250 well-wishers had crowded into the Knights of Columbus hall to honor Joe and Virginia. The hall was legally limited to an occupancy of 180 people, but no one seemed to care about the occupancy limit or the lack of elbowroom. As was typical for that time period, the guests were not treated to a sit-down dinner or a buffet; rather, they were served homemade sandwiches on hard rolls, wrapped in white paper. Members of the newlywed's extended families distributed the wrapped sandwiches to the guests from large cardboard boxes. Such wedding receptions had come to be known as "football weddings." The name evolved from the manner in which the sandwiches were distributed and passed around among the guests. Usually, the sandwiches, which came in five or six varieties, would be dumped on every table without any concern for the guests' desires as to choice. So, it was inevitable that some guests would go around the hall from table to table trying to find sandwiches to their liking. Typically, one would hear a guest yell out, "I've got a ham-and-cheese I wanna trade for a salami sandwich. Anybody wanna trade?"

"Here you go!" might be the reply from a half-drunk guest who would proceed to toss his unwanted salami sandwich across several tables. A couple of seconds later, the ham-and-cheese sandwich would come flying back in return. With many sandwiches being tossed to and fro, the moniker, "football wedding," seemed to be quite appropriate.

Joe's mind began to wander while he was disassembling a battery. He thought about how he would have liked to celebrate his wedding anniversary in a big way, but with one toddler and another child due in four months, it was quite clear to him that there was no way that he and Virginia could go on a second honeymoon— especially given the meager salary that he earned. It was painfully obvious to him that their one-week honeymoon in Niagara Falls would be their last vacation for a long time.

As he began to pour out the caustic sulfuric acid from the disassembled battery casing, he misjudged the location of the beaker into which he was to pour the acid. Some of the acid bounced off the countertop and onto his left hand, causing an instantaneous burning sensation that made him wince. He immediately sprang across the shop to the slop sink and ran cold water on his hand for a couple of minutes. He shook his head in disbelief at his clumsiness. In his four years working at the battery shop, something like that had never happened to him. In fact, he was so self-assured of his expertise that he had long ago given up wearing gloves on the job.

Placing his hand quickly under cold running water had minimized the damage to his skin. There would likely be little or no permanent scarring. After regaining his composure, he put on a pair of work gloves and cleaned up the countertop with a cotton rag. He then proceeded to clean the lead plates of the dismantled battery and remove the mushy lead-oxide residue. At that point, the shop owner, Luigi, walked by and casually looked at Joe's work product.

"Hey, Joey, I've noticed that you been doin' a sloppy job lately. Maybe, it's time for new eyeglasses."

Luigi's comment took Joe by surprise, for he believed that he was doing his usual first-class job.

"Luigi, you must be kiddin' me. The lead plates and the bottom of case look clean to me."

"Joey, you know I got a good sense of humor…but you also know that I never, never joke about work. I take my job very seriously. If the word should ever get out that my reconditioned batteries are unreliable, I'll be out of business in no time…So, do us both a favor and go over to the eyeglass store on Arthur Avenue after work and get your eyes examined by the opto…opto…"

"The optometrist?" interjected Joe.

"Yeah, that's what you call those guys…optometrists."

"Okay, Luigi, I'll go."

Joe readily agreed because he realized that his vision had been getting progressively worse over the past year—with the vision of his left eye being blurrier and cloudier than that of his right.

"Joey, leave work two hours early so you'll be sure to see the optometrist, today. Don't worry; I won't dock you for the two hours. After all, it's to my advantage that you should wear the right glasses…I don't know how much thicker they can make your glasses… They're already fuckin' Coke bottles," added Luigi with a grin.

Joe arrived at the eyeglass store at a few minutes past three. The store was located diagonally across the street from the building where he had lived with his parents until he married. The owner and optometrist, Doctor Quattrocchi—which, ironically translates from Italian to English to Doctor

Four-Eyes—had been examining Joe's eyes and fitting him with eyeglasses for as long as Joe could remember.

Joe greeted the optician behind the counter, whom he knew quite well. "Hey, Vinnie, is the Doc in? I need an eye exam. My vision has gotten worse, lately."

"Yeah, Joe, he'll be able to see you in about ten minutes."

Twenty minutes later, Joe was summoned to the examination room in the back of the store. Dr. Quattrocchi, an old-world gentleman in his mid-60s, who had emigrated from Naples around the turn of the century, greeted him warmly. The gray-haired, bespectacled doctor spoke English with a refined Italian accent, indicative of an educated man.

"Joe, what's the problem?"

"Well, I been noticing that my vision has been gettin' worse… kind of blurry and cloudy."

"When did you first notice this?"

"It's hard to say…maybe, a year ago. I should've come in sooner, Doc, but I been busy. My wife and my little daughter take up most of my free time…even more now, since Virginia is pregnant again and due to give birth in about four months."

"Joe, as you know, you are very, very nearsighted…what we optometrists refer to as a minus 13 correction…Well, let me take a look."

As Dr. Quattrocchi examined Joe's eyes in the darkened room, he heard him utter, "Hmm," several times. Joe immediately stiffened up, sensing that something was wrong.

"Joe, it's hard to believe, but I'm quite sure you've developed cataracts in both eyes…The left eye appears to be worse than the right eye."

"Cataracts? I've heard of cataracts, but I'm not quite sure what they are…Plus, I thought that only *old* people got 'em."

"A cataract is a clouding of the lens of the eye. The lens is behind the cornea and the iris. It works similar to a camera lens. It focuses light onto the retina, which to put it simply, acts like the film of a camera…Here, look at this model of the eye and you will better understand what I just told you. By the way, it's true that cataracts mostly develop in older people, but there are exceptions."

After looking at the model, which was about the size of a softball, Joe, who still didn't comprehend the situation, asked, "Do I need stronger glasses, Doc?"

"No, stronger eyeglasses won't solve your problem. You need to see an ophthalmologist who specializes in cataract surgery. I recommend that you get examined by Dr. Giovanni Montefusco. His office is in Manhattan, and he performs surgery at the New York Eye and Ear Infirmary. He's a good friend of mine, and a *paisano,* who studied at the University of Bologna. He's considered to be one of the best eye surgeons in New York. I'll make the arrangements. He is a very busy man, but I'm sure that he'll see you next week as a favor to me."

Dr. Quattrocchi managed to get Joe an appointment with Dr. Montefusco for the Wednesday of the following week. Joe and Virginia, arrived at the doctor's office at 3 o'clock on that Wednesday—a half-hour before Joe's appointment. They were both very nervous because of the gravity of Joe's problem, and had allotted extra time for their subway commute to ensure that they would not be late for the appointment with the prestigious doctor. The doctor's office was located in a well-maintained brownstone building on East 15th Street between First and Second Avenues, within three blocks of the New York Eye and Ear Infirmary.

Dr. Montefusco was the type of doctor who gave his patients his complete attention, thoroughly explaining proposed medical procedures and answering all questions. Consequently, his appointment schedule would usually slip through the course of the day. After an hour-and-a-half in the waiting room, Joe's name was finally called.

"It's about time!"

His palms were sweating and his heart was pounding as he and Virginia were ushered into the examination room. After a cordial exchange of greetings and pleasantries, Dr. Montefusco asked Joe some questions relating to his vision problem. He then began to examine Joe's eyes and within several minutes, he confirmed Dr. Quattrocchi's preliminary assessment.

"Mr. Sorrentino, I'm sorry to tell you that you have cataracts in both eyes. The cataract in your left eye is more advanced than the one in your right eye...I see from your chart that you are twenty-three years old. It's rare for cataracts to develop in young people. Sometimes cataracts are inherited…perhaps, one of your ancestors back in Italy had cataracts at an early age. In rare cases, cataracts can be caused by trauma to the eye, or even trauma to the head. I can tell that you haven't suffered any eye trauma, but have you ever had any head trauma?"

He thought for a while. "Actually, I don't know what you mean by 'trauma.'"

"Well, Mr. Sorrentino…"

"Doc, please call me 'Joe.' Mr. Sorrentino is my father."

"Okay, Joe, trauma is just a fancy medical term for injury. So, to put it simply, did you ever get hit in the head?"

"Yeah, about four years ago…on May 20th to be exact…I got hit in the head with a baseball while Virginia and I were on the field just before the start of a ballgame. The reason I can remember the date is that I had given Virginia her engagement ring the night before. We were well outside the foul line, showing off the engagement ring to my best friend, Nicky 'Moon,' when I was hit in the back of the head with a line drive."

"What happened next?"

"I fell forward, hittin' the front of my head, hard…real hard… on a steel fence post…and then I fell backwards, hittin' the back of my head on a couple of bricks on the ground. I was knocked unconscious, Doc… unconscious."

After listening to the rest of Joe's account of the incident, the doctor said, "Well, Joe, I cannot say for sure, but getting hit with the baseball, plus striking your head on the fence post and then the ground could—and I must emphasize *could*—could be the underlying cause of your cataracts. On the other hand, the whole baseball incident may be irrelevant. You just may have been destined to develop cataracts for reasons we doctors do not understand."

Joe stiffened his lips and stared at the ceiling. After about thirty seconds of silence, during which his thoughts ranged from, *Why me?* to *I've got to take it like a man*, Joe uttered, "How do you fix the problem, Doc?"

"If we do nothing, you'll go blind in the near future. First you will lose your vision in the left eye because that cataract is more advanced than that of your right eye. Then, perhaps a year later, you will lose the vision in your right eye."

"Oh my God!" exclaimed Virginia.

"Don't get yourself too excited, Virginia, the doctor is explaining what would happen if we *don't* do nuttin about the cataracts… right, Doc?"

"Right. Don't worry, Virginia, let me finish what I have to say and then you'll realize that things aren't so bad."

"Sorry, Doctor, I just couldn't help it. I'm so nervous."

"I understand, Virginia…Now, I want to explain that a person who becomes blind as a result of cataracts can distinguish day from night, and can usually see shadows. So, that person is not living in a world of total blackness. However, such a person is functionally blind in that he or she would not be able to do most of the things that a normal sighted person could do…But, the good news is that we can remove the cataracts by performing eye surgery."

"Oh, those are the best words I've heard so far," Joe sighed in relief.

"I will spare you the details of the operation, but suffice it to say that you won't feel a thing. I will remove the cataract from your left eye, and about six months later, I'll perform the same operation on your right eye. I want you to know that the worst aspect of the cataract surgery is the post-operative recovery phase."

"Whatta ya mean, Doc?"

"Well, you will have to lay perfectly still on your back for ten days—and I mean *perfectly still*. To keep you from moving your head, we will place sand bags on the left and right sides of your head. Your eyes will have to remain completely covered during the ten days. You'll be fed, by hand, a non-constipating diet, and drink through a straw. Your wastes will be deposited in a bed pan. Your body will be cleaned to some extent, but since the object is not to move you… actually, to keep your eyeballs totally immobilized…you will, quite frankly, begin to stink to high heaven. To make things worse, there will likely be three other people with you in the Recovery Room who will be in the same situation. The odors in that room are so bad that the nurses usually refer to it as the 'Rotting Room.' However, the sense of smell is such that after a day or so, the patients become totally used to the stench…they become oblivious to it.”

“Oh, boy. Oh, boy…And to think, I have to go through this twice. Can't you operate on both eyes at the same time?”

“No, that's not standard medical practice.”

“What happens after the ten–day recovery?” inquired Virginia.

“Well, assuming that he doesn't get an eye infection, pneumonia or some other complication, he will be able to see through the use of very thick eyeglasses. Now when I say very thick eyeglasses, I mean *very thick* eyeglasses. Joe, you must think that your eyeglasses are very thick, but let me show you what kind of glasses our patients typically would wear after cataract surgery.”

Dr. Montefusco grabbed a pair of ultra-thick eyeglasses from the shelf to his right and handed them to Joe, who remarked, “Some of my friends tease me about my thick glasses. They call 'em ‘Coke bottles.’ What the hell are they gonna call these?”

“Actually, many of my colleagues and I usually refer to *these* glasses as ‘Coke-bottle cataract glasses’. You can probably understand that a person wearing such glasses would lose some peripheral vision.”

“What's peripheral vision?”

“It's the vision to the sides. The effect of looking through these glasses would be, somewhat, like looking through a tunnel, but not quite so bad. Patients quickly learn to compensate by moving their heads rather than their eyes.”

“Oh, what a way to go through life…walkin' around with those freaky-lookin' glasses.”

“That may be true, Joe, but it certainly beats going through life as a blind man…Now, I don't want you to get your hopes too high, but in your particular case, there is a fair chance that you may not need to wear the ‘Coke-bottle glasses’ after the operation. The fact that you are so severely nearsighted might work in your favor. When we remove the lens from your eye…which is what we actually do in cataract surgery…you might be one of those very few lucky people who would actually see better without the lens than with the lens. To truly understand how this could be, you would need to have a knowledge of optics and a knowledge of the structure of the eye.

Therefore, I believe that the medical explanation is a bit too complicated for me to explain to you, but suffice it to say that the bottom line is that not only might the surgery save your vision, it might improve your vision. But, don't count on that happening. Please don't. Such a thing only has happened to two of my cataract patients in my thirty-year career. However, in your favor is the fact that the degree of nearsightedness of both of those patients was quite similar to yours. Unfortunately, I cannot predict what will happen in your case. The surgery will provide the answer."

"When should I have the surgery?"

"You could wait until your vision gets worse, but I would suggest undergoing the first operation in July and the next operation in January…right after the holidays."

"Whatta ya think, Virginia?"

"Since you gotta have the operations, anyway, I say, why wait? Get the whole thing over with as soon as possible…Plus, with the baby due in mid-September, that schedule should work out pretty good for me."

"Okay, Doc, let's set it up for July."

"Let me look at my calendar…I see that Wednesday, July 13th is open."

"Yeah, that'll be fine…What about the cost?"

"Don't worry about the cost. The New York Eye and Ear Infirmary is supported by charities, so the cost to use the facility will be minimal. My guess is that your whole stay at the Infirmary will cost you about $75 for each operation…And as a favor to my good friend, Dr. Quattrocchi, I will perform the operations *pro bono*… at no cost. However, you will have to pay about $150 for each operation to cover the combined services of the doctors who will be assisting me…They are giving you a bargain at my request."

Joe and Virginia left the doctor's office feeling somewhat dispirited and depressed. But, by the time they exited the subway in the Bronx, they were both resigned to Joe's fate and were hoping for the best.

On the morning of July 13th, Joe and Virginia headed off to Manhattan. Virginia was more sullen than Joe, but he managed to cheer her up during the subway ride by comically commenting on the appearances of many of their fellow passengers. After exiting at Union Square, the couple walked arm-in-arm several blocks east to the New York Eye and Ear Infirmary.

Virginia was feeling a bit strained from the walk since she had gained thirty pounds from her pregnancy, thus far. When they reached the corner of Second Avenue and 13th Street, they were struck by the understated majesty of the Infirmary.

The facility had been constructed in 1856 as a three-story building. However, in 1890, it had undergone a total renovation, which included the addition of three more stories, and changes to the interior and the façade. The architect for the 1890 renovation was the distinguished architect, Stanford White, who in 1906 would be shot and killed by the jealous multi-millionaire husband of the famous actress, Evelyn Nesbit. The trial of the murderer, Harry Kendall Thaw, had been labeled as "The Trial of the Century" by the newspapers of the day.

Joe's cataract surgery commenced at around one o'clock. Dr. Montefusco carefully made an incision into the left eye. As he proceeded to expand the incision, the worst thing that could have happened, happened: In medical terms, a massive expulsive choroidal hemorrhage. This rupturing of the blood vessels within the eye was caused by the sudden decrease in the pressure within the eye as a result of the incision. The pressure released from within the eye literally pushed the contents of the eye outward, causing extensive damage to the eye. Such hemorrhaging was extremely rare, occurring less than once in every thousand operations, and its occurrence usually had nothing to do with the surgeon's skill. On the contrary, the cause of the hemorrhaging related to the weak internal structure of the eye's blood vessels—a condition that could not be predetermined by the doctors of that era.

Dr. Montefusco and his assistants did their best to stop the bleeding and to minimize damage to the eye. After about twenty minutes, the hemorrhaging abated, but Dr. Montefusco feared that the eye may have been irreparably damaged.

Joe's left eye was bandaged, and he was wheeled into the Recovery Room, where his head was immobilized with sandbags. But since the cataract had not been removed, he would only have to remain immobilized for two days. By that time, the eye would likely be sufficiently "healed" for Dr. Montefusco to assess the damage.

Joe slowly awakened from the anesthesia about an hour later. Peering out of his right eye, he saw a blurry image of Virginia seated at his side. Although he couldn't see her clearly, he was able to discern a worried expression on her face.

"What's wrong, Virginia?" asked Joe in a groggy tone.

"Joe, I spoke to Dr. Montefusco right after he stepped out of the Operating Room. He told me the operation failed because your eye hemorrhaged."

"Whatta ya mean?"

"Your eye began to bleed during the operation. He couldn't continue with the operation. He said it was a very rare complication... somethin' he didn't expect...He said that it wasn't his fault."

"Oh, no!" moaned Joe, "What happens next?"

"I don't know. I don't know, dear."

The next two days passed very slowly for both Joe and Virginia. Virginia had remained at his side until the early evening on the day of the operation, and on the following day, she returned accompanied by Joe's parents and her father. Her mother would also have liked to visit him, but she remained at home babysitting little Anna. Joe's visitors found the stench in the Recovery Room to be appalling, but after 24 hours in that room, Joe had become used to it.

On Friday, Virginia and Joe's parents arrived at the Infirmary at one o'clock—just in time to see Joe being wheeled off to be examined by Dr. Montefusco. They followed closely behind the orderly as he steered the gurney through the swinging doors leading to Room 207.

"I think it would be best if you people have a seat in the waiting room at the end of the hall," said the orderly. "I'll tell the doctor that you'll be waitin' there. He'll come over to talk to you after he finishes the examination."

About twenty minutes later, Dr. Montefusco entered the waiting room and walked slowly over to Virginia. He had a sad look on his face.

"How is he?" asked Virginia, as her heart began to beat rapidly.

"I have very bad news for you. The hemorrhage caused extensive eye damage...He is totally blind in that eye...He will never be able to see out of that eye again."

"*O Dio!*" screamed Joe's mother.

"What about the right eye?" asked a tearful Virginia.

"Well, the odds are very, very high that if we tried to remove the cataract on the other eye, he would suffer another hemorrhage. My recommendation is not to perform cataract surgery on that eye. He will likely go blind in that eye in about eighteen months, or perhaps, two years. He will be able to distinguish day from night and possibly see shadows from that eye, but he essentially will have to live life as a blind man from that point on…I'm so sorry…It wasn't my fault…These things just happen."

"Wouldn't it be worth taking a chance on removing the cataract from his right eye…say, soon after he goes blind?" asked Joe's shaken father.

"No, I don't recommend it…at least, not in the near future. You should understand that there will likely be improvements made in cataract surgery over the coming decades. There may be new procedures, someday, that would minimize the possibility of hemorrhaging. If we should try to remove the cataract from his right eye in the near future, I am reasonably certain that another hemorrhage would occur. Then, there would be no hope of him ever regaining his eyesight in that eye because it will very likely be irreparably damaged. But, if we forgo the operation, there may come a time…"

"Doctor," interrupted Virginia, "Do you have any idea how many years it will take for medical science to come up with some new procedures?"

"No, that's the problem. I can't make a prediction on when the next breakthrough will be made. But, it's better to leave room for hope than to totally eliminate it by undergoing a surgery that will very likely fail because the blood vessels and structure of his right eye, most probably, are almost identical to that of his left eye…You see, God is usually consistent."

"Does Joe know the score?"

"Yes, Mr. Sorrentino, he does…and I think he has resigned himself to his fate and will cling to the hope that someday after he loses his sight, the day will come when the cataract in his right eye can be safely removed."

Chapter 4: I Want You!

Joe stared aimlessly at the window while sitting on his favorite living room chair. He could tell that the afternoon sunshine coming through the window was bright—in contrast to the shadows of the walls—but that was, essentially, the limit of his vision. As usual, he was listening to the radio, his crutch for getting through the tedium of the day. The audio, that day, was punctuated with an annoying amount of static—enough static to cause him to get out of his chair and head over to the radio. Although he couldn't see the radio, he knew exactly where it was: atop the credenza, five short steps from where he was seated. Upon reaching the radio, he ran his hand down the side of the cathedral-shaped wooden cabinet of the ten-year-old Philco. Sliding his hand over to the face of the radio, he found the tuning knob and turned it just enough to eliminate the static. He returned to his chair without bumping into any furniture. Living as a blind man for about three years, he had mastered the skill of being able to memorize his surroundings. He knew every square inch of his apartment and he could navigate it nearly as well as a sighted person. But, his loss of vision had led him into a state of deep depression. He found his life to be filled with emptiness and monotony, despite his wife's best efforts to create a pleasant home for him and to have him live as normal a life as possible.

He was no longer employed. He had returned to work in August of 1938, after only two weeks of recuperation following his unsuccessful cataract operation. At that time, the remaining vision in "good eye"—his right eye—was still good enough for him to do his job, especially since it entailed following a set procedure that he had mastered many years before. The only time he needed to be cautious was when he was handling the battery acid.

Within two months of returning to work, Virginia gave birth to their second daughter. He had secretly hoped that his second child would be a boy, but like most every parent, he was happy to learn that the baby had been born healthy. Softening his disappointment was the fact that his daughter had been born on September 19th—an auspicious day—the feast day of San Gennaro, the patron saint of Naples. In his mind, nothing but good fortune lay ahead for his little Clara.

Despite his progressive loss of vision in his right eye, he had been able to work throughout 1939, although during the last few months of that year, many of the batteries he had reconditioned didn't quite meet the standards of the battery shop's owner. Furthermore, he had spilled battery acid far too many times, burning his hands and disrupting the operation of the shop.

In the summer of 1939, Luigi had come to realize that Joe had become a burden on the operation of the battery shop, but the kindhearted old man just couldn't bring himself to giving Joe the axe. Finally, two weeks after Christmas, he reluctantly told Joe that he would have to let him go.

Joe graciously remarked, "Luigi, you've been like a second father to me. I know you're only doin' what you gotta do in these tough times. I know I haven't been pullin' my weight around here for a long time…So, I'm really grateful to you for allowin' me to hang on for as long as you did."

The static on the radio returned, but this time Joe decided to ignore it, since the station was running commercials. A minute later, the WNBC announcer returned with the latest war news. Speaking in an overly authoritative baritone voice—an affectation typical of newsmen of the day—he stated:

> "Yesterday, Wednesday, May 12, 1943…Tunisa… German General Von Arnim, along with 25 other Axis generals, was captured…More than 130,000 German soldiers and 120,000 Italian soldiers have surrendered…The once mighty Afrika Korps is no more."

"Way to go!" exclaimed Joe, feeling exuberant about the good war news. But feeling a twinge of sadness for his Italian brethren, he added, "That fuckin' Mussolini ruined Italy!"

Then, he heard the jingling sound of keys, quickly followed by the turning of the lock of his apartment door.

"Hi Honey, I'm home," announced Virginia, who had left the apartment for about a half-hour to pick up their daughter, Anna, from school, while young Clara, slept.

Anna, who would turn seven the next week, raced over to Joe and gave him a big kiss on the cheek as Virginia continued, "You know, I still haven't gotten used to this neighborhood even though we've been livin' here for more than two years. I really miss Arthur Avenue and our Belmont Avenue apartment."

"Well, I know this part of the Bronx doesn't compare with our old neighborhood, but my Uncle Pete offered us a deal that we just could not turn down. Right?"

"Yeah, I know, Joe, I know."

Joe's bachelor uncle, Pete, had always been extremely fond of his godson. In April of 1940, when Joe lost vision in his right eye— with the exception of being able to see some shadows and being able to distinguish daytime from night with that eye—Uncle Pete was devastated, and he vowed to help Joe and his family as much as he could. Of course, Joe's parents and Virginia's parents were providing some financial assistance to the struggling couple, but Uncle Pete had the means to do more. He was fairly wealthy in terms of cash and real estate. In fact, he owned six apartment buildings, although he was hardly able to eke out much of a profit from those low-rent tenements. Even so, he was still relatively well off. So he decided to provide Joe and Virginia with a rent-free apartment in one of his buildings. The apartment had five spacious rooms; whereas, Joe and Virginia's apartment on Belmont Avenue had only three small rooms. The only drawback of the rent-free apartment was that it was in a building located on Furman Avenue between East 237th Street and East 238th Street—five miles north of Arthur Avenue.

They had initially resisted Uncle Pete's offer, preferring the tight quarters of their Bronx Little Italy apartment to the spacious rent-free apartment miles away. However, after about six months, they came to their senses, realizing that Uncle Pete's offer was simply too good to pass up. In the five-room apartment, the girls would each have their own large bedroom, while in their Belmont Avenue apartment, they would have to continue to sleep in the living room—something that would certainly be a big problem when they got older.

Shortly after Joe and his family had moved into the Furman Avenue apartment, Uncle Pete sweetened the deal. He made Joe the manager of the building. His duties were simple: to collect the monthly rents and to field tenant complaints. He would be more than adequately compensated for his services, receiving $50 a month, in cash. He relished the responsibility of being the building's manager. He took the job very seriously. He even enjoyed dealing with the tenants and trying to solve their complaints. The job gave him some sense of worth, but it didn't require enough effort to fill the many lonely and empty hours of the day.

Joe, whose sense of hearing had sharpened since he lost his vision, was able to recognize that Virginia was in the process of opening the day's mail. "Anything important in the mail, Virginia?…and I don't mean bills."

"Nah, just the usual stuff…Oh…Oh, wait a minute, you got a letter from the draft board."

"The draft board?"

"Yeah, the draft board."

"I wonder what the hell they want from me…Open it, Virginia! Open it!"

"Okay. Let me see…It's an order for you to report for a physical on May 24th at 8 a.m." She then started to mumble as she speed-read the letter.

"What does it say? What does it say?"

Laughing heartily, she replied, "I guess if you pass the physical, you'll be drafted into the Army."

"Don't they know I'm blind?"

"I guess they don't. I suppose I should give them a phone call or send them a letter explaining your situation."

"Yeah, I guess so."

Later, at dinner, Joe told Virginia that he wanted to go down to the draft board in person to straighten out the matter. "I'll get Nicky "Moon" to bring me there. I know you can't take me there since you have to take care of the kids."

At just before 8 o'clock, on Monday morning, May 24th, Nicky and Joe arrived at the draft board. Before they entered the building, Joe said, "I'm gonna have some fun with these guys…I wanna see how far I can get before they realize I'm blind."

Nicky chuckled and said, "Now, that's the Joe I remember!"

Staying close behind Joe, Nicky discreetly guided him to the front desk, acting as if he, too, had received a letter to report for a physical.

"Show me your letter, young man," demanded the administrator at the front desk.

Joe pulled-out the folded-up letter from his pocket and handed it over to the man.

"I'll need to see some form of identification…a birth certificate…a driver's license."

"No problem, sir…here's my driver's license."

Nicky could hardly contain his laughter, for he knew the true story behind Joe's driver's license. The obvious question: How did it come to pass that a blind person would be licensed to drive a car in the State of New York—or any other state for that matter? The answer was quite simple: At Joe's request, Nicky had gone over to the New York State Department of Motor Vehicles the year before, and pretending to be Joe, he passed the mandatory eye test, and went from line to line until the license renewal had been processed. While doing so, not one of the agents had noticed that Nicky was 5'-9" tall, whereas the license renewal application indicated Joe to be 5'-3" tall. When Nicky presented the renewed driver's license to Joe, he was ecstatic. Joe had no intention of getting behind the wheel, but he figured that showing off his license to unsuspecting individuals could lead to some humorous situations. And Joe really loved a good laugh, especially if it was at someone else's expense.

After examining the drivers license, the administrator said, "Okay, Mr. Sorrentino, proceed to the line over there," pointing to a line of young men to his right.

Nicky whispered, "The line's to your left," as he started to guide Joe to the back of the line.

"Where are you going!" the administrator yelled at Nicky, "I haven't seen your letter, yet!"

"Actually, I didn't receive a letter. I just came here to keep my friend company."

"Oh? Well, in that case, go take a seat on that bench until your friend has completed the process."

The young men on the line that Joe had joined were directed into a locker room and told to undress down to their shorts and put their clothes into any available locker, being reassured that a member of the Military Police would safeguard their valuables. Joe undressed and managed to put his clothes into an empty locker

"Okay men, line-up for your medical examinations!"

Using all his senses, he found a place on the line leading to the medical examiners without anyone noticing that he couldn't see. The first examiner checked his blood pressure, which was found to be normal. The second examiner checked his musculature, reflexes and feet. He passed that examination. Finally, he reached the doctor. The doctor began his examination by listening to Joe's heart with a stethoscope; he followed with a check of Joe's testicles and rectum; then he proceeded to check his eyes. One quick glance at Joe's eyes and the doctor immediately knew that he was examining a blind man.

"What the hell are you doing here!" exclaimed the doctor, with a tone of incredulity.

Realizing that the jig was up, Joe replied, "Well…Well, I want to serve my country."

"Sorry, your blindness makes you ineligible to be in the armed forces."

On one hand, Joe had gone through the ruse for the fun of it—as a way of relieving his boredom and to have a good story to tell his friends. But, on the other hand, he truly *was* willing to serve his country, if the Army could find a job for him. *Surely*, he thought, *There must be somethin' I could do for the Army…even somethin' as simple as operatin' a radio or manning a telephone, stateside.*

"Doctor, isn't there somethin' I could do in the Army? After all, not every soldier is sent to the front."

The doctor was touched by Joe's sense of patriotism. He replied in a mellow tone, "Actually, it's true that there are certain jobs in the Army that a blind man could handle, but, unfortunately, Army regulations don't permit anyone who has failed the medical examination to serve. Many men have been rejected for far less than blindness, young man. I truly admire your patriotism, but I have no choice but to reject you…Good luck to you."

Joe was escorted to the front office and was met by Nicky, who was dying to find out what had happened behind the closed doors.

"Hey, Joe, how did it go?"

"Well, believe it or not, they want me…and, they're gonna make me a sergeant."

"Really?"

"No, you knucklehead…they don't want me. There is no place in the fuckin' Army for a blind man…You know, you're stupider than you look."

"How do you know how I look?"

"Oh, I know how you look…Anyway, I made it all the way through to the doctor. Now, that's quite a story, ain't it?"

"It sure is…You know, Joe, you were one of the funniest guys in the neighborhood when we were growin' up, and you still haven't lost your sense of humor, even after the bad hand you been dealt."

"Well, to tell you the truth, my sense of humor is helpin' me to go on livin'. But, there are times when I get very depressed. I ask God, 'Why me, God? Why me?'"

"Did he ever answer you?" asked Nicky, trying to inject some humor.

"No, not yet…Not yet…Hey, Nicky, instead of bringin' me back home, let's go to Arthur Avenue for some lunch and some vino. It's my treat."

"Sounds good! You don't have to twist my arm."

"Yeah, I know. You're a great pal, but you're one cheap bastard!"

Chapter 5: Naples, June 1943

Eighteen-year-old Serafina Piccarelli walked slowly up the twelve worn concrete steps from the cellar of her family's residence on Vico Giardinetto in Naples, Italy, ready to face another day in the war-torn city of her birth. She welcomed the warm breeze and brightness of the morning sunshine on this typical June day. It was an uplifting feeling just to be outside—a sharp contrast to the dark and uncomfortably humid cellar where she, along with seven other family members, had taken refuge since their three-story masonry house had been leveled to an uninhabitable pile of rubble by American bombers a few days before Christmas Day in 1942.

Like most houses constructed in 19th century Italy, her family's house, in the neighborhood known as Quartieri Spagnoli, had been extremely well built—especially when compared with modern-day construction. Its 12"-thick concrete ground floor was strong enough to support the rubble of the house's collapsed upper floors. Thus, the cellar was undamaged and safe enough to provide shelter, although it lacked cooking and toilet facilities, as well as water and electricity.

Fortunately, no family members had been inside the house when it was leveled. They, along with many of their neighbors, had taken refuge in a nearby tunnel about five minutes before the bombers—American B-24 *Liberators*—were overhead. The principal targets of the bombers were the piers and wharves located about a kilometer (a little more than ½-mile) away from the Quartieri Spagnoli. But, as a result of the poor visibility on that foggy day, many bombs had missed their targets, resulting in much collateral damage, which included the Piccarelli family's house.

Serafina, like most Neapolitans, had become quite used to the continual bombings. Naples was a major target due to its strategic importance. The bombings began on November 1, 1940, when twin-engine British bombers, flying out of Malta, attacked the port facilities in an effort to disrupt the Axis supply line for the North African campaign. The British continued their air raids through 1941. Unfortunately, Serafina's father, Giuseppe, was killed during a British air attack in the summer of 1941 while working as a longshoreman.

As she walked towards Vico Tre Regine, she casually glanced at the other bombed-out buildings on her block. Some of the buildings were totally uninhabitable; others, like her building, had habitable cellars; and two buildings had thus far incurred virtually no damage at all. Such were the fortunes of war. When she reached Vico Tre Regine, she reached into her purse and pulled out a pack of cigarettes. She was down to the last cigarette of her last pack; she decided to smoke it. She savored every puff, realizing that it might be her last cigarette for quite some time. Everything in Naples had become very expensive as the war progressed. Goods and the basic necessities of life were in short supply. Most families were in dire straits. As a result of rampant unemployment, many Neapolitans were surviving by exhausting their life savings and/or by committing petty crimes. Also a vast number of young Neapolitan women had reluctantly taken up the world's oldest profession—mostly servicing Italian and German soldiers.

After pausing a while at the intersection, she turned around and headed back to her house, dragging on her cigarette until the lit end reached her fingernails. As she surveyed the destruction, she cursed Mussolini—*Il Duce*—for having gotten Italy into the dreadful world war. Years before, her parents, like most Italians, had been enamored with Mussolini and his efforts to colonize parts of North Africa and to establish Italy as a world power—using the Roman Empire as his template and as an example to inspire nationalistic fervor in the Italian people. Throughout her schooling, Serafina, like all Italian school children, had been indoctrinated into an unquestioning admiration and respect for Italy's great leader. Now, it was obvious to her that even if he had in fact been a great leader in his early years, he had devolved into Hitler's lackey.

As Serafina reached her building, her dearest cousin, Lucia, emerged from the cellar. Lucia, who was also eighteen years old, was like a sister to her. They had lived in separate apartments in the same building for their entire lives. Serafina and her family, which included her mother's parents, had occupied the ground floor, with Lucia and her family living in the apartment right above. The smaller top floor had housed their two spinster aunts—*Zia* Giuseppina and *Zia* Maria.

Lucia was also a Piccarelli. Her father, Amadeo, had died of pancreatic cancer shortly before the war. Her only sibling, Marco, was serving in the Italian Army, but the family had no idea of his whereabouts, since they had not received a letter from him in more than three months. Lucia's mother, Assunta, had always gotten along quite well with Serafina's mother, Susanna. They were distant cousins who had known each other their entire lives. Their lives had always been very parallel; now they shared the common bond of widowhood and the anguish of having a son—or in Susanna's case, two sons—fighting in the war. Susanna would occasionally receive separate letters from her sons, Paolo and Pietro, who were serving in different army units. Often, the letters would contain two or three hundred lire; but sometimes the letters would arrive sans lire—the money having been pilfered somewhere along the way.

Serafina, with a dour expression on her face, looked deeply into Lucia's eyes and began to lay out a plan to save the family from the plight of slow starvation, which would be a certainty in the very near future, since the family's pooled funds—the combined money of all eight family members—amounted to about 2,500 lire (approximately $20).

"Lucia, our family will soon be out of money. There's no work to be found. We have sold everything of value. There's nothing more we can sell…except…"

"Except?…Except, what?"

Wagging the fingers of her right hand several times towards her crotch, she replied in a sad tone, "This…our bodies."

"Are you saying that we should become *puttane?*"

After a long pause, Serafina replied, "Yes, that's what I'm saying."

"I don't want to be a *puttana*. I don't want to be a sinner. I want to save myself for the man I will marry, someday."

"Lucia, don't you think that's what I would want to do, also? The very thought of becoming a prostitute turns my stomach and causes me to wonder how God will judge me. But, if we don't sell our bodies, we will starve and our families will starve…and, the older ones in our family will probably get sick and die."

After a long period of silence, Lucia sheepishly remarked, "I really don't have any idea of how to do it. Nobody ever explained sex to me."

"Well, I certainly can't explain it to you…I'm a virgin just like you…I figure that all we have to do is lie on the ground, lift-up our skirts and let the man do the rest."

"If I go along with this…and I am not saying that I will… where would we go to do this *thing*? Certainly not around here where everyone knows us."

"No, not around here. I've heard rumors that the *Il Cimitero degli Inglese*…the English Cemetery…is a popular spot for such *activities*. Most of the men who go to the cemetery are Italian soldiers, but there are some German soldiers who also go there…and occasionally, some wealthy Italian men, such as doctors, are serviced by *le puttane del cimitero*. I heard that men will pay 150 lire, and sometimes, a man might be willing to pay 200 lire, or more, depending on the circumstances. A woman could earn 600 lire (about $5) or more in an afternoon."

"That's a lot of money, but I don't think I could do it…become a *puttana*."

"*Va bene*, Lucia, I'm not going to force you. You don't have to become a *puttana*. But, would you at least come with me to the cemetery this afternoon to keep me company."

"This afternoon?"

"Yes, I want to get started today before I change my mind."

At around 2 o'clock, the two cousins started their 3-kilometer (approximately 2-mile) walk to the cemetery. Both women, who strongly resembled each other, were thin, yet shapely—their thinness being the result of the scarcity of food in their household. They each had unmistakably Italian faces, framed by long and wavy dark brown hair. After about 45 minutes of walking at a brisk pace in a meandering, but generally northeasterly route, they arrived at the cemetery, which, surprisingly—or perhaps, not so surprisingly—was fairly crowded with young women and soldiers loitering along its high outer wall.

The English Cemetery was a Protestant cemetery that was established in 1826 when a British Consul bought the land, which was serving as a garden for the church of Santa Maria delle Fede. The proper Italian name for the cemetery was *Il Cimitero Acattolico* di *Santa Maria delle Fede*. The cemetery contained the remains of Protestant foreigners who had lived in Naples or those that had died in Naples while touring. It was filled with many ornate and massive tombstones. Since the last burials at the cemetery had occurred in 1893, it was extremely unlikely that any of the people that Serafina and Lucia saw standing outside the cemetery were there to pay their respects.

"Let's stand over here, Lucia, and see what's going on."

After a few minutes, they observed a woman, who was standing off to their left, being approached by a pleasant looking Italian soldier. After exchanging a few words, the woman and the soldier walked away, arm-in-arm, heading into the cemetery.

"I guess they made a deal, Serafina."

"I'm *sure* they made a deal…and it didn't seem too hard. All she had to do was to stand there and wait."

Five minutes later, the two cousins were approached by two Italian soldiers, who conversed to them in the Sicilian. They were able to understand the soldiers, and the soldiers were able to understand them, but doing so required some effort for all—somewhat akin to a couple of New Englanders engaging in a conversation with a couple of people from the Heart of Dixie. The soldiers quickly got right to the point, asking how much it would cost for sex.

Serafina responded, "150 lire," while Lucia silently stood by with a dazed expression on her face.

"*Va bene*," said the taller soldier as he grabbed Serafina by the arm.

Lucia resisted the other soldier's approach, which caused him to utter a few expletives that she didn't understand—the expletives being Sicilian expressions that were foreign to her. At that point Serafina yelled at Lucia, in a no-nonsense tone, "*Andiamo via! Andiamo via!* Let's go! Let's go!"

"I only came here to keep you company, Serafina."

"Very well, you can wait out here for me and let me do this by myself, or you can do your part for the good of the family!"

Lucia wanted to run but she coyly took the soldier's hand and the two couples quickly walked to a section of the cemetery that offered some privacy. On the way, they walked past two "couples" engaged in sexual intercourse, and a woman performing oral sex on a German soldier who was standing ever so straight—as if being inspected by his commandant.

Both women were nervous. Serafina was able to hide her nervousness, but Lucia could not. When they reached a relatively lonely area, the two couples separated from each other, walking down different aisles of tombstones, in opposite directions. They wound up about 25 yards apart, shielded from each other's view by many large marble tombstones.

Serafina, who wanted to get the deed done as quickly as possible, laid down on the ground in front of an ornately carved, five-foot tall tombstone with the family name *Blake* carved on it. She positioned herself such that her head was almost touching the base of the tombstone. Then, she bravely lifted-up her skirt revealing her pink panties. That was all the encouragement that the young soldier needed. He was immediately aroused. He dropped to his knees, pulled down her panties, and quickly pulled out his engorged member, pausing a couple of seconds so that Serafina could get a good view of his manhood. This was a new experience for her since she had never seen an erect penis—not even in paintings or statues.

With a look of lust and some pride in his eyes, the young Sicilian mounted her. He was surprised at the difficulty he encountered in entering her. Serafina, sensing the forthcoming pain, closed her eyes and gritted her teeth. As the young soldier forced his way through the blockage, Serafina winced, but found the pain to be bearable.

Meanwhile, Lucia's experience was more akin to rape than consensual sex. She had gotten cold feet when the "moment of truth" had arrived. The soldier had to force her to the ground, and while on the ground, he smacked her across the face a couple of times to cause her to submit. She sobbed uncontrollably as the soldier had his way with her. Serafina could hear her whimpering in the distance, causing her to focus more on her cousin's plight than her own.

Both soldiers finished at about the same time. Serafina could feel the pulses of warm fluid being squirted deep within her. Lucia, who was totally numbed by her experience, was oblivious to everything that had happened.

Serafina arose as soon as the soldier had gotten off of her and demanded her 150 lire. The soldier laughed and began walking away. She ran behind him and tugged at the back of his uniform jacket, at which point he spun around and smacked her face with the back of his right hand. The forceful blow to her right cheek caused her to spin around and drop to one knee. Stunned momentarily, she instinctively began to rub her cheek. As the soldier was walking away from her, she spewed out a string of curses directed at him and his mother. He might have tolerated her curses had they been limited to him. But to hear someone curse his mother caused his Sicilian blood to boil. He turned around and approached her from behind intending to avenge his mother's honor. He swung his right leg back in a pendulum motion and gave her a swift kick in the ass with his heavy army boot. As she screamed in pain, he followed up with a second kick, causing her to fall flat on her face.

"*Vaffanculo! Vaffanculo!*" he exclaimed, which can be translated to mean anything from "Go to hell!" to "Up your ass!"—the latter translation seemingly more appropriate in this particular instance.

"*Siciliano bastardo!*" she countered.

"*Napolitana puttana!*" shouted the soldier as he gave her one more forceful kick in the rear, this time with his heel.

Meanwhile, Lucia just lay on the ground sobbing, never demanding payment for her services. As the young soldier walked away, he began to feel sorry for her. He decided to deviate from the plan that he and his buddy had concocted before encountering Serafina and Lucia: to have sex without paying for it. Feeling guilty about having claimed the young woman's virginity, he turned around and slowly walked back to Lucia, who was still lying frozen on the ground. He couldn't help but think of his two young sisters back in Sicily, and of how their purity was a matter of honor to his family. He realized that the young woman whom he had just forcibly deflowered was probably a "good girl" who had been pressured into prostitution as a matter of survival.

"I'm sorry," he said softly, as he pulled 150 lire out of his pocket and gently placed the money in her hand.

Sensing the genuineness of his remorse, Lucia tearfully responded, "*Grazie.*"

When the two cousins met, they embraced each other and recounted their first experiences in the world of prostitution. Serafina couldn't get over the fact that she had been duped. On their way back to the front gate of the cemetery, she wouldn't stop repeating, "*Siciliano bastardo,*" as her stomach turned at the very thought of that Sicilian who had taken advantage of her. Neapolitans generally distrusted and looked down upon Sicilians. It was a regional thing. Now, in Serafina's mind, she had a legitimate reason to *hate* Sicilians.

"Lucia, I'm going to do it again with the next man who approaches us. This time, I'll be smarter. I'll collect the 150 lire up front and hand it over to you for safekeeping."

A handsome Italian officer approached them after about a fifteen-minute wait near the front gate. Serafina took charge of the situation, requesting payment in advance. Without hesitating, the officer agreed to pay her 150 lire up front. She handed Lucia the 150 lire, which she quickly put inside her bra.

Serafina's encounter with the officer was totally different from her experience with the young Sicilian soldier. The officer, who appeared to be about 30 years old, was gentle and well mannered. After a few minutes of intercourse, she relaxed and actually experienced a twinge of pleasure.

The cousins walked home from the cemetery richer by 300 lire—enough money to buy a half-liter of olive oil, a couple of loaves of bread and a few eggs. Serafina insisted that they should return to the cemetery the next day, but Lucia needed to be convinced.

"Lucia, you did it once; you can do it again. Trust me, the second time will be much easier."

"I don't want to be a *puttana.*"

Smiling, Serafina replied, "Let's face it, you already are one. You are no longer a virgin, and you had sex for money."

The next day, Lucia reluctantly returned to the cemetery with Serafina. On that day they each earned 450 lire and they had become somewhat accustomed to their new *lucrative* profession. As it turned out, prostitution was not as lucrative a profession as they had first thought. On the third day of venturing to the cemetery, they were approached by two Neapolitan thugs who demanded protection money from them. The men were likely members of the *Camorra*—Naples' version of the Mafia. The two well-dressed, middle-aged men brandished knives while promising to slash their faces if they didn't fork over half of their daily earnings to them. Realizing that these men meant business, they agreed to pay the protection money. In return, the pimps promised to ensure their safety and to "take care" of any customers who would try to rob them.

Aside from being forced to give half of their earnings to their pimps, they were ordered to spend some of their money to upgrade their looks and sex appeal. The pimps demanded that Serafina and Lucia wear high-heeled shoes, silk stockings and plenty of makeup while plying their trade. The pimps allowed them two weeks to make the necessary purchases, since they were well aware that such items were quite costly and hard to find in war-torn Naples.

The two novices spent much of what that they had earned from their first two weeks of whoring on purchases of stiletto-heeled shoes, black silk stockings, and lots of makeup. However, making their appearances more sexy did, indeed, attract many more customers; so, the cost of primping up, probably, more than paid for itself in the long run. Of course, it didn't take very long for the family to realize what Serafina and Lucia were up to. Their sexy attire and heavy makeup was a dead giveaway. But, the family turned a blind eye, realizing that Serafina and Lucia, like a multitude of other young Neapolitan women, were selling their bodies for their own survival and their family's survival.

After working the cemetery for six days a week for the first month, they had become seasoned prostitutes, having gained experience in the various sexual positions, as well as in performing oral sex—the fine points of the latter having been taught to them by their pimps. They had been playing Russian Roulette as far as getting pregnant was concerned, since very few of their customers used protection. Fortunately—and perhaps, miraculously— neither of them had gotten pregnant after their first month of whoring. But they were playing with fire, and the odds were that either or both of them would soon become pregnant, given all of the unprotected intercourse that they were having.

Early into their second month of prostitution, they became friendly with a prostitute named Maria. Maria, who was twenty-five years old, had been working the cemetery for more than two years. After exchanging some small talk, Lucia broached the subject of pregnancy. Maria gladly gave the two young cousins a quick course in the sexual workings of a woman's body. She explained the menstrual cycle in great detail and told them to avoid unprotected sex when they would be most fertile. She advised that it would be *safe* for a working girl—or for that matter, any woman who didn't want to become pregnant—to have unprotected sex within the first ten days of the start of her period; during the following eight days, a woman would be quite fertile and could possibly become pregnant. She indicated that during those eight days, a woman who didn't want to get pregnant should either abstain from sex or have her partner use a condom; after those eight days, it would again be safe to have unprotected sex. She explained that since abstinence would cut into a woman's earnings, most prostitutes continue to work during their fertile period by only having sex with customers who agree to use condoms. She suggested that it would be wise for them to give condoms to their customers during their fertile periods, and she indicated that they might have to reduce their rate to as low as 100 lire, since most men don't like to use condoms.

Both cousins simultaneously asked, "What's a condom?"

Maria tried to explain to them what a condom is and how it is used, but she realized that it would be best if she showed them one. So, she pulled one out of her purse, removed it from its wrapper and unrolled it over two of her fingers, while explaining how a man would actually put one on. Serafina and Lucia got the point.

"Where can we get some condoms?" asked Serafina.

"You can get them from your pimps. Of course, you will have to pay for them…Nothing is free in Naples!" she added, as she gestured with both hands wagging up and down.

The cousins were very grateful for the sex education that Maria had just given them, and they decided to follow it, since the last thing that either of them would need would be a baby to care for, and to further disgrace their family.

Chapter 6: Grand Opening

Virginia led the way as she and Joe walked arm-in-arm, towards the elevated IRT Subway station at 238th Street and White Plains Road. The morning of July 2, 1951 was refreshingly mild, with a temperature of only 70 degrees. The walk from their apartment to the station had taken only five minutes. When they reached the stairway, they could hear and feel the vibrations and metallic noises above as a train pulled into the station. Joe could sense from the direction of the sounds that they had not missed their train—that the train pulling into the station was not a Manhattan-bound train.

"Hold on to me Joe…it's a long flight of stairs."

"I know…I know."

The couple boarded the downtown local at exactly 9 o'clock and began their long ride down to Manhattan's Little Italy where Joe was to begin operating a newsstand at the northeast corner of Spring and Lafayette Streets. After eleven years of fighting the boredom of living as a blind man and being mostly confined to his apartment, Joe had seized the opportunity given to him by the city to operate a newsstand. Although he had hoped for a newsstand in the Bronx— preferably, one on Arthur Avenue—his only choices at the time were a 23rd Street location and the Lafayette Street location. He opted for the Lafayette Street newsstand because it was within the boundaries of Little Italy, being only one block west of Mulberry Street— the heart of Little Italy, and one of the most famous and infamous streets in the City of New York.

"Joe, you better keep count of all of the stops because you're gonna be on your own tomorrow."

"Okay…but you count, too."

The subway commute required two train changes and a total of twenty-seven stops. After an hour-and-twenty minutes of noisy tedium, they finally arrived at the Spring Street station. Immediately upon exiting, Virginia spotted the newsstand on the other side of Lafayette Street, and said, "Joe, the newsstand looks nice. It's painted dark green and it looks like it's about 6 feet wide and more than 6 feet high. I think you'll be able to stand up inside when you're tired of sittin'."

She carefully led Joe across the busy two-way street and right up to the padlocked door of the newsstand. Using the key he had received in the mail, he managed to open the lock after fumbling around with it for a few seconds. He stepped inside and smiled. For the first time in a long time he was beaming with joy, buoyed by the realization that he was about to become his own boss—albeit the boss of a tiny enterprise—and that he would be earning his keep for the first time in many, many years.

After Virginia helped him open up the front of the newsstand and secure the newspaper counter, he was open for business; but he had one problem: no newspapers. However, within the next hour, three local newspaper deliverymen introduced themselves to him and provided him with 50 copies each of the early editions of the *Journal American*, the *World Telegram and Sun,* and the *Post.* He would later make arrangements for morning deliveries of the *Daily News* and the *Daily Mirror,* which would begin the following day.

After they ate the sandwiches and fruit that Virginia had packed for lunch, she headed off to Grand Street to do some food shopping. The little shops on Grand Street, between Mott and Mulberry Streets, arguably, sold the best imported Italian products that could be found anywhere in New York City and, possibly, in the entire United States.

Business in the early afternoon wasn't very good. Joe had managed to sell only two-dozen newspapers; however, he was confident that business would pick up when people would be heading home from work in the late afternoon and early evening.

"Scus-ah me. You-ah new-ah here?"

Joe responded to the friendly voice of the young—obviously Italian—woman. "Yeah, today's my first day here. I'll be open six days a week…

Monday through Saturday…but this week, I'll be closed on Wednesday for the Fourth of July holiday."

"Fourth-ah- July is-ah big-ah day-ah for me. My daughter, Felicia, will-ah be-ah four on-ah that-ah day-ah."

"Signora, what part of Italy are you from?"

"Napoli."

Upon hearing that the woman came from Naples, Joe switched to the Neapolitan dialect, much to the delight of the young woman. Speaking in her native tongue, the conversation became much more fluid and animated.

"How is it that you speak Neapolitan so well?"

"I learned it from my parents who were born in Naples. By the way, my name is Joe…Joe Sorrentino."

"My name is Serafina…Serafina Daniels."

"Daniels? That's an American name."

"Yes, I married an American soldier back in Naples in 1945. His name is Zeke. We live three buildings from here…over there," pointing north on Lafayette Street.

"Where?"

"Over there," again pointing up the street.

"Sorry, Signora, I'm blind. I don't know where you're pointing to."

"You're blind?"

"Yes."

"Were you born blind?"

At that point, Joe told her an abbreviated version of his life story, beginning with the baseball incident. "Now that you've learned a lot about me, tell me about yourself and how you managed to wind up living here."

Serafina told him that she was born in Naples nearly twenty-seven years ago, and that her maiden name was Piccarelli. She indicated that living in war-torn Naples had been like living in and endless nightmare; her father had been killed in an Allied air raid and her family had lived hand-to-mouth within the remains of their bombed-out house. Then, taking some liberties with the truth to mask her sordid past, she stated that in August 1944, she had met an American Army corporal as she was strolling along Via della Marinella, simply to gaze at the sea and to take her mind off the destruction all around her.

"Did he speak Italian?"

"No. That was a problem…and I only knew a few words of English…But, somehow, we managed to communicate."

"And then what happened?"

"We began seeing each other regularly. He proposed marriage to me on Christmas Day 1944, but I didn't say 'yes' until two weeks later. It was a tough decision because I knew I would be leaving my family and my beloved Naples…perhaps, forever."

"Oh, that must have been a hard decision for you."

"It was very hard. Anyway, Zeke got permission from the Army to marry me and we were married in March of 1945 in one of the few churches in Naples that had not been damaged during the war. His good friend, Corporal Butch Johnson, was the best man, and my dearest cousin, Lucia, was my maid of honor."

"Was the fighting pretty much over in Naples by that time?"

"Yes, the war had moved north by that time."

"Did you live in the Army base after the marriage?"

"No, I wasn't allowed to live there…he continued to live at the base, while I lived with my mother."

Joe, who found the story intriguing, continued probing for more details. "How did you get to America?"

"Well, a couple of weeks after the war ended in Europe…on May 8th, I believe…Zeke's unit was ordered to return home. Unfortunately, his ship to America was only for soldiers. So, I had to wait until late December to board a ship to America. The voyage took fifteen agonizing days. The ocean was rough, and the food…whatever I forced myself to eat of it…was terrible. I, like most of the passengers, was seasick all the time. When I saw the Statue of Liberty, I dropped to my knees and made the Sign of the Cross."

"So, that's how you got here?"

"No, not exactly…Zeke is from a small town in Tennessee named Gatlinburg. After we met at the dock in Manhattan, we went to the bus depot and headed for his hometown. We traveled for nearly three days, taking four different buses."

"How did you like his town?"

"I didn't like it at all. In fact, I hated it. The difference between Gatlinburg and Naples was like the difference between night and day. I couldn't see myself living there for the rest of my life. I knew I could never get used to that place."

"Did his family welcome you? Were they upset that Zeke had married an Italian girl instead of a girl from Tennessee?"

"They were very polite to me, but they weren't warm. *Americani* are much different from *Italiani*…plus, we couldn't understand each other. I'm sure they would have preferred Zeke to have married a girl from his hometown."

"Well, I bet that your family would have wanted you to marry a *paisano*."

"You're right. They even would have accepted a lousy *Siciliano* over Zeke!"

After they both laughed heartily over that remark, she continued.

"Anyway, although I was surrounded by many people in Gatlinburg, I was very lonely and homesick."

"I suppose you convinced your husband that you should move here."

"Yes, I did. Before I left Naples, my mother had given me the name and address of a *paisan'* who lived on Mulberry Street. Her name is Lena Rossi. She came here before the war. So, I sent Lena a letter from Tennessee telling her how much I hated it there and that I wanted to move to Little Italy…and, she helped me out. She did a lot for me that fine woman, God bless her. She found me the apartment that I'm now living in, and more important, she got Zeke a job working in Orazio Martucci's commercial heating and plumbing business. Orazio is also a *paisan'* and he's from my section of Naples. His office is on the other side of Spring Street, halfway between here and Mulberry. Zeke's been working for him for more than five years."

"Lena certainly did do a lot for you."

"She certainly did. I'm eternally grateful to her."

Unfortunately for Serafina, although Lena *did* do a great deal for her, she had also managed to damage Serafina's reputation in her newfound neighborhood. After having written to her aunt back in Naples about how she had helped Serafina come to Little Italy, her aunt informed her of Serafina's past. The kind-hearted Lena had one major character flaw: she loved to gossip. Rumors of Serafina's whoring days back in Naples soon spread throughout the neighborhood. The neighborhood women—who had never known the hardships of war—simply couldn't understand nor forgive her past. They would continually whisper about her. In their minds, once a *puttana*, always a *puttana*.

"How many children do you have, Serafina?"

"I have two daughters…Felicia, the four-year old, and Francesca who is only fourteen months old. My neighbor is watching them for an hour while I go shopping."

"I also have two daughters…Anna is a teenager, and Clara will become a teenager on September 19th."

"Oh, she was born on San Gennaro's feast day."

"Yes."

"She is destined to have a good life."

"Does your husband like living in Manhattan? Has he gotten used to city life?"

"Well, he is getting used to it, but I'm sure he misses Tennessee. He doesn't fit in with the men around here very well…But, he moved here to save our marriage and to make me happy. I was so miserable in Tennessee that even I had trouble living with myself."

At that moment, Virginia returned with two shopping bags, which were full to the brim with various imported cheeses, including a piece of sharp provolone, plus olive oil, jarred roasted peppers, *soprassata* and pepperoni. Joe introduced Virginia to Serafina, and they exchanged pleasantries, also in the Neapolitan dialect. As Serafina departed for her shopping trip, Joe remarked, "It was nice meeting you and I hope that you will stop by often. I enjoy speaking Neapolitan."

"So do I," replied Serafina. "That's why I chose to live in this neighborhood. Zeke and I have been married six years and he still has trouble putting two Neapolitan words together. Fortunately, he can understand most of what I say if I speak slowly, and I can understand much of what he says in English, if he speaks slowly."

Chapter 7: John-John

"Principal Davis; Assistant Principal Infante; teachers; fellow graduates and their families and friends…today marks the beginning of…" *Oh that doesn't sound so good. I think I'll change it a bit.*

"Mr. Davis, principal of our beloved school; Mrs. Infante, our assistant principal…"

Fourteen-year-old John-John Cara was standing in the middle of the tiny living room of his family's Mulberry Street apartment staring at the faded rectangular mirror on the wall as he was rehearsing his valedictory speech for the final time. P.S. 130's 8th grade graduation ceremony was scheduled for 10 a.m. on the last Thursday of June. He was very nervous. Public speaking was not his strong point. But, he was committed to giving the speech. The ceremony, which had been rehearsed several times during the past week, was to last about an hour. The Class of 1959 would march down the auditorium's center aisle to the tune of *Pomp and Circumstance*, played on the piano by the school's music teacher. The principal would then give his canned speech about the future and the impact that the students could make on the world. Medals would then be given out, and the ceremony would end with John-John's speech.

John "John-John" Cara was born on May 9, 1945 to John and Angelina Cara. Just before going into labor at Manhattan's Columbus Hospital, Angelina had gotten the word that the war in Europe had just come to an end. May 8th had been declared VE Day—Victory in Europe Day. Her spirits were lifted because she knew that her husband would soon be returning from his stint with the Army's 10th Mountain Division, which had been engaged in almost non-stop combat with the Germans in northern Italy for four months.

After more than twelve hours of labor, Angelina delivered a boy whom she would name John, after his father. She had considered naming her son after his paternal grandfather, but she broke with Italian tradition because she felt that naming her son Saverio would make his life difficult, even in New York's Little Italy.

John, Sr. had served with distinction in World War II, having been awarded the Bronze Star for valor. His division had trained in Colorado where the troops learned the fundamentals of being alpine soldiers. John, a former truck driver, learned to ski "the Army way" in the mountainous terrain of the Army's Colorado camp—Camp Hale—a place that would be transformed after the war into the ski resort town named Vail.

When John returned from the war at the end of 1945, Angelina, along with her seven-month-old baby boy, left her parents' Broome Street apartment to begin her life with her husband in their own apartment—Apartment 4E, at 214 Mulberry Street. The tiny apartment consisted of three "railroad" rooms, totaling only 350 square feet. They considered their new place to be only a "starter" apartment because they had aspirations of buying a house in Brooklyn, someday.

Their little boy, who came to be called John-John as a way of distinguishing him from his father, proved to be a very precocious and intelligent child. He could read simple sentences and count to one hundred by the age of three. He was a standout student at his first school, P.S. 21, which was located just two blocks away on Mott Street. At school, he was studious and shy. These qualities, plus the fact that he almost always got a grade of 100% on exams, won all the spelling bees and every class contest, such as naming all the presidents, caused his classmates to dislike him and treat him like an outcast. He just didn't fit in. He was a square peg in a round hole. The fact that he wore eyeglasses didn't help the situation either. He was often the target of bullies, but fortunately, his father had taught him how to use his fists at an early age; so, he was able to defend himself, although he didn't like to fight.

Angelina, who preferred to be called Angie, was extremely proud of her son's academic skills—and in some ways, she took ownership of them. She claimed that he had taken after her, since she, too, had been a standout student. She had been the valedictorian of her 8th grade class, but being a girl and given the fact that she had graduated in the heart of the Great Depression, her Sicilian-born parents insisted that she join her two sisters working as seamstresses in a nearby sweatshop. High school was definitely out of the question for young Angelina—her teacher's protestations to her parents notwithstanding.

John-John had only one friend at school—a blonde, blue-eyed boy named Willie Sanders. Willie, who was one year behind John-John, was his academic equal. He, too, had problems fitting in at school, but he had one problem that John-John didn't have: Willie was the only blonde-and-blue-eyed kid in the neighborhood—and the fact that his name didn't end in a vowel only exacerbated the situation. Unlike John-John, Willie couldn't defend himself very well. He often came home from school with a bloody nose or a black eye, after being picked on by one of his classmates just because he was different.

Willie's parents were true Bohemians. His mother worked as a secretary to support Willie's father, Jim, who was a "modern artist" specializing in cubism. The fascinating thing about Jim was that although he had been born right-handed, he had learned to draw and paint left-handed after having lost three fingers in a fireworks explosion when he was eighteen years old.

There was no TV in the Sanders' apartment, but there was, however, a library of at least three hundred volumes. By the 5th grade, Willie had already read half of the books in his home library and he encouraged John-John to read as many of them as he wished. Willie taught John-John how to play Scrabble and chess, and Jim taught him the fundamentals of perspective and how to sculpt with clay. Going to Willie's Spring Street apartment was certainly an educational experience, and John-John's trips uptown with Willie and his parents to the various museums and the Hayden Planetarium surely helped him to develop an appreciation for art, history and science, and to broaden his horizons at an early age.

When John-John was about eleven years old, Willie nonchalantly showed him a painting that his father had recently completed. Surprisingly, the painting was done in the traditional style. It was a well-rendered painting of a female nude, depicting full frontal nudity. He had seen similar paintings before at the museums, but his jaw nearly hit the floor when he realized who the shapely blonde model was: Willie's mother! He could never imagine *his* mother posing for such a painting, but to the avant-garde Sanders family, posing in the nude was no big deal.

His friendship with Willie ended in the summer of 1957 when Willie's mother grew tired of supporting her artist husband—an artist who had only sold one painting in his entire life. She and Willie moved to New Jersey in late August after she initiated divorce proceedings. Although John-John and Willie had promised to "stay in touch," their friendship soon withered away, and John-John really grew to miss his one and only buddy.

John-John moved on to P.S. 130 in September of 1957 after graduating from P.S. 21. His new school was (and still is) located at Hester and Baxter Streets at the southern end of Little Italy. He soon had the same problems with fitting in as he had had at P.S. 21, especially since half of his 7th grade classmates were from his former school. With the exception of a few girls, only the Chinese-American students—who comprised about 20% of the student body due to the school's proximity to Chinatown—were friendly to him. Furthermore, they seemed to respect him for his obvious intelligence.

During the outdoor gym sessions, which were held on the school's fenced-in roof, only the Chinese boys would welcome John-John to play punch ball with them. The Chinese boys were relegated to playing on the north half of the roof because they were never chosen to participate in the punch ball games at the south half of the roof; those games seemed to be restricted to Italian boys—probably, due to prejudice. Though John-John was of Italian descent, the team captains would never choose him either, even though he was known to be a decent ballplayer. He just wasn't liked because he was considered to be too much of a nerd and a teachers' pet. When he would complain about not being chosen, he would often hear, "Ah, go play with the Chinks on the other side of the roof."

In April of 1959, John-John was summoned to the Principal's Office. *I wonder why I'm being called to the Principal's Office,* he thought, as he nervously entered the office, trying to figure out what he might have done wrong. He nervousness immediately disappeared when he noticed that the Principal had a broad smile on his face. "John, I have great news for you! You've been accepted into Stuyvesant High School. You are the only one of our students to 'make' Stuyvesant in the past four years."

John-John was on Cloud Nine. He could hardly believe he had passed the Stuyvesant High School entrance exam. Passing that difficult citywide exam was the only criterion for gaining entry into Stuyvesant—one of the best high schools in New York City, and, arguably, one of the top-ten public high schools in the country. After gaining his composure, he thought about the Principal's comment about him being the only student from P.S. 130 to make Stuyvesant in the past four years. He soon realized that the student who had passed the Stuyvesant exam four years earlier was his older cousin, Carmine, who would soon be going on to college at night, having just accepted an entry-level job with IBM. He knew from Cousin Carmine that at Stuyvesant he would be surrounded by students of equal or greater intelligence, and that they all had one thing in common: a strong desire to learn.

The graduation ceremony went as planned. John-John's father couldn't attend the graduation ceremony because he was unable to get a day off from his job as a Manhattan bus driver. His place was taken by John-John's maternal grandmother who was particularly proud to see her grandson being given the highest medal—the Medal for General Excellence. His mother was quite impressed with his speech, as was his grandmother, despite the fact that she could hardly understand a word of English.

Chapter 8: Friends for Life

John-John was sprawled out on the living room sofa deeply engrossed in the classic novel, *Mutiny on the Bounty*. Physically, he was in his very hot and humid apartment; mentally, he was on a beach in Tahiti basking in the sun, admiring the topless native girls. Reading was his escape. It allowed him to leave his world of clustered tenements and dirty streets.

"Angie, I don't understand this son of ours. Here it is, the middle of July, and he's in the house readin'…He should be outside playin' ball or somethin'…Hangin' out with some boys his own age…whatever."

"Whatta ya want from me? I keep tellin' him to go out, but he just mopes around the house either readin' or watching TV. The only time he goes out is when he goes to the library…Meanwhile, Vivian is out all day enjoyin' the summer."

John Sr. was ready for his day behind the wheel of his New York City bus, wearing his olive-drab bus driver's uniform, which fit his trim physique quite well. He would be working the First and Second Avenue route from 1:30 p.m. to 9:30 p.m. As he checked himself in front of the bedroom mirror, it dawned on him that he had forgotten to give John-John his daily boxing lesson.

"C'mon, it's time for a quick boxin' lesson."

"Can't we skip it today?"

"Nope. If I've told you once, I've told you a thousand times…a fella's gotta know how to handle himself in a fight…especially in this neighborhood."

"I know, Pop, I know. I've had quite a few fights and I was able to defend myself."

"What did you do?"

"I blocked the punches and counter-punched just like you taught me."

"Then what?"

"Somebody usually broke it up…The fight usually ended with no one getting hurt much."

"Next time, if somebody gets wise with you, you teach him a lesson! Give him a roundhouse square on the nose…right away… not once, but as many times as you can. Then, the word will get around the neighborhood that you're good with your fists…and trust me, that might be the last time that anybody picks a fight with you around here."

"But, Pop, I really don't want to hurt anybody."

"Listen, to survive in this neighborhood, you gotta be tough. You gotta deal with a lot of mean guys. They only respect toughness around here. That's how they measure you as a kid growin' up, and that's how they measure you as a man…In fact, did you ever notice that none of the men around here ever smile? That they all act like they have a chip on their shoulder and that you better not mess with them?"

"Yeah, now that you mention it…yeah, all the old guys have that look."

"Okay, now, let's get some boxin' in. Start off with a couple of combinations."

After a five-minute lesson, John Sr. exclaimed, "Now, go downstairs and get some air! Play some ball! You can read later."

An hour later, Angie had to scold her son: "You heard what your father said…Put down that book and go outside!"

He reluctantly put down his book and left the apartment. Slowly descending the three flights of stairs, he counted each step, as was his habit, finding that there were still fifty. Finally, he stationed himself right in front of the building and took in the scene: nothing more than a bunch of cars and trucks stuck in traffic; some women scurrying about or occasionally stopping a minute to gossip; and several well-dressed "big shots" standing across the street in front of Nick's Drugstore, conducting "mob business."

His thoughts wandered back to the past summer—his graduation year. His father had "hit the numbers" for $500 and he had spent that summer in Long Branch on the Jersey shore with his mother and sister in a small bungalow near the beach. His father joined them the first two weeks of July, and then every weekend after that. It was great to have gotten away from the hot and steamy city, but this year his father couldn't scrape up enough cash for a summer vacation, mostly because his lucky number—214—had not come out all year.

A couple of boys his age walked by him, paying him no mind. He stared down at the sidewalk. He slowly walked to the nearby corner of Spring Street and stood in front of Aldo's Butcher Shop. His new location didn't change his view very much. He was still bored silly. All he wanted was to get back to his novel, but he knew he couldn't return home for a least an hour to avoid making his mother angry.

Several minutes later, he heard a squeaky voice yelling something that was difficult to hear over the noisy Spring Street traffic. The squeaky voice was coming from a boy, about his age, who was standing across from him in front of Chappy's Bar.

"Yo! Hey you!" pointing at John-John. "Let me see if you can catch this ball."

In the blink of an eye, the boy hurled a pink rubber ball about four stories into the air towards John-John. John-John followed the ball, moved a couple of steps to his left and caught it. He then threw the ball five stories into the air as he yelled, "Let's see you catch this one!"

The other boy caught the ball with ease and continued the routine. After they each had caught the ball about a half-dozen times, the kid crossed over. With a broad, friendly smile, he said, "Hey, you're a pretty good ballplayer."

"Thanks. So are you."

"My name is Joey Russo, but the guys call me Joey 'Limp.'"

"I'm John-John Cara…Hey, why do they call you Joey 'Limp'?"

"Well, I hurt my hip last year while slidin' into third base. The doctors put a few stainless-steel pins in it. Since then, I walk a little funny. I really don't limp, but one of the guys, Danny, started callin' me that, and the name stuck."

"You live around here?'

"Yeah, I live at Spring and Lafayette. I hang out at Joe's Newsstand, right across from my building."

John-John seldom walked on Lafayette Street, but he knew the newsstand. He just didn't know that quite a few boys in his own age hung out there.

"C'mon," said Joey, "I'll introduce you to Joe and who else might be standin' around…By the way, Joe is blind, but sometimes it's hard to tell. He doesn't use a cane and he rides the subway from all the way up the Bronx to get here. He's a lot of fun. He loves to break our balls and we love to tease him. But, if we tease him too much, he'll throw his piss at us."

"What do you mean, 'throw his piss at you'?"

"Well, Joe pees in a pickle jar because he can't leave the newsstand. If you get him mad enough, he'll fling the piss right out the front window at you."

During their one-block walk on Spring Street towards the newsstand, John-John learned that Joey, like himself, was fifteen years old. He had graduated from nearby Saint Patrick's School a year earlier in June and he would be starting his sophomore year in September at Power Memorial High School in uptown Manhattan. He also learned that all the guys who hung out at the newsstand had gone to Saint Patrick's.

Joey introduced him to Joe, who smiled and just said, "Hi."

John-John took note of Joe's appearance: middle-aged; short; slightly rotund; and almost as bald as an eagle.

Joe's once athletic build had atrophied during the years that he was mostly confined to his apartment. Fortunately for Joe, working at the newsstand, coupled with his long commute, had curbed his weight gain and had even caused him to lose a few pounds.

About five minutes later, four members of the "newsstand crew" stopped by and John-John was introduced to each one.

"Hi, I'm Danny Potenza…sometimes they call me 'Plumber' or Danny 'the Plumber'."

"Yo, I'm Lennie 'Squirm.' My last name is Muccio."

It was obvious how Lennie had gotten his nickname; he was extremely thin and wiry, and only about 5'-4" tall; plus, he had an oily complexion and straight, black greasy hair. As for Danny's nickname, "Plumber," it was simply based on the fact that Danny's father was a plumber—Tony "the Plumber"—and his father's nickname had been passed on to him.

"Hi, John-John, I'm Frankie Martinez." Then, adding with a laugh, "Sometimes they call me 'Bubbles' because of my bubbly personality and sometimes they call me '*huevos*.'"

"Way-vose?" inquired John-John.

"Yeah…close enough," answered the short-and-stocky guy to John-John's right. "In regular Spanish *huevos* means *eggs*, but in Puerto Rican slang, it means *balls*…and in Frankie's case, *big balls*…By the way, my name is Eddie Rodriguez, but everybody calls me 'Shortie.'"

"Your nickname should be 'Fatso'!" teased Joe.

"Be nice, Joe, be nice."

John-John silently disagreed with Joe. The nickname "Shortie" was far more appropriate. Eddie was a short, heavy-set guy, but he wasn't fat. John-John looked closely at Frankie and wondered how such a little guy—who was even smaller than Lennie—could have earned such a crazy nickname. He guessed that both Frankie and Eddie were Puerto Rican. There weren't very many Puerto Ricans in the neighborhood, and they generally stuck to themselves. Usually, none of the Italians in the neighborhood would associate with Puerto Ricans, but at the newsstand, things were apparently different.

Hanging out with the guys, John-John learned that Danny was a student at Aviation High School, Frankie attended Seward Park High School and Eddie went to Metropolitan Vocational High School. Eddie's school was unique. It was the only high school in the United States that utilized a ship as a floating school. The former Liberty Ship, *SS John W. Brown*, which was permanently docked at an East River pier, was used for the study of maritime trades. Just like John-John and Joey, all three of these guys would be entering their sophomore year after the summer.

"Hey, Lennie, what about you?" asked John-John.

"Who, me? I don't go to high school."

"He's a truant," remarked Joe, while shaking his head.

"Yeah, I'm a truant. I stopped going to school after the fourth grade."

"Didn't the truant officers come after you?" asked John-John.

"Yeah, they've tried many times, but I'm too fuckin' smart for them."

"Smart my ass!" yelled Joe. "You're gonna grow up to be an illiterate dumb bell, Lennie."

John-John told the group that he was a product of the public school system, adding, "I guess if I had gone to Saint Patrick's, I would've known all you guys"

"What high school do you go to?" asked Shortie.

"Stuyvesant."

"Oh, I hear you gotta be very smart to go to that school…you gotta pass a tough test to get in," remarked Frankie.

"Well, it is a pretty tough test…You know, the bad thing about going to Stuyvesant is that no one else from this neighborhood goes there. My best friends at school live in Queens, the Bronx and Staten Island."

At that point, a thin, tomboyish-looking young girl approached the newsstand.

"Hi, Joe."

"Hi, Felicia."

"Joe, do you have any copies of *Il Progresso* left?"

"Yeah, I got one copy left. I've been holdin' it inside the stand for your mother. I know she likes to read the news in Italian."

John-John noticed that the skinny young girl, with the ash blonde hair, whom he judged to be about twelve or thirteen years old, was staring at him in a funny way—almost as though she had some sort of a crush on him. But she didn't say anything to him. Soon, Danny interrupted her staring by teasing her.

"Hey 'Stick,' how's it goin'?"

"Don't call me 'stick,' Danny!"

"Okay, then…Hey 'Skank,' how's it goin'?"

Flustered and embarrassed, she scurried back to her building, just up the block.

"Who's that girl, Joey?"

"Oh, she's Felicia Daniels. Her father is Zeke Daniels…a hick from Tennessee. He met her mother, Serafina, during the war. They were married in Naples."

"The rumor around the neighborhood is that her mother was a big who-ah back in Naples," added Danny in an insulting tone.

Ignoring Danny's remark, Joey continued, "She's got a ten-year-old sister named Francesca and a seven-year-old brother they call Little Zeke."

"Her parents really bust our chops," interjected Shortie. "They don't want us playin' anywhere near their buildin'."

"They're always yellin' at us…threatenin' to call the cops on us…tellin' us that we should go play somewheres else. But there ain't no places to play around here. The streets and the sidewalks are our fuckin' playgrounds," said an animated Frankie.

"There's that tiny park over there," said Joe, pointing in the general direction of the mini-park at nearby Cleveland Place.

Frankie replied, "Joe, if you could see, you would realize that that park is hardly longer than a couple of city buses, and it's only about 25 feet wide. You can't play any kind of ballgame there."

"Yeah," agreed Danny, "So we play wherever we can…When Zeke and his wife tell us to get away from their buildin', I tell 'em that they don't own the streets or the sidewalks…And if Serafina really gets me mad, I tell her to go back to Italy! That really gets her angry and she starts screamin' curses at me and my family in Neapolitan."

"Yeah, she's got some mouth on her…like a sailor," added Joe.

"So, what do you do when she curses at you and your family?" asked John-John.

"I curse back at her in Neapolitan…yellin' twice as many curses at her and her family than she yelled at me."

"Hey Danny, tell him what you guys have been doin' to get even with Serafina and her husband," commanded Joe with a sly smile on his face.

"Well, Zeke's side job is bein' the janitor of his building. So, sometimes, we take his garbage cans and carry 'em over to Prince Street and leave 'em there. Or, sometimes we'll take some garbage out of that trash can by the traffic light pole and throw it in the hallway of his buildin'."

"Tell him the rest, Danny," encouraged Joe.

"Okay. I know you just met Joe and you probably think he's just a kind old blindman. But, don't be fooled. Joe may be a kind old blindman, but he's also a master at breaking balls, and he's got a little bit of the devil in him."

Joe smiled, saying, "Yeah, I got a lot of the devil in me."

"Yeah," added Frankie, "He comes up with some crazy stuff… things he used to do when he was a kid up in the Bronx."

"Well," Danny continued, "Many times, we put his crazy ideas into action."

Shortie chimed in: "Yeah, like this…One time, we collected all the dog shit we could find in the neighborhood and put it in a brown paper shoppin' bag. At around 9 o'clock at night, we put the bag on the sidewalk right in front of Zeke's building. We put a newspaper over the bag, set the newspaper on fire and rang Zeke's bell…Then, we all yelled 'fire,' doing our best to change our voices…We ran back here and hid around the corner…But, we peeked to see what was happenin'."

Joe, who could not contain his laughter, finished the story, saying, "I heard that when that dumb hillbilly stomped out the fire, he was up to his ankles in dog shit…hot dog shit!"

"Wow, you guys are crazy!" said John-John, as he tried to figure out if his newfound friends might be a bit *too* crazy for him.

"There's more!" added Danny with a sense of pride. "About once a month, Lennie orders two pizzas from different pizzerias in the neighborhood and has them delivered to Zeke and Serafina's apartment."

"Yeah, I order the pizzas from that phone booth," pointing to the phone booth in front of the East River Savings Bank, directly across from the newsstand.

"One time, after the delivery boy was turned away by Zeke or Serafina, he threw the two boxes of pizza in the trashcan by the traffic light pole. As soon as he was out of sight, we went into the can and pulled out the pizza boxes. None of the garbage touched the pizzas. The only thing wrong was that the pizzas were a little lopsided.

"That's true, Danny, but that was some of the best pizza I ever ate," said Joey, adding, "The best part was that it didn't cost us nuttin…You can't beat free pizza!"

John-John was getting cold feet about hooking up with the newsstand crew. The guys seemed too wild, but, they were also friendly to him. Sure he loved his books, but he also realized that his father was probably right: there was much to be learned on the streets—things you can't learn from books. Plus, he wanted friends. He didn't want to be the weird loner kid. So, he decided to give hanging-out with these guys a chance.

Over the next two weeks, he became fully involved with the newsstand crew. He got to meet all of the "regulars" including Charlie "the Ox" whose nickname came from his squat physique and unusual strength; Vinnie "Lemons" who always looked like he had just sucked on a sour lemon; Donny "Knobhead" whose head was shaped like a doorknob; Nicky "White Cap" who always sported a white baseball hat and supposedly even slept with it on his head; and Tommy "Yeah-Yeah" who couldn't put two sentences together without uttering "yeah-yeah" somewhere in those sentences.

John-John's prowess as a ballplayer helped him gain status with the guys. He was quite good at all of the city games played with a rubber ball, better known as a "spaldine": punch ball, stickball, stoopball, box ball and Chinese handball. As the weeks went by, he ventured a bit onto the "wild side," grabbing one of Zeke's garbage cans and bringing it to Prince Street one night, and on another night, tying a free-standing, four-foot-high bus stop sign to the back bumper of a Lafayette Street bus. The bus stop sign prank was his own idea and all the guys got a big laugh as the heavy steel sign bounced over the cobblestone pavement, clanging its way up Lafayette Street.

One evening in mid-August, John-John and Frankie were standing in front of the closed newsstand after playing stoopball on Crosby Street until no one could see the ball. After the game, six of the guys walked over to Mott Street for sodas, leaving John-John and Frankie to wait for them by the newsstand. As the two were talking, they moved away from the newsstand close to the traffic light pole and adjacent trashcan. At that point, they noticed two young guys crossing Lafayette Street, heading almost directly at them. John-John recognized them as they drew near: the two guys were "Crazy" Mike and Sonny "Splits". Mike may not have been truly crazy, but he certainly had a reputation for acting crazy, while Sonny had earned his moniker by having split many heads, lips and other body parts of those unfortunates who had pissed him off for one reason or another.

Mike and Sonny had graduated from P.S. 130 the previous year along with John-John, but they were both two years older than him, each having been left back twice. Given their age advantage and their mean dispositions, they were the two most feared guys in the school. They had really disliked John-John at school because he represented everything they were not. John-John had gone to great lengths to avoid them throughout his two years at P.S. 130. If he saw them standing in front of one school entrance, he would walk around the block and go into the school through the other entrance. He would avoid the schoolyard and he would always go back to his homeroom at the end of the day and remain there for ten or fifteen minutes before cautiously exiting the school.

"Hey, Sonny, look who's here…the fuckin' four-eyed boy genius!"

John-John stiffened up, not knowing how to respond. Without any provocation, Mike forcefully shoved him, pushing him back several feet. That move incited Sonny, causing him to shove John-John, too. John-John, who at 5'-8" tall and about 175 pounds was relatively big for his age, instinctively pushed back.

This angered Sonny, who shouted, "So, you think you're a smart guy…You're nuttin but a fuckin' four-eyed mope!"

Instead of standing by John-John's side, Frankie slipped out of sight. John-John then figured that it was going to be two against one. He couldn't believe that Frankie hadn't stood by him, but he had no time to fret about it. Sonny threw a punch, which John-John skillfully evaded. Then, "Crazy" Mike grabbed hold of John-John from the back while Sonny tried to land some punches; but John-John managed to keep him at bay by kicking wildly. Mike then slid his arms upward, managing to get John-John in a headlock.

While John-John was busy trying to defend himself against the two thugs, Frankie was in front of the newsstand reaching up behind the fascia of the newsstand's steel awning. He quickly found the stickball bat that the guys kept there. As John-John was about to get the beating of his life, Frankie came to his aid, bat in hand. Swinging the bat with all of his might, and with reckless abandon, he struck Mike across his left ear. As Mike let out a scream of pain, Frankie took two swings at Sonny, catching him first on the shoulder and then squarely on the right knee.

Heeding his father's advice, John-John decided to *finish* this fight. He repeatedly punched Mike in the face, causing his nose to bleed and his upper lip to split. Sonny, who wasn't finished fighting, attacked John-John from behind. But Frankie protected John-John's back by literally cracking the stickball bat—Danny's mother's old broomstick—over Sonny's head.

"Okay, we had enough," muttered Mike.

"Okay! Okay, it's over!" yelled Sonny. But, showing defiance, he chose to spit at Frankie and then yell, "Fuck you! You fuckin' spic bastard!"

Without even batting an eyelash, Frankie hit Sonny right across the nose with what remained of the broken stickball bat.

"Okay, now it's *really* over! Go back to fuckin' Hester Street where you guys belong!"

The rest of the crew returned with sodas in hand, not realizing what they had just missed. But they got the gist of what had happened when they got a close-up look at "Crazy" Mike and Sonny "Splits," both of whom were bloodied—especially Sonny "Splits".

When the two were about a half-block away, Sonny yelled, "It ain't over. We'll be back!"

Frankie responded, "You better bring a fuckin' army because you're gonna have to fight all of us standing here, plus five or ten more guys!"

"Ah, go fuck yourselves!" shouted Mike.

"I'd rather fuck your sister!" yelled Frankie.

A shaken John-John worried about the repercussions of the melee because he knew that Mike and Sonny were treacherous. Shortie, who was very streetwise, gave his opinion of what Mike and Sonny might do: "Don't worry, they won't come back. In fact, they're probably so ashamed of what happened here that they'll probably *sneak* back home…and they won't show their faces until their wounds have healed."

"Why would they do that?"

"Because if any of the guys down at their end of the neighborhood saw that somebody threw them such a fuckin' beatin,' they would lose their reputations as tough guys."

"I hope you're right, Shortie. I hope you're right."

"I know I'm right, John-John. Anyway, judging by the way they looked, I know you can handle yourself, big guy."

"Yeah, I guess I can handle myself in a fair fight, but those guys don't fight fair…plus, I really hate fighting."

"I don't like fightin' either," said Frankie, "But you gotta do what you gotta do…especially in this neighborhood…By the way, if I was you, I wouldn't go walkin' around Hester Street for a while. Shortie is probably right about them not comin' back here, but if you go there, they'll probably gang-up on you."

John-John walked over to Frankie and gave him a big hug. "Frankie, thanks for saving me."

"Hey, we all stick together around here…All for one and one for all! Like the fuckin' Three Musketeers."

"I guess I know how you earned your nickname, 'Way-vose.'"

"Yeah, now you know," responded Frankie with a broad grin. "When you're small like me, you gotta be a little *loco*. My father told me that since I'm small, I should use a bat, a brick, a pipe, or whatever I can get my hands on when I get in a fight. He said it's only fair that I should use an 'equalizer.'" Then Frankie began to laugh, saying, "My father…my father and his equalizer."

I think I have found friends for life right here at the newsstand, thought John-John. After mulling over what had just happened, he made a decision to never again wear his eyeglasses when out on the streets, concluding that the glasses made him look weak. Given that his vision was 20-40, forgoing his eyeglasses wouldn't be much of a problem.

Chapter 9: Kick the Can

It was a hot weekday evening in early September. Joe had just closed up the newsstand and was on his way back home to the Bronx. The "newsstand crew" was hanging out in front of the stand doing nothing in particular—one of the joys of being youths without any responsibilities. This would change on the coming Monday when most of the guys—Lennie "Squirm" being the exception—would be starting the new school year.

The eight guys on the corner couldn't contain themselves, being quite animated and loud as they engaged in their favorite pastime— making fun of each other and any odd-looking people who walked by. Adding to the din was Danny's new portable transistor radio, which was tuned at full volume to the *Murray the K* program on WINS. Zeke and Serafina, seated nearby in front of their building, had just come down from their hot and stuffy apartment in hope of catching a cool breeze. They knew they would have to deal with the noisy Lafayette Street traffic, but they saw no reason why they had to put up with the extra noise from the gathering on the corner. Zeke could have let the situation slide, but he decided to try to get the guys to move across the street.

"Now why must y'all hang out on *this* corner? Me and my wife can't rightly hear each other talk."

Danny, who was always ready with a nasty response, blurted out, "What does it matter? You can't understand each other, anyway!"

Zeke yelled over the laughter, "Git your asses across the street over there by the bank buildin'!"

"Hey, John-John, where ya goin'? Stay here! He doesn't own the fuckin' streets," remarked Donny 'Knobhead.'"

"Yeah, go call a cop!" yelled Charlie "the Ox" with an air of defiance.

"Maybe, I will call the po-lice and teach you youngins a lesson."

"Ah, go ahead!" yelled four of the guys in unison.

Zeke's blood was boiling, but he didn't call the cops, despite Serafina's urgings. After a half-hour, the two went back up to their apartment.

Danny laughed, saying, "I guess they had enough."

At that point, Shortie, who was quite a jokester, feigned, "Hey, John-John, it looks like "Crazy" Mike and Sonny "Splits" are comin' up the block lookin' for you."

"Where?" John-John nervously replied.

"Only kiddin'…Only kiddin'. As I said a couple of weeks ago, those guys ain't gonna show their fuckin' faces around here."

"Hey, why don't we play a game of kick the can," suggested Frankie.

Kick the can was a popular inner-city game, which probably originated around the turn of the century. All that was needed to play the game was an empty can of some sort. The game, as played in Little Italy, was somewhat akin to baseball. An offensive player would place the can at "home base" and kick it towards the defending fielders. He would try to reach first base before being tagged with the can by one of the fielders, or before the "catcher" could tap on home base with the can tossed to him by one of the fielders. A "run" would be scored when a player would reach home base safely. As in baseball, each team was allotted three outs. A typical game consisted of five innings.

Instead of playing the game across the Lafayette Street–Spring Street intersection, with each corner being a base, the guys decided to play the game on the sidewalk because there was too much traffic at the intersection. Since the sidewalk was relatively narrow, they modified the game to have only two bases. A square in the concrete sidewalk in front of the newsstand served as home base and a similarly-sized square directly in front of Zeke and Serafina's building was chosen for first base.

Frankie found an empty Rheingold beer can that had been thrown in the gutter, and the game soon began. This quirky street game was actually a lot of fun—in some respects, more fun than some organized sports. After John-John's team had scored two runs, it was his turn to kick the can. He swung his right leg backward and then followed through with a mighty kick sending the can about 20 feet into the air. Unfortunately, the can flew right through the Daniels' open bay window and into their living room.

A bay window was a rare architectural feature that could only be found on a handful of buildings in the neighborhood. The Daniels' apartment, which was one-story above street level, had the only bay window on Lafayette Street. The bay window created a mini-alcove within the living room, and its side windows—which were usually kept open in the summer—provided a clear view of Lafayette Street, including whoever might be hanging out in front of the newsstand.

In less than a minute, Zeke came down from his apartment with the beer can in hand.

"Now, which one of you guys done threw this can into my livin' room?"

"What makes you think *we* did it, Zeke?" exclaimed Donny.

"Who else would've done it? Now fess up!"

John-John sheepishly admitted that he was the guilty party, while trying to explain that it was an accident.

"Now, this shit's gotta stop. Go play somewheres else!"

At that point, John-John's father, still in his bus driver's uniform, had just come out of the subway after a tough day behind the wheel. As he crossed Lafayette Street, he couldn't miss the commotion straight ahead, and he couldn't help but notice that John-John was right in the middle of it.

"What's goin' on here?" questioned John Sr.

"Are you this boy's father?" asked Zeke, pointing to John-John.

"Yeah, what's the problem?"

"He either threw or kicked this here can right through my livin' room window. It done hit the TV set, but luckily, it didn't damage it."

"Is that true, John-John?"

"Yeah, Pop, but it was an accident. It happened during a game of kick the can."

"Listen, if you're gonna play kick the can, you should go play it on Crosby Street, not around here."

The guys then crossed over to the bank building, leaving Zeke and John Sr. standing together in front of the newsstand.

"Look, I'm not a hard-ass. I was a youngin once. But these young fellas are always in my hair…and they are very disrespectful to both me and my wife."

"Disrespectful? Has my son been disrespectful?"

"Nope, I can't say that he has."

"Say, I can tell that you're not from around here. In fact, your accent reminds me of an old Army buddy of mine…He was from Tennessee."

"You got a good ear for accents, sir. I'm from Tennessee…and I, too, was in the Army."

That said, the two veterans briefly recapped their military service in World War II and exchanged names.

"You know, I was thinkin' about joining the VFW over on Kenmare Street," remarked Zeke.

"Ah, don't waste your time. Many of the men who now hang out there aren't even vets. The place has changed a lot. It's become a bookie parlor and a place to play cards for serious money."

"Well, that's not what I was a lookin' for…I think I'll go back upstairs, now. Nice to meet you, John."

"Likewise, Zeke…and if my son *ever* gives you or your wife a problem, let me know and I'll make sure it won't happen again."

Later that evening, John Sr. told John-John that he and his friends should stop annoying Zeke and that they should show him and his wife some respect.

"You know, that man went through hell fightin' for this country…same as I did. I don't never wanna hear that you been disrespectin' him or his wife."

"Okay, Pop."

The following afternoon, John-John was at the newsstand talking to Joe. None of the guys were around. In the midst of their conversation about the Yankees, Felicia walked over and surprised John-John by speaking to him for the first time ever.

"That wasn't nice of you to kick that beer can into our livin' room. You could have hurt someone."

"It was an accident."

"Yeah, Felicia, from what I hear, it wasn't done on spite," added Joe.

"Well, my father cooled off after talkin' to your father, but my mother is still angry with you…That's the way she is…If you do her wrong, she don't forget…In fact, she refers to you as a '*Siciliano bastardo*'…a Sicilian bastard."

"I know what it means. How does she know that I'm Sicilian?"

"I told her", volunteered Joe. "When she started noticing that you were hanging out here, she asked me about you."

"Well, I told my mother you seemed nice and that she shouldn't call you that."

"Thanks, Felicia."

At that point, Felicia giggled, tilted her head, and looked at him with fluttering eyes. Then she abruptly turned around and left. John-John got the feeling that the tomboyish-looking young girl might have a crush on him.

That evening at about ten, the guys were in the mood to do some singing. Usually, they would sing at the first landing of the entrance to the uptown IRT Subway because the acoustics there made almost any voice sound good. However, because it was hot and very humid, they chose to sing outside on the stoop in front of the closed hero shop, which was about halfway between the newsstand and the Daniels' building. The guys' awful attempts at four-part harmony filtered into all of the nearby apartments, particularly unnerving Zeke and Serafina, who were glued to their TV set trying to follow a crime drama.

The singing group consisted of John-John, Shortie, Frankie and Charlie "the Ox". Danny would occasionally try to chime in, but since he couldn't carry a tune if his life depended on it, he was usually told to sing "far away"—a double entendre and a cute way of telling him to "shut up." The singers, trying as hard as they could, just couldn't come close to duplicating the complex harmonies of their favorite song, *Where or When*, as sung by Dion and the Belmonts. They just couldn't do the song any justice, and their attempts at harmony turned to cacophony when Danny would try to get into the act.

After about fifteen minutes of what Serafina considered to be howling, she had had enough. She went over to the bay window, picked up one of the numerous flowerpots from the windowsill, and flung it towards the "offending" singing group. The ceramic pot just missed Shortie, landing inches from his feet.

"Hey, are you crazy, lady! You could've killed me!"

"Ah, Go home-ah you-ah *figli di puttane!*"

Even the two Puerto Ricans, Frankie and Shortie, knew that Serafina was calling them "sons of whores," having learned the insulting phrase, "*figli di puttane,*" from Joe, who frequently punctuated his speech with Neapolitan insults and curse words.

"Drop dead you old witch!" yelled Frankie.

'Serafina, *Tu sei una puttana!*" added Danny, feeling more than justified in calling Serafina a whore, given that she had referred to all of the guys' mothers as whores.

John-John didn't utter a word. He just sat on the stoop with his mouth wide open, wondering how such a seemingly innocuous thing as singing could have led to such a tense situation.

Chapter 10: Uncle Joe

The winter of 1963 was a typical New York City winter. Despite the normal frigid temperatures and gloomy days, New Yorkers were generally in good spirits. They, along with everyone else in the country, were breathing a bit easier now that October 1962's Cuban Missile Crisis was a few months behind them, thanks to President Kennedy's courage and leadership.

About two-and-a-half years had passed since John-John's introduction to the newsstand crew. During that time, he had truly become "one of the boys." In many respects he had become the de facto leader of the group because all the guys looked up to him—both literally and figuratively. At seventeen, he was already one of the biggest guys in the neighborhood. He had had a "sudden" growth spurt about six months earlier, adding 6 inches to his height. He had grown so rapidly the summer before his senior year in high school that he actually had developed stretch marks on his shoulders. From Frankie's perspective, John-John's 6'-2", 200-pound physique made him some sort of a giant. To Lennie "Squirm" and Shortie, he was not quite a giant, but he most certainly was *big*. Had he had the mindset of a typical neighborhood tough guy, he could easily have terrorized many of the neighborhood's youths, given his size and his boxing ability.

He had learned how to compartmentalize his life. He fit right in with his intelligent classmates, quite a few of whom could be classified as nerds. He enjoyed exchanging ideas with his intellectual equals; discussing Shakespeare, politics, advances in the sciences, and the fine points of mathematics. He wondered what school would have been like had girls been permitted to attend his prestigious high school. He concluded that had the school been coed, he certainly would have been dating by now—his senior year; but on the other hand, since girls would have comprised about fifty percent of his class, perhaps, he wouldn't have gotten into Stuyvesant—his place in the Class of 1963 might have been taken by a girl with a higher admission test score.

As well as he fit in with his high school classmates, he was equally adept at fitting in with the boys on the corner. He made an effort to speak neighborhood slang, at times intentionally making grammatical errors, and occasionally lacing his sentences with cuss words for effect. He tried to downplay his intelligence and thirst for knowledge, although he sometimes forgot himself. But doing so didn't lower his standing in the newsstand crew; the guys actually respected his academic accomplishments and interest in learning. However, he was smart enough to understand that he should never act as though he were better than any of his pals—not even the illiterate Lennie "Squirm." The same held true in his dealings with everyone else in the neighborhood. It was one of the keys to fitting in and surviving on the "mean streets" of Little Italy.* His father's advice to him many years earlier had struck a chord: "You wanna get along in life… don't 'high-hat' nobody around here or anywhere else. Never act like you're better than anyone."

John-John had really grown close to Joe over the years, in part because of Joe's avuncular personality, which all the guys found endearing. In fact, the guys would often refer to him as "Uncle Joe." But they all were well aware that besides being a mischievous and fun-loving man, Joe was a complex person with many facets to his character, including a mean and dark side.

His mean and dark side surfaced the week before the Christmas of 1962 when a newsstand was erected directly across the street from his newsstand, adjacent to the cigar store and the downtown IRT subway station. The proprietors of this new newsstand were an elderly married couple whose physical handicap was that they were midgets—a word that has since become pejorative, being replaced by the term "little people." Joe quickly realized that another newsstand at the intersection would hurt his business—and this angered him to no end.

A decade later, the opening scene of Martin Scorsese's benchmark film, Mean Streets—a tale about the very same neighborhood—would be filmed in front of a bar, located within a block of the newsstand.

He would continually rage, "I don't see why those fuckin' midgets had to open up a newsstand right across the street from me! I gotta get 'em outta here!"

After the little people were in business for about a month, New York City was hit with a snowstorm that blanketed it with an 8-inch layer of whiteness, which would turn to a gray slush the following day. Joe decided to have some "fun" at the expense of his new competition. Pointing to the building next to the newsstand, he demanded, "Hey, guys, do me a favor. Go up the roof and bomb the fuckin' midgets' newsstand with snowballs for about an hour. I'll give a copy of *Playboy* to whoever hits the newsstand with the most snowballs."

Since Joe would never let any of the guys thumb through his *Playboy* magazines, fearing that their dirty hands would make the magazines look used, it was a tempting offer that none of them could pass it up.

"Try not to hurt nobody…But, if you do a good job, I'm sure most of their customers are gonna come over here to buy their papers."

Danny, Frankie, Shortie, Lennie and John-John scurried up to the roof and began their barrage. They laughed heartily as passersby and would-be customers ran across the intersection while protecting their heads with their hands. Occasionally, someone would accidentally get hit by a snowball, which packed quite a wallop from the momentum of its four-story drop. A few times, a passerby who looked "a bit odd" to the guys, would intentionally be targeted.

When the hour-long onslaught had ended, it was determined that Danny had won the *Playboy*, scoring forty-six direct hits on the newsstand. Joe gave the magazine to Danny with a smile, saying, "Danny, it was worth it. I could hear those fuckin' midgets yellin' and screamin' from here…and I think I sold thirty or forty more papers than I sold this time yesterday."

While the guys were chuckling about their rooftop misdeed, they heard a squeaky female voice yelling at them from behind.

"Hey, you guys were throwing snowballs at my newsstand from the roof!"

"You're wrong. It wasn't us, lady."

"I know it was you! I saw your faces!"

Then, pointing at John-John, who towered over her, she came up with the best insult that she could muster: "You, longie! You, longie!"

John-John stood dumbfounded, not knowing how to respond, or even if he should. But, the quick-witted Danny bent down to the woman's eye level and retorted, "Ah, go back across the fuckin' street…You, shortie! You, shortie!"

As the weeks went by, Joe's new competitors really ate into his business, especially during evenings. Most people coming home from work exited from the subway kiosk right behind the little people's newsstand. Also, the factory workers returning from work would first have to pass the little people's newsstand before reaching Joe's stand. Joe figured that his sales had dropped about thirty percent as a result of his new competition, and he decided—as a matter of his survival—that he had to find a way to drive them out of business.

His initial sortie in his war against his competition entailed getting Lennie "Squirm" to glom a bundle of the little people's newspapers every day before they opened. Lennie who didn't go to school and usually walked his dog in the early morning, was happy to do Joe's dirty work. Every morning, he would nonchalantly pick up a bundle of fifty *Daily News* or fifty *Daily Mirrors* and carry them over to Crosby Street where he would leave them in front of a factory building, after removing fifteen copies for Joe. Even if Joe didn't sell the "extra" copies, he would receive seven cents for each newspaper he returned to the distributor the following day. On very rainy days, Lennie would divert from his Crosby Street routine by soaking both bundles of morning newspapers in nearby rain-filled potholes, rendering the newspapers unsaleable.

Later on, Joe upped the ante by convincing Vinnie "Lemons" and Tommy "Yeah-Yeah" to set fire to the little people's newsstand. Following Joe's plan, Vinnie and Tommy placed the corner trashcan against the newsstand and set the trash on fire. The newsstand was only damaged superficially by the flames, but it was substantially damaged by the firemen who put out the fire.

When Joe exited the subway on the following morning and walked past the little people's newsstand, he smelled the lingering odor of burnt wood and metal. He smiled from ear-to-ear, as he thought, *I guess Vinnie and Tommy really came through for me last night.* To his delight, the little people abandoned their operation shortly after the fire, opening up another newsstand on East 14th Street.

John-John had been privy to all the details of Joe's attempts to drive the little people out of business. Although he had participated in the snowball assault, he, along with most of the other guys, wanted no part of the rest of Joe's plans. John-John, who had just completed reading Charles Dickens' *Oliver Twist* in school, came to the conclusion that Joe had some of the same attributes as the evil character, Fagin, who encouraged his young followers to engage in petty criminal activities.

One day, Joe convinced Joey "Limp" to "borrow" a copy of the paperback book, *The ABC's of Sex*, by Jake Lee, from the cigar store across the street. Joey, who worked at the cigar store on a parttime basis, had no trouble hiding the book under his jacket at the end of his workday. Joe took delight in having Joey, John-John or Danny read him chapters of the book, which addressed just about every topic related to human sexuality and reproduction. He would comment on nearly every paragraph, adding his own experiences to illustrate certain points. Thus, Joe, with the aid of the book—which was never returned—gave the guys a great sex education. He answered questions that none of the guys would have dared asked their fathers, who, to a man, believed that their sons should learn the facts of life on the streets—just as they had.

Joe always got even—in spades—with anyone who did him wrong or played a trick on him. There was the time when Donny "Knobhead" kept tickling Joe's nose with a feather, trying to get him to believe that he was dealing with a pesky mosquito. Joe fell for the ruse a couple of times, but when Donny giggled, he knew that he wasn't dealing with a mosquito.

"Cut it out 'Knobhead'!"

"How'd you know it was me?"

"I recognized your giggle, you fuckin' dummy!"

Joe filed the incident away until he could get the opportunity to exact some revenge. That opportunity soon came when one of his customers, Louie "Gyp," told him that he was about to throw a radio into the trashcan because it was filled with cockroaches and wasn't working properly. The roaches apparently had discovered that the heat of the radio tubes gave them a warm home. Louie didn't want to throw the radio into one of the garbage cans in his building's hallway because he feared that the roaches would further infest his building.

"Louie, don't throw the radio away. Just leave it with me."

"Why?"

"I know somebody who might be able to clean out the radio and make it work right. I'll give the radio back to you if he fixes it."

After Louie left, Joe put the radio in a large brown paper bag and tightly wrinkled the top of the bag to affect a seal. When Donny stopped by, Joe asked him to try to fix the radio, indicating that it was his radio from home. Donny, who was a student at George Westinghouse Vocational High School, was heavily into the study of electricity and electronics. He had a mini workbench at home that he used when he tinkered with TVs, radios and small appliances. Fixing Joe's radio would be a welcomed challenge for him.

Early that evening, Donny, placed the radio on his workbench. He methodically unscrewed the radio's back covering, unwittingly surprising the roaches within. The small radio contained at least a hundred roaches, which began speeding off in all directions. Donny yelled, "Fuckin' roaches!" as he raced to the window and tossed the radio down to the sidewalk without even bothering to check who might be below. Fortunately, the radio crashed onto the sidewalk without hitting anyone. Donny and the other members of his family tried to kill all the roaches that had escaped from the radio, but they were only partly successful. At least a dozen of those fast-moving insects had escaped from being crushed, taking refuge under the refrigerator and in other hiding places.

Joe played dumb the next day when he inquired about the status of *his* radio.

"Joe, I tossed your radio out the window. It was filled with fuckin' cockroaches. Now my house is infested with them!"

Joe acted as though he was surprised and sorry, but he was really happy inside. He got extra satisfaction when he later told some of the newsstand crew how he had duped Donny, knowing that they would immediately turn around and tease Donny about the incident. Of course, Joe convincingly denied his culpability in the matter, when an angered Donny returned to yell at him. However, by telling the guys how he had set up Donny, they clearly got the message that they, too, would suffer a similar fate if they ever dared to anger Joe too much.

Joe truly enjoyed mischief. Mischief, as well as controversy, seemed to feed his soul, serving to take his mind off his blindness. When the guys would inevitably get involved in one controversy or another with Zeke and Serafina, Joe would usually play the role of instigator, bringing the situation to a higher level by throwing "gasoline on the fire" whenever he could. What John-John had heard when he first met Joe had proved to be true: He wasn't just a kind old blindman. In fact, fifteen years later, when the hit TV comedy series *Taxi* hit the airwaves, John-John and the rest of the old newsstand crew would come to agree that Joe's temperament—and to some extent, his appearance—had been quite similar to that of the character Louie, as played by Danny DeVito in that popular sitcom.

All of the guys were well acquainted with the general story of how Joe had gotten blind, but John-John would continually probe him for more and more details. Joe eventually told him the complete story and he let him in on his two little secrets: the fact that he could distinguish day from night with his right eye; and the fact that he could vaguely—very vaguely—make out shadows with that eye. John-John promised Joe that he would never let the rest of the crew in on his secret—and he kept his word.

"Joe, is there anything that the doctors can do to restore the vision in your right eye?"

"Nah, it's too fuckin' dangerous. My right eye could explode and hemorrhage during an operation, just as my left eye did. Then, I would lose the very little I got goin' for me in my right eye."

"I'm sure things must have changed over the past two decades… there must have been some advances in medical science."

"I don't think so."

"When was the last time that you went to an eye doctor?"

"About ten years ago."

"Ten years ago?"

"Listen, I don't want no part of doctors. As far as I'm concerned, they're all a bunch of fuckin' shoemakers!"

"Joe, I think you really should go visit a top eye surgeon."

"Ah, leave me the fuck alone. I'm happy the way I am."

Chapter 11: Have a Hot Dog

Sam "the Hot Dog Man" was open for business, standing alongside his pushcart on Mulberry Street near the corner of Spring. It was noontime on the last Saturday of April. Sam and his hot dog pushcart could be found at the same spot every Saturday, except for the winter months, for as long as anyone could remember. He and his hot dog pushcart, which was clad with stainless steel and topped with a large, multi-colored umbrella, had become part of the neighborhood fabric—a fixture, so to speak. He sold only hot dogs, potato chips and soda. The hot dogs were said to be kosher—although, that was of little importance in Little Italy. Sam, like all other New York City hot dog vendors, kept his previously boiled hot dogs warm in a heated stainless-steel bin filled with water. Throughout the city, such hot dogs were commonly referred to as "dirty-water hot dogs," because the warm water inside the bin was opaque and slimy. However, very few New Yorkers seemed to care about the quality of the water; the wonderful smell of the hot dogs, enhanced by the enticing aromas of cooked onions, sauerkraut, and spicy mustard, quelled most people's concerns about sanitary conditions.

Sam was a sixty-something-year-old, jovial, Jewish man who had immigrated to America from Poland in the early 1930s, fortunately missing the Holocaust by a several years. Despite being in America for more than a quarter-century, he spoke English with a thick Yiddish accent. However, to those who had the opportunity to engage him in a serious conversation, it was apparent that his Yiddish accent masked a wise and learned man who seemed to be working at a job that was "beneath him." But, he was making a very decent living from his little pushcart, making enough money to spend his winters in Miami.

When John-John walked out of his building, he was instantly attracted to the savory aromas being blown his way by the pleasant spring winds. He had just finished his lunch—a peppers-and-eggs hero sandwich. His mother, Angie, had prepared it just the way he liked it—smothered in olive oil. But, John-John was a "growing boy," and he certainly had enough room for one of Sam's hot dogs. At home, he was sometimes referred to as "the eating machine." In fact, before leaving his apartment, he had sneaked a big bite of his sister Vivian's hero when she had left the kitchen to answer the phone.

John-John walked over to the pushcart, greeted Sam, and placed his order. Within seconds, Sam had a hot dog on a bun, topped with sauerkraut and mustard in John-John's hand. He then dug deep into the soda bin and pulled out an ice-cold bottle of Coca-Cola. As John-John handed him 40 cents, he attempted to engage Sam in a bit of conversation, but he soon realized that with three customers lined-up behind him, the conversation would have to wait until next Saturday.

When John-John turned around, he noticed that Vinnie "Lemons" was the third person in line behind him. Vinnie was one of Sam's favorite customers because he would typically eat three or four of his hot dogs every Saturday.

"Hey, Vinnie, are you gonna come to Lafayette Street for some stickball practice at around one?"

"Yeah, I'll be there…I know we're gonna start playin' some games for money soon. Have you booked any, yet?"

"Almost…I'm close to setting up a game with one of the teams from Prince and Elizabeth for $2 a man…They call themselves The Magnificent Seven."

"Maybe, we should play for five bucks a man 'cause I hear they ain't that fuckin' magnificent."

"Nah, that's too much money for me. I'll have a hard enough time coming up with the $2…Besides, they're a real good team, despite what you say."

When Vinnie reached the head of the line, he ordered a hot dog with nothing on it. Sam was surprised by the order because he knew that Vinnie usually wanted his hot dogs with "the works," that is, overflowing with onions, sauerkraut and mustard. When Sam handed him the plain hot dog on a bun, Vinnie quickly pulled the hot dog out of the bun and gobbled it down in two bites.

"Vutz you doin', Vinnie?" asked a perplexed Sam."

Without answering, Vinnie smiled and pulled an unwrapped cigar out of his pocket and placed it on the hot dog bun.

"Sam, put plenty of onions, sauerkraut, and mustard on it…and don't skimp!"

"Are you playin' some keinz-ah joke on some-vun?" asked Sam as he followed Vinnie's directions.

"Yeah, you got it right, Sam."

John-John got the feeling that the odds were that Vinnie was going to give the doctored-up "hot dog" to Joe—an easy target.

"Hey, Vinnie, I hope you're not gonna give that *hot dog* to Joe."

"Yeah, I wanna have some fun with him."

"That's not nice…The man's blind."

"So what he's blind. He's a real ball buster. He likes to dish it out, so he should be able to take it…Now, I don't want you spoilin' my joke. It took me a long fuckin' time to come up with this idea."

Should I tip Joe off? thought John-John, torn inside about what to do. He knew that it was obviously unfair to pick on a blind man. But, he also knew that Joe didn't mind being the butt of an occasional practical joke because it made him feel like "one of the boys" instead of a handicapped person to be pitied. He was also well aware that Joe had initiated, or been a part of, several practical jokes played on the guys or on Felicia. So, as John-John walked with Vinnie to the newsstand, he decided not to tip-off Joe. When they arrived at the newsstand, Vinnie tapped on the door and asked Joe to let him inside. John-John joined Danny, Frankie and Shortie who were milling about in front of the stand.

"Okay c'mon in, Vinnie…Are you eatin' a hot dog? I smell onions and sauerkraut."

"Nah, Joe, I already ate two of 'em…I bought this hot dog for you. I know how much you like Sam's hot dogs."

Joe was a little suspicious, wondering why Vinnie, who was known to be a "cheap bastard," would be treating him to a hot dog. It was certainly out of character for Vinnie to do so. Joe sniffed the 'hot dog' back and forth a couple of times, concluding that it smelled okay.

The guys outside the newsstand, who had been tipped-off by John-John about what was about to happen, had their eyes glued on Joe, waiting for him to bite into the cigar. But, Joe still harbored some suspicions. So, he decided to share the hot dog with Vinnie, reasoning that if it were doctored-up, Vinnie wouldn't want any part of it.

"Here, Vinnie, have half."

Before Vinnie could say a word, Joe began to tear the hot dog and bun in half with his hands; but he soon noticed that the 'hot dog' felt unusually stiff. As he continued to apply force, he felt— and heard—a snap. At that point, Vinnie and all of the guys began laughing. Joe quickly brought the split 'hot dog' up to his nose and was now able to smell the tobacco, despite the strong aromas of the toppings.

"You tried to make me eat a fuckin' cigar, you fuckin' low-life bastard!" yelled Joe, as he threw both halves of the pseudo-hot dog at Vinnie as he was trying to get out of the newsstand. Joe managed to hit Vinnie right in the back, staining his light blue t-shirt with globs of mustard, onions and sauerkraut.

"Joe, you got him good!" remarked Frankie.

"Hey, Vinnie, Joe's too smart for you!" added John-John, in a mocking tone.

Everyone knew that if you messed with Joe, he would get even two-fold or three-fold. True to form, Joe still wanted to exact some more revenge on Vinnie. To do so, he pretended that he found Vinnie's practical joke to be funny, even though it had backfired. While chuckling, Joe stealthily unscrewed the cap of his "pee jar," waiting for his target, Vinnie, to venture close to the open front window of the stand. When he was confident that Vinnie was within range, he grabbed the half-full jar and flung its contents out towards Vinnie. Fortunately for Vinnie, his quick reflexes saved him from being totally drenched, but he didn't get off unscathed; the right shoulder of his t-shirt received an ample dousing of Joe's warm, smelly piss.

"Did I get him in the face?"

"No, you only got him on the right shoulder. Most of the piss wound up on the sidewalk," replied Danny.

"Hey, Vinnie, you asshole, you're lucky my aim ain't what it used to be."

Everyone had a good laugh at Vinnie, and they jokingly warned him that Joe probably wasn't finished with him, yet. Then, changing the subject, John-John asked Danny, "Did you pick-up our stickball team shirts?"

"Yeah, I did. They're in my apartment. I'll run upstairs and get 'em."

Within five minutes, Danny returned to the newsstand with eleven stickball uniform shirts. The shirts were bright green jerseys with white lettering and trim. On the front of each shirt was an embroidered rendition of an Arab's face, with crossed swords below it. Above the Arab's face, there was the word "THE" printed in block letters, and below the crossed swords, there was the word "SHEIKS," also printed in block letters. Each shirt had a number on the back. The numbers of the first ten shirts ran consecutively from "0" to "9", but the eleventh shirt sported the number "37". That shirt was earmarked for Joe who, as a joke, was going to be drafted into service as the team's third base coach.

"Hey Joe, we got our stickball shirts," said Danny, "And there's one for you, too."

"For me?"

"Yeah," said Frankie, "You're gonna be our third base coach…You're gonna tell us whether to stop at third base or go home."

"Don't be a fuckin' wise ass, Frankie!"

"Joe, he's only kidding," said John-John, "But we did get you a shirt. It has Casey Stengel's number on it and it has 'Coach' written on the left sleeve. We want you to wear it when we're playing a game…You'll be our good luck charm."

Joe, who had overheard the guys describing the shirts as they looked at them for the first time, remarked, "Now, let me get this straight. The name that's on the shirts is 'The Sheiks.' Why did you have them put the word 'the' on the shirts? No uniforms that I can remember have the word 'the' in front of their team's name…The uniform of the New York Giants just has the word 'Giants' printed across the front—not '*The* Giants'...same with the Dodgers…You guys are just a bunch of knuckleheads."

"We're not knuckleheads," said Frankie, "We're *The* Sheiks! The one and only Sheiks."

"And, what's with that stupid fuckin' name?"

Danny chimed in, "Well, a few months ago, many of us saw the old movies, *The Sheik*, and *The Son of the Sheik*, on TV…both starring Rudolf Valentino. We chose the name in honor of him. We want to be like him…great lovers."

"We want to emulate him, Joe," added John-John.

"There you go again John-John, using big fuckin' words. I'm not sure what *emulate* means, but I'm sure of this…When it comes to girls, you guys got two speeds…slow and reverse! And I doubt if any of you guys could get laid in a women's penitentiary, even if you had a fistful of pardons!"

At that point, Felicia walked by the newsstand. She said hello to everyone, but she seemed to pay particular attention to John-John in a way that girls do when they subliminally signal a guy that they like him as more than just a friend.

"Hey, Felicia, do you know how to use a camera?"

"Danny, I only took about three pictures in my whole life."

"Well, as soon as Lennie 'Squirm' arrives, we'll have the whole team here. I'd like you to take a picture of the team in our brand-new shirts…and the team includes Joe, our third base coach."

The temperature was about 60 degrees—slightly chilly for just wearing a t-shirt—but the guys didn't mind the chill. They gladly donned their Sheik shirts after removing whatever they were wearing on top. Joe, after some urging, reluctantly pulled his Sheik shirt over his long-sleeved shirt and apron. When Lennie arrived, they all posed in front of the newsstand—five guys kneeling, and the rest, including Joe, standing behind them.

"Hey, Felicia, don't take a picture of your thumb," advised Shortie with a laugh.

After taking three photos, Felicia gave the camera back to Danny. Just then, Peter Florio approached.

"Hey Joe, here comes the toy soldier," yelled Danny.

The guys considered Peter to be a real "wuss." Moreover, he was one of the most uncoordinated and unathletic guys in the neighborhood—a neighborhood where being tough and having athletic prowess were the two most important yardsticks of acceptance for boys. Although Peter continually tried to fit in with the guys at the newsstand, he never was able to assimilate into the group. The guys often teased him because he went to Xavier High School—an all-boys Catholic school on West 16th Street, where the students wore military-style uniforms. Most of the newsstand crew thought that it was hokey to be a teenager in New York City walking around in a military uniform, worrying about how much starch was in your collar and how shiny your shoes were. However, Joe liked Peter because he was very dependable and trustworthy.

"Peter and Felicia, can you both do me a favor?"

"What is it, Joe?" they responded in unison.

"Felicia, would you walk me to Mott Street…to the T-Bone Supermarket? And Peter, would you mind the stand for me?"

They both agreed. Felicia escorted Joe to the supermarket where he bought some fresh vegetables, a box of spaghetti, a bag of lentils and a dozen eggs. Twenty minutes later they were back at the newsstand.

Meanwhile, the guys, sporting their Sheik shirts, were practicing stickball on Lafayette Street, between Spring and Kenmare Streets. Five of the guys were positioned at Spring Street and the other five were at Kenmare Street. Taking turns, one guy would hit the ball from Spring Street towards the guys on Kenmare. Then, one of them would hit the ball back towards Spring.

The actual game, which was always played for money, was commonly referred to as "longways," because the "ball field" ran the length of the street. Each team fielded seven players. There was no pitcher. Unlike baseball or softball, a batter would attempt to hit the ball either fungo-style, or by bouncing the ball in front of him on the pavement and then swinging at it. The ball, a pink rubber Spalding, was commonly referred to as a "Spaldine." A batter was allowed only one swing. If he swung at the ball and missed, or if he hit the ball foul, he was out. If a fly ball bounced off a building or off a fire escape located in "fair territory," the ball would be in play; the same rule applied to balls hitting parked cars. As long as the ball could be caught before it hit the ground, an out was made. It certainly wasn't baseball, but in some respects, it was much more fun—and it required a special kind of skill and agility to catch a ball that might suddenly carom off of a fire escape or a parked car at a crazy angle.

John-John and Charlie "the Ox" were the top-two power hitters of the team. During this practice they were both stationed at the Kenmare Street end of "the field." On John-John's first swing of the practice session, he totally swung over the ball, causing Joey "Limp" to tease him about the number "0" that he had selected for his Sheiks shirt.

"Yo, John-John, you're livin' up to your number…You're a big fuckin' zero…You're good for nuttin!"

John-John laughed at Joey's remark. He then lobbed the ball upward in front of him, and on its third bounce, "golfed" a shot more than 100 feet into the air. The ball landed on the roof of the four-story building next to the newsstand—the building above Seymour's Luncheonette. That was the first time that any of the guys had hit a ball onto that roof. In a game, it would have been a home run. John-John would later compute—after taking some measurements and using geometry—that the ball would have traveled about 320 feet if it hadn't landed on the roof. As remarkable as John-John's shot was, Charlie "the Ox" managed to top him. Aided by a sudden gust of wind, he hit a ball over 400 feet, on a fly, up Lafayette Street. Had he hit that shot in a game, even the slow-footed Charlie might have been able to trot around the bases twice before the ball was retrieved.

After about an hour-and-a-half of practice, the guys had had enough. John-John, Danny, Frankie and Shortie decided to hang out in front of the newsstand, while the rest of the team went into Seymour's Luncheonette.

"Hey, Joe, are you finished with Vinnie?" asked Frankie, in an inciting tone.

"Nah, I wanna get him one more time, but I'm not sure how."

"Vinnie is sittin' in a booth with Lennie 'Squirm' and Donny 'Knobhead.' Suppose we bring you into Seymour's and you throw a glass of water in Vinnie's face. He'll never expect it."

"That's a good idea, Danny…Let me see…I don't think I have any water handy, but I just bought a dozen eggs. I guess my wife won't mind if there's one egg missin'."

"Joe, you're crazier than the rest of us put together!"

"Well, John-John, when I was young, I was quite a character… quite a character…Okay, take me in and bring me within 5 feet of him. Then, one of you guys call him. When he answers, I'll know exactly where he is."

All five of them entered the luncheonette. Vinnie was seated in a booth with his back to the door.

Initiating Joe's plan, Frankie yelled out, "Hey, Vinnie, you gonna buy me a soda?"

"Buy your own soda!" exclaimed Vinnie, turning his head slightly back towards Frankie.

"What?" replied Frankie, holding back a laugh as best as he could.

"You heard me! Whatta I look like…a fuckin' bank?"

After hearing Vinnie's voice twice, Joe was able to zero-in on him. He fired the egg with exceptional accuracy, guided by his own version of sonar. The egg hit Vinnie squarely on the back of the head. The only words that Vinnie could utter were, "What the fuck!"

Everyone in the luncheonette had a hearty laugh, except for one unfortunate customer who had been splattered with some of the egg—and Seymour, of course, who didn't find any humor in what had just happened. The irate customer headed for Joe and started yelling at him. At that point, the guys closed ranks around Joe to protect him just in case the customer—who was not from the neighborhood—might decide to take a swing at Joe.

John-John quickly intervened, saying, "Mister, please…the man is blind. He didn't mean to have the egg splash on you."

"Well, it's no big deal…I guess." Shaking his head, he continued, "But, I don't think anyone should be throwing an egg at anybody in the first place, let alone a blind man throwing an egg in a crowded luncheonette!"

"I'm sorry, mister…You're right," said Joe, as he pretended to feel remorse.

"Sir, let me clean your shirt with some seltzer," interjected Seymour. "And as for you, Joe, act your age!"

As Joe and his entourage departed, Joe's expression turned from one of remorse to one of glee. He kept asking the guys to describe to him exactly where the egg had hit Vinnie and what Vinnie's reaction had been.

Shortie remarked, "Joe, I'm surprised you didn't tell Seymour off when he told you to act your age."

"Well, normally, I would've told him to go scratch his ass with a broken bottle. But, I gotta be able to use his terlit when I gotta take a dump…so I held my tongue."

"Hey, Joe, here comes Vinnie," whispered John-John.

"Vinnie, now we're even."

"Okay, Joe, we're even," adding with a laugh, "Suppose, next Saturday, I buy you a knish?"

"Do us both a fuckin' favor, Vinnie, don't buy me nuttin!"

"Okay, Joe, okay."

Chapter 12: The High School Cafeteria

The bell rang throughout Basilica High School, marking the end of the fourth period. Felicia, a sub-par student, raced out of her "boring" history class and headed for lunch—the highpoint of her school day. It was the Friday before Memorial Day. She would soon be completing her sophomore year at this all-girls' Catholic high school, established in 1915 by the Sisters of Mercy. The handsome Faux Gothic school building was at East 50th Street and Lexington Avenue in Manhattan, just a block away from the IRT Subway stop. The school provided a solid college preparatory education, counterbalanced by religious and moral teachings. It featured strict discipline, which was a selling point for many of the students' parents, particularly those who were concerned with the safety of their daughters. Movies such as 1955's *Blackboard Jungle* and 1958's *High School Confidential,* plus many stories in the *Daily News* and *Daily Mirror* about gang violence and juvenile delinquency in the public schools, had created a climate of fear for parents. For a $15 monthly tuition, parents could rest assured that their daughters would get a good Catholic education in a safe environment.

Despite making her way to the cafeteria as quickly as possible, Felicia found herself to be about the fifteenth girl on the lunch line. Her three usual lunch mates were near the front of the line and would be sitting down to eat about five minutes ahead of her; however, she knew they would save a seat for her at their usual table.

As she slowly progressed through the lunch line, she found the aromas of the institutional-grade food to be unusually nauseating. Perhaps, the high heat and humidity of the day, coupled with the lack of air conditioning, heightened her sense of smell. Oh, how she longed for a dish of her mother's *pasta fasool,* instead of the cafeteria's ho-hum food.

After paying thirty-five cents for her lunch, she joined her friends, all of whom were juniors: Judy Kowalski, Angie Colucci and Maria Rizzo. Maria, the studious one of the group—a member of the National Honor Society, who had ambitions of becoming a marine biologist—was attempting to steer the conversation towards the coming final exams; however, no one was interested. Instead, the conversation quickly drifted to a topic that was of interest to all the girls at the table—boys!

Angie, who was often referred to as "Fat Angie," behind her back, led off the conversation with a shocking statement: "You all know I been goin' out with Bobby "Beans" from Kenmare and Mulberry. Well, he's been pressuring me to 'go all the way'.

"Oh?" replied Judy.

"Yeah, and, I just might."

"Are you crazy!" said Felicia and Judy in unison, as their jaws almost hit the table.

"No, I'm not crazy. I'm serious."

"Really?" said Maria, totally astonished by Angie's matter-of-fact attitude.

"Yeah, really."

Felicia and Judy just stood there with their mouths agape, while Maria nervously tugged at her large horn-rimmed glasses.

Oh, excuse me a minute. I'm still very hungry. I'm gonna go get myself another piece of cherry pie."

When Angie left the table, the girls wondered aloud if she had made up the story for effect. Felicia said that she knew Bobby "Beans" and that he was quite good looking. The consensus was that at 5'-1" and around 180 pounds, it seemed very unlikely that Angie would attract anyone—especially someone as good looking as Bobby "Beans."

When Angie returned, Judy took the floor. She was an attractive blonde of Polish-Ukrainian extraction, from Second Avenue and East Second Street. She had an effervescent personality and a well-proportioned figure. Her fine Slavic facial features were, unfortunately, marred by a severe acne condition, which she tried to cover-up with globs and globs of *Clearasil* and makeup. At seventeen, she was the oldest of the group and its natural leader. Angie, who was several months younger than Judy, would be turning seventeen in

August, while Maria would not be seventeen until October. Felicia would be "Sweet Sixteen" on the Fourth of July, and she was hoping that her parents would acknowledge this important milestone with a big party.

"I've just met a new guy," said Judy. "He's from Prince and Mott…your neighborhood," pointing to Angie and Felicia. "His name is Sal DiMaggio. His family is from Sicily. I'm sure my father won't approve of him because he's Italian, and I guess Sal's family won't approve of me because I *ain't* Italian."

Judy then flipped out a wallet-sized photo of Sal and showed it to Angie and Felicia.

"Hey, he's good-lookin'," said Angie.

You can tell he's Italian with that Roman nose and dark wavy hair," remarked Felicia. "Here, Maria, have a look."

"No, that's okay, I've actually met him."

Maria did her best to mask the envy she felt over her long-time best friend's popularity with boys. She could easily recall the names of the five other boys Judy had dated before Sal and the details of those dates that Judy had shared with her. She wondered if she would ever find *any* boy that would like her. So far, no one had ever asked her out on a date. Whenever she would find herself among teenage boys—a rare situation—she had a tendency to slouch and look down. She was shy and insecure, and her deportment signaled a lack of self-confidence, discouraging any boy who might have noticed her. She felt like an ugly duckling, but she was just an awkward and somewhat dowdy, young auburn-haired girl who was yet to blossom.

Maria recalled the pain she had felt when she and Judy had gone to the LaSalle High School dance two weeks earlier. Her experience redefined the term "wallflower." While Judy danced just about every dance, Maria hadn't even been asked to dance once, causing her to wonder why she had begged and pleaded with her parents to let her go to the dance.

She further recalled how badly she had felt when Brother Donovan, the chief chaperon at the dance, in a clumsy attempt to rectify the situation, had brought over a gangly and shy boy to dance with her. They *did* dance, but the fact that the boy had to be forced to dance with her only lessened her self-esteem.

Perhaps, Maria's overall insecurity about her appearance was exacerbated by the fact that she wore braces. The braces certainly detracted from her appearance, but they were a temporary thing; however, when she looked at herself in a mirror, she would often think of the cruel comment that Louie, a young boy from her building, had made about her braces: "Maria, when you smile, your face looks like the front of a 1953 Buick."

Upon seeing the photo of Sal, Felicia decided to get some respect at the table. So, she whipped out a photo from her wallet and passed it around the table.

"Who's he?" asked Judy, in an admiring tone.

"He's John-John Cara…my boyfriend."

"I've seen him around the neighborhood. I think he lives on Mulberry Street, near Spring."

"Yeah, you're right, Angie. By the way, John-John is senior at Stuyvesant High School. He's 6'-2" and built like an athlete…which he is. He'll be goin' to Columbia University this September to study engineering. My mother likes him even though his family is Sicilian."

"A Stuyvesant guy! He must be some sort of genius."

"Nah, I don't think he's a genius, Judy, but he's real smart."

"I heard that only one out of every twenty students who take the test for Stuyvesant get in," remarked Maria.

"Is he a nerd?" asked Judy.

"No, not at all. He's actually quite cool. He's hangs out with a bunch of wild and funny guys who call themselves the Sheiks." "Why the Sheiks?" questioned Maria.

"Well, they have this thing about Rudolph Valentino…you know, the actor who played a sheik in the silent movies." Giggling, she added, "They want to be great lovers like him."

When Maria saw the photo, she thought, *Felicia is really lucky to have found a guy like him.* She was drawn to his friendly face, "cute" curly hair and broad shoulders. In a swooning, girlish way, she secretly wished that she were his girlfriend. She knew that her parents, who were both born in Sicily, would like him right from the start because he was of Sicilian ancestry. Throughout her childhood, it had been stressed that she should marry a Sicilian. Marrying anyone but a Sicilian would greatly disappoint her parents. Of course, if she couldn't find a Sicilian mate, her parents would begrudgingly accept someone whose roots were from another part of Italy; but they likely would never welcome a non-Italian into the Rizzo family.

Little did the girls at the table know that Felicia had told them a white lie: She wasn't dating John-John. He had simply given her one of his fifty, wallet-sized, graduation photos. However, over the past few months, she had spoken to him many times at the newsstand and she sensed, by the way he looked into her eyes when they spoke, that there was some chemistry between them.

Chapter 13: Crosby Street

Felicia arrived at her Spring Street subway stop at about 3:30 p.m. ready to start the Memorial Day weekend. She crossed Lafayette and stopped at the newsstand. The only person at the stand, aside from Joe, was Tony "Gallons," who had arrived there only seconds earlier.

"Joe, what's leadin'?" asked Tony.

"'Six' and 'two'," Joe quickly responded.

"Great! I have a dollar on 626. If I 'hit the number,' I'll win five hundred smackers."

Tony, a seventy-something-year-old former prizefighter, was a big gambler. He would bet on almost anything. He loved betting on horses almost as much as he loved playing the numbers. He usually chose his numbers based on what he had dreamt about the night before. But, sometimes, he would pick numbers from a license plate he had seen, or the number of a bus or subway car he had recently ridden.

As Tony waited for the third and final number to come out, he couldn't stop thinking of what he would do if he won the money. *First, I'll pay off the hundred clams I owe to Benny "Sticks." Then, I'll take the train to Monmouth Racetrack and bet the whole wad.*

Joe supplemented his meager newsstand income by "taking numbers"— working as an assistant to a "runner" for one of the neighborhood's bookies. The runners—not the bookies—had the responsibility of dealing directly with the bettors; that is, taking the bets and paying-off the winners. Most runners had assistants working for them, so they could handle a greater number of bets than if working alone, and thus earn more money for themselves.

The way the numbers racket worked was that a runner would be paid twenty percent of whatever his players had won. The twenty percent didn't come out of the players' winnings; rather, it would come directly from the bookie, whose payout to winners was far from commensurate with the one-chance-in-a-thousand odds of hitting a three-digit number. If the payouts were consistent with the odds of winning, a dollar bet should have yielded a lucky player a thousand dollars—not the five-hundred-dollar payout he would actually receive; but it was the only game in town, so nobody complained.

A runner didn't get any percentage of his players' losses; thus, he would genuinely hope that his players would win. Since Joe's runner would usually give him one-quarter of his "end" from the bookie for a player's win, Joe was really rooting hard for Tony. If the number "six" were to be the third number, Joe would get twenty-five dollars of his runner's hundred-dollar earnings for the win.

"Joe, have you seen any of the guys?" asked Felicia.

"Nah, I haven't seen any of them yet, but I'm sure some of the guys will be here soon."

None of the newsstand "regulars" ever considered that asking a blind man if he had *seen* a certain person was a poor choice of words. But, Joe was used to it, and he generally responded without making an issue over the use of the word *seen*. Once in a while, however, he would wisecrack, "I haven't *seen* anyone in years!"

"What are you doin' for the holiday weekend, Felicia?"

"Nuttin special. My mother went to visit her brother, Paolo, in Brooklyn, so I'll have to cook dinner, tonight. Maybe, on Memorial Day, we'll go to South Beach, in Staten Island. The water at the beach is a little polluted, but my father says it's okay to swim in it."

She then scurried off to her apartment to start preparing dinner. Her mother had left her all the ingredients for making linguine *con vongole*—more commonly referred to as linguine with clams—and fried filet of flounder. Felicia, for her age, was already quite a good cook. Her mother had seen to that.

Felicia had dinner on the table at 5:30 p.m. Her father, who had returned from a hard day's work an hour earlier, was quite pleased with the meal, as were her younger sister, Francesca and her brother, Little Zeke. Zeke, who spoke in an accent resembling that of the character, Sheriff Andy Taylor, on the *Andy Griffith Show*, complimented Felicia at the end of the meal saying, "Your cookin' is almost like your mama's. It's so-oo good!"

"Thanks, Dad."

While Francesca washed the pots and dishes, and Felicia dried them, Zeke went to the couch to watch TV. The hard day's work, coupled with the three glasses of wine he had drunk at dinner, caused him to become very drowsy. He soon fell fast asleep on the comfortable soft couch.

At around seven, Fluffy, the family's cute little white dog was giving signals that she needed to be walked. Usually, no one volunteered for the chore, but this time, Felicia said she would gladly take Fluffy for a walk. She just wanted to get out of the house after spending so much time in the kitchen. With Fluffy on a leash, she made a left out of her building and headed to the newsstand.

"Joe, did Tony's number come out?" she asked.

"Nah, the last number was "seven." He missed by one, and I'm out twenty-five bucks! I should've known not to get my hopes up too high. That Tony is a loser, with a capital 'L' and he'll always be a loser...He left here in a huff, worrying how he was gonna pay off his shylock, Benny "Sticks."

"By the way, Joe, I don't understand anything about playin' the numbers."

"Well, let me tell ya, Felicia, that there are two different numbers game racquets in the city...You got the Brooklyn Numbers racquet and the New York Numbers racquet...Hardly anyone around here plays the Brooklyn numbers, but I'll tell ya that they get the daily Brooklyn number from the last three digits of all the money bet at a certain racetrack on that day. You can actually find that number in the sports section of the *Daily News* and the *Mirror* on the following day."

"What about the New York number?"

"Give me a chance to finish, Felicia...Well, in this neighborhood, most of the people play the New York numbers. It's basically the same as the

Brooklyn numbers game, but instead of using the last three digits of the total money bet at a certain racetrack, they use the last digit of the total money bet on three different races…I think, the first, fourth and seventh races. Each number comes out a few minutes after those races, and the number is spread by word of mouth very quickly. So with the New York numbers, you actually get a chance to root for your number, as Tony did. With the Brooklyn numbers, you find out all three numbers at once. So, in my opinion, playin' the New York numbers is more fun, but it can be a slow death, as Tony just found out."

Just then, John-John arrived at the newsstand. "Hi Joe. Hi Felicia. Any of the guys been around?"

"No, you're the first one to stop by," replied Joe.

John-John reached down to pet Fluffy, who seemed to like the attention. She became very animated, wagging her tail and barking in a friendly way.

"John-John, I'm gonna take Fluffy for a little walk. Do you wanna come with us?"

"No, I think I'll hang out here and wait for Danny and Frankie."

Joe interjected with a laugh, "Go! If any of your friends come by, I'll tell 'em you went for a walk with your *girlfriend* and that you'll be right back."

Felicia blushed as John-John quickly replied, "She's not my girlfriend!"

However, John-John decided to go for the walk, anyway, mostly to get away from Joe's kidding. When they reached Prince Street, he thought they would be making a U-turn and heading back. He was quite surprised when Felicia turned to her left and began walking across Lafayette Street.

"Where are we taking Fluffy?"

"I think Fluffy wants to cross the street," Felicia responded with a laugh.

"Let's head to Crosby Street. Fluffy needs the exercise."

Crosby Street runs parallel to Lafayette Street and is one block west of it. Unlike present-day Crosby Street, with its numerous trendy and expensive converted lofts, Crosby Street of the '60s consisted mostly of factories and warehouses. After seven, it was usually deserted, making it the neighborhood's premier "make-out spot." John-John started to suspect that Felicia might have something other than Fluffy's need for exercise on her mind. When they reached Crosby Street, they turned left towards Spring.

About halfway down the block, Fluffy began to run in a circle. Her leash served as a lasso, bringing Felicia and John-John in close contact, face-to-face. As they laughed, they looked into each other's eyes. Then, instinctively, Felicia tilted her head, closed her eyes and drew herself ever so close to him. John-John, who had never kissed a girl, quickly closed the gap between them, puckered his lips, and kissed her.

He wondered what her reaction would be. *Will she pull back? Will she smack me in the face?* When her lips pressed tightly against his, he knew that she truly was enjoying *their* first kiss.

She pulled away and whispered, "John-John, I think I fell in love with you the very first time I saw you at the newsstand, three years ago. John-John was silent for quite a while. Then, he managed to spurt out, "Felicia, I like you a great deal…a great deal." That was the best he could say in response to her use of the word "love." To him, the word "love" was not a word to be used lightly. He realized that what he was feeling at that moment was a combination of lust, passion and a sense of accomplishment. He felt that love was something that developed over time. He knew there was the possibility that their first kiss could be the first step to true love, but at this time, he felt that saying, "I like you a great deal," was enough.

Somehow, Felicia was buoyed by his response, despite his use of the word "like." They embraced tightly and kissed with so much passion that Fluffy, perhaps thinking that Felicia was being harmed, began to growl.

"Let's head back," said John-John in a soft voice.

As they approached the corner of Crosby and Spring, Felicia decided that it would be smarter to walk the last block back to her building, alone. She didn't want the word to get back to her parents that she had been seen walking back from Crosby Street with John-John. As she walked towards Lafayette Street, she thought of all that had happened that day and how ironic it was that her lie at the lunch table was no longer a lie: she was, indeed, John-John Cara's girlfriend—or, at least, very close to being his girlfriend.

After giving Felicia a three-minute head start, John-John began walking towards the newsstand. By the time he got there, Felicia and Fluffy had already made their way upstairs. Felicia found Ole Zeke still asleep on the couch, "sawing wood," and she was happy to learn that her mother had not yet returned from Brooklyn.

Danny had arrived at the newsstand about the same time that Felicia had walked by with Fluffy. He sensed that something was going on between Felicia and John-John. *Why would they both be walking back from Crosby Street?* he wondered.

"Hey Joe, I'm back…Hi Danny. What's cooking?"

"You tell me what's cookin'!"

"Yeah, where did you go with her?" asked Joe

"I bet you took a walk with Felicia on Crosby Street," Danny added.

"Yeah, you hit the nail right on the head." "Did you make-out?" asked Joe.

"Yeah. We kissed a few times on Crosby Street, and guess what? She told me that she has loved me from the first time she saw me at the newsstand, three years ago!"

"Did she let you feel her up?" asked Danny, with a smirk on his face.

John-John stammered a bit, and then proceeded to lie, saying, "Yeah, she let me feel her ass. It felt soft, yet firm. You know, it's hard to describe exactly how it felt."

At this point, Joe chimed in: "John-John, you're gettin' to be as big a bullshit artist as Vinnie 'Lemons.' All I know is that when it comes to girls, you are as slow as shit! If Felicia *did* let you kiss her, I would lay 50-to-1 that it was your first kiss…and, I would lay 100-to-1 that she didn't let you get to 'second base'!"

"Joe, you don't know what you are talking about. I've been with many girls. Don't forget, I *am* one of the Sheiks!" John-John asserted.

"Sheiks my ass!"

Joe was right about John-John. It was his first kiss—at age eighteen, no less. He was impressed by Joe's perception; for a person who couldn't see, Joe *saw* better than most people.

When Frankie "Bubbles" and Donny "Knobhead" arrived at the newsstand, John-John repeated the details of his "conquest," this time with more bravado.

Serafina returned home at around 8:30 p.m., sweaty and exhausted from her ride on the steamy, hot BMT Subway train. Felicia wondered just how her mother would have reacted had she known of her romantic encounter with John-John. She knew, for sure, that she would have been furious. The only question was: how furious?

Serafina wasn't above smacking her children as a way of teaching them to be obedient and respectful to her. Felicia was aware of her mother's rule about dating: she wasn't allowed to date until she was at least seventeen. Kissing John-John a month before her sixteenth birthday clearly violated the rule. The violation was more egregious because Serafina truly disliked John-John. She disliked all of the boys who hung-out at Joe's Newsstand because she felt they were too noisy, boisterous, and disrespectful. She had told them many times to go hang-out on another corner and had even called the cops on them on several occasions. She particularly disliked John-John because she believed that he was the ringleader of the group, and more important, because he was a *Siciliano.*

Her deep dislike of Sicilians was visceral. It was likely that her initial dislike of Sicilians had been passed down to her from her parents and grandparents, who had learned it from their forebears. The animosity between Neapolitans and Sicilians, probably, stemmed all the way back to the 15th century, when Naples and Sicily had become parts of the same kingdom. Who knows how such things begin? However, Serafina's bad experience with her Sicilian soldier "customer" in the Naples cemetery had certainly cemented her hatred for Sicilians.

Serafina usually watched Felicia like a hawk. The sexy, sometimes flirtatious, former Neapolitan prostitute didn't want her daughter to get involved with boys at a young age. She knew that young boys, and men—even old men—were only interested in one thing: S-E-X. She sought to protect her daughter's virginity to ensure there would be no possibility that she would be forced into an early marriage due to pregnancy. She wanted her to marry no earlier than age twenty-one; to marry wisely; and to live the American Dream: a house in the suburbs with a white picket fence; and a loving husband who had a white-collar job that provided for all of the necessities and comforts of life.

Serafina, in contrast, was not living the American Dream. She had married a Tennessee hillbilly as a way of escaping the poverty of postwar Naples. Zeke was a nice-enough fellow, but she was never deeply in love with him. She never felt the passion. Perhaps, all of her sexual encounters as a prostitute had numbed her. Nevertheless, her union with Zeke had produced three "beautiful" children, and she had, indeed, escaped postwar Naples; but her life in America was far from the American Dream. Zeke, with only a fifth-grade education, was only suited for manual labor. His non-union job as a plumber's helper for Martucci and Sons, Commercial Heating and Plumbing Contractors, didn't pay well. The only way for the family to make ends meet was for Serafina to work in a sweatshop as a seamstress.

As Felicia lay in bed that evening, her mind began to wander. She envisioned herself as Mrs. John-John Cara, living in the suburbs with their three adorable, curly-haired children.

As John-John laid his head on his pillow, he reflected upon how much things had changed. He had been barely aware of Felicia's existence until about a year ago. In fact, it wasn't until the beginning of the previous summer that he had paid any attention to her—when her body was transforming from a somewhat scrawny tomboy to that of a young woman with curves in all the right places.

His thoughts then shifted to how he would try to get to "second base" with Felicia on their next walk down Crosby Street. Joe, who had taught him more about the facts of life than his father, had once explained the love—baseball analogy to him, thusly: "first base" was just hugging and kissing; "second base" was petting a girl's private areas over her clothes; "third base" was like second base, but with the hands adventuring under a girl's bra and panties; and a "home run" was, obviously, intercourse.

The neighborhood was relatively quiet on Saturday morning. Joe opened the newsstand at around ten. There weren't many customers. It seemed that many people had gone down to the New Jersey shore or up to the Catskills. John-John, Danny, Frankie and Vinnie "Lemons" all arrived at the newsstand, almost simultaneously, at around eleven. None of them had any plans for the Memorial Day Weekend. Their families didn't have enough money for a weekend getaway; they could barely make ends meet, despite living in rent-controlled tenement apartments.

"Let's play some stickball John-John! Me and Vinnie against you and Danny," challenged Frankie.

"Okay," said Danny, "A dollar a man."

John-John balked, "Let's play for fun."

"Nah, a buck a man, you cheap bastard!" yelled Vinnie.

John-John reluctantly agreed to play for money. He never liked the idea of playing for money. He felt that sports should be played simply for fun. Unfortunately, it was an unwritten rule in the neighborhood that once you became a teenager, you *had* to play for money. It was part of the betting mentality that pervaded the neighborhood. They walked down Lafayette Street to the parking lot on Kenmare Street. There were very few cars parked in the lot, and fortunately, none of the cars were blocking the "home plate" painted on one of the brick walls that bounded the parking lot.

The game was quite simple. Balls and strikes were determined by whether or not the pitched ball hit the painted home plate. Each team was allotted two outs per inning. If a ground ball, line drive or fly ball was fielded cleanly, the batter was out. There was no base running in the game. A ground ball that got past a fielder was a single. A ball hit less than 20 feet above the building wall behind the pitcher was a double; above that level, it was a triple. If the ball rebounded far enough off the wall to hit the building wall by the batter, it was a home run. To make the game more interesting, a ball caught off the wall on a fly was an out.

John-John and Danny won the game 3 to 1. They decided to put their winnings to good use by going to the Loew's Commodore on Second Avenue and East Sixth Street. (This theater would become quite famous five years later when it would be renamed The Fillmore East.) The movie that afternoon was *The Evil of Frankenstein*, which was so-so, but the air conditioning was absolutely wonderful, especially in an era when hardly anyone in the neighborhood had a home air conditioner. They returned to the newsstand at about four and greeted Joe.

"How was the movie?"

"It sucked…well, almost sucked," said Danny.

"Yeah, but the air conditioning was great."

"Too bad you couldn't bring me back some nice cold air in a bag or somethin'."

Shortly thereafter, Felicia stopped by. John-John greeted her warmly and asked if she would be walking Fluffy in the early evening. She responded, "Probably, after I wash the dishes…but, if you want to walk with me, it would be better if you waited for me at the corner of Prince. I don't want my mother to see us walking together."

"Okay, I'll be there at seven."

John-John, who didn't leave much to chance, arrived at the corner early. Shortly after seven, he saw the silhouettes of Felicia and Fluffy making their way up Lafayette Street. When they met at the corner, Felicia said with a grin, "I think Fluffy wants to walk on Crosby Street again."

They walked about halfway down Crosby Street and began to kiss. John-John soon made his move towards "Second Base" and was surprised that Felicia didn't object to his roaming hands. Ironically, her bottom *did* feel soft, yet firm—just as he had said in his fib at the newsstand the day before. After a few minutes of passion, they both agreed that it would be smart to retrace their route, with her returning home from Prince Street alone with Fluffy.

Unbeknown to the young couple, a pair of eyes had spotted them as they rounded Crosby Street onto Prince. Those eyes belonged to Tessie Fasano, who was returning home from her part-time job at Gimbel's Department Store. She was making her way home from the BMT Subway station when she saw John-John and Felicia walking arm-in-arm, with Fluffy trailing close behind. Tessie was one of the three Fasano sisters who lived on Spring Street, a few buildings away from Joe's Newsstand. She, along with her two sisters, were said to be the three biggest gossips in the neighborhood. She was unmarried, and at age forty-five, she was considered an "old maid." God had not been kind to her when it came to looks. She was known throughout the neighborhood as Tessie "the Bulldozer" because it was said that she looked as if she had been French-kissed by a bulldozer. Unfortunately for her, she had developed a pushy and acerbic personality to go along with her bad looks. By contrast, her two sisters, Anna, forty-two, and Fannie, thirty-nine, were among the prettiest women in the neighborhood. Both of them were married, and each had two children.

Typically, the Fasano sisters could be found in front of their building sitting on bridge chairs for much of the day and night. They usually passed comments on just about everyone who walked by. They particularly enjoyed talking about neighborhood people, mixing facts and fiction to make their stories spicier and more interesting. The sisters were well acquainted with the Daniels family; in some sense, they were friends with them. Occasionally, Serafina and Zeke would sit with the sisters and join in the gossip; but, as soon as they would leave, the sisters would gossip about them, particularly about Serafina's rumored sordid past.

Chapter 14: Bragging

John-John was awakened by the bright sunlight passing through the kitchen windows. The Memorial Day weekend was over. It had been short, but eventful for him. Now it was time to get back to school. He looked up at the clock on the kitchen wall. It was 6:05. He knew his mother would soon be getting up to make breakfast. Rather than getting out of bed, he decided to rest for ten more minutes.

At 6:15 the alarm clock rang in the bedroom—the only bedroom in the tiny apartment. Angelina got up from bed leaving her husband to sleep until noon because he had gone to sleep at 4 a.m. after driving the night shift. She slowly worked her way from the bedroom to the kitchen. It was a short walk since the apartment had only three "railroad" rooms. As she entered the living room, she eyed her fifteen-year-old daughter, Vivian, fast asleep on the convertible sofa. She shook her in a less-than-gentle manner, saying, "Get up… The holiday's over…Time to go to school."

When she entered the kitchen, she was happy to see that John-John was up and in the process of folding-up his rollaway bed. Although sleeping in the kitchen would seem rather strange to most Americans, especially those living in houses in Middle America, it was quite common in Little Italy and other such neighborhoods. How else could people raise families with two or more children in tiny three or four-room apartments?

John-John lingered over his breakfast of coffee, juice, a softboiled egg and toast. After some chitchat, he dressed and went off to school, boarding the IRT Subway at the Spring Street Station, right behind Joe's stand. He arrived at Union Square within five minutes, and after a ten-minute walk, he entered the school at the East 15th Street entrance. He walked with a bit of a swagger, buoyed by his weekend romantic escapade with Felicia. Although it had only amounted to just a few kisses and some petting, he felt that he had gone through a rite of passage.

Many of his fellow seniors had opted for light workloads, taking only those courses necessary to fulfill New York State curriculum requirements, but John-John was taking full advantage of the school's offerings by taking several electives. In addition to taking English, World History, French and Gym, he had elected Qualitative Chemical Analysis, Calculus and Advanced Mechanical Drawing.

Lunch came none too soon for John-John, who was always hungry. With lunch tray in hand, he joined his usual fourth period lunch mates: Gary Schindelheim; Stanley Mizel; Tommy Tedesco; and Bernie Goldberg.

"Hey John, how was your weekend?"

"Great, Gary."

"Where did you go?"

"Nowhere. I never left the neighborhood."

"Well, *that* doesn't sound like much of a holiday weekend."

"Well, I didn't go anywhere, but I did have a couple of hot make-out sessions with Felicia."

"Who's Felicia?" asked Tommy.

"She's a girl from my neighborhood. Although she lives only about 50 feet from the newsstand where I hang-out, I never paid much attention to her until recently."

"How come?" asked Gary.

"Well, she's two years younger than me. Up until recently, she had a boyish figure…flat as a board…and she acted like a tomboy. In fact, she could catch a "spaldine" as well as most guys."

"So, one could infer that things have since changed," remarked the erudite Stanley.

"Yes. She has developed into a cute and sexy-looking babe. It's hard to believe how much her body has changed."

"How's her face?" asked Gary.

Before he could answer, Bernie, who always brought things to the lowest common denominator, chimed in: "Who cares, you can't fuck a face!"

"Yeah, I've heard that before, Bernie, but for the record, her face is actually quite nice. She has high cheekbones, sensuous lips, blue eyes and long, sandy-blonde hair."

"How far did you get?" inquired Gary, who loved to ask questions—especially when it involved girls.

John-John wanted to tell the truth, but he knew the true version wouldn't be much of a story. He wanted the guys to think of him as a stud, so he decided to exaggerate after concluding that it would do no harm to Felicia since none of the guys knew her.

"Well…she let me feel her up through her clothes…and then I managed to get my right hand into her bra and actually play with her tits…which are quite big.

"I guess you did have a great weekend, after all," said Gary.

"Way to go, John!" added Bernie.

The Stuyvesant students were a special breed. Most were intellectually gifted; many of them were even smarter than their teachers. However, when it came to girls, most of the students were socially inept, not knowing how to interact with girls. Perhaps, this was partly due to the fact that Stuyvesant High School, at that time, was not coed; so, there was no interaction with the opposite sex; or, perhaps, most of the Stuyvesant boys just never found time for girls because they were too busy with their studies.

At about the same time that John-John was doing his lunchtime bragging, Felicia was truly enjoying lunch at Basilica High School with her usual bevy of girlfriends. It wasn't that she found the food anymore pleasing—it was still the same old institutional-grade slop; it was the fact that she didn't have to make-up a story about some boy she was dating. She could actually tell the truth this time.

"Did you have a nice weekend, Felicia?" asked Maria.

"Yeah…I actually had a great weekend. I had two dates with John-John."

"Oh? Where did he take you?" asked Judy.

"Well, we didn't go anywhere special…We went to Crosby Street, twice, where we made out hot and heavy…if you know what I mean."

"Goin' to Crosby Street for a make-out session is not a date in my book," interjected Angie, with a bit of attitude in her voice. "A date is when a guy takes you out to a movie, or to dinner, or someplace."

"Okay, so they weren't what *you* would call official dates, but I had a wonderful time, anyway. When John-John hugs and kisses you…you've been hugged and kissed. I love the feeling of his strong arms and chest." Do you wanna see his picture?"

"Nah, we saw it last week," the girls replied in unison.

Acting as if she hadn't heard them, she reached in her handbag and pulled out John-John's graduation photo.

The photo was passed around the table rather quickly. Only Maria paused to take a good look at it. She felt strangely attracted to the young man in the photo. She wondered how it would have been if she had been with him on Crosby Street. *I wish I could get a guy like him to like me.* The shy young girl had developed a bit of a crush on John-John, even though she had never met him.

Chapter 15: The Lay-off

Serafina left her apartment at about 7:45 a.m. and began her leisurely three-block walk to the dress factory, J & L, Inc., where she had been working as a seamstress for the past five years. The morning of June 3rd was already quite warm and humid, so she knew she would be sweating all day behind her sewing machine in the stifling factory. After all, these factories weren't called "sweatshops" for no reason.

She arrived at the factory on Broadway and Broome Street about five minutes before the 8 o'clock starting time. When she exited the elevator on the fourth floor, she noticed something unusual: about fifteen of her coworkers were milling about in front of the factory door. *Something must be going on,* she thought. Just then, Izzie, the manager, opened the factory door and walked into the hallway.

"Listen!" the diminutive, seventy-year-old shouted. "I have some bad news. I will have to lay-off almost everyone. I can only keep eight workers. To make it easy, I've made this list of the names of the eight employees who *aren't* being laid off. If your name isn't on this list, please go home. Please! Please! Maybe, in a month or two, business will be better and I can call all of you back to work."

With that short announcement, Izzie posted the list on the hallway wall and quickly went inside the factory, locking the door behind him. Serafina pushed her way to the posted list and checked for her name. It wasn't there. She had been laid-off. None of the other women's names were on the list either. They, along with the late arrivers, had all been laid off. Unbeknown to these women, the eight fortunate individuals who had been retained had been pre-notified and told to report to work at 10 o'clock.

A few of the women tried to open the door. It was locked, and banging on the door did no good except for releasing some of the anger they felt.

"They're treating us like a bunch of dogs!" yelled one angry woman.

"No respect!" added another.

"What are we gonna do?" was a question repeated over and over again. The consensus was that they could get some meager help from the International Ladies' Garment Workers Union (ILGWU) and that they would eventually qualify for unemployment insurance; however, these payments wouldn't amount to much. The women resigned themselves to the fact that they had no choice but to go home and hope to be re-hired in the near future. The chances of finding work at another dress factory were slim since all the other sweatshops were feeling the same economic slow-down.

Serafina returned to an empty apartment. Her children were at school and Zeke was on one of Martucci's trucks en route to a job up the Bronx. She pondered her situation: The family absolutely needed her salary; it couldn't get by on Zeke's salary alone.

She went into the top drawer of her dresser and found the family's bankbook. She opened the blue East River Savings Bank bankbook and zeroed in on the balance: $187.42. *That's all! I thought we had more than that.*

She considered the family's options: Borrowing money from her two brothers was out of the question since they were hardly making ends meet; and borrowing money from one of the neighborhood's many shylocks would be a dreadful mistake because their interest rates were astronomical. She knew that once one got started with the shylocks, it was almost impossible to get off the merry-go-round of accumulating interest—and there was always the threat of physical harm to the borrower or his family if payment deadlines were missed.

She concluded that the only viable option was to find a way for Zeke to earn more money. Perhaps, Martucci could give Zeke some overtime work; or if there were no overtime to be had, perhaps, he would advance Zeke some money, especially since he had been a hardworking, conscientious employee for about seventeen years.

At around eleven, Serafina strolled past the newsstand without even bothering to greet Joe. She was a woman on a mission. She crossed to other side of Spring Street and hastily walked towards Mulberry. Upon reaching the small office of Martucci and Sons, Commercial Heating and Plumbing Company, she walked down a few steps, took a deep breath, and opened the door of the small dingy office. She was warmly greeted, in Italian, by the 52-year-old proprietor, Orazio Martucci, who was seated at the front desk going through some invoices. There was no one else in the front office.

"Buon giorno, Serafina."

"Buon giorno, Orazio. Come stai?"

"Sto Bene," responded Orazio, *"E tu?"*

"Non sono contenta," replied Serafina, indicating that she was unhappy.

At that point, the conversation shifted seamlessly from Italian to the Neapolitan dialect that they both felt more comfortable speaking.

"Why are you unhappy, Serafina?"

"My factory laid-off almost everyone, including me. My family needs my salary to survive."

At that point, Orazio noticed that her eyes were beginning to well up with tears. He said, "Let's go into the back room. I'll make us some espresso, and you can calm down."

He opened the door to the back room. There were no workers in the room, which was small, somewhat dirty, and without windows. The centerpiece of the dimly lit room was a 6-foot-long wooden table with piles of papers and blueprints.

He pulled out a small coffee pot—a *macchinetta*—from the file cabinet along with a can of Medaglia d'Oro espresso coffee, walked over to the small kitchenette along the wall and began brewing the espresso.

"Have a seat, Serafina."

Within minutes they were sipping espresso, and he actually managed to make her laugh when he told her a rather salty joke.

"Now, Serafina, how can I help you?"

"I was wondering if you might be able to let Zeke work some more hours and, possibly, Saturdays."

"Well, normally, my answer would be 'no,' but your problem has occurred at the right time as far as my business is concerned. You see, my big job in the Bronx is falling way behind schedule. I was just about to order three of my crew to work ten-hour days and Saturdays, so that we could get back on schedule. Zeke was not going to be one of the three, but since I know that your family desperately needs the money, I'll replace Joey with Zeke. It won't be a problem because Joey doesn't know that I was going to ask him to work overtime."

"Orazio, you are my savior!"

At that point, they both stood up and embraced. She felt a spark. She had always found Orazio to be quite attractive, despite the fact that he was thirteen years older. He had classic Italian features, dark wavy hair, streaked with gray, and a strong physique honed by his early years of hard labor. He did have some flab around the stomach, which had accumulated because he was now spending far more time in the office than on the jobsites. In some ways, he reminded her of her late father just before he had become a casualty of war at the age of fifty.

There had been some sexual tension between the two of them over the years—flirtatious talk and innuendo—doing so, even in front of Zeke, who didn't quite grasp the nuances of their conversations.

"Besides losing your job, is there anything else new? Something good?"

"Yes, there is something good. My dearest cousin, Lucia, and her husband, Vincenzo, are coming to visit us from Naples in a few weeks. They will be staying with us for a month. She and I lived in the same building back in Naples. We are the same age…and we shared a lot during the war. Since neither of us has any sisters, we are more like sisters than cousins…Actually, we get along better than most sisters."

Serafina didn't tell Orazio that she and Lucia—working as a pair—had been prostitutes during the war. However, although he knew nothing of Cousin Lucia's past, he *had* heard many rumors about Serafina's wartime days as a prostitute.

After a second cup of espresso and some banter, Serafina got up from her chair, saying, "I think it's about time that I go home. I can't thank you enough for your help."

Orazio walked over to her and embraced her. He had a lustful gleam in his eyes—a gleam that she had seen many times in the cemetery in Naples. He hugged her so tightly that it would have been nearly impossible to slide a piece of paper between them. He then began to kiss her on the lips. She didn't pull back, and she never uttered a single word of protestation, thinking, *I must not resist him.*

Excited by her lack of resistance, he forced his tongue into her mouth and in one smooth move, picked her up and sat her on the table, without any regard for his papers and blueprints. Then, he gently pushed her shoulders down upon the table and lifted her skirt. As he tugged at her panties, she yelled, "*Aspetta!* Wait!" Orazio thought that she was putting on the brakes, but when she quickly added, "Let me do it. I don't want you to rip them," he knew that she, too, was into the moment. They hugged tightly as he penetrated her. After about ten minutes of heavy breathing and moaning, she began to convulse in ecstasy as she was experiencing the greatest orgasm of her life. Despite having been with countless men, she had rarely felt the pleasure of an orgasm. Sex as a prostitute had been work, not love. She had trained herself to become numb during those encounters as a way of protecting her inner self. In the marriage bed, she enjoyed sex with Zeke to some extent, but he was a "slam-bam, thank-you ma'am" kind of a guy, who never quite lit the fire in her soul.

Orazio pulled out while still erect. Without saying a word, she got off the table, knelt down in front of him and began sucking him in an amorous way. She was quite adept at performing the act, having done so in her whoring days far too many times to count.

After about three minutes, Orazio began to climax, making sounds that seemed more like giggles than moans. *What shall I do?* she thought. Back in her days as a prostitute, she had always spat out the "stuff" in a defiant manner to show her customers how much she detested them and the act she had been "forced" to perform due to her unfortunate circumstances; however, this time she decided to swallow every drop, not wanting to risk offending Orazio.

All aglow with contentment, Orazio remarked, "Serafina, if you're happy with Zeke's next paycheck, maybe, you can stop by the following week to have some espresso coffee with me…Come about this time of day because I'll likely be alone."

"Well, I suppose I can stop by next week." Then, she sighed with a sly smile, "You men are all alike."

As she walked out of the office, she caught the attention of the nosy Fasano sisters who were at their usual post across the street in front of their building. Fannie remarked, "Look at Serafina, her hair's a lot messier now than when she walked into Martucci's office."

"Yeah," agreed Tessie. "Looks like her skirt is a little crooked, too."

"She was in his office for almost an hour," added Anna.

"This proves that she must be having an affair with him. Why else would he hire that dumb hillbilly husband of hers?" said Tessie, with an all-knowing look on her face.

The Fasano sisters had seen Serafina visiting Martucci's office quite often over the past years. Being the gossips that they were, and being well aware of Serafina's past—thanks to Lena Rossi's gossiping ways—they had long ago started a rumor about Serafina having an affair with Orazio. What they didn't know was that Serafina's visits, until that day, had been purely social. She simply enjoyed speaking with him in their common dialect. Although, on occasion, their conversations would be somewhat flirtatious, most of the time they were engaged in innocent small talk.

Serafina sensed that the Fasano sisters were eyeing her as she walked, but rather than crossing the street to talk to them, she stayed on Martucci's side of the block. Crossing at the corner, she buzzed past the newsstand without saying anything to Joe. When she got into her apartment, she gargled several times with mouthwash and took a long, hot bath. She didn't want Zeke to pick-up any clues.

She had found her tryst with Orazio to be very exhilarating and physically satisfying. She suppressed her feelings of guilt by justifying what she had done as being for the good of her family—the same justification that she had relied on in Naples, twenty years earlier. She figured that she would have to go on seeing Orazio at least until she got her job back, assuming that Orazio gave Zeke the overtime he had promised. The prospect of taking Orazio as her lover for a while didn't faze her. On one level, she found it exciting. She just hoped that the affair wouldn't lead to pregnancy; but if it did, she would simply tell Zeke that the "rhythm method" had failed and that they would be expecting their fourth child. She felt confident, however, that there would be little chance of Orazio getting her pregnant because he seemed to be a man who could exercise self-control and withdraw before ejaculating. She knew that he wouldn't want to father a child outside of marriage, especially since his hot-tempered wife, Concetta, would never put up with such a disgrace; she would scratch his eyes out—or worse!

Chapter 16: Wolverton Mountain

John-John, Danny and Frankie were at their usual post in front of the newsstand. It was Friday evening—and happily for all—the first day of summer. Joe would soon be closing up and heading home to the Bronx. John-John was eagerly anticipating his high school graduation, which would be held at Carnegie Hall the following Thursday. He was quite relaxed knowing that he had most likely "aced" his final exams. With the pressure of school behind him, he was ready to devote more time to cultivating his relationship with Felicia.

Felicia stopped by the newsstand shortly after seven, more dressed-up than usual. She was wearing a turquoise blouse, a white cotton skirt and dark nylon stockings. The skirt was so sheer and clingy that the silhouette of her panties was quite visible.

"Hi Felicia, Why are you so dressed-up?" asked John-John.

"Well, we're expectin' my mother's cousin and her husband from Italy. They're flyin' in from Naples, by way of Rome. They probably landed at Idlewild about a half-hour ago and should get here sometime after eight."

Frankie remarked, "I notice that your father and mother are sitting with the Fasano sisters in front of their Spring Street stoop. Why didn't your father go pick 'em up?"

"I don't know. He ain't too thrilled that they'll be stayin' in our apartment for a month. I guess he figures that they are savin' a lot of money by stayin' with us, so they should spring for a cab."

"I notice that Zeke really dressed-up for the occasion. He's wearing a new t-shirt!" commented Danny in his typically ridiculing way.

"That's the way he is," replied Felicia, in a protective tone. "But, he's a great dad."

"How do you think you did on your finals?" asked John-John.

"I think I got 70s or 75s on all of my exams, except for my Italian final. I might have flunked it. My mother will go crazy if I flunked Italian. After all, I can speak Neapolitan quite good."

"Maybe, that's the problem. The Neapolitan dialect is so different from "high Italian" …the Italian of Dante Alighieri…you most likely get confused and mixed up."

Of all the Sheiks, only John-John would have made the reference to Dante Alighieri. Surely, none of them, especially the likes of Vinnie "Lemons" or Lenny "Squirm" would have the foggiest idea of who Dante Alighieri was.

"I think you're right, sweetheart."

"Don't let your mother hear you call him 'sweetheart,'" said Joe, with a wry smile.

Felicia felt that John-John *truly* was her boyfriend. Since the Memorial Day weekend, she and John-John had managed to take Fluffy for five more walks on Crosby Street without her parents suspecting a thing. However, what she didn't know was that Tessie Fasano had spotted her walking arm-in-arm with John-John on Crosby Street the previous Friday. That was the second time she had seen the pair walking together on Crosby. At that point, she was convinced that the two were dating."

"Why don't you and John-John take a walk on Crosby Street?" urged Joe, who loved to play cupid.

"No, my parents might come lookin' for me, especially if the relatives get here early."

Danny remarked, "I got an idea, Felicia. Forget about Crosby Street. Save time…have John-John meet you in your hallway. Don't worry, I'll keep an eye on your parents."

"Yeah, I'll keep an eye on them too," said Joe, causing everyone to laugh.

"What do you think, Felicia?"

"It's really risky, John-John…Let me think about it a minute."

"John-John, if Zeke gets off his chair and starts heading home, I'll run over to the buildin' and signal you…same, if Serafina is coming," said Danny.

John-John and Danny had worked out the "signal" two weeks beforehand, when they were in a very silly mood. Rather than just yelling, "Watch out!"; "Scram!"; "Cheese it!"; or any words to that effect, they came up with the kooky idea of Danny singing *Wolverton Mountain*, if Zeke should be approaching when John-John and Felicia were together. *Wolverton Mountain*, the 1962 country song made popular by Claude King, was about a hillbilly named Clifton Clowers who lived atop a mountain and guarded his pretty young daughter from would-be suitors with a gun and a knife. Zeke reminded John-John and Danny of good ole Clifton Clowers, although Zeke never flashed a gun or a knife. Should Serafina be coming, Danny was to sing *O Sole Mio*. The only problem was that Danny was undisputedly the worst singer among the newsstand crew, and possibly the entire neighborhood.

"Felicia, why don't you head for your building and wait for me in the hallway. Don't worry about your parents, Danny and Frankie will stand guard."

"Okay, but we're takin' a big chance."

"Don't worry, Felicia, I won't let 'em turn the corner until John-John gets out of your hallway," said Frankie. "I'll trip 'em if I gotta."

"Don't forget Felicia, we *are* the Sheiks…all for one, and one for all!"

"Yeah, go. Go have some fun," added Joe.

Felicia nervously waited two minutes alone in her hallway. When John-John arrived, he pulled her into his arms, without saying a word, and began kissing her passionately. The danger of making out with her, with Zeke and Serafina close by, excited him, but the fact that she was wearing a skirt, instead of her usual pants or jeans, excited him even more. He soon became fixated upon getting his hands up her skirt. He started maneuvering slowly, putting his right hand on her left thigh, just above her knee. He found the silky feeling of her nylon stocking to be sensuous. When he dared venture farther up her thigh, she abruptly stopped his advance with her hand. He didn't want to force the issue, so he stopped—but only for the moment, thinking, *I need to distract her so she doesn't notice where my hand is going.*

He diverted her attention by quickly spinning her ninety degrees towards the mailbox wall. She didn't seem to notice his hand moving up towards the back of her thigh to where her garter belt fastened to her nylon stocking.

Even if she had, she didn't stop him. She began to breathe heavily—as did he. He slowly worked his hand farther up, until he reached her silk panties. After several minutes of fondling her behind while they French kissed, he decided to make his move towards his ultimate goal. He slowly shifted his hand to the front, while again distracting her with another spin. He then tried to sneak two fingers between her thighs.

"John-John," she faintly uttered in a tone that sounded as if she was about to stop him.

But, he paid her no mind, and she let him have his way with her. As he gently rubbed her in a to-and-fro motion, he could feel her wetness through her delicately sheer panties. It was a new and pleasant feeling for him and his thoughts shifted to going for "Third Base."

While they were going at it hot and heavy, Tessie Fasano steered the conversation with Serafina and Zeke away from the usual, run-of-the-mill gossip: "Serafina, I guess Felicia is datin' John-John."

"What-ah you mean-ah?" responded Serafina with a touch of anger in her voice.

"Well, I saw them, two times, walkin' on Crosby Street, arm-in-arm…walkin' your dog."

"Are you sure-ah?" she snarled. "Felicia is-ah no allowed-ah to go with-ah boys…and-ah I can't-ah stand-ah that John-John—that *Siciliano bastardo*."

"Are you sure they weren't *just* takin' a walk?" asked Zeke, trying to calm the situation.

"Listen, everyone in the neighborhood knows that in the evenin', Crosby Street is for young guys and girls who are in love…and for a few bums who sleep in the cubbyholes 'cause they're too drunk to make it back to the Bowery," said Tessie, with an all-knowing look on her face.

Arising from her seat, Serafina bit her lip and said, "I'm-ah gonn-ah ask her nice, but-ah if its-ah true, I'm gonn-ah pull her by-ah the hair and give her *un schiaffo in faccia*. I'll-ah slap-ah her face real hard-ah!"

That said, she and Zeke sped off to their apartment to confront Felicia. Danny and Frankie weren't close enough to hear what had been said, but they surmised by the scowl on Serafina's face, that something was up and that John-John had better get out of the hallway—fast! So, they tried to execute the plan. Danny scampered towards the hallway. Meanwhile, Frankie tried to slow down Serafina and Zeke. True to his word, he *did* try to trip them, but Serafina had brushed right by him and Zeke had managed to jump over his short legs.

As they turned the corner, they were surprised to see Danny in front of their building, "singing" at the top of his lungs.

"What the hell is that boy up to, Serafina?"

When he could make out the words of the song, *Wolverton Mountain*, he yelled out, "What are you sassin' me boy?"

"No, I'm not sassin' you, Zeke." Then, Danny attempted to sing *O Sole Mio*.

"Now Danny, I'm rightly tired of your crap!"

"Listen, Zeke, there's no law against singin' in the street. Is there? This is a free country! I can sing wherever and whatever I want!"

"This shit's gotta stop, Danny! I know that you're making fun of me and my wife."

Then, Serafina added, "Go sing-ah in front-ah your hous-ah, you-ah *disgraziato!*"

As Danny started to retreat, he just had to get the last word. He turned around and yelled at Serafina, "This is America. Learn to speak English!"

She yelled back, "*Bastardo!*"

With that, Danny yelled, "Nice t-shirt, Zeke! It's about time you bought a new one. Your other ones have more holes in them than a slice of Swiss Cheese!"

Meanwhile, John-John and Felicia were in a panic. The kooky plan had backfired. It may have worked under normal circumstances, but they hadn't anticipated that Serafina and Zeke would have *raced* back home as a result of Tessie stirring up the pot. If John-John went out the front door, Zeke and Serafina would be all over him, but more important, Felicia would be in deep, deep trouble. He imagined Serafina beating the hell out of her, and that only Zeke, who greatly favored his first-born child, would be able to put an end to the beating—that is, only after Serafina had at least gotten some satisfaction.

Thinking quickly, John-John came up with Plan "B": "Felicia, go into your apartment and sit on the sofa! Read a magazine or watch TV! I'll go up the roof."

She stood there frozen. "C'mon, let's go Felicia, Danny can't stall them much longer!"

They quickly ran up the stairs. As Felicia reached her apartment door, John-John blew her a kiss and said, "Remember, whatever happens, you're my girl."

As he reached the third floor, he could hear Serafina and Zeke entering the hallway. He proceeded to the roof as quietly as he could. For a big guy, he could be stealthy. He opened the heavy steel door and reached the safe haven of the roof. He hadn't thought the plan through, but he had made the only viable choice. Now, he had to figure out how to come down from the roof. He could wait on the roof until about midnight and then go down the stairs when everyone was asleep; or, he could cross over to the roof of the adjacent building and go down its stairway. Seeing no need to wait up on the roof, he climbed over the low fence separating the two roofs and walked over to that roof's door.

"Oh shit, it's locked!"

His final option was to get onto the roof of the corner building, which was 5 feet lower than the other two roofs and directly above the newsstand. He jumped off the parapet, landing on the lower roof with a thud. He tugged at the roof door only to find that it, too, was locked. Peering down from the roof, he saw that the coast was clear—no Zeke; no Serafina. So, he whistled and called down in a low voice, "Danny, Frankie, come up and open the roof door so I can get down from here."

They looked at each other and laughed, deciding to let John-John squirm a bit. They ignored several of his pleas. Finally, Danny yelled up, "That's what you get when you get involved with that crazy family!" Then, Danny made his way up to the roof door, slid the latch-bolt and pushed open the door.

"Thanks, Danny. I know that Felicia is part of a wacky family, but I've really fallen for her. It's hard to believe that a year ago she was the butt of our jokes and teasing."

"Yeah, now she's your girlfriend. Who would've thought it?"

"By the way Danny, what happened to our plan? Shortly after I heard you singing, I heard Zeke yelling at you."

"Well, for whatever reason, Serafina and Zeke bolted from the Fasano sisters and raced towards the newsstand. Frankie told me that he actually did try to trip 'em, but he failed."

John-John shook his head as he approached Frankie back at the newsstand.

"Sorry, John-John, I tried to slow 'em down, but ..."

"That's okay, Frankie," John-John interrupted.

At that point, Joe began his inquisition. His questions were probing. He relished hearing all the details—the spicier the better. John-John didn't hold back. He gave Joe, along with Danny and Frankie, a play-by-play account. He had no qualms about telling Joe everything because he was his mentor when it came to sexual matters; and of course, he just *had* to tell his two best buddies all the details.

Joe shook his head approvingly when John-John detailed his maneuvers under Felicia's skirt. He then asked, "Did you whip it out?"

"What do you mean, Joe?"

"You should have unzipped and have her play with your 'salami' while she was hot."

"Joe, I don't think she's that kind of girl."

"Listen, they're all that kind of girl!"

"For a blind man you're pretty dirty when it comes to the subject of women."

"What does bein' blind have to do with it? I'm still a man, ain't I?"

Frankie joined in, "Joe, I heard that about five or six years ago, you went to a whorehouse with the older guys that used to hang out here before us."

"Yeah, it's true. Vinnie "Pip" and Louie "Beak" took me up to a whorehouse on 27th Street and Lexington Avenue. They paid ten dollars each, but I talked the girl into givin' me a discount 'cause I couldn't see what was goin' on…She only charged me five bucks!"

This was the first time that John-John had heard of Joe's exploit at the whorehouse, and it lowered his opinion of him.

"But Joe, you're a married man. I can't believe you did that!" said John-John. Then, he really pissed Joe off when he added, "As a blind man you should be grateful that you have a loving wife and family who take care of you."

"You don't know what the fuck you're talkin' about John-John. My wife treats me like shit and my children treat me only slightly better."

"Really, Joe?"

"Yeah, really…You see, when I went blind, my wife realized that I would be a burden on her for the rest of our married life. In the beginning, she was very understandin' and comfortin'. But as the years went by, things changed. She developed a nasty edge. She's always yellin' at me and remindin' me of the miserable life I've given her. She treats me like a dog. The only joy I get is right here at the newsstand, thanks to you guys."

"Gee, Joe, I had no idea how badly you are treated at home," remarked John-John.

"Me too," said Danny and Frankie, almost at the same time.

"To make things worse, I think my wife might be cheatin' on me…but I'm not sure."

"Maybe, you should follow her," joked Frankie.

Not appreciating the kidding, Joe shot back, "Frankie, why don't you go fuck yourself, you short, four-eyed bastard!"

Meanwhile, back at the Daniels' apartment, Serafina was interrogating Felicia like an FBI agent.

"I hear-ah that you-ah see-ah John-John. That he is-ah your-ah boyfriend-ah."

"Where did you hear that?"

"Tessie Fasano told-ah me that she saw-ah you with-ah John-John on Crosby Street-ah, twice-ah!"

"It's not true! I don't know what she saw or what she thinks she saw, but I wasn't on Crosby Street with John-John. She needs glasses!"

Serafina raised her voice and said, "Listen to me, if I find-ah out-ah that it-sah true, I'll-ah break-ah you face!"

"It's not true! I don't like John-John. I never liked him or any of the boys that hang out at the newsstand.!"

"Okay for now-ah, but I donn-ah want to see-ah you anywhere near that-ah *Siciliano bastardo. Capisci?*"

"Yeah, okay. I understand"

The interrogation was over *for now*, but Felicia knew that from that day forward it would be very difficult to hook-up with John-John. Her mother would be keeping very close tabs on her.

Chapter 17: Father Monetvecchio

Serafina paced back-and-forth in front of her building anxiously awaiting the arrival of her cousin, Lucia, whom she hadn't seen in eighteen years. Zeke, who wasn't as anxious, sat on a chair just staring at the nearby intersection. Soon, a cab slowed down and double-parked directly in front of the building. Serafina's heart raced when she spotted her cousin waving and yelling at her from the cab.

"Lucia! Lucia!"

"Serafina! Serafina!"

Serafina ran over to the cab as her cousin was opening the door. Before Lucia's right foot could hit the pavement, Serafina fell over her, smothering her with hugs and kisses, and winding up partly inside the cab.

Once the *cugini* were both out of the cab, the greeting frenzy really began; and just when it had simmered down a bit, it started all over again when the children came down to meet their Italian cousins. The greetings were accompanied by Italian-style kisses on both cheeks. Zeke never liked this tradition, especially when it came to greeting men. Back in Tennessee, *real* men didn't hug and kiss. A firm handshake accompanied by the words, "How ya'll doin'?" was the customary greeting. But, Zeke went through the motions, mostly for Serafina's sake.

The *cugini* were very exhausted from their long journey. They had taken a local train from Naples to Rome, while lugging four large, beat-up suitcases. Five hours later, they were in the air on their nine-hour flight to Idlewild Airport. After spending nearly two hours deplaning and wending their way through Immigration, the baggage carousel, and U. S. Customs, they had their first New York City experience: hooking up with an unscrupulous cab driver, who couldn't pass up the opportunity of fleecing the foreigners. Despite having been shown the Daniels' address clearly printed on a card that had been sent to them by Serafina, the cabbie had taken them on quite a "tour" of New York City.

Serafina and the cousins began speaking in their Neapolitan dialect, very loudly, and at a fast pace. Many Italians, not familiar with the dialect, would have had trouble understanding the conversation. After several minutes, Serafina asked the *cugini* to speak more slowly, and she began to sprinkle-in some broken English so that Zeke and the children could better understand what was being said.

While she and her cousins were busy talking, Felicia and Francesca made some espresso and put out a platter of Italian pastries. Everyone sat at the table and enjoyed the fine selection of pastries from Caffé Roma, which Lucia said were just as good as the ones in her favorite Naples *pasticceria.*

By eleven, the children were totally bored and headed off to bed. Zeke's eyes were weary but he pushed himself to stay awake because if Lucia and Vincenzo could still be so full of energy after so many hours of traveling, he certainly wasn't about to be a party-pooper.

Felicia twisted and turned in bed as her thoughts focused on her latest encounter with John-John. She realized that their make-out session had gotten far too hot and heavy. She hadn't anticipated that he would have put his hands all over her most private areas—and that she would have enjoyed it. Her conscience was bothering her. Her mind was in turmoil. She thought, *Surely, good girls would never let boys get that far. Huggin' and kissin' should be enough.*

She eventually fell asleep. Once asleep, she slept soundly through the night, only awakening upon hearing the din of the singsong Neapolitan conversation coming from the kitchen. Serafina and Lucia were talking loudly and non-stop, trying to catch-up on what had been going on in their lives over the past eighteen years. Their letters to each other had been few and far between because neither of them could write very well.

Felicia did her best to converse with Lucia and Vincenzo throughout the morning. It wasn't easy, but she managed. She later excused herself to "go get some air"—a pretext to possibly meet-up with John-John. Sure enough, she found him right away. He, along with Danny, Frankie and Shortie were standing in front of the newsstand, teasing Joe. She didn't know what was going on, but whatever it was, it apparently had angered Joe so much that, just as she was nearing the stand, he picked up the weight holding down a stack of *Daily Mirrors* and flung it, trying to hit anyone of the guys that he could. Fortunately, he missed, and the weight clanged harmlessly on the sidewalk.

"John-John, I need to talk to you."

"What's up?"

They moved behind the newsstand so that they could speak privately.

"Yesterday, we went too far. You had your hands all over me… and I didn't stop you."

"Well, I couldn't help myself. One thing led to another…and another.

"I got the feelin' that if my parents hadn't come back, you might have gone even further."

Nah, "I don't think so.

"Well, I think so. You seemed so… so…"

"Intense?"

"Yeah, that's what I was about to say…intense."

"I guess you never do know what can happen in the heat of the moment. Guys my age have raging hormones. I've read that in several magazine articles…and according to the magazine articles, girls your age have raging hormones, too. Anyway, you seemed to be enjoying yourself just as much as me."

"I suppose so, but I think we'd better cool it for a while. My mother knows about us thanks to Tessie Fasano."

"Tessie Fasano?"

"Yeah, Tessie saw us walking back from Crosby Street, twice, and she put two-and-two together."

"I guess even a half-brain like Tessie can add two and two," snickered John-John.

"It's not funny. My mother is furious. She would've killed me if she knew how far we went. She doesn't want me messin' around with boys…especially you. She can't stand you. She hates your guts."

"Well, I always sensed that she didn't like me…but, she actually *hates my guts?*"

"Yeah, she thinks you're a 'Smart Alec' and a big troublemaker. Anytime the guys are up to somethin', she thinks you're behind it."

"Well, sometimes it's true, and sometimes it ain't. She's giving me too much credit."

"She always refers to you as that '*Siciliano Bastardo*.' You know, she can't stand Sicilians."

"Why?"

"I don't know. She just hates them. Anyway, we have to cool it for a while. I doubt my mother will ever let me out of her sight now that she suspects that you're my boyfriend. Even with the cousins here, she'll still be watching me like a hawk."

"Maybe, we can find a way to meet for a few minutes while your mother is busy with her cousins."

"I doubt it. If she can't watch me, she'll have Little Zeke follow me."

As if on cue, Little Zeke turned the corner and yelled out to Felicia, "Mama wants you to come home…and she means right now!"

"Zekie, you're not going to tell her that I was talking to John-John."

"No, not this time," implying that he had given Felicia her one free pass.

There was a lot going on in the kitchen when Felicia returned. Serafina, Lucia, and Francesca were busily preparing the early afternoon meal—*il pranzo*. The meal was served shortly after one o'clock. It consisted of hot and cold antipasti, lasagna, *melanzane* (eggplant), *salsicce* (sausages), *braciole* (beef rolls in meat sauce) and *patate al forno* (roasted potatoes). A mixed salad was served at the end of the meal. Unlike the American tradition, the Italian tradition is to serve the salad at the end of the meal, believing that doing so is beneficial to digestion. It is very difficult to get a waiter in Italy to serve you a salad at the beginning of dinner. The waiter may shake his head as if to agree, but more often than not, the salad will be served at the end of the meal. The Italians just can't understand why anyone would want to start his meal with a salad.

After a half-hour of animated conversation during which they all munched on fresh fruit and drank small cups of espresso, Serafina served dessert: Italian cookies and miniature pastries. After that, the men retreated into the living room to watch TV, while the women remained in the kitchen to clean up.

At around four, Felicia told Serafina that she wanted to walk over to Saint Patrick's to go to confession. It wasn't unusual for her to go to confession. She typically did so twice a month because her grammar school nuns had "hammered" the importance of going to confession deep inside her brain.

"Okay-ah, Felicia, but-ah, Francesca, you go-ah too," ordered Serafina.

Felicia and Francesca began their three-block walk to Saint Patrick's Old Cathedral, which is located between Mulberry and Mott Streets, off Prince Street. The cathedral's construction was begun in 1809, when the neighborhood was an Irish enclave. It was completed in 1815 and served as the seat of the Roman Catholic Archdiocese of New York until the present-day Saint Patrick's Cathedral replaced it in 1879, at a then-quiet location that is now in the midst of noisy midtown Manhattan. Unlike the current cathedral, Old Saint Patrick's has rather plain exterior architecture. However, the interior is magnificent. It features a series of huge stone columns, similar in style to those of the present-day cathedral. The columns support the inner vault, which is about 85 feet high at its peak. Many moviegoers would later become familiar with the interior of Saint Patrick's Old Cathedral, as it was the location of the famous Baptism Scene of *The Godfather,* and it was also featured in *The Godfather, Part III.*

The sisters walked along Prince Street, besides the red brick wall that bounded the church and its adjoining cemetery. The wall, which was wavy and tilted, was said to have been constructed to protect the cathedral from Protestant enemies. When they entered the church on Mott Street, they noticed parishioners lined up in front of two confessionals. The confessional with the longer line was that of Father Montevecchio. Father Montevecchio was loved by everyone in the parish—particularly, the women. The 40-year-old priest was strikingly handsome. He had dark, wavy hair, a Roman nose and a personality that exuded friendliness and warmth. He was in good physical condition and a decent athlete. He frequently played stickball with the teenagers in front of the Mulberry Street Rectory, and he amazed them by hitting some balls 300 feet up the street—not bad for anyone, especially a priest.

The other confessional was that of Monsignor Cordani, a short, 70-year-old with a huge, hooked nose, bald head and a nasty temperament. The line at his confessional was short—three people—because he had a reputation of scolding and reprimanding parishioners for even a minor sin. He was known for asking many probing questions and for requiring staggering amounts of prayers for penance. Missing just one Sunday mass could yield a penance of twenty *Hail Marys* and twenty *Our Fathers*. Legend had it that the sins of one of the neighborhood's mobsters had been so egregious, that Monsignor Cordani had required him to paint the rooms of the Rectory to gain forgiveness.

Without hesitation, Felicia and Francesca lined up in front of Father Montevecchio's confessional, despite there being about ten parishioners ahead of them. Felicia intentionally let Francesca lineup in front of her because she didn't want to risk the chance of her sister overhearing her confession.

Each confessional had closed, unlit booths on either side of the priest. While one person would be confessing to the priest, the next person would be waiting in the other booth preparing for confession by contemplating his or her sins. Upon the completion of one's confession, the priest would judge the severity of the sins and require a specific number of prayers as penance, which were to be said inside the church immediately after exiting the confessional. Every confession ended with the confessor (sometimes referred to as the "penitent") reciting *The Act of Contrition*. Upon its completion, the priest would close the screen between him and the confessor and then open the screen of the other booth. On many occasions, the person waiting to confess could hear much of what was being said by the other person and the priest. But with Francesca ahead of her, Felicia knew she wouldn't have to worry about her sister eavesdropping on her confession.

After about fifteen minutes in line, Felicia entered the confessional. She could faintly hear parts of her sister's confession. Francesca's sins couldn't have amounted to much because she was out of the booth in less than three minutes. Seconds later, Father Montevecchio opened the screen on Felicia's side. She could clearly see his familiar profile—the dim lighting in his cubical giving him a somewhat mystical aura.

She began reciting the mandatory introduction to confession: "Bless me Father for I have sinned; it has been two weeks since my last confession."

After a two-second pause, she continued, "Um…well…I ate meat on Friday one time, but I forgot that it was Friday."

"Okay, if you didn't know it was Friday, it's really not a sin. It would be a sin if you did it intentionally. However, you should know that the Vatican is in the process of making some important changes. I'm quite sure that in the very near future, eating meat on Friday will no longer be a sin…Anything else?

"Well, I disobeyed my mother."

"How did you disobey her?"

"Father, I recently began dating. My mother doesn't want me to date until I'm at least seventeen."

"When you say 'dating,' what do you mean, exactly? Going to the movies? A dance?"

"No Father, it was nuttin like that. We took walks on Crosby Street."

"*Only* walks?"

"No Father, we hugged and kissed."

"Anything else?"

"Well, one day we made out hot and heavy in the hallway of my building."

"What did he do?"

"He put his hands all over me. He reached all the way up my skirt."

"Did you try to stop him?"

"Yeah, at first, but then I let him put his hands wherever he wanted.

"How old is he?"

"He's eighteen."

"And, how old are you, Felicia?"

"I'll be sixteen in two weeks…but Father, how do you know who I am?"

"Well, about ten minutes ago, between confessions, I peeked out the slats in my door to see how long the line was. I couldn't help but see you and your sister standing near the end of the line. Anyway, even if I hadn't seen you, I would have recognized your voice. As you know, I've had Sunday dinner at your house at least half a dozen times."

"Yeah, whenever you come over for dinner, it's like we're celebrating a holiday. My mother always gets so excited."

"Felicia, your mother is a fine woman. As you know, she comes from the same part of Naples that my mother came from. Speaking to her in our common dialect and eating her delicious food reminds me of the good old days when my mother was alive."

Father Montevecchio continued, "Listen, your mother knows what's best for you. You're too young to be dating an eighteen-year-old. In fact, you're much too young for one-on-one dating. It can only lead to trouble. I've heard the confessions of quite a few young girls who have gotten into trouble by engaging in pre-marital sex…some who have gotten pregnant …and some who even had abortions. You're too young to get started down that road. Aren't you, Felicia?"

"Yes, Father," she sighed.

"Felicia, can you recite the last words of the *Act of Contrition* for me?"

She couldn't recite the last words without going through the entire prayer in her mind, so she quickly and silently raced through the prayer:

> *O my God, I am heartily sorry for having offended Thee, and I detest all of my sins, because of Thy just punishments; but most of all because they offend Thee, my God, who art all good and deserving of all my love. I firmly resolve, with the help of Thy grace, to sin no more and to avoid the near occasions of sin.*
>
> *Amen.*

"Father, the last words are, 'to avoid the near occasions of sin'."

"Correct. Do you understand what those words mean, Felicia?"

"I've never given those words much thought, Father."

"Well, simply put, those words mean that one should avoid situations that could lead to sin."

"I understand, Father."

"Now, for your penance, please say ten *Hail Marys* and ten *Our Fathers*…and now say a good, heartfelt *Act of Contrition*."

That's not so bad, she thought, feeling relieved.

She recited the prayer and was just about to stand up and leave. But before Father Montevecchio closed the screen, he added, "Felicia, you need to stay away from that boy until you're seventeen…you understand me. This is not just a recommendation. It is part of your penance!"

"But Father, if I leave him for a year he'll surely find someone else. He's so handsome and so nice."

"Felicia, if it's meant to be, it's meant to be. He will be there for you next year, if it's meant to be."

She opened the door of the confessional and slammed it shut— the noise echoing throughout the cavernous church. She had tears in her eyes, which she hid by covering her eyes with both hands, as if she were contemplating her confessed sins. She entered a pew in a section of the church where no one else was sitting and began to recite her prayers. She said the words of the prayers by rote, not giving any thought to the meaning of the words.

While she was praying, she couldn't help but think of what had just happened. *Father Montevecchio has just ruined my life. I was so happy with John-John this past month. I know I let things get out of hand, but…*She mulled over her options: Obey her priest and "cool it" with John-John for a year or disobey her priest and continue the relationship. Being a devout Catholic, she knew what she *had* to do—however painful it would be.

At about the same time that Felicia was facing Father Montevecchio, Serafina was involved in her own confession: She was telling her cousin about her recent sexual encounter with Orazio Martucci.

She began her story with the details of her layoff from the factory, speaking softly in Neapolitan dialect, and with a rapidity that would ensure that Zeke wouldn't get the gist of the conversation should he, by chance, hear what she was saying. She proceeded to tell Lucia how Orazio had seduced her and how she had complied without any resistance.

Lucia nodded in an understandingly manner, occasionally asking for more details. After Serafina had spilled her guts out, Lucia remarked, "I would have done the same thing if I were in your shoes. Don't worry, after what we did in Naples, we are both going to Hell…or maybe, if we are lucky, we will spend many, many years in Purgatory."

Serafina managed half a smile and said, "You're right. We did a lot of bad things in our lives. But, we are not bad people. We merely did what we had to do to survive and to help our family survive."

They then began to reminisce about their days as prostitutes. Somehow, with the distance of time, they were even able to laugh about some of their exploits in the English Cemetery.

"Serafina, do you remember how nervous Zeke was the first time he had sex with you in the cemetery?"

"Yes, I had to teach him everything. He didn't know what he was doing…. It was his first time with a woman. His friend, Corporal Butch Johnson, had to force him to come to the cemetery with him."

"By chance, Zeke's friend wound up doing it with me…Perhaps, if Zeke had gone with me instead of you, I would be living here as *la signora* Daniels."

"Maybe, but I guess it was *my* fate…You remember, he proposed to me in the cemetery on the fouth time he went with me, right when we were in the middle of doing it."

"Of course, I remember."

"He said, '*Sposami Serafina, sposami*,' in pretty good Italian. I was shocked that he would want to marry me."

"Of course, who would want to marry a *puttana?*"

"But, then he pulled a folded letter out of his pocket and handed it to me."

"Oh yes, the letter…Do you still have it?"

Serafina nodded, "It's somewhere in my dresser."

"I would love to see it again after all these years."

"Okay, let me see if I can find it."

After a few minutes, Serafina returned with the wrinkled old letter, which was neatly written in perfect Italian. They read it together:

My Dearest Serafina:
I love you with all my heart and soul. I want to marry you. But
first, I want you to give up the life you are leading. I know that
you are only doing what you are doing to survive and to help
your family survive. I am sure that deep down inside you are a
good girl with a warm heart. If you will agree to stop what you

are doing and see <u>only</u> me—with the hope of us getting married
in the future—I will give you 30,000 lire, plus 5,000 lire every
month.
With love, Zeke

"Lucia, it is written in much better Italian than I can write. I later learned that he had an Italian-American soldier named Louie LaPinto write the letter for him…but they were Zeke's words."

Serafina turned to the back of the letter, revealing the response that she had hastily scribbled to Zeke several minutes after reading his words. The gist of her reply was that she would accept his proposition if he would increase the upfront money from 30,000 lire (about $250 at that time) to 60,000 lire, so that Lucia could also get out of prostitution at the same time— emphasizing that much of the money would have to be given to their pimps as a form of compensation for "allowing" them to quit the profession.

"Serafina, I remember that he gave you the 60,000 lire on the following Saturday."

"Yes, and I gave him a phony home address…on the other side of Naples…so that he wouldn't be able to find me. I couldn't pass up the opportunity to cheat that stupid *Americano*…But, somehow he found me two weeks later."

"He tracked you down on Christmas Day. Right?"

"Right. I didn't know what to do. I couldn't give him back *all* of his money…You remember that I gave our pimps 30,000 lire to buy our freedom…So, I acted like I was very thrilled that he had found me and that I just *couldn't* understand how he had gotten confused over where I lived."

"I guess he was so stupid and so in love with you that he believed you."

"Yes, he was so blinded by his love for me that he didn't realize that I had tried to swindle him…But, he turned out to be my ticket out of Naples."

"I remember that he left Naples, along with many American soldiers, in June 1945…only a few months after you were married… and that you lived with us until a week before Christmas."

"Yes, unfortunately, my ship to America left right before Christmas. It was a very sad day when I left Naples to start my new life… one of the saddest days of my life. But…"

"Listen, Serafina, make sure that no one finds out what is going on between you and Orazio…and end it as soon as you get back to work. Be discreet. You don't want Zeke to find out that he's a *cornuto*—a cuckold."

"No, Lucia, he must never find out. He's a good husband and a good father. It would destroy him if he ever found out. My only problem is that this neighborhood is full of nosy gossipers. I've got to be extra careful. Orazio will not be satisfied with *having me* just one or two times. I know that he expects to see me every week."

"All I can say, Serafina, is be careful…very careful."

Chapter 18: Officer Casey

John-John was feeling quite good about himself. He had passed all his final exams with flying colors, achieving an average of 93.2% in his final semester at Stuyvesant. There was no school on this day or the next; all that remained was his graduation ceremony on Wednesday, June 25th, at New York's prestigious Carnegie Hall.

It seems that there were two answers to the question: Can you tell me how to get to Carnegie Hall? The usual response of a Borscht Belt comedian would be, "Practice! Practice! Practice!" The far less common response would be, "Graduate from Stuyvesant High School."

John-John was standing in front of the newsstand awaiting Joe's arrival. Rather than waiting for him by the subway kiosk, he chose to stay by the newsstand just in case Felicia would walk by. He had hoped to see her on Sunday, but their paths had never crossed.

As expected, Joe exited the subway at just about ten, after his long trek from the Bronx. For whatever reason—some say it was vanity—Joe never used a cane. He said he didn't need one because he had the entire trip to the newsstand memorized—knowing exactly how many of his steps were required in each segment of his commute. When he would reach the curb on the west side of Lafayette Street, he would wait for someone to assist him. Usually, one of the neighborhood people would be there to help him across the busy street; or sometimes, he would enlist the help of a stranger.

"Wait, Joe! I'll be there in a few seconds," yelled John-John.
Joe nodded and waited for him.

Grabbing Joe under the arm, he asked, "How was your subway ride?"

As they walked across the street, arm-in-arm, Joe replied, "Same old shit. As you know, I take three trains. It's a long and boring trip, especially since I can't see nuttin. When I used to ride the subway in the old days, I would check out all the passengers, especially the pretty girls, and I would read the advertisements. The ride flew by a lot quicker then, no matter where I was goin'."

"Yeah, it must be tough for you, Joe."

"Well, you heard what happened to me back in April, didn't you?"

"No. What happened?"

"On my way home, I made my usual change to the express train at Union Square. When the doors of the train opened, I walked in and reached for the pole. Instead of grabbing the pole, I accidentally grabbed a woman's tit. It felt real nice, so I guess I squeezed it a bit longer than I should've."

"What, did she do?"

"She smacked me in the face and started yellin' at me in Spanish, a mile a minute. I think she was a Puerto Rican. I kept yellin', 'I'm blind! I'm blind!' When she realized she had smacked a blind man, she apologized to me to no end…Oh, she felt so bad."

"Did she feel so bad that she let you feel her other tit?"

"Don't be a wise ass, John-John!"

"Sorry, Joe, it *really* must be tough for you."

"You have no idea how tough it is…no idea. Close your eyes for a minute. Here's the key to the newsstand's padlock. Try to unlock it and open the door."

After quite a bit of groping for the padlock and then trying to find the keyhole, John-John eventually was able to open the door.

"That was really hard, Joe. I'm amazed at how you can do all that you do."

"Well, I've adapted, but it hasn't been easy."

"The most amazing thing I've ever seen you do was to change the porcelain light bulb socket of the outside light. You were able to use a screwdriver and pliers better than most people who can see."

"Yeah, that's because I was pretty handy with tools before I lost my sight…By the way, how ya doin' with Felicia?"

"I don't know. I think we may have to cool things for a while. Serafina wants her to stay away from me. Felicia says that her mother hates me. Would you believe it? She actually *hates* me. She refers to me as that *Siciliano bastardo*."

With a huge grin on his moon-shaped face, Joe remarked, "That Serafina is one tough cookie, but maybe if you're extra nice and polite to her, she might get to like you, even though you *are a Siciliano bastardo*."

Joe found it quite funny that Serafina referred to John-John as a *Siciliano bastardo*. Forever a teaser and ball buster, he would thereafter call John-John "*Siciliano bastardo*" at least once a day, while emphasizing that Sicilians should not even consider themselves to be Italians, while, of course, the Neapolitans were truly Italians.

Shortly after John-John and Joe had neatly stacked all the newspapers on the counter, the first customer of the day arrived.

"Good mornin', Joe. It's gonna be a hot one today."

Joe immediately recognized the voice of Police Officer Casey, as he recognized the voices of nearly all of the people who frequented his newsstand. "Good mornin', Casey. Yeah, I'm sweatin' already and it's only 10:30 in the mornin'."

"Good morning, Officer Casey."

"Good mornin', kid."

Police Officer Casey, who worked out of the 5th Precinct, called everyone under the age of twenty, "kid." He was a tall, burly, well-seasoned, forty-year-old New York City Police Officer, with a ruddy complexion and facial features that were unmistakably Irish. One might say that he had the map of Ireland on his face. The funny thing about Officer Casey was that his surname wasn't really Casey; it was actually Jones; and his full name was Aloysius Malachy Jones. With a "handle" like that, it was obvious that some sort of nickname would have been needed for him to survive childhood and adolescence. The nickname "Casey" was given to him when he was growing up in Hell's Kitchen—the moniker obviously being derived from the name of the legendary locomotive engineer, Casey Jones.

Officer Casey picked up a *Daily News* and started thumbing through it. Then, while glancing towards Cleveland Place, he said with a sense of hurry in his voice, "Gotta go, Joe! I see one of my customers down the block." With that, he quickly walked off, taking the newspaper without paying for it.

"Hey, Joe, Officer Casey took the paper and didn't pay for it!"

"I know, I know, he never pays for newspapers."

"Why not?"

"Cops in this neighborhood never pay for nuttin. They're all crooked…Givin' him a newspaper every day is no big deal. It only costs me pennies a day. I gotta keep on his good side. I don't want him to 'pinch' me for bookin' numbers."

"Joe, what did Officer Casey mean when he said that he saw one of his customers?"

"I guess you don't know that Casey has a little parkin' racket goin' for him. I heard that he lets five neighborhood people park their cars on Cleveland Place in front of the 'No Parking' signs, for twenty bucks a month. That adds up to a C-note a month, which I suppose he has to share with some other cops. But, that's not all of the side money he makes. How do you think he got to own two houses in Queens…plus a bungalow in Rockaway…certainly not on a cop's salary."

"How do you know about the parking racket, Joe?"

"Tony 'Gallons' and Jimmy 'Cans' told me about it. They both pay him to park on Cleveland Place. It works out good for him and good for them. They say it's worth twenty bucks a month not to look for a parking space every day."

"Joe, do you really think all the cops in this neighborhood are crooked?"

"Nah, not all of 'em. But, it seems that when they find an honest cop who won't scam with the rest of 'em, they do their best to have him transferred, or they give him some kind of assignment where he can't see what the rest of 'em are up to."

"So, I guess that honesty is not the best policy in the 5th Precinct."

"Well, you've seen some crooked cops in action yourself, haven't you?"

"Sure. Last month, I saw 'Little' Alex make a payoff to two cops in a patrol car, stopped right in front of his social club, which is right across from my building."

"How did he make the payoff?"

"Oh, it was done in a rather clever way. Alex went over to the police car and leaned over to talk to the cop behind the wheel. While he was talking to him, he put his right fist through the open back window. As he lowered his fist out of sight, he began gesturing with his left hand…as a distraction, I guess. Two seconds later, he pulled out his right hand…no longer held in a fist. Both cops nodded and the car slowly made its way up Mulberry, stopping near the corner of Prince in front of 'Fat' Benny's social club."

"Did you actually see any money?"

"No, but after the cops pulled away, I went over to Alex and asked him what was going on. Since, he has known me since I was born, and because he has known my parents for years and years, he didn't mind me asking him such a question. He told me that he had two, ten-dollar bills crumpled in his fist…one for each cop…and that he had simply dropped them down onto the car's floorboard."

"John-John, the cops in this neighborhood are very smart. They're making a decent salary plus loads of money on the side. If I was a cop in this neighborhood, I'd do the same thing."

"I don't know if I could be a dishonest cop, Joe. I would find it hard to go against the oath that all police officers take when they graduate from the Police Academy."

"You won't have to worry about that. Someday you'll be an engineer …and I'm sure you'll be a great one!"

"Thanks, Joe. I hope I do well at Columbia. Engineering is a difficult program and Columbia's program is one of the most difficult in the country. I've been told that more than half of the freshman will flunk-out by the middle of their sophomore year."

"Don't worry, you'll do fine…Gettin' back to crooked cops, have you seen anythin' else…any more payoffs?"

"Yeah, the other day I saw good ole Officer Casey coming out of the 'Swag Shop' near my building. He was carrying a full shopping bag. You know, you never see a cop in uniform carrying a shopping bag."

"I hear that shop does a good business whenever it's open. You know, I even buy things there…the bargains are great."

The "Swag Shop" wasn't really a shop in the true sense. Rather, it was an outlet for the fencing of stolen goods. The shop, which was only open to neighborhood people, was very non-descript; it had no signs, and the windows were painted black. Whenever there was a new shipment to be fenced, the word would quickly get out on the street, and before long, many neighborhood people—particularly women—would be scurrying to the shop to take advantage of the bargains. On one day, there might be a truckload of sheets and pillowcases; a few days later, there might be a load of wool suits. One side effect of the shop's bargain prices, and limited clientele was that many of the neighborhood people would wind up with the same, or similar, goods. For example, about a week after the shop had sold out a shipment of Italian-knit shirts, many of the neighborhood men and boys were walking around wearing identical shirts—in either, red, green or blue—the only colors available. It was actually a funny sight to those who knew the story behind the shirts. But, at a price of just two bucks apiece, no one seemed to mind that his shirt was far from unique.

"Joe, I guess Officer Casey had a load of swag in that shopping bag."

"Of course he had…and I'm sure he didn't pay for it…plus, I bet there was an envelope with some cash in that shoppin' bag, too."

"I suppose you're right, Joe."

"Of course I'm right. Casey doesn't miss a fuckin' trick. If there's some money to be made, or a chance for a freebie, he won't let it slip by him…Ah, more power to him. I would do the same thing if I was in his shoes."

Chapter 19: Carnegie Hall

"Hey, Ma, how does my suit look?"

"It looks great! You're gonna be the best dressed and best-lookin' student at the graduation…Nobody's gonna know that your nice blue suit cost me only twenty bucks on Orchard Street."

"Was it a second, Ma?"

"Yeah, the back pockets are a little crooked…but the jacket covers the pockets…Don't worry, nobody's gonna notice."

It was John-John's long-awaited day—Graduation Day. His family was excited, even more so because the ceremony would be held at Carnegie Hall.

John-John's dad, who had managed to get the day off, donned his finest suit, a white-on-white shirt, a red silk tie, and his best pair of shoes—black Florsheim wingtips—for the special event. The clothes really did "make the man." What a change from his *Ralph Kramden* olive green bus drivers' uniform! Now, all spiffed up, he looked like a cross between a business executive and a *Mafioso*.

Angelina was wearing a green satin dress, which she had made herself. The green of her dress accentuated her bright red hair, which she owed to *Miss Clairol*—not her Sicilian heritage. At age 46, she still had the looks and figure that many men would find attractive.

"Johnny, let's take a cab up to Carnegie Hall."

"No, you know I hate cab drivers. I argue with two or three cabbies every day. They're always cutting off my bus."

"So, because *you* can't stand cab drivers, we all gotta take the train on Houston Street."

"Yeah…anyway, the train will get us there quicker."

"C'mon Vivian, get away from that mirror so I can use the bathroom…It's my graduation, not yours."

"Vivian, get out of the terlit…let your brother use it!"

John-John's cute, vivacious, 15-year-old sister, Vivian, was hogging up the bathroom—or the "terlit" as it was commonly called— trying to get her hair "just right." Vivian had recently completed her freshman year at Saint Anthony's Commercial High School, in nearby Greenwich Village. Her goal was to become a secretary—a typical job at that time for an Italian-American girl from a bluecollar family. It would be rare for such a girl to go on to college. She usually would be discouraged to do so by her family because it was believed that a girl's goal should be to find a husband and to raise a family as soon as possible.

After a bit of yelling and screaming, the Caras managed to leave the apartment right on time. John Sr., whose work revolved around schedules, had made sure of that.

They soon walked past Joe's closed newsstand and headed up Lafayette Street. As they approached Felicia's building, John-John spotted her peering down from her open bay window. She smiled at him, blew him a kiss and yelled, "Congratulations, John-John!"

The "harmless" blown kiss triggered Angelina's anger and caused her to admonish her pride and joy: "Listen, John-John, I don't want you foolin' around with that Felicia. I hear she's a nice girl, but she comes from a really lousy, low-class family. Her father is a hillbilly and her mother…well, I hear her mother is a *puttana*…a who-ah. It's common knowledge that she used to work the streets of Naples durin' the war, and now I'm hearin' rumors about her and Orazio Martucci! I don't want you gettin' involved with that family…You hear me?"

"But Ma…"

"*Basta.* Enough for now. Let's go and enjoy your graduation.

"Oh, okay, Ma."

Angelina continued, "I'm so proud of you. You're the first one on both sides of the family to go to college, full time. Not just any college, but Columbia University…a great Ivy League school. Thank God we won't have to pay for your education. The scholarships that you've won will cover almost everything."

When the Cara family arrived at Carnegie Hall, the entrance was teeming with well-dressed people wedging their way towards the doorways. Each of the approximate 700 graduating students had been allotted three tickets. Thus, with a capacity of about 2,800 people, nearly every seat of the Main Hall would be filled.

Carnegie Hall was built by philanthropist Andrew Carnegie in 1891. It is located in the heart of Manhattan at 57th Street and Seventh Avenue. The Italian Renaissance-style, masonry structure had been the home of the New York Philharmonic Orchestra until 1962, when it moved to New York's Lincoln Center. Even with the loss of the Philharmonic Orchestra, it was (and still is) a major venue for top quality music events in New York City.

The graduation ceremony was uneventful. Several years earlier, the graduation had been *quite eventful*, to put it mildly. That graduating class had begun chanting, "Down with the Flea! Down with the Flea!" when Stuyvesant's principal, Leonard J. Fliedner, tried to speak at the ceremony. The nickname "the Flea" had been pinned on Dr. Fliedner many years earlier. The reasons for that class's particular animosity towards him were not obvious—especially to the guests; but the continuous chanting by the rowdy seniors led to the cancellation of the rest of the graduation ceremony and some bad press and television coverage that marred Stuyvesant's great reputation.

On this day, the speeches made by Dr. Fliedner, various department heads, and the valedictorian and salutatorian were typical of any high school in America—filled with nostalgia, challenges to the graduates and much forgettable hyperbole. The most memorable aspect of the graduation was the venue.

At the same time that John-John was at his Carnegie Hall ceremony, Danny, Shortie, Joey "Limp" and Charlie "the Ox" were graduating from their respective high schools. However, Frankie, who was a Seward Park High School senior, didn't graduate. He would have to remain at Seward for another semester, or two, because he had failed too many subjects. The guys would later jokingly refer to him as "Super Senior."

When the Carnegie Hall ceremony had ended, the graduates and their families lingered along the 57th Street sidewalk for a while. It was a chaotic and noisy assemblage, with the din of the crowd being supplemented by the ever-present background sounds of the Manhattan traffic. The graduates shuffled through the crowd, each seeking to say some parting words to their buddies. After hugging and shaking the hands of as many friends as he could find, and promising to "stay in touch forever," John-John joined his family waiting for him along the curb.

"John-John, would you like to have lunch in an Italian restaurant or a Chinese restaurant?"

"Well, Pop, since we eat Italian food just about every day, let's go have lunch in Chinatown…and, anyway, the few times that we've eaten in an Italian restaurant, the sauce wasn't nearly as good as Mom's."

"Okay, let's go eat Chinks."

"Eating Chinks," or "Going to the Chinks" were not considered to be pejorative expressions in the sixties—that is, not to *most* New Yorkers. No prejudice was intended. It was just common vernacular at that time.

"Johnny, let's take a cab…and I don't wanna hear about how much you hate cabbies…It's hot and these high heel shoes are killin' me."

"Okay, Angie…okay."

John Sr. begrudgingly hailed a cab. Within twenty minutes, the taxi, —a Checker Cab with fold-down jump seats—arrived at the foot of Chinatown. John Sr. paid the driver the fare, but only a 5% tip because "he took the long way to Chinatown." The family then proceeded down the steps to their favorite Chinese restaurant, Yat Bun Sing, at 16 Mott Street.

"For this special day we're gonna celebrate with a real treat… Lobster Cantonese, plus the usual things we order! It's gonna cost me a few more bucks, but it's not every day that my son graduates Stuyvesant."

After a perfunctory look at the menu, John Sr. got the attention of the waiter. "Hey, Charlie, we're ready to order."

"How do you know his name is Charlie, Pop?"

"Oh, they all answer to 'Charlie'…it comes from the Charlie Chan movies."

"You think they mind you calling them 'Charlie'?"

"Nah, not at all."

While the Caras were enjoying their Chinese lunch, Felicia was trying her best to sidestep Serafina's questions about her report card. "How-ah you do-ah in school-ah, Felicia?"

"I did good, Mama."

"Let-ah me see-ah your report-ah card," Serafina demanded.

"I misplaced it. I can't find it,"

"You-ah not gon-nah leave this-ah house until you-ah find it!"

Felicia knew where her report card was. She hadn't misplaced it. She was just too scared to show it to her mother because she had passed all of her subjects, except for Italian. After "looking" all around the house for her "misplaced" report card for about fifteen minutes, she figured that it was time to face the music.

"Mama, I found it!"

She handed her mother the report card while Serafina was talking to Cousin Lucia in the living room. As Felicia quickly disappeared into the kitchen, Serafina's eyes zeroed-in on the grade that was written in red ink.

"You-ah gotta a 60 in *Italiano! Disgraziata!* You-ah Italiana. How-ah could you-ah fail-ah Italiano, *la bella lingua?*" And-ah, your other grades-ah no so good-ah!"

"I don't know why I have trouble with Italian, Mama. I find it hard…very difficult. Maybe, it's because I know the Neapolitan dialect and it confuses my understanding of 'high' Italian."

Cousin Lucia felt left out of the conversation, so she asked Serafina what was going on. Serafina explained the situation to Lucia who then expressed empathy for Felicia because she, herself, had always found it difficult to speak, read and write proper Italian.

"*Hai ragione*, Felicia—You are right. *Italiano e` difficile,*" said Cousin Lucia, while gesturing with her hands for emphasis.

"Mama, don't worry. I can still work my summer job at the lingerie shop. I won't have to go to summer school. I'll repeat the course next year."

As Serafina accepted the reality of Felicia's failure to master the Italian language, the Caras were finishing their special lunch. The tab, with tip, amounted to $8.50—almost twice the usual amount.

But, to them, it was well worth it.

Chapter 21: Hoppin' a Sale

While most of the guys were at their graduation ceremonies, eighteen-year-old Lennie "Squirm" was hanging out in front of the newsstand trying to figure out how he could make a few bucks.

Lennie, the grammar school dropout was unemployed by choice, although, his job prospects were quite limited. He viewed work as something for other people—certainly not for him. He figured he could make his way through life using his street smarts and wits. His formal education had ended when he completed the fourth grade at P.S. 21. Occasionally, thereafter, he would pop into school for a few days just to mollify the truant officers, but he would pay absolutely no attention to what was being taught. As a result, he was basically illiterate; he could only read and write a few words. The newsstand crew often mocked his illiteracy, and even Joe got into the act once when he derisively challenged Lenny to a "speed-reading contest."

One story that was often repeated as a way of teasing Lennie about his illiteracy related to the time when some of the guys had decided to go fishing on Staten Island. The fishing party consisted of Lennie, Danny, Frankie, Charlie "the Ox" and John-John. They had only two fishing rods—which they intended to share—but they didn't have any bait. When the ferry landed at the Staten Island Terminal, the guys disembarked and followed the rest of the passengers as they made their way to the exit. After walking with the departing passengers for about two minutes, Lennie pointed to a sign and exclaimed, "Ooh look! Bait and tackle." The guys looked at the sign and they each began to laugh. Then, Danny fired back, "Listen numb skull, the sign reads, 'Buses and Trains!'"

Lennie had been given the nickname "Squirm" because of the way that he was built. Physically, he was a lean and wiry bag of bones. His body resembled that of Don Knotts in his portrayal of Deputy Sheriff Barney Fife on the *Andy Griffith Show*. However, unlike Don Knotts, Lennie was quite handsome. He had Roman features, a nice tan complexion and thick, shiny black hair, which he combed straight back.

Lennie was soft-spoken and somewhat shy. Yet, he was fun to be with, and one could not ask for a better, or more loyal, friend. Even though he was usually worrying about where his next buck would come from, if he had some cash in his pocket, he wouldn't think twice about lending some of it to a friend in need. On the other hand, he wouldn't think twice about borrowing some money from his friends—which was more often the case. Occasionally, he would borrow money from the local shylocks, even though their interest rate—or "vig"—was well above what banks would charge. A one-week loan would be made at interest rates ranging from 20% to 25%. If the loan wasn't paid back on time, the borrower would have to deal with one of the shylock's "enforcers." Usually, some threats would be made if the payment date was missed and the interest owed would be increased dramatically; but if the borrower tried to string the shylock along for too long a time, he risked a broken kneecap— or worse.

After about twenty minutes of shooting the breeze, Frankie and Nicky "White Cap" stopped by the newsstand.

"Hey Lennie! Hey Joe! What's cookin'?"

"Same old shit, Frankie" replied Joe, as Lennie shook his head as if to agree.

"Yo, Lennie…Frankie…let's go to Canal Street and 'hop' some sales."
"Not me, Nicky. I don't like to cheat people," Frankie quickly replied.

"If they're stupid enough to fall for the scam, they deserve to be cheated!" exclaimed Lennie.

"Hoppin' a sale" was neighborhood lingo used to describe the scam of cheating unsuspecting fireworks buyers out of their money. The scam was simple and it usually worked. Within several weeks of the Fourth of July holiday, many teens from the outer boroughs would head for Chinatown to buy fireworks. The nearest subway stops for Chinatown are on Canal Street. Usually, a half-dozen of neighborhood teens, working in pairs, would wait by a subway kiosk and approach exiting youths, asking them if they wanted to buy fireworks. Those who bit at the offer would be told, for one specious reason or another, that they would have to pay for the fireworks in advance. The "pigeons" would then be told to wait about ten minutes on the corner until the "sellers" would return with the fireworks. Of course, they would never return, pocketing from five to ten dollars each time they pulled-off the scam. The scam artists were smart enough to limit their scamming to a couple of times a day because they didn't want to chance running into anyone they had cheated. On the rare occasion that this would happen, the scammers were usually smart enough to come up with some story that their naïve customers would fall for, hook, line and sinker. One typical cover story was that the cops had spotted them making the sale and that they had to ditch the bag of fireworks; but, if they—the customers—would wait fifteen minutes on the corner, they would be back with the fireworks. Of course, the scammers wouldn't return for the rest of the day.

So, Lennie and Nicky started walking towards Canal Street with hopes of making some easy money. To Lennie, cheating, scheming and stealing were perfectly acceptable things that one would need to do to survive. His sense of morality had been forged by the examples that his parents and close relatives had instilled in him at an early age. His father was a "three-time loser," meaning that he had been convicted of felonies three times. His aunt ran a grocery store that served as a front for a bookie operation. The most unusual thing about the grocery store was that it lacked refrigeration. Thus, one couldn't buy a container of milk at the store. Also, the store only stocked two types of pasta—spaghetti and ziti; such a meager selection of pasta was unheard of in a grocery store, especially one in Little Italy.

Lennie's older cousins, the Muccio brothers, were three low-level criminals whose escapade several years earlier had made them the laughingstock of the neighborhood. They had been engaged in a crime that required both stealth and strength. They would break into factory lofts in the middle of the night, targeting office safes. If they couldn't crack a safe, they would carry it out of the building with great effort, usually lugging it down a fire escape, or sometimes lowering it down with ropes. They would transport the safes in a van to a rented cellar on Thompson Street, just to the south of Greenwich Village, in an area that would later become known as SoHo.

Rather than breaking open a safe on the night they had stolen it—or shortly thereafter—they had decided to accumulate as many safes as they could before Christmas, and open all of them about a week before Christmas. They jokingly referred to this scheme as their "Christmas Club." Unfortunately for the "Moochers," as they were often referred to in the neighborhood, the police, acting on a tip from someone living across from the cellar, caught them one early December night as they were carrying their thirteenth safe into the cellar. The sergeant on the scene couldn't stop laughing when Joey Muccio volunteered that the reason they hadn't opened the safes was that they were "saving" the money inside them to buy Christmas presents.

Lennie and Nicky returned to the newsstand about an hour after they had left. None of the guys were there.

"Yo, Joe! Where's everybody?" Lennie inquired.

"Today is graduation day for John-John, Danny, Shortie, Joey and Charlie."

"It must be nice to graduate high school. I wish I was graduatin' high school."

"Listen dummy, if you go back to school this coming September, with hard work and some brown-nosin', you might graduate when you're thirty!" Then Joe added with a laugh, "At age thirty, you'd be older than many of the teachers!"

"Hey Joe, me and "White Cap" just made fifteen bucks from some dopey kids from Queens in less than an hour. High school graduates will probably be makin' a buck an hour!"

"Lennie, you made some easy money, today, but in the long run, your buddies will make a decent livin' while you'll be schemin' and scammin' the rest of your life. Also, if you don't watch out, you'll wind-up spending a lot of time in jail just like your father did."

"Ah, whatta ya know, Joe!"

"I know plenty!"

Chapter 21: The Invitations

The telephone rang in the Rizzo's apartment at around ten in the morning on the last Saturday in June. Vincenzo Rizzo, who was staring aimlessly out the living room window towards the factory building directly across the street, let the phone ring six times before answering it.

"*Pronto. Chi parla?*" Vincenzo asked, with a touch of sadness and raspiness in his voice.

"*E` Felicia, Signor Rizzo. Come sta?*"
Vincenzo's reply was almost inaudible.

"Can I please speak to Maria?" Felicia continued in English.
"*Maria, e` tua amica, Felicia.*" Maria, who was lingering at the kitchen table drinking coffee with her mother, Rosaria, quickly headed towards the living room, walking through the two bedrooms in between the kitchen and living room in the railroad apartment.

"Hi, Felicia. How are you?" Maria asked in a subdued tone as she picked up the receiver from the end table.

"Well, my parents are throwin' me a Sweet Sixteen Party on the Fourth of July, which, you know, is my actual birthday. You're invited. So are Angie and Judy and a lot of other people."

"I would have loved to come to your party, but I won't be able to make it. Me and my parents will be going to Sicily as soon as my father can make the flight arrangements. A couple of hours ago, we got a telephone call from my father's sister in Sicily. Well, when he heard her voice on the phone, he just knew it had to be bad news because no one from Sicily ever calls unless it's bad news. His sister was crying so much that he could hardly understand her. She told him that their brother...my Uncle Pino...had passed away, suddenly, today, at about noon, Italian time."

"Oh God! I'm so sorry to hear that. No wonder your father's voice sounded so sad. I thought there might be somethin' wrong. He usually gives me a warm greetin' and chats with me a bit in Italian before handing you the phone."

"Yeah, we're all so sad and shocked. Uncle Pino was only sixty-four years old. He was the closest one in age to my father, who is sixty-two. They both came to America back in the late thirties to make some money to support their families back in Sicily. My father left my mother and my brother behind, while my uncle left his wife and three children behind. They had it hard here. They worked like dogs…twelve hours a day, six days a week, for many years. They lived with two *paisani* in a cold-water flat and sent almost all the money they made back to Sicily."

"Yeah, I know it was hard back in those days. My mother's life in Italy was no picnic either, especially durin' the war. She seldom talks about the war years. Every time I ask her questions about that time in her life, she changes the subject."

To lighten things up a bit, Maria changed the subject. "Where's the party being held?"

"My parents are renting a luncheonette on Spring Street…the one right next to the subway station…not the one on the corner. The luncheonette will be closed on the Fourth of July, so the owner, Jake, was happy to rent out the place to my parents for the day."

"That sounds good, Felicia. I'm sorry I'll miss your party. I didn't get a party when I turned sixteen last October. My parents don't know that such a thing as a Sweet Sixteen Party even exists."

"By the way, Maria, I tried callin' Judy yesterday, and again, just before I called you. No one answered the phone. Do you know where she is?"

"Don't you remember, Felicia, she told us on the last day of school that she and her family were going up to the Poconos for three weeks."

"Oh, now I remember. I guess the only one from our lunch table group that will be comin' to my party is 'Fat' Angie."

"You know, she can be the life of the party, if she's in a good mood."

"That's for sure…How long will you be in Sicily, Maria?"

"I'm not sure…at least two weeks, but possibly, five weeks or more. My father is studying the calendar as we speak. It all depends on how much time he can take off from his job. So, if you don't hear from me for a while, you can figure that I'm still in Sicily.

"Okay."

"Oh, Felicia, guess what? Yesterday I finally got my braces taken off. My mouth feels so great, and I think I look so much better now without that horrible, ugly shiny metal around my teeth."

"I can't wait to see the *new* Maria. Good luck, and please give my condolences to your father, and also to your mother."

As Felicia hung-up the phone, she noticed that her mother, Cousin Lucia and her husband, Vincenzo, were about to leave the apartment. "Where are you goin'?" Felicia asked.

"We gon-ah take-ah a walk-ah in the neighborhood," Serafina replied

"Una passeggiata," added Lucia.

The group didn't include Zeke. True to his promise, Orazio Martucci had given Zeke plenty of overtime. Since Serafina's "visit" to Martucci's office, Zeke had been working ten hours a day on weekdays, plus eight hours on Saturdays. This was great for the Daniels family, financially, but it made it somewhat boring for Cousin Vincenzo because Zeke was hardly at home during the cousins' visit.

The trio's first stop was at Joe's Newsstand. Joe surprised *i cugini* with his ability to speak in the Neapolitan dialect. After exchanging pleasantries with Joe and responding to his question about the length of their stay in America, Serafina and *i cugini* proceeded along Spring Street and stopped to greet the Fasano sisters, who were comfortably seated at their usual post in front of their building. From there, they walked diagonally across the street to Martucci's office.

"Buon giorno, Orazio! Vorrei presentare a te mia cugina Lucia e suo marito, Vincenzo," exclaimed Serafina, happily introducing her cousin and her husband to Orazio.

"Piacere. Molto lieto," responded Orazio with a broad, toothy smile. He rose from his seat behind the desk and hugged and kissed *i cugini* in a manner that was customary throughout Italy. The conversation continued in the Neapolitan dialect. Orazio's Neapolitan was absolutely perfect; he spoke the

dialect like someone who had never left the shores of Naples. The reason for this was that since 1950, he would spend a month in Naples every year, visiting his many relatives. In sharp contrast to Orazio, Serafina, who had never returned to Naples, had lost some of the present-day nuances of the dialect.

Orazio excused himself for a moment and went into the back room to begin brewing a pot of espresso and to clear-off the table— the same table where a few weeks earlier, he had had his way with Serafina. Two minutes later, he popped out of the back room, saying, "Come on in and have a seat at the table."

He placed a box of Italian cookies on the table, and then, as if on cue, the radio began to play Jimmy Roselli's rendition of *Mala Femmina,* a popular Neapolitan song about a man's love for a "bad" woman. When the espresso was ready, he poured it into beautiful black-and-gold demitasse cups, which were more suitable for an elegant dining room than the back room.

The conversation focused on Naples and the beautiful towns along its outskirts—Positano, Sorrento and Amalfi. They talked and sipped espresso for close to an hour. After a typical "Italian goodbye," with hugs and double-kisses, the visitors headed for the outside door. Vincenzo led the way, with Lucia following close behind him. Serafina lagged a bit to have a quick, private word with Orazio.

Speaking in English to ensure the privacy of his conversation with Serafina, Orazio asked when he might see her alone.

"Sunday, Zeke-ah and I-ah are drivin-ah Lucia and Vincenzo to Brook-ah-lene. They-ah gon-ah stay-ah with my brother, Paolo, until-ah the Fourth-ah-July. I try-ah to com-ah here Monday morning while-ah Zeke-ah work-ah."

"Va bene, Serafina. Va bene."
After leaving the office, they headed down Mulberry Street, stopping in every shop between Spring and Hester. *I cugini* really enjoyed the *passeggiata.* They felt like they were walking along the streets of Naples.

While her mother was busy giving her cousins a tour of the neighborhood, Felicia was peering down from her bay window every five minutes, or so, to see if John-John was in front of the newsstand. When she finally spotted him standing there along with most of his buddies, she knew that she had the chance to talk to him out of the sight of her ever-vigilant mother. So, she raced down to the newsstand and walked over to him, greeting him with a quick hug and a peck on the cheek.

John-John, who was a little surprised by her display of affection, said, "How are you, sweetheart?"

"Oh, I'm fine...I'm fine." Then, she addressed the group: "Guys, I want all of you to come to my Sweet Sixteen Party on the Fourth of July at 3 o'clock. It's gonna be held at Jake's Soda Fountain, which will be closed for the holiday."

Then, reconsidering her invitation, she said, "Sorry, Danny, I can't invite you. My father and mother are still very mad at you. They didn't like what you said to them while you were trying to protect me and John-John from gettin' caught by them in my hallway."

"Felicia, won't your mother be upset if *I* come to the party?"

"Well, John-John, they won't be crazy about the idea, but I think they'll let me have my way on my birthday."

"But, hold on!" John-John added. "We're the Sheiks...all for one, one for all. We can't go to your party without Danny." "Yeah, we're not flat-leavers," added Donny.

"You said it "Knobhead"! If Danny ain't invited, we all shouldn't go," said Frankie, reinforcing the consensus of opinion.

Vinnie "Lemons" and Lennie "Squirm" shook their heads in agreement. Then, Joe put his two cents in: "Fellas, don't ruin her party. Go without Danny."

"No, I don't think we should go," interjected Shortie.

Danny, surprisingly, felt bad about the situation. He noticed that Felicia was about to cry. So, he called for a pow-wow. The guys huddled out of Felicia's earshot.

"Look, I don't wanna ruin her party. Go without me. When the time is right, I'll sneak in right under the noses of Serafina and Zeke. It'll be fun."

"Okay, Danny, but make sure you do manage to sneak into the party," said John-John, speaking for the entire crew.

Returning to Felicia, John-John said, "Okay, we'll come to your party without Danny…Now, let's go into your hallway. I want to talk to you in private."

He was surprised that she didn't balk at his request. Once inside the hallway, he gazed into her eyes and said, "Felicia, oh how I've missed you." When he embraced her tightly and kissed her, he noticed a difference in her kisses. It seemed like she was holding back. She was. Rather than enjoying the moment, she was haunted by Father Montevecchio's voice in her head telling her to "avoid the near occasion of sin." So taking heed of Father Montevecchio's admonitions, she parried every one of John-John's attempts to get past "first base." He soon gave up trying.

"Felicia, I think I should get back to the newsstand while the gettin' is good. You never know when your mother and her cousins might pop up."

"Okay. Take care. See ya soon."

He exited the building, rather disappointed, wondering what had happened to their relationship. As the hallway door closed, Felicia bit her lower lip while thinking about how she was going to hold onto the love of her life. She recalled Father Montevecchio's words from her last confession: *Felicia, if it's meant to be, it's meant to be. He will be there for you next year, if it's meant to be.* The thought that he soon would be going off to college where he would meet more worldly and sophisticated girls made her feel even more depressed, and only exacerbated the situation as she saw it.

Chapter 22: Encore

Serafina sat by herself at the kitchen table drinking her second cup of coffee of the morning. The apartment was eerily quiet. For the first time in quite a while, she was alone. The day before, Sunday, the entire family, along with *i cugini*, had piled into Zeke's pride and joy — his 1954 Plymouth Belvedere—to visit Serafina's brother, Paolo. Although the Plymouth was nine years old, he kept it in tip-top condition. Every week, he would either be under the hood tinkering with the engine, or busily polishing the car. In fact, the car's light blue paint still retained a new car luster. *I cugini*, who, obviously, were not familiar with American car styles, thought the Plymouth was a brand-new car.

The six-passenger, four-door sedan was somehow able to fit seven passengers on the trip to Paolo's house, which was in the Bensonhurst section of Brooklyn. Passenger space wouldn't be a problem on the return trip because Francesca and Little Zeke, along with *i cugini*, would remain at Paolo's house until Felicia's Sweet Sixteen party. Their four-night stay would be a pleasant change for the children, who would get a chance to spend some time with their three cousins; and Lucia and Vincenzo would greatly enjoy reconnecting with Cousin Paolo and his wife, Laura.

Zeke had left for work at seven. When he kissed Serafina good-bye, he told her that he would likely work at least two hours overtime, depending upon how the job was going. Felicia had left for work shortly before nine, anxiously anticipating her first day at J and B's Lingerie Shop, which was located just two blocks away at Broadway and Spring.

Serafina realized that she needed to ensure that Zeke's overtime would continue, and to do so, she would have to keep Orazio "happy." After thinking about the situation for a while, she decided to go see Orazio that morning, figuring that 10 o'clock would be a quiet time in his office. She rationalized what she was about to do: *I'm doing it for the good of my family….Anyway, I've been with many, many men, so, one more isn't going to make any difference in the eyes of God.* On one level, she was actually looking forward to the tryst. Orazio was a very attractive man in her eyes and she really enjoyed his Neapolitan ways; plus, the very idea of clandestine sex made her heart race in anticipation, especially after being in a dull marriage for so many years.

She stepped into the bathroom and began applying her makeup, putting on plenty of rouge, mascara, eye shadow and brilliant red lipstick. She then spent about ten minutes fussing with her hair. After that, she removed her nightgown and sprayed Chanel No.5 all over her body. She went to her bedroom dresser and began looking through the bottom left drawer. Beneath a half-dozen pairs of everyday underwear, she found what she was looking for: the pair of red, lacy bikini panties that Zeke had bought her for Valentine's Day. The panties still had the tags on them.

After slipping on the panties, she took a good long look at herself in the full-length mirror behind the bedroom door. She was quite pleased with what she saw. For a mother of three, she still had a pretty good figure. Her belly did curve outward a bit, but only enough to accentuate her voluptuousness. Her full breasts had yet to succumb to gravity, although they were not as perky as they had been when she was "working" the English Cemetery in Naples.

She went into her closet and found the dowdiest looking housedress she owned—a loose-fitting, blue cotton dress with a row of white buttons on the front. She put on the dress and slipped into a pair of tan wedge shoes. She then went back to view herself in the mirror. She was happy to see that the looseness and style of the housedress camouflaged the fact that she was braless.

As she left the building, her thoughts focused on how she might avoid the watchful eyes of the ever-present Fasano sisters. She decided that she would take a circuitous route to Orazio's office. Rather than walking past the Fasano's building, she chose to walk south down Cleveland Place; she then turned left onto Kenmare, and then left again onto Mulberry. When she reached the corner of Spring and Mulberry Streets, she was within 100 feet of Orazio's office and on the same side of the street. She could see the Fasano sisters in the distance seated in front of their building on the other side of the street. They didn't seem to notice her. Soon, a bus stopped in front of the nearby Spring Street subway station. She figured if she timed it right, she would be shielded from the Fasano sisters for a few seconds as the bus pulled away from the bus stop—which, hopefully, would be long enough for her to enter Orazio's office without being seen by the nosy sisters.

Her timing was perfect. She managed to enter Orazio's office without being seen by the sisters. Orazio glanced upward and smiled as she stepped in front of his desk. He was very happy that she had kept her promise to see him. He was puzzled by her plain-looking housedress, which seemed to be inconsistent with her make-up, hairdo, and the amount of perfume she was obviously wearing.

They exchanged pleasantries in English and then began to speak in the Neapolitan dialect.

"I'm so glad to see you, Serafina. Would you like some espresso?"

"No, thank you. I don't want to be here too long. This neighborhood has too many gossipers…too many eyes. I don't want to start any rumors about us."

"I understand. By the way, are you happy with the amount of overtime work that I've given to Zeke?"

"Of course I'm happy. That overtime has really helped us to get through these hard times. We would be in deep trouble without it. Thank you, Orazio, thank you…I hope the overtime will continue because it looks like my lay-off won't end soon."

"Oh, I think the overtime could last for a couple more months, depending on how things go."

She wasn't sure what he meant when he said, "depending on how things go." Was he referring to the workload of his business or to his relationship with her?

"Orazio, let's go into the back room. I have a surprise for you."

She opened the door to the back room, and while entering, she began unbuttoning her dowdy blue housedress. As he turned around to lock the door, she quickly flung the dress against the wall and spun around to face him.

His jaw dropped and his eyes opened widely, astonished by the surprising, lovely sight before him. He immediately focused upon Serafina's bulbous breasts with their large protruding nipples. He then gazed down at her very sexy red bikini panties, which highlighted her curvaceous body. He couldn't help but compare his wife's obese body to that of the shapely beauty in front of him. He was immediately aroused, and he began kissing her passionately. She returned his kisses with equal passion. She had subconsciously become quite enamored with Orazio and her feelings began to surface, spurred on by the excitement of the situation. For a few seconds, she thought of Zeke and how ironic it was that she had never gotten around to wearing the Valentine's Day panties for him; and now, she was wearing them to delight his boss.

Orazio began fondling her breasts with one hand while placing the other hand inside her panties. He then gently pushed her down onto the table—again, not worrying about removing the papers and blueprints—and he began kissing her breasts. After a couple of minutes of caressing her breasts, he removed her panties and easily entered her. Their lovemaking was so intense and in sync that after about five minutes of heaving and gyrating, both climaxed simultaneously. As Serafina was moaning, she could feel five or six pulses of his warm fluid shooting deep within her.

She quickly put her dress back on, and said good-bye to Orazio, trying to leave as inconspicuously as possible. The entire tryst had taken about fifteen minutes. She retraced her route and, somehow, managed to avoid being spotted by the Fasano sisters. Unfortunately for Serafina, Connie Landano, a first cousin of the Fasano sisters, *had* seen her. Connie crossed Spring Street and stopped to gossip with her cousins.

"Hey, did you see Serafina comin' out of Orazio Martucci's office?"

"No," they answered in unison.

"Well, I just saw her walkin' out of his office and she seemed to be actin' a little strange. She was walkin' quickly towards Mulberry with her head down. She passed right by me without even seein' me. Based on what you been tellin' me about her and Orazio, I really think she's screwin' around with him."

"Yeah, I bet he's fuckin' her right in the back room," remarked an animated Tessie.

When Serafina completed her circuitous walk back to her apartment, she immediately headed for the tub and began to fill it with very hot water—as hot as she could stand. She hadn't expected Orazio to "come" inside her and she felt that taking a hot bath would minimize her chances of getting pregnant. As she sat in the tub, she concocted a scheme that would protect her from Zeke's suspicions, should she become pregnant. She would "seduce" Zeke at night, no matter how tired he might be. Her logic was flawless: If she did get pregnant, Zeke would be the proud father, whether he actually was or wasn't. To ensure his interest, she would don the Valentine's Day panties, which she would wash and dry before he came home from work—not wanting to chance that he might notice any stains or scents.

Chapter 23: The Sweet Sixteen Party

Little Italy's Fourth of July holiday celebration usually began around noon with sporadic fireworks being set off throughout the neighborhood. During the evening, there would be an endless barrage of deafening blasts, seemingly coming from all directions. The neighborhood had a reputation of having one of the loudest July 4th celebrations in the city, and every year it tried to live up to that reputation. It wasn't that the neighborhood people were any more patriotic than the rest of the city's populous; they weren't. The fact was that quite a few people in the neighborhood sold or distributed fireworks—an enterprise that was rather lucrative, but illegal. These "entrepreneurs" disliked and even discouraged the neighborhood scam artists who would "hop sales" from naïve buyers on Canal Street. Their logic was that scamming was small potatoes. Selling firecrackers by the mat, cherry bombs and ash cans by the gross, and box loads of rockets and assorted fireworks, was where the real money could be made.

When all the fireworks that could be sold had been sold, there usually was a fair amount of fireworks left over. Rather than storing them until next year, the sellers would give away bags and bags of fireworks to the neighborhood kids and keep a sizeable amount for their own use. Typically, the sellers would place a trashcan in front of their social clubs and set the trash on fire. Then, they would throw mat after mat of firecrackers into the flaming trashcan. A mat consisted of 80 packs of firecrackers, each of which contained 20 firecrackers. Thus, every time a mat would be thrown in the trashcan, the result would be 1,600 firecracker bangs—many occurring at nearly the same time.

At around one o'clock, Felicia returned from the beauty parlor sporting a very becoming "up-do" which made her look more sophisticated and at least two years older. With the help of her sister, she put on her birthday dress, which was pale yellow with white trim. She then slipped a pair of white, open-toed, high-heel shoes over her light nylon stockings. She looked at herself in a full-length mirror and was quite pleased.

Zeke was taken aback when she entered the living room. "My, how my lil' gal has grown up!" he said, as images of Felicia as a toddler flashed before his eyes. Serafina also praised her, but she couldn't help but comment that the dress was a bit too tight. Uncle Paolo, Aunt Laura and *i cugini* each repeated "*Bella, Bella!*" three times, and even Little Zeke said, "You're lookin' great, Sis!"

Felicia sat down on the living room couch and began watching TV, taking care not to wrinkle her dress. The rest of the women returned to the kitchen to put the finishing touches on the food they were preparing for the party. The aromas coming from the kitchen were absolutely wonderful and made everyone wish they could begin eating right at the moment. The dishes being prepared included baked ziti, eggplant parmigiana, sausage and peppers, and chicken Francaise.

Zeke, Paolo and his three children, Vincenzo and Little Zeke went off to the luncheonette carrying cases of soda and bags of ice. They would remain there to complete the decorating and to set up the hot trays.

At about two, the guys began to gather on the stoops in front of the East River Savings Bank, directly across the street from the newsstand, which was closed for the holiday. Within a half-hour, the entire crew was there. Danny then began to reminisce about Felicia's *fifteenth* birthday. "Hey, John-John, do you remember what we gave Felicia for her birthday last year?

"Of course. How could I forget."

"Well, I hope you do better than that this year!"

When the laughter ended, John-John replied, "Danny, we shouldn't have listened to Joe. I know it was only a practical joke… and I laughed my ass off at the time…but I felt bad, later."

"Not me," countered Danny, "It was a great practical joke and Felicia should've just laughed it off…not cry over it like a little girl."

"Well, in many ways, she *was* a little girl at that time…but not anymore."

The year before, the ever-mischievous Joe had planted a seed in John-John and Danny's heads when he told them how he had once given a girl a box of garbage for her birthday as a practical joke. Joe had wrapped the "gift box" with bright wrapping paper, ribbons, and bows. "You should've seen her face when she opened the box!" Joe had laughingly recalled. He then goaded John-John and Danny into playing the same trick on Felicia for her fifteenth birthday.

Of course, they were up for it. At that time, they considered her to be almost one of the boys because she spent a lot of time at the newsstand. The guys would constantly tease her and often make her the butt of their practical jokes—but that didn't deter her from continuing to hang-out at the newsstand. For example, there was the time that Danny rolled-up a paper napkin into a wad, soaked it with ketchup, and sneakily dropped it between her feet from behind. John-John then asked, "Did you drop something, Felicia?" Upon seeing the "bloody sanitary napkin" at her feet—appearing as if it had dropped down from under her skirt—she turned beet red, and quickly ran home, dying of embarrassment, as the two immature youths laughed their heads off. Yet, within an hour, she was back at the newsstand doing her best to tease John-John and Danny.

Creating Felicia's "special" birthday present had taken some effort. Following Joe's point-by-point instructions, John-John and Danny first went to the tobacco shop across the street and got an empty cigar box. They then went to Aldo's Butcher Shop and got some meat scraps free of charge. Then, rummaging through trashcans and seeing what could be had in the gutter, they found a gooey eggshell, some orange peels, an apple core, and the soggy butt of a fat cigar. After stuffing all that garbage into the cigar box, they went inside the newsstand to gain Joe's approval.

Joe sniffed the contents of the box and said, "Somethin' is missin.' It needs to smell bad for Felicia to get the full effect." So, Joe turned to his left, opened up his "pee jar" and then sprinkled a generous amount of his piss all over the contents of the box.

John-John and Danny then went down Spring Street to Nick's Drugstore and bought 35 cents worth of wrapping paper and ribbon. Shortie, who was working part-time at the drugstore, wrapped the gift.

Felicia was totally thrilled when they gave her the birthday present at the newsstand. She held the box against her chest and smiled from ear-to-ear. She was adamant about not opening the gift until her mother returned from work, despite John-John, Danny and Joe imploring her to open it at the newsstand. When Serafina stopped by the newsstand on her way home from work, Felicia showed her the well-wrapped gift that John-John and Danny had so "thoughtfully" given her for her birthday. Serafina seemed touched, and said, "You-ah boys-ah no so bad-ah." John-John felt like a heel. He wished the box really did contain a gift.

Joe then whispered while giggling, "Wait till they see what's in the box." About two minutes after Felicia and Serafina had headed for their apartment, John-John and Danny positioned themselves beneath the Daniels' open bay window. Since the Daniels' apartment was one flight above street level, it would be easy to eavesdrop on Felicia and Serafina's reaction when they opened the box.

After waiting about two minutes under the window, they heard Serafina scream, "*Figli di puttane! Figli di puttane!*"

They weren't shocked to hear Serafina call them "sons of whores." They quickly ran back to the newsstand to report what Serafina had yelled. Joe got a big kick out of what Serafina had said and taking no responsibility for having orchestrated the practical joke, he laughingly remarked, "You guys are in a lot of trouble. You better stay away from Serafina…and Zeke, too!"

A few minutes later, Felicia came down with the garbage-filled cigar box. With tears in her eyes, she threw the box at John-John and Danny, missing John-John's head by inches. She then said, "How could you guys be so cruel? How could you be so cruel?"

John-John replied, "We're sorry. It was supposed to be a joke… just a joke." Danny then repeated John-John's exact words, but based on his tone of voice, he didn't seem to be totally sorry. To make amends, the next day they chipped-in $2 each and bought Felicia a bottle of perfume as a real birthday present. She forgave them, but Serafina did not. In her book, it was one more black mark for Danny and John-John—the *Siciliano bastardo.*

While Danny was finishing recounting the story, John-John's mind began to wander. He thought about his present romantic feelings for Felicia and he wondered what the future would bring.

"Hey, John-John, what did you buy Felicia for her birthday?" asked Frankie.

"I had my mother go down to Orchard Street to buy her a birthday present. She bought her a green silk blouse for only three bucks."

"You only spent three bucks on your girlfriend…you cheap bastard!" Joey "Limp" interjected.

"Well, she's gonna think I paid $14 for it, Joey."

"How come?"

"You know that this week I started my summer job with Swift Feet Messenger Service. Well, one of my deliveries was to Bergdorf Goodman's on Fifth Avenue. When I made the delivery, I asked one of the mailroom guys if I could have a Bergdorf-Goodman's box. He gladly gave me one. When I got home, I put the $3 blouse in the box and, magically, it looked like an expensive blouse."

"Why would she think it cost you fourteen bucks?" asked Shortie.

"That's easy. I used an old trick that my father taught me. On the back of the box I wrote '$14' in pencil, pressing down as hard as I could. Then, I erased the '$14' just enough so that the price could still be read…even though it was light."

"John-John, that's a cool move!" exclaimed Lennie "Squirm," who always appreciated a good scam.

"Me and Tommy also got her blouses, and they didn't cost us a dime. We went into a store on Delancey Street, yesterday. While 'Yeah-Yeah' got the woman's attention by knockin' over some earrings on the counter, I swiped two blouses."

John-John smiled and nodded his head. He couldn't judge them, for he, too, had shoplifted—albeit only once in his life, just to prove he was 'one of the boys.'"

"What are you bringing, Shortie?"

"John-John, my gift also cost me nuttin. I glommed a bottle of Chanel No. 5 from the drugstore when Nick wasn't lookin'…Felicia will be thrilled."

"Hey, I bought her three 45-records," added Donny "Knobhead."

Thereafter, all the guys announced what they had bought for Felicia.

"Yo, John-John, why is someone with your brains workin' as a fuckin' messenger boy?" asked Nicky "White Cap," adding, "I thought you would be workin' in an office, or somethin'."

"Nicky, summer jobs are hard to find, especially jobs in an office. Two months before I graduated, my mother stopped by the office of our state assemblyman, Paul DeStefano, and asked if he could get me a summer job. She told him that I had won several scholarships, including the New York State Regents Scholarship and an academic scholarship from Columbia. He told her that he had no summer job for me and that she should go see Big Sal to see what he could do for me. My mother was very surprised that a state assemblyman would tell her to go see a *capo* to get me a summer job…So was I when she told me. I guess DeStefano must be involved with the mob guys in some way."

"Did she go see Big Sal?" asked Tommy.

"No, she decided not to. She felt it would be better for me if I didn't owe him anything."

"Yeah, yeah, I think she did the right thing."

Felicia walked from her building to the luncheonette accompanied by her mother, sister, Aunt Laura, and Cousin Lucia. Her posture exuded an air of confidence. She looked pretty and she knew it. As John-John gazed at her from across the street, he was amazed at how great she looked, and he was proud that she was his girlfriend.

"Hey, John-John," Frankie exclaimed, "Get a load of Felicia!"

"Yeah, she looks gorgeous!"

"Should we go to the party now?" asked Lennie.

"Nah, let's wait about twenty minutes before we go."

"Why should we wait twenty minutes, John-John?" asked Shortie.

"I think we should wait for the place to become more crowded before we go in. I don't want Serafina and Zeke focusing on us."

"Makes sense to me," said "Knobhead."

The luncheonette began to quickly fill up. "Fat" Angie arrived, gift in hand, soon followed by a bevy of young neighborhood girls, including Phyllis

Falzone, Mary LaRocca, Lauren Festa and Annette Guido. Following right behind them were the three Fasano sisters and Serafina's good friends: Lena Rossi; Patti Mauro; Dolly Zito; and Jenny La Malfa. Two of Zeke's coworkers, Phil Di Chiaro and Larry Bianco soon entered with their wives. Shortly thereafter, Serafina's other brother, Pietro, who lived in Long Island, arrived with his wife, Sophia, and their two children.

With the luncheonette now relatively full, John-John said, "Guys, I think it's about time to go to the party."

"I'll wait about a half-hour, and when the coast is clear, I'll sneak in right under Zeke and Serafina's noses," Danny announced in his usual jocular manner.

When the guys entered the luncheonette, Serafina and Zeke contorted their faces showing the contempt they held for the newsstand crew. Nevertheless, in deference to Felicia's wishes, the boys were ushered into the place by Zeke, who warned," Go find some tables in the back and behave yourselves or I'm gonna throw y'all outta here."

On the way to the back, Felicia greeted the guys, warmly, kissing each of them on the cheek as they presented her with gifts. John-John was a little disappointed by her greeting. He had wanted a kiss on the lips, but he understood that she couldn't do so under the watchful eyes of her parents. After claiming two tables along the back wall, the guys made a beeline to the food and began loading up their plates. John-John, who was known for his ravenous appetite, piled more food on his plate than any of his buddies, and ten minutes later he pushed his way through the food line for a second helping. Felicia then drifted towards the back of the luncheonette to chat with the guys.

"How do I look, John-John?"

"You look absolutely beautiful…better than I've ever seen you look," replied John-John while swallowing a spoonful of baked ziti. "Let's dance, John-John."

"Okay, but give me about five minutes to finish eating."

"Don't worry!" exclaimed 'Knobhead,' "No one's gonna eat your food. I'll guard it with my life. Get up and dance!"

As John-John arose, his favorite song, *Where or When*, by Dion and the Belmonts began to play on the RCA 45 Victrola.

John-John grabbed Felicia tightly and they looked into each other's eyes as they danced slowly near the back of the luncheonette. Dancing next to them were Shortie and "Fat" Angie. Shortie, who was about 5'-7" tall and 220 pounds, found the effervescent Angie attractive, despite her weight—or maybe because of it. Joey "Limp," who seldom had a nice thing to say about anybody, commented, "Shortie and Angie look like a pair of matching bookends!"

About halfway through the song, Serafina noticed that Felicia was dancing with John-John. The sight of him dancing closely with her daughter irked her to no end. She excused herself from her conversation with Patti and Jenny and quickly walked over to the dancing couple. She put her hands between them and pushed them apart so that there was at least a 6-inch gap between them. "That-sah the way-ah you gonn-ah dance with-ah Felicia, o you get out-ah!" Serafina admonished.

"Okay, Serafina, okay. No problem. Anyway, the song is ending."

Meanwhile, Danny was outside the luncheonette waiting for his chance to sneak into the place. A few minutes after Serafina had separated John-John and Felicia on the dance floor, Danny noticed that Serafina and Zeke had their backs to the door, re-stocking the cooler with ice and soda. So, he quickly sneaked into the luncheonette without either of them noticing him.

"Hey, Danny, you made it!" exclaimed Frankie.

"Sit here. We'll try to block you," said Shortie, who was seated next to Angie.

"Get me some food, John-John. I'm starving!"

John-John went back to the food trays for the third time, catching the attention of Zeke.

"Boy, you sure can eat! Why don't you save some food for the rest of them there guests?" said Zeke, obviously annoyed that John-John was hogging up so much food at his expense.

"Here you go, Danny Boy. Enjoy it, but eat quickly, just in case you get spotted by Zeke or Serafina."

Felicia, who had worked her way towards the back again, after speaking to some friends and relatives near the entrance, was shocked to see Danny comfortably seated in the back corner, chowing down.

"Danny, why are you here? You know my parents don't want you at the party. Please…please…try not to let 'em notice you. I don't want a scene."

"Don't worry, I'll lay low."

Then, John-John, who was trying to find a way to be alone with Felicia, got a bright idea. He told all the guys, with the exception of Danny, to stand up and face the front, to provide some blocking for him and Felicia. They complied, and "Fat" Angie, whose girth provided some additional blocking, joined them. John-John then grabbed Felicia by the hand and led her to a couple of empty chairs next to Danny. He told her to sit down, and he sat down next to her. He turned to her and they began kissing passionately while Danny tried his best to look the other way.

After about three minutes of making out, Felicia said, "I better get back to the party." As she arose John-John gave her a pat on the behind. She turned around, looked at him, and just smiled.

When everyone of the crew returned to his seat, Frankie whipped out a cigar. Not just any cigar, but a DeNobli Cigar—a cigar that was commonly referred to as a "Guinea Stinker."

"Frankie, you're not gonna light that up in here, are you?" asked Lennie "Squirm."

"Sure am."

Frankie lit-up the cigar, and within less than a minute the entire luncheonette wreaked with the awful aroma of the DeNobili.

Zeke, accompanied by Vincenzo and Paolo, soon made it to the back and confronted Frankie.

"Now, Frankie, put out that dang cee-gar!"

"Why?" replied Frankie, faking a look of bewilderment?

As Zeke was about to answer, he spotted Danny. The fact that Danny was at the party despite being told by Felicia that he wasn't welcome, made his blood boil. He grabbed Danny by the arm and yelled, "You better get outta here, boy! And that goes for the rest of you boys!"

Danny replied, "Okay, Zeke, okay. It's no big deal. The party stinks, anyhow."

Felicia's face became flushed as the guys got up to leave, and then her eyes began to well-up.

Angie left with Shortie, shouting over the din to Felicia, "I'll be back. We're gonna exchange phone numbers outside."

As each of the guys walked out the door, they mockingly said to Serafina and Zeke, "Nice party. Thank you for inviting us."
Serafina yelled back, "Go-ah…Just-ah go-ah!"

As Danny stepped out he turned around to Zeke and said, "Why don't you buy a sports shirt or somethin'? All you ever wear are white t-shirts. I bet when Felicia marries John-John, you'll wear a white t-shirt and a bow tie!"

"She'll-ah marry John-John over my-ah dead-ah body!" Serafina screamed out.

Most of the guys felt bad for Felicia because their departure cast a pall over the party, but on the other hand, they were angered by the way they had been thrown out—especially since most of them had been well behaved.

The guys soon gathered in front of the newsstand. After a few minutes, Frankie said, "I got an idea. I got two more packs of DeNobli's up in my apartment. Whatta ya think if we all light-up the DeNobli's and smoke 'em right in front of the luncheonette to stink 'em out?"

"Frankie, for a guy who ain't too smart, you certainly come up with some great ideas!" exclaimed Charlie.

"Okay, are all you guys gonna do it?" Frankie questioned, knowing full well that they would.

"Sure!" Lennie answered quickly, as if speaking for all.

Within five minutes, Frankie made it up and back from his apartment. He handed each of the guys a DeNobli and showed the three non-smokers in the group how to light-up. John-John, a non-smoker, lit his cigar and immediately began to choke and gag. He was not the only one who choked and gagged on the acrid smoke. Most of the guys either choked, gagged, or coughed; even those who were accustomed to smoking a pack of cigarettes a day. Those DeNoblis were one tough smoke.

The guys walked over to the luncheonette and planted themselves on the sidewalk, directly in front of the door, which had been kept open because the luncheonette's air conditioner was broken. Two large, greasy floor fans provided some ventilation, but they didn't make much of a difference on that humid, sultry afternoon. Once the boys began puffing their cigars, it took only about two minutes for the smoke to waft into the luncheonette.

"What's that awful smell?" Lena asked the woman seated next to her at a table near the front of the place.

Jenny, who faced the door said, "It's those wise kids who were just thrown outta here. They're all in front of the place smokin' cigars and aimin' the smoke towards the door."

When the cigar smoke reached Zeke, he quickly ran outside and yelled, "Hey, boys, go smoke them cee-gars somewheres else!"

"Ah, you don't own the sidewalk!" Danny quickly countered.

At that moment, Zeke wanted to give Danny a swift boot in the ass, but he restrained himself. He tried a different tack.

"John-John, you got the most brains of all you youngins and I know that you're kinda sweet on my Felicia. Why don't y'all just move on? Don't ruin Felicia's party any more than y'all ready have."

John-John tried to encourage the guys to move away from the luncheonette, but they seemed to enjoy the situation and stood their ground. Zeke's brother-in-law stepped outside and began to yell and curse at the boys with no effect. Suddenly, Cousin Vincenzo emerged brandishing a long carving knife and yelling in Neapolitan. From the look in his eyes, the redness of his face and the way the veins in his forearms were protruding, the boys knew he meant business.

"Yo, I think that mad wop is lookin' to cut us up! Let's go!" yelled Lennie.

"Yeah, let's go!" seconded John-John. "Let's get away from him!"

The guys didn't run, but they certainly didn't linger by the front door. When they reached the newsstand, Lennie "Squirm," who was one of the Sheiks who had a key to the newsstand, unlocked the padlock and opened the door. He reached inside and pulled out a shopping bag filled with assorted fireworks.

"It's showtime!" Frankie shouted as he went over to the corner trashcan and started to set the trash on fire with his cigar. Within a couple of minutes, the trashcan was ablaze. Then, Lennie distributed the fireworks to all the guys, and they each began to flip pack after pack into the trashcan, resulting in continuous bangs, which were only interrupted when the guys occasionally flipped-in the heavy artillery—cherry bombs and ash cans.

When the shopping bag was about half empty, several of the guys headed for Sonny's social club on Kenmare Street to get some more fireworks. They soon returned with nine bags of free fireworks—enough fireworks to last well into the night, if they paced themselves.

At about 9 o'clock, the Sweet Sixteen Party was over. Felicia and her sister walked quickly past the guys and the exploding trashcan without saying a word. Soon, Serafina, Zeke and the rest of the relatives rounded the corner.

Zeke yelled, "I'm gonna call the po-lice on you guys!"

"Ah go ahead, Zeke. They won't come," yelled Danny.

"We're patriots!" added Frankie.

"You guys ain't no patriots. Y'all don't know the first thing about bein' patriots!"

"Ah, you're nothin' but a rebel. Why don't you go back to Tennessee!" yelled Lennie.

Zeke just bit down on his lip and headed for his apartment. He had decided that it would be a waste of time to call the cops. He knew they wouldn't come. So, the fireworks bombardment continued until all the bags were emptied—which was at around midnight.

Chapter 24: Capaci, Italy

Maria was alone on the top floor of her late Uncle Pino's three-story house a few minutes after excusing herself from the gathering of sad relatives and friends who were recounting her uncle's "short life" and sudden death. Pino had been very well liked and respected throughout Capaci, a small seaside town along Sicily's mountainous north coast, located about three miles west of Palermo. Many of his friends would refer to him as *Il Sindaco*—the Mayor—because the affable man would voice his opinion on just about everything, particularly local issues, and because he had the demeanor and deportment of a small-town mayor.

Maria and her parents would have full use of the top floor during their extended stay in Sicily, which would amount to seven weeks. Her father, Vincenzo had been given nearly two months off from work because the owner of the fish store where he was employed was a fellow *paisano* who understood that when one makes the long trip to Sicily, the visit should be for a substantial amount of time. Vincenzo had hoped that his married son, also named, Vincenzo, would have been able to come to the funeral and spend some time in Sicily; but, unfortunately, the married father of two, who was working as a truck driver in Manhattan, couldn't get enough time off from his job.

As Maria sat on the plush velvet sofa trying to catch a breeze on that stifling July 4th evening, she could barely keep her eyes open. The whirlwind trip to Sicily, the jet lag, and the long dreary funeral had taken its toll. Unlike July 4th in Manhattan, there would be no fireworks to help keep her awake. However, on July 15th, there would be plenty of evening fireworks in Palermo and its neighboring towns as part of a big celebration in honor of Palermo's patron saint, Santa Rosalia. According to Sicilian lore, *La Santuzza*—as she was commonly referred to by the locals—had interceded to save Palermo from being ravaged by a plague in 1624.

Maria decided that it would be a good time to take a hot bath. Before stepping into the four-legged, antique tub, she took a long look at herself in the mirror of the dimly lit bathroom. She was pleased to see that she appeared to be a little thinner, yet more curvaceous.

As she sat in the warm tub water, the events of the past four days flashed before her eyes: The Rizzo family had departed Idlewild Airport on a Pan Am Boeing 707 at about 5 p.m. on Sunday. They had landed in Rome at about 7 a.m. on Monday and had made it to Palermo's airport at noon. Cousin Ciro was there to greet them at the terminal, which was only about the size of an American supermarket. After exchanging hugs and kisses, they walked over to his car for the ride to Capaci. All four and their luggage had somehow managed to squeeze into the rickety, old Fiat, although Vincenzo had to keep one of their three large suitcases on his lap. Shortly after leaving the airport, Maria couldn't help but be impressed with the beauty of Sicily's coast, in particular, the way in which its low, rugged mountains plunged into the beautiful azure Mediterranean Sea. But after ten minutes of riding with Cousin Ciro, she could no longer focus on the beautiful sites; instead, she worried about being killed in a car crash. Cousin Ciro was a typical Sicilian driver. He drove his little car with reckless abandon, weaving and skirting through the chaotic traffic and unbelievably tight streets. He didn't concern himself with stop signs—no one seemed to stop at stop signs—and he seemed to ignore the few red traffic lights that they came upon. She would later learn that many Sicilian drivers joked that in Sicily, a red light is only a "suggestion" to stop—not a requirement to stop.

The drive from the airport to Uncle Pino's house had taken about twenty minutes. The first thing that Maria noticed upon arriving was a group of men, women, and children—most of whom were dressed in black—standing in front of 21 Via Grazziani. She would soon learn from her parents that most of these people were her Sicilian relatives whom she had never met.

When the Rizzo family got out of the car, every person in the group, plus quite a few people who had crossed the street to see who had arrived, greeted them warmly. Vincenzo, who had last been to Italy in 1960, on a two-week solo trip to take care of some financial matters, introduced young Maria to her newfound relatives and *paisani.* She smiled and hugged-and-kissed everyone while saying, *"Piacere."* Her head was spinning as she tried to put the names with the faces, but, she reasoned that it would be a safe bet to address any female relative that she would later re-encounter, as "Maria," since at least four of the women to whom she had been introduced were named Maria. Similarly, for men the odds favored that their names would either be Giuseppe, Vincenzo, or Nino.

The worst part of that day had been when Maria and her parents entered Uncle Pino's house and made their way into the living room. There, right in the center of the room, was a dark wooden casket with the lifeless body of her uncle who had died suddenly from a heart attack at age sixty-four. Maria could see that he had been a robust and handsome man, and dressed-up in his dark blue suit, he looked like he was just taking a nap, especially since the ashen color of his face wasn't obvious in the dimly lit room.

Seated in front of the casket, with tissues in hand and reddened eyes, were Pino's fifty-eight-year-old wife, Costanza, his eldest child, Giuseppina, his seventy-five-year-old brother, Antonio, and his seventy-year-old sister, Antoinetta. His two sons, Giuseppe and Vincenzo were standing in front of the casket, along with their "kid sister," nineteen-year-old Maria, who appeared to be in a state of shock and disbelief. When Vincenzo made his way to the casket, he began to cry loudly and uncontrollably. His wife, Rosaria, tried to calm him down, but to no avail. Young Maria was struck by the sight of her father crying—something she had never seen. He had always projected both physical and emotional strength, along with a quiet, stoic persona.

Pino and Vincenzo had been as close to each other as brothers could be. Although they both loved and greatly respected their oldest brother, Antonio, the fact that he was so much older than them made him seem more like an uncle than a brother to them. Life in the 1930s had been particularly harsh in Sicily. So, in 1936, Pino and Vincenzo made the very difficult decision to temporarily leave Sicily to make "their fortunes" in America. They left their wives and children behind with the promise that they would send most of their earnings back to Sicily to support their families.

When the brothers arrived in America in October of 1936, they made their way from Ellis Island to the lower east side of Manhattan, walking through the unfamiliar streets, lugging their large valises. After walking nearly three miles, they arrived at the apartment of two *paisani* on East Third Street and First Avenue. The two *paisani*, who were also brothers, had been living there for about a year, while sending most of their earnings back home. They welcomed Pino and Vincenzo to share the tiny apartment with them provided that they would pay for half the rent and the other living expenses.

Pino and Vincenzo soon learned that the streets in America were not paved with gold, especially since America had not as yet emerged from the Great Depression. Still, they managed to find jobs in a fish store that was owned by a *paisano* who had been in America for many years. Working long hours, they managed to eke out a living, and by living frugally, they each provided for their families back home. By the summer of 1939, Pino could no longer bear being an ocean apart from his family; so, he returned to Sicily. Uncharacteristically, Vincenzo had decided not to follow in his brother's footsteps. Ostensibly, he wanted to remain in America for a couple of years to earn more money, but secretly, he was weighing the possibility of eventually making a new life for himself and his family in America.

When war broke out in Europe, Vincenzo tried to return to Sicily, but he found it impossible. He was quite worried about his wife and son, but he took comfort in knowing that Pino would do everything he could to ensure Rosaria and young Vincenzo's wellbeing.

Surprisingly, in early 1943, forty-two-year-old Vincenzo was drafted into the United States Army. Fortunately for him, he was assigned as an MP patrolling the Brooklyn piers. By becoming a member of the U. S. Armed Forces, he was accorded the privilege of American citizenship, which after the war made it quite easy for his wife and son to join him in America. Rosaria and young Vincenzo arrived in New York in January 1946 to begin a new life.

While still enjoying her long, warm bath, Maria's thoughts flashed forward from the two-day wake to the day of the funeral mass and burial, Wednesday, July 3rd. On that morning, the family and close friends of Pino gathered around his open casket for the last time. The priest led the mourners in prayer, and shortly thereafter, Pino's two sons closed the casket to the lugubrious laments of Pino's closest family. The two sons, Pino's two brothers and two cousins lifted the heavy casket and carried it out the door and onto a horse drawn, black funeral wagon, which had clear glass sides framed with beautifully carved wood. Maria had never seen anything like it. In New York, all of the hearses were gray or black Cadillacs or Lincolns. The wagon driver, who was dressed completely in black, including an unusual black hat, yelled *"vai"* to his two magnificent white horses, and the wagon slowly began its five-block journey to Sant'Erasmo's Church for the funeral mass.

The mourners walked behind the wagon as it slowly made its way through the tight winding streets, which, by American standards, were more akin to alleys than streets. Many of the mourners were carrying lit candles. Maria walked next to her parents among the second row of mourners. She was given the honor of carrying one of the lighted candles. Within ten minutes, the cortege reached Capaci's small piazza, which is rather unexceptional.

The focal point of the piazza is Sant'Erasmo's, an 18th century church of Baroque design, featuring an octagonal nave. The slightly ornate façade of the church is flanked by two winding, steep, stone stairways. These stairways proved to be a challenge to the pallbearers, but, fortunately, they managed to negotiate them without incident.

After the mass, the cortege slowly walked about a kilometer (a little more than half a mile) to Santa Rosalia's Cemetery. The cortege grew and grew en route to the cemetery as many bystanders along the streets joined the group of mourners. When Father Balsano finished his prayers at the gravesite, four cemetery workers lowered the casket into the pre-dug hole. At that moment, with the entire throng wailing, Pino's wife, Costanza, tried to throw herself onto the casket as it sat on the bottom of the grave. Her two sons grabbed her, as she was about to make the plunge and dragged her away into the arms of consoling relatives. The image of her aunt trying to throw herself into the grave would be something that young Maria would never forget.

After about a half-hour of soaking in the tub, Maria put on her underwear and nightgown and returned to the sofa. She was soon yawning and straining to keep her eyes open. She didn't want to fall asleep. She wanted to wait for her parents to come upstairs so that she could talk to them and hug them, tightly. Uncle Pino's sudden death had made her come to realize that life is, indeed, short. To help her remain awake in the interim, she decided to write a letter to her best friend, Judy. In her two-page letter she described her trip to Sicily and the Sicilian-style funeral, and she informed Judy that she would not be returning until the end of August.

Shortly after completing the letter, her parents entered the room. She sprang up from the sofa and warmly hugged and kissed them. No words were spoken. No words needed to be spoken.

Chapter 25: The Big Bangs

It was a typically hot July evening. The neighborhood streets were cloaked with an invisible veil—a combination of odors typical for a summer day: vehicle exhaust; rotting pieces of garbage that the Department of Sanitation had failed to sweep-up from the gutters; foul-smelling gases seeping out of the catch basins, and tarry vapors coming from the blacktop pavement. Alongside the newsstand, there was one additional odor: Joe's urine. Every evening, just before heading home, Joe would empty his "pee jar" along the curb near the back of the stand. Since he emptied the jar in basically the same spot day after day, the urine had percolated deep into the blacktop. In the winter, the smell would hardly be noticeable; but on hot summer days, it was quite noticeable.

John-John and several of his good buddies were hanging out at the newsstand, giving Joe a play-by-play account of Felicia's Sweet Sixteen Party.

"Don't skip a thing! I wanna know everything that happened at the party…and after the party," said Joe, who lived vicariously through the guys and their exploits, and considered himself to be their *consigliere*.

He took delight in how John-John had fooled Felicia into thinking that his $3 gift bought on Orchard Street had cost him $14 at Bergdorf-Goodmans.

"Great trick! but he mockingly added, "I gotta say you're one cheap bastard!"

He got a kick out of hearing how Serafina had insisted that John-John and Felicia dance at least 6 inches apart, and he laughed hard when told how the guys stood outside the party blowing DeNobili cigar smoke towards the open door.

"You guys are somethin' else," said Joe, "You always manage to get the last laugh."

"Hey Joe, speaking about last laughs, I got an idea."

"What's your idea, Danny?"

"Well, I been noticing that Serafina and her cousin…I think her name is Lucia…come down with folding chairs at exactly 7:30 to sit in front of the building. They're usually joined by Zeke and the cousin's husband at about 8 o'clock."

"What are you gettin' at?" asked Shortie, knowing that Danny had something devilish in mind.

"Why don't we plant a cherry bomb at the curb where Serafina and her cousin will be sittin'."

"How are we gonna set it off?" asked Lennie.

"Simple. We get a lit cigarette and push the fuse of the cherry bomb into the cigarette about an inch from the lit end. Then, we put it by the curb close to where they'll be sittin'. We must put the cherry bomb right next to the curb so that they won't spot it. Timin' is everything, so we oughtta plant the cherry bomb about three minutes before Serafina and her cousin come down…What do you think, John-John?"

"I think it'll be a lot of fun to see how they react to the 'big bang' and I also think you're some sort of a genius when it comes to getting even with people."

Joe interjected, "I think you guys are goin' too far. I'm sure that Serafina and her cousin are still shell-shocked from their days in Naples durin' the war. You shouldn't do it."

"C'mon, let's do it!" said Frankie, ignoring Joe's concerns. "Just say 'when' and I'll light up a cigarette."

At exactly 7:26, Frankie lit-up a cigarette and puffed on it until Lennie handed him the cherry bomb. About thirty seconds later, Frankie carefully inserted the end of the fuse into the cigarette and nonchalantly walked up Lafayette Street, pausing a second to place the firework in the gutter as planned. He then walked across the street where he was soon joined by the rest of the crew. Sure enough, at exactly 7:30, Serafina and her cousin, each carrying a folding chair, came down to sit in front of the building. At that point, the guys walked about 100 feet north of where they had gathered; they did so to gain more separation from the explosive device, so that they could deny any involvement. They purposely made a lot of noise so that Serafina and her cousin would be well aware that they were across the street and up the block from them.

The cigarette burned ever so slowly. Just when the guys were beginning to think that it might have gone out, there was a tremendously loud "boom" within 10 feet of where the two women were sitting. The unanticipated explosion shocked Serafina and her cousin. They screamed at the top of their lungs as they sprang up from their chair, yelling "O Dio! O Dio!" The two then cupped their ears and braced themselves for the next blast, which they anticipated would be coming soon because back in their war days in Naples, one blast was usually followed by another, and then another one or more.

The guys thought that it was one of the funniest and cleverest pranks they had ever pulled off. They had a big laugh over the screaming reaction of the women. The callous youths didn't seem to care—or maybe, didn't fully comprehend—that they were resurrecting the women's wartime terrors. They enjoyed their prank so much that they decided that a repeat performance was in order.

On the following evening, they raised the ante, so to speak, by planting two "time bombs" in the gutter—this time, using "ash cans" instead of cherry bombs. The guys were shrewd enough not to place the ash cans—which are slightly more powerful than cherry bombs—at the same location they had used the evening before. This time, they placed one device about 10 feet farther up the street from the original location, and the other about 10 feet farther down the street. They set the fuses such that the time bombs would explode about five minutes apart—the idea being that just when the women would be back on their chairs thinking that all was well, the second blast would occur.

The plan worked perfectly. The two women screamed upon hearing the first blast, but after a couple of minutes they sat down again. They were puzzled by the blasts. They couldn't figure out how yesterday's blast and today's blast had happened. Upon hearing the blast and the screams, Zeke and Vincenzo ran downstairs to see what was going on. After calming down the frightened women, Zeke remarked, as he pointed across the street, "You know, Serafina, I reckon that somehow them guys are settin' off them there fireworks… I just know it."

"But-ah, they-ah cross-ah the street-ah."

"I know, but…"

Before Zeke could finish his sentence, a second booming explosion occurred. This one seemed even louder than the first one, perhaps due to the echoing effect of the blast wave bouncing off the metal-clad entrance of the nearby loft. Once again the women screamed. The two men, though shocked, didn't scream or yell. Instead, they let out a string of cuss words; Zeke, in English and Vincenzo, in the Neapolitan dialect. Zeke's gut told him that the newsstand crew had set off the fireworks, so he quickly scooted across the street to confront them.

"Hey, guys, I know that y'all are causing them there fireworks to go off in front of my buildin'!"

"You're wrong, Zeke," replied Danny, calmly.

"Wrong my ass!"

"Okay," demanded Shortie, "Tell us how we're shootin' off those fireworks by your buildin' when we're over here almost a half a block away."

"Well, I don't rightly know how y'all are doin' it. But if it ain't you, then who?"

John-John trying hard to keep a straight face, interjected, "Zeke, you've been blaming us for everything that happens around here for years."

"Well, I done had good enough reasons to blame y'all."

Danny decided to push the envelope: "You know, Zeke, I think this time you owe us an apology."

"Apology! Apology my ass! I'll apologize to you guys when bears don't shit in the woods anymore!"

Zeke walked away with smoke coming out of his ears, totally frustrated by the situation. Danny suggested to the group that they should pull off the prank a third time on Monday, but John-John talked the guys out of it.

"Enough is enough. Let's quit while we're ahead…Zeke is gonna be up all night trying to figure out how we did it."

"Yeah, John-John," seconded Donny "Knobhead," "Two times is enough."

About ten minutes later, Charlie "the Ox" and Joey "Limp" joined the group. They were immediately filled-in on all the details of the time-bomb prank. They felt cheated that they had missed out on the fun on both days. Charlie and Joey, who both fancied themselves as excellent pool players, had been at Pop's Pool Hall near City Hall until late Friday night, and they had just returned from an afternoon pool session that had lasted longer than expected. Joey, who was looking to unwind from his day of shooting pool, and in particular, his crushing defeats by Charlie, suggested a game of Johnny on the Pony.

Johnny on the Pony is a rough "street game" game which is rarely played anymore. The underlying, but usually unstated objective of the game, is to physically punish the opposing team to the greatest extent possible. Teams usually consist of four individuals— almost always-teenage boys or young men. A coin flip decides which team will be the "pony." The smallest team member—known as "the pillow"—puts his back against the wall. The second team member bends over at the waist at about 90 degrees and plants his head into the stomach of the first team member, whose stomach serves as a cushion or pillow—hence the name given to the first team member. The third team member bends over close to 90 degrees and wraps his arms around the torso of the second team member. The fourth does likewise with the third team member, forming, in effect, a "pony"— albeit a six-legged pony.

The opposing team members, one at a time, run towards the pony from a distance of at least 20 feet, and just before reaching the pony, jump as high into the air as possible, and land on the back of one member of the pony. If the pony should cave-in before all four of the opponents have landed on it, they get to do the whole thing over again. The opposing team also gets to go again if the pony cannot hold the entire team for ten seconds after the fourth team member has landed on the pony. If the pony holds the load through the ten-count, the opposing team then becomes the pony. It is obvious that if the teams are mismatched in terms of weight and/or strength, one team could wind up taking most of the punishment while the opposing team would be dishing out most of the punishment.

Joey managed to choose two heavyweight partners: Charlie "the Ox" and Shortie. He chose Lennie "Squirm" to be his team's pillow. John-John wound up with Danny, Donny "Knobhead" and Frankie as his teammates. In terms of weight, the teams were clearly mismatched. Joey's team, excluding the pillow, averaged about 220 pounds per man, while John-John's team, sans pillow, averaged about 170 pounds per man.

John-John's team lost the coin flip. Frankie, serving as the pillow, put his back against the huge cardboard *La Primadora Cigar* sign on the side of the cigar store. The team formed its "pony" with John-John in the first position, followed by Donny and Danny. Joey "Limp, who weighed 210 pounds, jumped first. Despite his nickname, he was able to run and jump very well, landing with full force on John-John's back. Just as the last member of the team, Shortie, landed on Danny's back, the pony buckled.

The next two rounds ended the same way. It seemed that John-John's team would never get its chance for revenge. At the beginning of the fourth round, Joey crossed over to curb on the other side of Lafayette Street, close to the Daniels' apartment building.

"Hey, Joey," yelled Frankie, "You can't run from there."

"Oh yes I can. There is no rule about how far away you can be from the pony when you start your run."

"That's not fair!" yelled John-John, as he broke out of the pony formation.

"It's fair. You guys are just a bunch of crybabies because you can't beat us."

"Okay, Joey, just go…just go," replied John-John.

Then Danny softly said, "Let's shift the pony while Joey's in mid-air."

Everyone thought it would be a great way to get even with Joey. Frankie would call the shift signal because he would be the only one of the team who could see Joey's run.

Joey looked both ways to check if any cars were coming. When he was sure that his path was clear, he dashed across the street with all of the speed that he could muster. Frankie, with perfect timing, quietly coordinated the shift: "One-two-three," followed by a yell of "Shift!" just as Joey began his leap. The guys moved, as a unit, about 4 feet to the right, just in time for

Joey—who was moving his legs in the air like a cartoon character—to go crashing head-on into the *La Primadora Cigar* sign. Everyone except Joey, was in stitches—even his own teammates. Joey, on the other hand, almost needed stitches. His head had put a hole in the cardboard sign, which sat in a metal frame that projected about 2 inches off the wall, thereby leaving some air space between the sign and the wall. Joey was writhing in pain; his nose was bleeding, and he seemed to be crying.

"Who's the crybaby now, Joey!" asked Danny in a sarcastic tone followed by a laugh.

"I guess you'll never do that again," remarked John-John.

Joey didn't answer. He just moaned and groaned while keeping his nose pointed up in the air to stop the bleeding. No one showed him any pity. The more he moaned and groaned, the harder they all laughed and made fun of him. It was the neighborhood way. Even Felicia, who had watched the game from her bay window, yelled, "Hey Joey, nice jump!"

"Wait til we tell Joe about this on Monday!" teased Donny 'Knobhead.'

"He'll laugh his ass off!"

Chapter 26: License and Registration

It seemed like just about everybody in the neighborhood was outside on this oppressively hot and humid late July evening. Those who remained in their apartments tried their best to cool off with fans. Very few families had air conditioners, and if they did, the units had a low cooling capacity because the electrical wiring in the neighborhood's turn-of-the-century tenements was inadequate for the bigger air conditioning units.

John-John, Danny, Frankie, and Shortie were at their usual post in front of the newsstand kibitzing with Joe. Although it was just 7 o'clock, Joe had had enough of the heat and had decided to close up early. Within five minutes, the guys helped Joe put all the unsold papers inside the stand. They then unfolded the counter and swung it upwards as Joe locked it in place from the inside. The counter and its supporting panel were hinged together and served two functions: a counter for the newspapers and the closure pieces for the front of the stand.

As the guys walked Joe to the subway kiosk behind the newsstand, they saw Jerry "Fats" with a wrench in his hand, turning on the water of the fire hydrant, which was almost directly in front of the seated Fasano sisters. The 45-year-old Jerry, a cousin of the Fasano sisters, had a reputation for being a little crazy, but he was generally okay unless one tried to "bust his chops."

"Hey, Jerry, great idea!" yelled Shortie.

The guys escorted Joe down the stairs to the subway. As Joe put his token in the turnstile, the token clerk "buzzed" a door open allowing the guys free entry into the station to help Joe board the train. Three minutes later, the train came and Joe was guided safely onboard. He would not have any guidance at the Union Square Station where he would transfer to the uptown express train en route to the Bronx.

After thanking the token clerk and exiting the subway station, the guys were immediately drawn to the sound and sight of the cool water gushing out of the hydrant. It looked all too inviting to them, especially since the temperature of the subway station where they had just spent the last few minutes must have been at least 110 degrees. So, without any hesitation and with little discussion among themselves, they decided to cool off "under the pump." (In neighborhood lingo, a fire hydrant was commonly referred to as a "Johnny Pump" or simply, a "pump.") In a matter of seconds, they were all completely soaked and cooled-off. The most annoying thing about going under the pump was the large amount of water that was inevitably trapped in one's sneakers and socks. One's clothes would usually dry off in about an hour, but the water inside the sneakers would "squish" the rest of the evening.

"Hey, here comes a bus! Let's wet the bus driver and the passengers!" yelled Frankie.

"No, Frankie, let's not do it," said John-John, empathizing mostly with the bus driver.

"Ah, don't listen to him…Quick, let's go find an empty soda can or a piece of wood," ordered Danny.

While the bus was stopped at the traffic light at the Lafayette Street intersection, Shortie managed to find an empty soda can in a nearby trashcan. He immediately squashed it with his foot and handed it to Frankie.

Then, Danny brought Frankie a piece of scrap wood that he had just found, saying, "Frankie, use this instead of the can. It'll be easier to hold and control."

"Frankie, let's wait until the bus pulls out of the bus stop before we wet it," said Shortie.

"Good idea," said Danny, "That way we won't have to deal with any of the passengers who are gettin' off here."

When the bus pulled into the stop, John-John started walking away from the hydrant, wanting to have deniability in case his father were to find out about the dousing of a fellow bus driver.

"Hey, John-John, where ya goin!" yelled Frankie.

"I can't be part of this. If my father would find out, I'd be on the *business end* of one of his boxing lessons."

The bus driver, who apparently had been through the drill many times before, quickly shut his side window and yelled to his passengers, "Shut the windows unless you don't mind takin' a bath!" For whatever reason, only about half of the passengers heeded his advice.

As the bus was slowly pulling out of the stop, Frankie knelt down behind the hydrant and wrapped his arms around it. Holding the piece of wood—one hand on each end—just below the stream of gushing water, he forcefully tilted it upwards to an angle of about 45 degrees, causing the stream of water to arc into the air and into the bus's open windows. Many of the passengers screamed as they were hit with the cold water. One man, who had gotten completely soaked, wanted to get off the bus and take on the youths; but the bus driver wouldn't let him off, having no pity for him, or any of the wet passengers, because they had ignored his warning.

About ten minutes later, Felicia and her sister, Francesca, turned the corner and were heading towards the gushing hydrant. Most neighborhood girls, and those boys who might be considered to be weaklings, knew that walking behind an open fire hydrant would be a risky proposition, because more often than not, they would be dragged under the pump and "soaked to the bone." For some reason, Felicia and her sister had ignored the risk; perhaps, Felicia was reassured by John-John's presence.

"Hey, let's get' em!" yelled Danny, pointing at the two sisters.

Frankie, Danny, and Shortie immediately ran over to Felicia and grabbed her, leaving John-John to drag Francesca under the pump. But, he decided to give her a free pass because he felt it wouldn't look right for a big guy to "pick" on such a young girl.

"John-John, help! Help!" yelled Felicia.

Before he could decide if he should try to save her from her dousing, it was too late. She was totally soaked. One of the reasons that girls were more often targeted than boys was that they obviously would offer less resistance. But, the primary reason was to get a view of the girls' bodies through their soaked clothes. Although not as revealing as the wet t-shirt contests that would become popular about a decade later, the near transparency of the victim's soaked garments left little to the imaginations of the leering guys. Unfortunately for Felicia, she was wearing white cotton pants and a light-blue, tightfitting blouse. Her outfit, when soaked, revealed most of her attributes, even though she was wearing a bra and panties. When the guys felt that she had had enough of a soaking, they let her go. Realizing that the guys were getting a "free show," she crossed her arms across her chest and headed home. After taking a few steps, she turned around and yelled, "John-John, I thought you would protect me!"

"I'm sorry, Felicia, it all happened so fast."

About two minutes later, a green, black, and white Plymouth patrol car approached the scene, stopping in the street just before the stream of gushing water. The flashing red roof light was turned on and the two police officers slowly stepped out of the patrol car. The guys instinctively moved about 20 feet from the hydrant. They recognized one of the police officers to be Officer Casey. The other police officer—the driver—they had never seen before.

"Okay, who opened the pump?" yelled Officer Casey, directing his question to everyone in the vicinity, including the Fasano sisters and their cousin Jerry "Fats."

"I don't know," replied Jerry.

"We don't know," remarked Tessie. "We just got here."

"What about you clowns?" pointing to the guys.

"It was open when we got here, Officer Casey. You can't blame us for taking advantage of the cool water."

"No, kid, I can't blame you for that. In fact, I wish I could get myself cooled-off, tonight."

Officer Casey walked back to the patrol car, opened the trunk, and pulled out a monkey wrench. He placed the wrench on the hexagonal stem at the top of the hydrant, and after six clockwise turns of the wrench, the water flow stopped.

Directing his remark at no one in particular, Officer Casey said, "Hey, do me a favor, don't turn it back on tonight. I've got more important things to do than goin' around shuttin' off damn hydrants!"

Felicia had waited behind the newsstand for about five minutes, not having the courage to face her parents. She was afraid that her father might over-react. When it became obvious to her that she had to face the music sooner or later, she turned the corner and headed towards her building. Her parents and *i cugini*, who were all seated by the doorway, were shocked to see her returning totally soaked, looking as if she had gone swimming with her clothes on.

"Who did this to you, girl?" asked an angry Zeke.

"Some of the guys from the newsstand…Danny, Shortie and Frankie…But, it was all in fun."

"Fun my ass! I'm gonna go teach 'em boys a lesson they won't surely forget!"

By the time Zeke reached the fire hydrant, only the Fasano sisters and Jerry "Fats" were there. The guys had gone over to Charlie's Candy Store on Mott Street for sodas and goodies. So, he reluctantly returned to his seat in front of his building and started ranting, mostly to Serafina. By that time, Felicia was upstairs removing her soaked clothes and drying herself off.

At about ten, Serafina, Zeke and i *cugini* decided to go upstairs for some espresso and biscotti. A few minutes later, the "hydrant bathers," who were now dry, except for their feet, congregated at the newsstand along with Vinnie "Lemons" and Joey "Limp." Soon, Lennie "Squirm" approached in his red-and-white 1958 Ford convertible, with the radio blasting at full volume. He pulled over and parked in front of the Daniels' apartment building. The guys were instantly drawn to Lennie's "new" car.

"Great wheels!" yelled Danny.

"Wow, Lennie, you got one of the best cars in the fuckin' neighborhood!" exclaimed Frankie.

"When did you get it?" asked John-John.

"I picked it up last night…Get in, I'll take you guys for a ride. But I can only fit five of yous."

"Where did you get the dough for these wheels?" asked Shortie.

"Oh, I got some money from my mother, and I borrowed $250 from "Spring Street" Larry. He's givin' me a break on the "vig." I gotta give him back three hundred bucks in two weeks…He's givin' me an extra week on the house."

"How are you gonna come up with the money?"

"I'll figure that out later, John-John…I'll cheat a little, scam a little, steal a little…whatever."

John-John, Danny and Shortie hopped in the back, while Frankie and Joey squeezed in alongside Lennie. After a ten-minute spin around the neighborhood, Lennie pulled into the same parking spot, keeping the radio set at maximum volume so his car would be the center of attention. The guys remained in the car and Vinnie joined the group, leaning up against the car's right front fender. Lennie kept the engine running, and about every thirty seconds, he would rev it up. He loved the big V-8's throaty sound, which was enhanced by the car's low-restriction, dual-exhaust system.

As the radio was, ironically, playing, *In the Still of the Night*, by the Five Satins, Zeke poked his head out the window and yelled, "Be quiet down there…and lower that dang radio!"

Danny replied, "Ah, leave us alone. It's a free country."

"You'll see just how free a country it is when I sic the po-lice on you boys!"

"Ah, go ahead and call the cops!" yelled Lennie as he revved-up the engine.

About fifteen minutes later, a patrol car arrived on the scene. Once again, it was Officer Casey and the "new cop."

"Hey, guys, we got a complaint that you're makin' a racket… revvin' up the engine…playin' the radio loud," said Officer Casey from the front passenger seat of the patrol car.

The other cop then got out of the patrol car and went over to Lennie.

"License and registration, please…and turn off the engine and the radio."

"Okay, officer."

Lennie reached into the glove compartment, found the registration, and handed it to the police officer. He then pulled his driver's license out of his wallet and gave it to the officer. By this time, Zeke had come downstairs, and the rest of the family was watching from the windows.

The young police officer was very conscientious. He checked and double-checked the registration. Then, shining his flashlight onto the VIN Number on the car's dashboard, he compared that number against the number that was written on the registration. Everything checked out to his satisfaction, so he handed the registration back to Lennie. He then began to check Lennie's driver's license. Lennie was worried, but he tried not to show it. The license was a phony. He had bought a blank driver's license from a neighborhood scammer, Rocky "Bumps," about a month before. The blank license was one of a dozen that had been stolen by Rocky's sister, a clerk at the nearby Department of Motor Vehicles office.

Shortly after Lennie had bought the blank driver's license, he had asked Danny to show him his driver's license:

"Hey, 'Plumber,' I wanna see how many numbers there are on a driver's license. Don't worry, I'm not gonna copy your license number exactly…I'll change the last three numbers. Plus, I'll have to change the letter at the beginning of the license number. I have seen enough licenses to know that the letter is the same as the first letter of the driver's last name."

When Danny checked out his driver's license number, he noticed that it began with a "P". "Lennie, you're not as dumb as I thought…I guess the "P" on my license number stands for Potenza…So, your number should begin with an 'M', for Muccio."

"Yeah, I figured out that thing about the letter all by myself."

Lennie was true to his word. When he had his sister type in all of the pertinent information on the blank license, he told her to copy Danny's number, but to change the "P" to an "M", and to change the last three digits of Danny's license's fifteen numerals from "462" to "359".

As the young officer was just about to hand the license back to Lennie, he said to Officer Casey, "There's something about this license that doesn't seem kosher."

"Whatta ya mean?"

"There seems to be something wrong with the number."

Officer Casey stepped out of the car and studied the license, saying, "Looks okay to me."

"Oh, now I know what's wrong…There's a discrepancy…Remember the code?"

"What code?"

"The first two digits after the letter of the license number are supposed to indicate the second letter of the driver's last name. For example, if the second letter of the driver's name is a 'J', then the first two digits should be a '1' and a '0', because 'J' is the tenth letter of the alphabet."

"Oh, now I remember. You know, it's been a long time since I graduated from the Police Academy."

"Well, since the driver's last name is Muccio, the first two digits should be a '2' and '1' because 'u' is the twenty-first letter of the alphabet…Instead, the numerals begin with a '1' and a '5'. For '1-5' to be correct, the *second* letter in his name must be an 'o'. This license must be a phony. We should arrest this kid on a forgery charge!"

When Zeke overheard what was being said he began licking his lips. Meanwhile, Danny was the only person present, other than Lennie, who had realized what had happened. The "1-5" which Lennie hadn't changed when he had partially copied Danny's license number, correlated to the "o"—the second letter of Danny's last name: Potenza.

"Kid," said Officer Casey, "It looks like I'm gonna have to arrest you for havin' a forged driver's license."

"Wait, Officer Casey. Let me get my father…Frankie, run over to Sonny's club and bring my father here as fast as you can!"

"Okay, kid, we'll wait a few minutes…only because I know ya."

In less than five minutes, Lennie's father, Dom, arrived at the scene and approached Officer Casey, saying, "Hey Casey, what the fuck's goin' on? I hear you wanna pinch my kid on some cheap charge."

"Hold on, sir," interjected the other officer. "It's no 'cheap charge,' as you put it. His license is forged and it has his name and address on it. That makes it a big deal. It would have been much better for him if he was driving without a license."

Dom wrapped his arm around Officer Casey's shoulders in a cordial manner and said, "Let's talk in private, Casey."

When they were about 25 feet beyond the patrol car, Officer Casey said, "Okay, Dom, whatta ya have in mind?"

"Well, what'll it take to make you and your partner, 'Dick Tracey' or whatever the fuck his name is, to say that you made a mistake…the license is legit?"

Casey mulled things over for about twenty seconds and said,

"$100 will do the trick."

"A hundred bucks for this penny-ante offense!"

"Yeah, and that's assuming I can convince my partner to take the money. He's new in the precinct. I'm not sure what to make of him, yet."

"Listen, I aint carrying that kind of dough. I was down forty bucks in the card game I was playin' before I was called over here… Give me ten minutes and wait for me on the corner of Kenmare and Mulberry. I'll be there with the C-note."

"Okay Dom, see you there in ten minutes."

"Let me ask you one thing…Why did you check-out Lennie?"

"We got a complaint, apparently from that man over there," pointing at Zeke. "Your son was playin' the radio too loud and revvin'-up the engine of his hot rod."

Later on, when Zeke realized that Lennie wasn't going to be arrested, he approached the officers to find out what had happened to change things. Officer Casey told him they had made an honest mistake and that the driver's license wasn't a forgery.

"This doesn't set well with me officers. I would like your names and badge numbers."

Hearing this, Dom went into a wild tirade. He realized that Zeke was trying to throw a monkey wrench into the deal by implying that he might take the matter to a higher level.

"You fuckin' hillbilly bastard! Why don't you mind your own fuckin' business! Why don't you go back to Georgia where you belong!"

"I ain't from Georgia, I'm from Tennessee…and by the way, why don't you teach your son how to behave himself?"

"I'd like to teach you somethin', you rat bastard!"

"Oh yeah! Just because you been in and out of prison a few times, you think you're a tough guy."

At that point Officer Casey tried to calm things down, but the situation was becoming more volatile. After a few more exchanges of profanities, Zeke took the initiative, putting himself right in Dom's face.

"Okay, you take the first swing, Dom, but then I'll kick your ass so bad that none of your kinfolk will recognize you!"

Everyone was surprised to see Dom back off. He had a reputation of being quite good with his fists, having spent many years moonlighting as a bouncer. Officer Casey then stepped in between them and he turned his attention to Zeke, threatening to arrest him if he didn't go back up to his apartment, immediately. Zeke reluctantly complied.

Danny commented to all in earshot, "That Zeke is a lot tougher than I thought!"

Later that evening, Lennie concluded that he must get a legitimate driver's license. The problem was that he was illiterate; he wouldn't be able to pass the written test for the learner's permit because he couldn't read the questions. If somehow he could overcome *that* hurdle, the rest would be easy. He would likely pass the road test with flying colors since he had already gotten a reputation of being quite a "wheel man."

Danny came up with a way to beat the system—a way for Lennie to pass the written test. He first outlined the plan to John-John, trusting his opinion above that of all the guys.

"Danny, I think it'll work because it's a very simple plan…They usually watch out for people trying to get a peek at other people's papers, but I don't think they'll spot what you plan to do."

The next morning, Danny and Lennie went to the New York State Department of Motor Vehicles Office on Worth Street, not far from City Hall. The two entered the exam room to take the written test for a learner's permit, despite the fact that Danny already had a driver's license. They were well aware of the fact that four or five different versions of the test were handed out in such a pattern that it was virtually impossible to cheat by copying answers from others; but their plan didn't involve trying to copy answers.

The tests were handed out and the clock began to tick. Lennie, who couldn't read the questions, randomly circled answers. Meanwhile, Danny breezed through the test. When the time was up, all the test takers lined-up on two, approximately equal, lines in front of the two clerks whose job was to grade the tests as they were presented to them by the test takers. Lennie was the fifth one in line and Danny was right behind him. They discreetly switched their test papers while waiting on the line. Just before the start of the exam, Danny had printed Lennie's name and address on the test paper. All that was missing was Lennie's signature—and Lennie did know how to sign his name.

Lennie handed in "his" test for grading after standing in line for a little more than five minutes. The clerk shook her head in an affirmative way upon finishing the scoring.

"Perfect!" she exclaimed, "You answered all twenty questions correctly…Oh, I see that you forgot to sign your paper. Please sign it and go over to Window 12 to pay the fee and get your learner's permit."

While in line, Danny noticed that Lennie had printed the name "John Cara" at the top of the test. Lennie wasn't trying to get John-John in any kind of trouble; he had chosen that name for its simplicity—a total of only eight letters. When Danny handed the test paper to the clerk, she immediately noticed that the "address block" wasn't filled in, and that the test wasn't signed. After Danny added a phony address and signature to the test paper, the clerk began the grading process.

"Boy, I think you've gotten the lowest score I've ever seen…A three! Did you study before taking this test?"

"Well, not very much, Ma'am."

"Here, take this pamphlet and study it hard for a week…then, come back and try again!"

Danny and Lennie had successfully scammed the Department of Motor Vehicles, and they proudly told everyone at the newsstand how they had pulled it off.

On Friday evening, John-John reminded the guys and Joe that he would be heading off on vacation with his family to the New Jersey seashore town, Long Branch. He would be spending the rest of the summer in Long Branch in a tiny, rented bungalow close to the ocean. Today had been his last day of his summer job.

"You lucky stiff," said Danny.

"Hey, we're gonna miss you," remarked Frankie.

"What are you gonna do about Felicia?" asked Joe. "Did you tell her you'll be gone for the rest of the summer?"

"No, I'll tell her tonight, if I see her."

"If you don't, I'll give her a kiss for you, John-John," said Lennie "Squirm" with a Cheshire Cat grin on his narrow face.

"Lennie, if you try to kiss her, she'll scratch your eyes out," said Joe.

John-John waited by the newsstand until eleven at night in hope of seeing Felicia. Although their relationship had cooled off, he still had feelings for her. For whatever reason, she never came down that night.

As he was running up the stairs to his apartment, his thoughts of Felicia were replaced by a vision of himself on a beach surrounded by a bevy of pretty girls in Long Branch. He hoped that that would be the case, and he hoped that he would "get lucky" with one or more of them.

Chapter 27: Under the Olive Tree

Maria was alone upstairs in her Uncle Pino's house in the middle of writing a letter to her best friend.

…Judy, I've been here for over a month, but it seems like two months. I haven't seen much of Capaci—let alone, Sicily. The only excitement around here was on July 15th, the feast day of Santa Rosalia. Santa Rosalia is the patron saint of Palermo and the nearby towns. There was a big procession that day. A statue of the saint was carried around the town. A lot of people marched behind the statue while a band played many of the songs that I've heard at the feasts in New York. At night, they shot off a lot of fireworks in the piazza, which is very close to where I'm staying.

The mood at my uncle's house is still very sad. Every member of the family is in mourning. During the first two weeks of the mourning period, I felt like I was living in a funeral parlor. There were loads of visitors at the house paying their respects and offering condolences to Aunt Costanza, her children, my father, and everyone else, including me. In the past two weeks, fewer people have come to the house—about two or three a day. They usually stop by at around 4 o'clock because in Sicily, it is customary to visit in the afternoon.

Of all of my relatives here, I feel closest to my cousin, Maria, probably, because she is only three years older than me. Also, we have the same first and last names. Sometimes, to avoid confusion around here, they refer to me as "Maria l'americana" or just, "l'americana." I'm not too crazy about Maria's thirty-eight-year-old sister, Giuseppina, who also lives here. Giuseppina has never married. She has a bossy personality and isn't very friendly to me or her sister. Maybe, she is jealous of Maria because Maria is the baby of the family. Plus, Maria is absolutely beautiful, while

Giuseppina is dowdy and overweight. Uncle Pino's two sons are very nice.
They are both married and live nearby.

In Sicily, people in mourning must wear something black for at least a
year, but I think Aunt Costanza will be dressed in black until she dies.
Her sons usually wear black suits when they are meeting visitors or walking
around town; or if it's too hot, black pants, white dress shirts and black ties.
At other times, they attach a black ribbon to their work shirts or sports
shirts. Giuseppina dresses like her mother—all in black—but Maria
avoids being all in black. For example, she might wear black pants and a
blue blouse, or white pants and a black blouse. She believes that it's what is
in your heart that counts— not how you dress.

As Maria was about to write the next paragraph, Cousin Maria entered the room. She put her hand on her younger cousin's shoulder and said, "I have an idea. Tomorrow let's go to the piazza and do some shopping…and, I'll give you a tour of the town, since I know you haven't seen very much of it."

"Oh, that would be great…but I'll need some money for shopping."

"Don't worry, I'll convince your father to give you some money. I can be quite persuasive. It's time you dressed in style. Your outfits do nothing for you."

Cousin Maria had no trouble convincing her uncle to give his daughter 40,000 lire (about $65 at that time) for a major shopping spree and a new hairdo. He realized that Maria's visit to Sicily had been mostly a somber experience, and that going shopping—her favorite pastime in America— would certainly lift her spirits. His only proviso was that she must spend the money wisely.

The last day of July was exceptionally hot—even for Sicily. As the two cousins walked arm-in-arm, towards the piazza in the latter part of the morning, the temperature was already about a hundred degrees and "*l'americana*" was feeling it.

"Maria, I can see that this heat is already getting to you."

"Yes, but it still feels good to get out of the house."

"Our first stop will be the lingerie shop. It's about time you stop wearing "old ladies" underwear…I've seen those ugly white cotton panties of yours. It's time for you to become a sexy young woman."

At the lingerie shop, the younger Maria sifted through many delicate panties and finally selected five pairs of silk bikini panties that were very sexy and sheer. She would never have considered buying such underwear had it not been for the encouragement of her cousin.

"Can I interest you in buying a bra?" asked the shopkeeper.

Maria thought about it for a few seconds: *My bras have certainly gotten tighter since I've been here. I don't need to put tissues in them, lately. Maybe, I've put on a little weight, or maybe, my female hormones are finally kicking in…whatever…I guess I should take a look at some bras and probably try on a bigger size.*

"*Si, signora,* let me see some bras."

Guided by Cousin Maria—who accompanied her inside the dressing room—she wound up buying three bras that fit her well and were quite sexy in a European way. The sexiest bra—a black one—was lacy and partly see-through.

The two Marias then walked over to a chic female clothing store where "*l'americana*" bought three stylish tops, a dress and two pairs of brightly colored hip-hugger pants.

After stopping at a *caffè* for espressos and pastries, the two made their way to the best hair stylist—*parrucchiere*—in town, whose tiny salon was on a very narrow street, Via Regina Margherita, about eight blocks from the piazza. Fausto, the hair stylist, doted on the younger Maria, slowly cutting her very long auburn tresses while asking her questions about New York City and America. Fausto was truly a master hair stylist, because when Maria stepped out of the chair, her shoulder-length auburn hair looked worthy of *Vogue* magazine.

"Maria, we got to do something about your eyeglasses. Do you really need to wear them all the time?"

"Well, my vision is 20-40 in both eyes."

"I don't know what those numbers mean. In Italy we use different numbers for vision…I guess because we use the metric system and you Americans don't."

"Well, 20-40 isn't that bad, but I just got used to wearing my glasses all the time."

"Take off your glasses…Can you see me? Can you read the sign across the street?"

"Yes, I can see you quite well…and I *can* read the sign across the street."

"Good. From now on, you only wear your glasses in the house, and then, only to read, to watch television or when your eyes are tired…Now, put your glasses in your handbag."

"Okay."

"You know, you look so much prettier without those ugly glasses."

Upon returning to the piazza, the girls headed for a small shoe store that featured well-crafted Italian shoes. The door to the store was open for ventilation, allowing the wonderful aroma of fine leather to permeate well beyond the store's entrance. Young Maria bought one pair of off-white, low-heel pumps. This final purchase left 2,000 lire "change" for her father.

As soon as the girls returned home, young Maria ran upstairs to put on her new clothes so that she could model them for the family members, most of whom were seated at the downstairs table lingering over espresso while discussing tidbits of the latest town gossip. The usually shy girl was so pleased with her "new look" that she confidently modeled the various combinations of her recent purchases to choruses of, *"Bella! Bella!"*

A few days later, the DiMartino family stopped by the house for a Sunday afternoon visit. Gustavo and Lucrezia DiMartino had paid a visit to Costanza and family within a week of the burial. This time, their nineteen-year-old son, Lorenzo, accompanied them. Lorenzo, was strikingly handsome and well-built. At nearly 6 feet tall, he was much taller than most Sicilian males. When he was introduced to *"l'americana"* he stared at her with wide-open eyes. He then managed to stay close to her no matter where she went in the room. He focused most of his attention on her, smiling all the time, while hardly speaking to anyone else. It was quite evident to everyone—except Maria—that he was smitten with her

About an hour into the visit, Lorenzo asked, *"Signor* Rizzo, would you and your family like to take a ride in my car to your brother's orchard?"

"Certo," replied Vincenzo.

After driving about two kilometers in Lorenzo's beat-up old Lancia, they reached Antonio's orchard, which was located at the east end of Capaci, close to the town of Isola delle Femmine. The orchard consisted of many groves of olive trees, and fruit trees of all varieties. It extended about 1,000 feet back from the entrance, all the way back to the road bordering the Mediterranean Sea, and it was about 500 feet wide.

"This orchard is huge! How big is it *Pappa?*"

"Antonio says that it's five hectares…but I don't know what that is in acres."

"Well, whatever size it is, it looks like you could fit half our neighborhood in it."

The group first walked over to the small stucco shack, which was close to the orchard's entrance. They found the shack to be locked.

Vincenzo shrugged his shoulders. "Well, there was never anything interesting inside this shack, anyway."

Vincenzo, happy to be back on familiar ground, began to walk ahead, with Rosaria, walking a step behind. Shielded by the shack, Lorenzo surprised Maria by quickly embracing her and kissing her on the lips. She had unexpectedly received her "first kiss" and it made her heart flutter a bit. She smiled at Lorenzo and squeezed his hand as they began to follow her parents. When they all reached the end of the orchard, they stood silently along the rundown old fence and admired the beautiful Mediterranean. While looking seaward, Maria's thoughts focused on her first kiss, and she wondered what the future might bring: *Would Lorenzo be my first boyfriend?*

The "future" came rather quickly. Two days later, Lorenzo paid a mid-afternoon visit to 21 Via Grazziani; this time, he was by himself. He entered the house carrying a large Sicilian-style pizza that his mother had made for the grieving family's evening dinner— *la cena*—which, during the summer months, was usually eaten at dusk. A true Sicilian-style pizza is thick and covered with tomato sauce, grated cheese, and onions. Unlike the American version, it is not topped with mozzarella cheese.

The pizza was well received by Costanza, who was truly grateful for Lucrezia's thoughtful gesture. She insisted that Lorenzo sit down and have a cup of espresso and some biscotti. The two Marias entered the room accompanied by Cousin Maria's boyfriend, Enzo, who was a good friend of Lorenzo. They all sat down with Lorenzo and soon were served espressos by Costanza. As they chitchatted, Lorenzo gave his full attention to *"l'americana,"* smiling and laughing at almost anything she said—whether it was funny or not.

After about a half-hour, Lorenzo asked Enzo and the two Marias if they would like to take a drive with him to the beach. Enzo immediately said 'yes.' After asking their parents, the two cousins were granted permission to go along—the understanding being that they would serve as each other's chaperone.

They arrived at the orchard in less than ten minutes. Lorenzo pulled into the dirt driveway and parked close to the shack. Once out of the car, Enzo offered everyone a cigarette. *"L'americana"* was quite surprised to see her cousin take one and light-up.

"Maria, would you like one?" asked Enzo, pointing the open pack at her.

"Oh no…I don't smoke."

"Well, it's about time you begin," said Cousin Maria. "Here, take a puff on mine."

"No, I really don't want to."

"Oh, come on…stop being a little girl."

Cousin Maria's last comment struck a chord. "Okay, one puff."

As she took a drag, she began to choke and cough. Everyone laughed, including *"l'americana"*—once she stopped choking and coughing.

"Listen, everyone chokes and coughs on the first puff, but if you want to be a sophisticated young woman, you should learn how to smoke."

Trusting her cousin, who had become her role model, she decided to try to smoke one cigarette. After two unsuccessful attempts, she succeeded in lighting her first cigarette. The smoke tasted a little acrid, but by her fifth puff, she began to find the smoking experience to be somewhat agreeable, and she noticed that it made her feel more relaxed than usual.

"Inhale, deeply Maria. Let the smoke go all the way down into your lungs."

She did so with a muffled cough, and a little redness on her face, but Cousin Maria was pleased with her protégé. "Now you're no longer a little girl! You're a sophisticated young woman…but don't let your parents find out that I taught you how to smoke!"

Enzo and Maria soon disappeared into the deep recesses of the orchard, leaving Lorenzo and the younger Maria alone. So much for chaperoning each other! It was obvious that Enzo and Cousin Maria wanted to be alone. It was less obvious—at least to the younger Maria—that her cousin wanted her to experience something more than kissing.

After Lorenzo and Maria had walked together for several minutes, Lorenzo stopped under an olive tree. He pulled Maria into his arms and hugged her tightly. He then gently pushed his tongue between her lips so that it touched her moist tongue. Maria had read about "French kissing" in a magazine, and now she was experiencing it. She liked the sensation. She could taste a tinge of smoke in his breath, and she supposed that he could taste the smokiness of her breath. As they kissed, Lorenzo began to feel her soft behind with his right hand while placing his left hand on her shoulder. Soon, he lowered that hand onto the front of her blouse and began fondling her. She was startled—no one had ever touched her there before—but, in the heat of the moment, she didn't try to stop him. Lorenzo, sensing Maria's inexperience, decided to see how far he could get. He became excited as he thought, *Maybe, I can be her "first"!*

After a few minutes of fondling her breasts over her blouse, he slid his hand down past the vee-neck collar and onto her bra. She didn't resist. Encouraged, he deftly slid his hand under her bra and began massaging her perky left breast. When she realized he was touching her *bare* breast, she tried to push his hand out of her bra. But, he resisted and distracted her by bending her backward and slowing easing her to the ground.

While on the ground, with Lorenzo on top of her, the level of passion rose. She could feel his hardened member rubbing against her thigh. She found herself breathing heavily, in sync with his heavy breathing. He then grabbed her left wrist and slowly pulled her hand towards his crotch. Her curiosity got the better of her, so she grazed his crotch with her palm. Having mixed emotions about what she had just done, she quickly pulled her hand away and stopped kissing him for a few seconds. He smiled and then resumed kissing and hugging her. Soon their level of passion was back to where it had been.

Lorenzo, who was, after all, a virile Sicilian young man, hadn't given up on his ultimate goal: claiming the virginity of *"l'americana."* So, after about five more minutes of passion, he sneakily began to push his hand under the waistband of her tight pants. He somehow managed to do so without her noticing. However, when he slipped his right hand under her lacy bikini panties, she *did* notice. She realized if she didn't stop him, she could soon lose her virginity to this Sicilian *Casanova.* So, she firmly and loudly exclaimed, "No, Lorenzo, no!" But, he continued his maneuvering, trying his best to stimulate her. At that point, she mustered up all of her strength and pushed him off of her, yelling, *"Basta! Basta!* Enough! Enough! You're moving too fast!"

"Mi dispiace! Mi dispiace! I'm sorry! I'm sorry! Your beauty overwhelmed me. You are so heavenly. Please forgive me."

Believing that his apology was sincere, and charmed by his flattering words, she said, "Okay, I forgive you...Now, let's go find Maria and Enzo."

She straightened out her clothing and the two of them began to walk arm-in-arm towards the beautiful Mediterranean. As they walked, she thought of the recent events: Three days ago, she had never been kissed, and now she had come fairly close to "going all the way." She now felt that she *could* be desirable to young men and that she no longer was the wallflower she had been not too long ago. But she also felt pangs of guilt. As a result of her strong Catholic upbringing, she believed that she had engaged in sinful behavior— sinful behavior that she would have to confess to a priest!

After wending their way about 100 meters through the grove, they spotted Enzo and Maria just ahead. Despite being blocked, somewhat, by the olive trees, Maria could see that Enzo and her cousin were adjusting their clothes. When they all met up, Lorenzo suggested that they should leave. Within ten minutes, they were back at 21 Via Grazziani.

The girls then said *"Ciao"* to Enzo and Lorenzo—being careful not to display any affection—and walked into the house. They found Costanza, Rosaria and Giuseppina seated at the kitchen table, gossiping. They decided to join them. During the course of the conversation, it registered with the younger Maria that Giuseppina seemed to resent her sister. She had noticed over the past month that Giuseppina would often direct snide remarks towards her sister—and now she was at it again. She concluded that Giuseppina was jealous of her sister. In young Maria's eyes, Giuseppina was a bitter, dowdy old maid who had long ago abandoned any thoughts of marriage, while her sister was young, vibrant, and beautiful.

Soon, Costanza signaled that they should start preparing *la cena*, which would consist of the pizza Lorenzo's mother had sent, a garden salad, assorted cheeses, and some sliced pepperoni. A liter of beer would be put on the dinner table, in addition to the usual red wine, since many Italians like the combination of beer and pizza.

The entire family gathered around the dining room table and soon the adults were in animated conversation about nothing of any importance. After the espresso and pastry, the men drifted into the ground floor living room, while the women cleaned-up, and washed and dried the dishes. After completing their chores, the two Marias made their way to one of two terraces on the top floor. They were by themselves. Cousin Maria began the conversation by asking what had transpired between Lorenzo and Maria in the orchard.

"We were making out very passionately under an olive tree. That was the first time I ever made-out with anyone. I enjoyed it, but he was moving too fast for me. He managed to get me on the ground, but when he put his hands inside my panties, I stopped him…and we ended things."

"Why did you stop him?"

"I was afraid that if I didn't stop him, I would no longer be a virgin."

She had expected that Cousin Maria would have been shocked and upset by Lorenzo's aggressive behavior. To her great surprise, she wasn't upset with Lorenzo—she was upset with her.

"You should have let Lorenzo have his way with you…What do you think Enzo and I were doing? Picking olives? No, we were making passionate love…*amore*. Trust me, sex is enjoyable and exciting. The sooner you lose your virginity, the sooner you will be enjoying the fruits of life…By the way, I was about your age when I lost my virginity, and I have no regrets."

"I have been taught that virginity is something to be preserved until marriage."

"Who taught you that? The priests! The nuns! What do *they* know? Listen to me, in Sicily, more than a few brides walking down the aisle in their fancy white gowns are *not* virgins. They present the appearance of being virgins to the public, whereas the truth is quite different. Appearance is everything here." Then, adding with a laugh, "My family still believes that *I'm* saving myself for my future husband."

Still somewhat in shock, young Maria remarked, "Well, *I* certainly didn't think that you were having sex…I thought you were a virgin."

"Well, things are not always what they appear to be…especially here in Sicily. By the way, in your stay thus far, have you ever seen any evidence of the existence of the Mafia?"

"No, I haven't."

"I assure you that the Mafia is here. Its tentacles are everywhere…but it isn't obvious…A great deal of effort goes into making it appear that the Mafia doesn't exist."

"I don't understand your point…Surely, the people know it exists."

"Sure they do, but…Oh, what I am trying to explain is that how things *appear* is far more important than how things really are…So, as long as you can present the appearance of being pure and chaste, no one will ever question your virtue."

"Well, be that as it may, I don't think that I'm ready to lose my virginity."

"Listen, you are missing out on something special. Why wait? Have your fun, now. You will probably be married in about four or five years. Life is too short. Look at my poor father who is no longer with us.

"True, life is short, but I don't think I'm ready to take that big step."

"*Va bene*. Very well. By the way, tomorrow Enzo and Lorenzo would like us to join them at the orchard again. What do you say? Do you want to go, or do you want to sit here all day talking to the old ladies?"

After weighing her options for about thirty seconds, and feeling pressured by her cousin, she responded in a reluctant tone, "Well…I guess I'll go."

"Good. I know that you've made the right decision. Trust me, you will have fun. I will make a sophisticated young woman out of you, yet. To avoid anyone getting any ideas about what's going on, the guys will meet us in front of *la parrucchieria*."

That night, young Maria tossed and turned in bed for about an hour before falling asleep. She felt like she was being pulled in two directions. Her cousin's *joie de vivre* attitude greatly conflicted with the morals that had been instilled in her by her parents and the Catholic Church. However, she did enjoy her encounter with Lorenzo very much, despite the fact that he had been more aggressive than she had expected. Her newfound amorous desires, bolstered by her cousin's urgings, outweighed any doubts that she was having about seeing Lorenzo, again.

The following afternoon, shortly after *pranzo*, the two girls excused themselves and soon were heading off to their rendezvous. During their fifteen-minute stroll to Via Regina Margherita, the younger Maria, who apparently had been mulling over the idea of letting Lorenzo "have his way with her," asked about the possibility of getting pregnant. Her worldly cousin advised that she, like many other women, relied on the "rhythm method" to avoid pregnancy. She explained that it would be safe to have unprotected sex within the first ten-days of the start of a woman's period, and then, the woman should abstain for eight days—the fertile period of the menstrual cycle; after that, it would again be safe to have unprotected sex.

She added, "Of course, if the guy uses a condom, you could have sex anytime without having to worry about getting pregnant."

"Oh my…I didn't know any of this."

"By the way, when did your last period begin?"

Counting on her fingers, she replied, "About twelve days ago, I believe."

"*O Dio*, it's a good thing I asked. Right now you are very fertile. You could become pregnant if you have sex today. Of course, you could ask Lorenzo to use a condom, but I think that your 'first time' should be without a condom, so that you can experience the full pleasure during this wonderful event in your life. Besides, most Italian men don't like to use condoms."

"How can I keep him under control, today, when we're making out?"

"Don't worry! Lorenzo is a gentleman. I've known him for most of my life. He won't force you to do anything you really don't want to do."

"But, in the heat of the moment, if his excitement gets the best of him, he might forget he's a gentleman. I won't be able to overpower him. He's much bigger and stronger than me."

"Well, if you're *that* afraid, maybe we shouldn't get into the car with the guys…maybe, you want to remain a little girl instead of becoming a woman." Then continuing her psychological manipulation, she offered, "If you want, we can tell the guys that something has come up and we need to be back home in a half-hour…Then, you can hang out with my sister for the day…perhaps, she can teach you how to crochet."

"Well, I really would like to go…but only if I could have some control of the situation."

"Listen, you want to control the situation? I'll tell you how. I just thought of a way to stop him in his tracks if you think he's trying to get into your pants, today."

"How?"

"Follow my advice, even though it may sound a little strange…If he's on top of you and he puts his hand on the zipper of your pants, surprise him by, somehow, rolling him over and maneuvering yourself on top of him…then, unzip his pants and pull out his "*salsiccia*."

"His *salsiccia?*"

"Yes," replied the devilish Maria, choosing to refer to Lorenzo's member as a "sausage," rather than by its anatomical name, to make the deed seem more playful to her protégé. "He will be so shocked," she continued with a laugh, "that his thoughts of entering you will vanish, being replaced by the expectations of what you're about to do to him."

"No, I don't think I'll be able to do that. I never…"

The older Maria cut off her cousin in mid-sentence, saying, "Listen, if you're unable to do that, then you won't be able to follow through with the rest of my plan."

"Well…I don't know. I don't know…Oh, what's the rest of your plan?"

"You simply grab his *salsiccia* with your hand and give it a kiss. Then, you put your lips around it and do what comes naturally."

"Do what comes naturally?"

"Yes. Don't be a prude. Think of it simply as advanced kissing… or a more intimate way of showing affection…nothing more, nothing less."

"It sounds like sex to me," recalling what she had learned about "blow jobs" from "Fat" Angie at the lunch table.

"No, it's not truly sex. It is, as I said, a more intimate way of showing affection."

"Oh no, I don't think I'm ready to do that."

"You're so naïve. Every woman does it sooner or later…Well, maybe not my sister…Why wait for later? When I was your age, I already had done it about a dozen times. Believe me, you will find it a very enjoyable and pleasurable experience, more so, when you see the pleased look on Lorenzo's face…Don't worry, his *salsiccia* won't bite you!" she added with a laugh.

The younger Maria said nothing as she mulled things over, although her thoughts were certainly being influenced by her cousin's sugarcoated descriptions of sex.

When they turned the corner of Via Regina Margherita, they immediately spotted Lorenzo's old Lancia, parked across from *la parrucchieria*. It was decision time for young Maria. She was extremely nervous. She could feel her heart pounding. She hesitated a couple of seconds, but then followed her cousin and slid into the back seat of the car, sitting right behind Lorenzo. Enzo turned around and gave each of the girls a cigarette, teasing the younger Maria, "Let's see if you can do a better job lighting your cigarette this time."

This time she was able to light the cigarette on her first try.

"Brava, Maria 'l'americana.' Brava!"

She began to inhale deeply without the slightest hint of a cough. She could feel the smoke going deep down her lungs. Following the example of the others, she waited about two seconds and slowly exhaled, puckering her lips to steer the path of the smoke. After about six or seven deep drags, she noticed that her nervousness had lessened considerably. She finished her cigarette just as Lorenzo was pulling into the orchard's driveway.

They found the shack to be locked, which was a good indication that there weren't any workers around. Once they were deep within the orchard, Enzo and Maria said *"Ciao"* and scampered on ahead. Lorenzo and "*l'americana*" walked at a slow pace, taking in the beauty and delightful aromas of the orchard.

A few minutes later, they arrived at the same olive tree where yesterday's encounter had taken place. Lorenzo gently grabbed her in his arms, and they began hugging and kissing. As had happened on the day before, she soon found herself down on the ground with Lorenzo on top of her. His hands were all over her as they kissed passionately. When she felt his hand tugging on her pants zipper, she knew what he had in mind. So, she made her surprise move. She rolled him over, taking advantage of the fact that the ground to his left sloped slightly downward. In one quick move, Lorenzo was on the bottom and she was on top.

She giggled and then commanded, "*Aspetta! Aspetta!* Wait! Wait!"

At that point she felt empowered by the fact that she was now in control of the situation. As Lorenzo looked on totally befuddled, she tilted her head downward, put her hand on his zipper and slithered down towards his knees. Instinctively, he spread his legs apart, allowing her knees to touch the ground. Biting down on her lower lip in reaction to the anxiety she was feeling, she quickly unzipped his pants, placed her hands into his underwear and pulled-out his stiffened member. He just lay there silently with his eyes wide open—totally astonished. Any thoughts of deflowering Maria had vanished from his mind—at least for the moment. It was the first time that Maria had ever seen a man's organ in the flesh—let alone touched one. She could hear Cousin Maria's words: *Every woman does it sooner or later…Why wait for later?*

She cringed, closed her eyes and then planted a kiss right on the head of his throbbing organ. She then picked up her head several inches and opened her eyes. She let out a slightly audible sigh of relief, realizing that through sheer willpower, she had overcome her fears and anxiety. She laughed inside, thinking that Cousin Maria was right: it really didn't bite.

At that point, Lorenzo gently pushed down on her head and she began to satisfy his want, in part to please him, but more so, to please Cousin Maria. Ten minutes later, they began to walk—slightly apart—towards the sea in search of Enzo and Maria. The couples soon met, and they continued to walk to the end of the property, and then across the road to Capaci's picturesque beach. Once on the beach, Enzo offered everyone a cigarette, which they all accepted. The two Marias began to walk ahead with cigarettes in hand. As before, the deep inhaling and exhaling tended to calm her down—and she was far from being calm after what she had just done.

"Maria, did you take my advice? Did you follow my plan?"

"Yes…Yes, I did."

"Did my plan work out just as I said it would?"

"Yes, it worked out *exactly* as you said it would…I caught him by surprise and turned him over before he could have his way with me, which I'm sure was his intention…Then, I played with his *salsiccia*…and I did, as you say, 'what comes naturally.'"

"Did you find it as enjoyable as I said it would be?"

Well…kind of…You know, I really didn't think I could go through with it, but…"

"As I've said, I will make a sophisticated young woman out of you, yet…Tell me, how did it end?"

"Well…when I felt him squirt, I jumped and pulled away. I spat out the stuff as he continued to squirt, mostly onto the ground…but some of it got on his pants. I then found some tissues in my purse and wiped off my lips and mouth as he stared at me."

Cousin Maria shook her head disapprovingly. "Oh no! Was he angry?"

"I think so. When he got up, he shook his head and talked to himself in words that I couldn't quite make out."

The older Maria responded with a laugh, saying, "Ah, don't worry, in Sicily we have a saying…Sex is like pizza…even when it's bad, it's still good."

Cousin Maria enjoyed saying bizarre things to her impressionable young cousin—often making them up as she went along. She was very outgoing, carefree, and had a somewhat devilish personality. As the youngest of four children, everyone in the family doted on her—except for her much older sister, who would usually try to boss her around as if she were her second mother. Her parents had never been very demanding of her, and she could get away with just about anything with her two brothers. In fact, to Giuseppe, who was twelve years her senior, and Vincenzo, who was ten year her senior, their kid sister would always be their little *principessa*—their little princess.

"Seriously, Maria, in Italy, when a woman arouses a man as you did, he expects her to finish the job properly…to keep his *salsiccia* in her mouth until he finishes his business.

"You never explained that to me."

"Must I explain everything to you? You should have figured *that* out for yourself. What did you think was going to happen at the end?"

"Well, I didn't give it much thought…but I guess I should have."

"Yes, you should have…no guy likes to see his seeds being spit-out in front of him. It's viewed as an insult…It's a psychological thing, I suppose."

"It's viewed as an insult? I didn't realize that."

Well, one way of finishing the job is to discreetly spit out the stuff into a tissue…you know, when the guy isn't looking at you…or you can simply swallow it."

"Oh, I don't think I could swallow that gooey stuff, plus I don't think it would be a healthy thing to do."

"Oh, I've done it so many times that I've lost count. And I can honestly say that it hasn't hurt my health in any way…Forgive me, but don't I look great."

The younger Maria agreed by nodding her head. To her eyes, her cousin was a ravishing beauty. At 5'-3" tall and about 110 pounds, she was thin, yet shapely. She had a very pretty face, sensuous lips, long black hair and a wonderful tan complexion. She certainly appeared to be "the picture of health."

Changing the subject, the younger Maria asked, "Do you think Lorenzo is telling Enzo what just happened between me and him in the orchard?"

"No. No. Don't worry about such a thing. Guys in Italy, especially in Sicily, are discreet…not like the guys in America who tell their friends every detail of their sexual adventures."

"How do you know what goes on in America?"

"Well, I've seen many American movies."

When they reached the Lancia, after taking the long way back to the front of the orchard, Enzo offered everyone a cigarette. Maria gladly accepted his offer. Sex and smoking had come to be connected in her mind. During the drive, Lorenzo announced that he would be going away for about eight or nine days with his family to their island retreat. The DiMartino's owned a cottage on the beautiful island of Favignana, which is off Sicily's west coast.

"Favignana is a beautiful place, Maria, but I wish I wasn't going. I would rather be here with you. But, don't worry, I'll be back before you leave for America…probably on Friday, August 16th. When are you going back?"

"August 18th."

"Good…I hope to see you on the 16th."

Every evening thereafter, when the two cousins would be chatting alone upstairs on one of the terraces, the older Maria would steer the conversation to her favorite topic—sex. She would often repeat, "It would be such a wonderful experience for you if you would let Lorenzo be your 'first' when he comes back from Favignana…I assure you, you won't regret it."

Cousin Maria's constant talk about the joys of sex was beginning to have its intended effect. A few days before Lorenzo was to return to Capaci, young Maria asked, "Does it hurt the first time? Will I bleed?"

At that point Cousin Maria knew that her protégé was seriously considering losing her virginity to Lorenzo. "No, it doesn't hurt much. A little pinch and then the pleasurable feelings take over… and don't expect much bleeding. That's an old wives' tale."

"But, shouldn't I save myself for my husband?"

"Listen, when you meet your true love later on in America, simply tell him that you're a virgin. Men believe what they want to believe. He will respect you and he will never know the difference. Anyhow, I don't know why so much fuss is made over a tiny piece of tissue!"

The days flew by quickly and soon it was Friday, August 16th. Enzo telephoned Cousin Maria about noon to tell her that Lorenzo had returned from Favignana and that he wanted the four of them to go to the orchard one last time—assuming that "*l'americana*" still wanted to see him. Presuming that Maria would want to see Lorenzo, she gave Enzo the "okay," telling him that they would meet them at the usual spot, at the usual time.

Young Maria didn't voice any objections when told that her last date with Lorenzo had been arranged. In fact, she was looking forward to seeing him; she had missed him.

Telling the family that they were off to the piazza, the two cousins began their leisurely walk to Via Regina Margherita. Within a few blocks of their destination, the older Maria began her last pitch about the beauty and joy of intercourse. She repeated and repeated that holding onto one's virginity was a foolish thing. Life was short and one must live for the moment. To some extent, she was practicing a form of brainwashing—but in her mind, her continual encouragement was aimed at a positive end.

A couple of minutes before reaching the rendezvous spot, Cousin Maria remarked, "You realize it's been more than twenty days since the start of your last period. There is no way…believe me, no way…that you can become pregnant, today! Trust me, you'll enjoy the experience and you will have me, and of course, Lorenzo, to thank for it…Don't be afraid. Become a woman, today! Remember, I haven't steered you wrong, yet."

The younger Maria said nothing. When they reached the car, she got in without hesitation. After the customary greetings, she gladly accepted a cigarette from Enzo, who seemed to have an endless supply of them. Once again, she inhaled slowly and deeply, enjoying the soothing effect of the smoke.

Cousin Maria then whispered, "See, you thought you wouldn't like smoking, and now you seem to like it more than I do. It will be the same thing for…for…for you know what. Trust me."

Despite all of the continual badgering, Maria still wasn't sold on the idea of losing her virginity to Lorenzo. Her "game plan," which she had firmed-up in her mind while riding in the car, was to give Lorenzo a "repeat performance," but, this time, with a better ending. Preparing ahead, she had filled her pants pockets with tissues. *I think he'll be pleased…pleased enough that when I return next summer, he'll probably want to continue where we left off…and maybe then, I'll let him be my "first."*

Within several minutes of arriving at the orchard, Enzo and Cousin Maria went off on their merry way, once again leaving Lorenzo and Maria behind. Lorenzo led Maria by the hand to their "favorite" olive tree, where they soon began kissing very passionately. As before, Maria wound up on her back with Lorenzo on top of her. Following the script of their last encounter, she managed to turn him over and wind up on top, while still in his embrace.

As she was moving her hand towards his zipper, Lorenzo squeezed his thighs tightly around her thighs and proceeded to roll the two of them over a couple of times, ending with him being back on top. His move had caught her by surprise. They both laughed as they rolled over—although Maria's laugh was triggered more by nervousness than anything else.

As he wiggled to position himself between her thighs, she tried to regain the superior position. However, the entwined couple had come to rest next to an olive tree in the adjacent row, slightly downhill from where they had started. To get back on top, she would have to fight gravity by trying to roll herself and Lorenzo uphill towards "their" olive tree. After several unsuccessful attempts, she resigned herself to being on the bottom. Realizing that this would be his last time with "*l'americana*," he decided to try his best to deflower her. When he pulled her pants down to her knees, she knew that the moment of truth had arrived. She felt like screaming at him and pushing him away, but that feeling was over-ridden thanks to her cousin's endless brainwashing.

She could hear her cousin's voice saying, *Relax…Let it happen… You'll enjoy the experience…Don't be a little girl…Be a woman…*as he quickly pulled down her black panties, revealing her patch of auburn hair. Operating quickly, before she could react, he eased the head of his throbbing member into her to the point where he could feel the blockage. She closed her eyes and gritted her teeth, anticipating great pain. He took a deep breath and rammed forward with force. He could feel the blockage give way. She was surprised that the pain had been quite bearable—and only momentary—and she soon came to enjoy the sensation of his rhythmic movements deep within her.

After about five minutes, she felt a sensation throughout her body that she had never felt before. She began to moan, and soon let out a scream of joy. Seconds later, she felt six pulses of warm fluid shooting deep inside her, as Lorenzo sighed with delight and then collapsed upon her. The two remained as one for a few minutes. Upon separating, Lorenzo noticed traces of blood on his limp member. Figuring that Maria would also have some blood to contend with, he handed her his handkerchief, saying, "Here Maria, wipe yourself with this."

After wiping herself, she looked down at the handkerchief. She noticed some gooey, red stains on it—but the extent of the staining was less than she had envisioned. She handed the handkerchief back to Lorenzo who surprised her by putting it back in his pocket without using it to wipe himself clean. Unbeknown to her, he intended to keep the stained handkerchief as a souvenir—a souvenir of the day that he deflowered his first virgin.

After she pulled-up her underwear and pants and straightened out her blouse, the two made their way towards the other end of the orchard, arm-in-arm, to seek out Enzo and Maria. Upon finding them, the couples made their way to the beach. With cigarettes in hand, the two Marias walked on ahead of the guys. Young Maria *really* needed that cigarette.

"Well, are you still a virgin?"

"No, not anymore."

"*Auguri!* Congratulations! You are no longer a little girl…Are you glad you did it? Was it as great an experience as I said it would be?"

"Yes, I'm glad I did it…and I really enjoyed it once Lorenzo got deep inside me, but now I'm feeling guilty about breaking a Commandment."

"Don't worry about *that* Commandment…It's not an important one like, *Thou shall not kill.*"

"Well, I still feel guilty about what I did."

"Don't! You were going to do it sooner or later…better sooner. Follow my philosophy…Live for the moment!"

"I hope my parents will never find out about this."

"Don't worry. They will never know…and don't worry about having gotten pregnant. I guarantee you that you'll get your period about a week after you return to New York."

"I hope so…but right now I still have feelings of guilt."

"Well, if it will make you feel better, when you get back to America go to confession. Tell the priest what happened today, and on the other days, with Lorenzo. The beauty of the Catholic religion is that the priest will absolve you of your sins…Of course, I don't think what you did was sinful…Anyway, as long as you're sorry when you confess, you will be forgiven."

"Maybe, I should go to confession at Sant'Erasmo's Church, tomorrow."

"No, I don't think you should."

"Why not?"

"Well, the priest at Sant'Erasmo's, Father Balsano, has loose lips when he drinks. The rumor is that after drinking lots of wine during *pranzo* at his cousin's house on Sundays, he gossips about the steamiest confessions he heard the day before. Surely, your confession would be leaked to his cousins during this Sunday's *pranzo*.

"How would he know it was me confessing?"

"He can see you."

"He can see me?"

"Certainly. The confession boxes aren't totally dark…plus, I'm quite sure he can see who's standing in line for confession through
the slats in the door in front of his chair."

"He knows who I am?"

"Of course he does. He knows you came here to attend my father's funeral. Father Balsano knows everything that goes on in Capaci. He would certainly tell his cousins that you are no longer a virgin. Then, word of your sexual escapades would soon spread all over Capaci, and eventually, back to your parents when they are home in America."

"Well, if that's the case, I better wait until I get back to America to go to confession."

"Good…and remember: Should you decide to make love again, I'm sure that some priest in America will forgive you again!" Cousin Maria jokingly exclaimed. "As you might have figured out by now, I'm not a religious person…and I don't have much respect for priests. I believe that many of them are hypocrites. But, that's me. Cling to your religion if you wish. Go to confession if it will make you feel better."

When they all got back into the car, only Maria *"l'americana"* asked for a cigarette. She knew it would be her last one for quite a while, so she savored it. As she slowly inhaled and exhaled a few times, her feelings of guilt were replaced with a feeling of accomplishment. The wallflower had, indeed, become a woman, and she had Cousin Maria to thank for it—and, of course, Lorenzo.

When they reached the piazza, Lorenzo double-parked the car and they all got out. He bade farewell to his "conquest" with deep sadness in his eyes, giving her one last kiss.

"*Arrivederci, Maria, mia innamorata.*"

"*Arrivederci, Lorenzo, mio innamorato.* I will never forget you."

"There will always be a very special place in my heart for you, Maria."

"There will always be a very special place in my heart for you, also," Maria responded with a tear in her eye and a crack in her voice.

Cousin Maria then interjected, "Lorenzo, do you know that Maria will be returning next summer?"

"No, I didn't know that."

"Yes, Lorenzo, I'll be coming back next year to spend the whole summer here as a graduation present from my parents."

"Good…Good…I'll be waiting for you, and perhaps, we can continue where we left off."

"Oh yes, *mio innamorato*, oh yes."

As the young women headed for 21 Via Grazziani, the older Maria—ever the mentor—offered the following advice: "As soon as we get home, take a long, hot bath. While in the bathroom, wash your panties in the sink. Wring them tightly and place them deep into your family's pile of dirty laundry. They should be dry by the time your mother starts packing."

"I feel like I could use a hot bath…and thanks for reminding me about my panties. I'm sure they got stained."

"By the way, what color are your panties?"

"They're black."

"How fortunate! There is little chance that your mother will spot any stains on them when she washes your clothes back in America."

"Thank God I didn't wear my white ones!"

Chapter 28: Back to School

The taxi pulled-up to the curb in front of 39 East First Street carrying three extremely exhausted passengers. Vincenzo Rizzo and family had just completed their sixteen-hour trip from Capaci, Sicily to Manhattan. They had left Capaci at 9 o'clock in the morning to what would be an unforgettable send-off. It seemed like every relative and friend had made their way to 21 Via Grazziani to wish them *"buon viaggio."* After much hugging and kissing, Vincenzo, Rosaria and Maria had squeezed into Cousin Ciro's old Fiat for their ride to the airport. They had come to Capaci laden with three suitcases. Now, they were returning to America with four suitcases and two shopping bags—the extra suitcase and the shopping bags being needed to carry all the gifts they had received, plus an assortment of Sicilian food specialties.

Their flight from Palermo to Rome was uneventful, as was their flight from Rome to New York. The Pan Am Boeing 707 landed at Idlewild Airport at around 4:30 p.m. When the plane's wheels touched down on the runway, many passengers applauded—which seems to be an Italian custom. They passed through Passport Control and collected their baggage relatively quickly, but everything came to a halt when U. S. Customs detained them for a baggage inspection. Perhaps, the presence of the shopping bags had triggered the inspection.

The Customs inspectors proceeded to carefully remove all the contents from the shopping bags, placing some of the items to their left and some to their right. All the items placed to the right were foodstuff that wasn't sealed or packaged by a product manufacturer. Among those items were olive oil from Antonio's orchard—which had been funneled into two soda bottles— and some cheese and pepperoni wrapped in wax paper.

After the shopping bag search had been completed, the older inspector, who appeared to be of Italian descent, pointed to the items to his right and announced, "Mr. Rizzo, we are confiscating these items. You cannot bring them into the country."

Vincenzo stoically accepted the Customs officials' decision, but Rosaria became very upset and agitated about losing more than half the contents of the shopping bags. Speaking in broken English in a very respectful tone, she remarked, "Signore, we-ah good-ah, decent people. We-ah no *criminali*. We no wanna do anything-ah wrongah."

Ignoring her plea, the inspectors turned their attention to the four suitcases. The younger inspector picked-up the dark blue suitcase and the maroon suitcase from the family's unmatched luggage pieces and placed them on the counter. The inspectors opened both suitcases; the older inspector began to carefully remove the contents from the blue suitcase, while the younger inspector did likewise with the maroon suitcase. Fortunately for the Rizzos, both suitcases contained only clothing, including the family's dirty laundry.

When the younger inspector began to sift through the dirty laundry, Maria became extremely uneasy. Her feeling of uneasiness soon changed to mortification when the younger inspector "unfurled" her lacy black bikini panties and raised them up to eye level, as if to put them on display to all people standing nearby. "Ooh, very sexy," he said with a sly smile.

Embarrassed, Maria looked over towards her father with her head down. She could tell from the expression on his face that he was shocked that "his precious little girl" had taken to wearing such sexy underwear.

When the inspectors didn't find any contraband in the two suitcases, the older inspector made the decision not to check the other two suitcases, one of which, as it turns out, was loaded with all kinds of Sicilian goodies. *I've done enough checking,* he thought. *If some illegal foodstuff is in the other suitcases, so be it…let the nice Italian lady have her cherished olive oil, pepperoni and cheeses.*

Within minutes of clearing Customs, the Rizzos were in a taxi headed for home. About forty minutes later, the taxi crossed over the Brooklyn Bridge into Manhattan. Maria thought, *My, how I've forgotten how tall the buildings are and how much quicker things move around here. The difference between Manhattan and Capaci is like night and day.*

When Maria stepped out of the taxi, she looked at her watch and noted that the time was 7:15 p.m. It had been a grueling day for her and her family. She figured out that she had been up for close to twenty hours. Before climbing up the exterior metal stairway leading to her building's front door, she took a long, hard look around her. She had forgotten how dirty her neighborhood was and how rancid the air smelled, especially on hot, humid summer days. She gathered that the temperature was around 35 degrees Centigrade—about 95 degrees Fahrenheit. After having been in Sicily for nearly two months, she had become accustomed to thinking in terms of degrees Centigrade, kilograms and meters.

With great effort, the family managed to lug their suitcases and shopping bags four flights up to their apartment. When they reached their door, their next-door neighbors, Virginia and Pietro Pucci, came out to greet them. With the neighbors speaking in Sicilian, it felt like they hadn't left Capaci. After some warm hugs and kisses, Virginia briefly went into her apartment, returning with a quart of milk, a loaf of Italian bread, a dozen eggs and a dish of cooked pasta and eggplant.

"These will help you get along until you get a chance to go shopping."

"*Grazie,* Virginia, that is so thoughtful of you."

When the Rizzos finally entered their apartment, they immediately found it to be very stuffy, and stifling hot. Vincenzo made his way into the living room to open both windows, while Rosaria opened the two kitchen windows and Maria turned on all the fans.

Everyone was too tired to eat. Rosaria put the milk, eggs, and the pasta into the refrigerator, which, fortunately, was working well; so well, that she put her head into it for a few seconds to cool her face. Maria desperately wanted to take a bath. So she asked, "Do you think I'll be able to take a bath, Mama?"

"No, Maria, not now. There is too much to do. Besides, your father will be going in and out of the kitchen as we unpack and do what we have to do to get things back to normal…Take your bath in the morning."

"Okay, Mama, I understand."

The Rizzo apartment, like many other Lower East Side and Little Italy tenement apartments, had the bathtub in the kitchen, right next to the sink. When not being used as a bathtub, it was covered with a white, porcelain-enameled, metal cover, which also served as a very useful kitchen countertop. Clearly, taking a bath at that time would have been very disruptive to Vincenzo because he would have had to stay out of the kitchen while Maria bathed.

After some minor unpacking, while moving back and forth throughout the apartment, all were in bed by nine. Although Maria had thought that she would fall fast asleep as soon as her head hit the pillow, she wound up tossing and turning in bed for more than a half-hour. She was tormented by the thought that Lorenzo might have gotten her pregnant, despite Cousin Maria's reassurances and guarantees to the contrary. She wondered what her parents' reaction would be if she were to be pregnant. She knew one thing for sure: her father and mother would be devastated; they would consider her to be a disgrace—*una disgraziata*—to the family.

When the alarm clock rang at 4:45 a.m., Maria opened her eyes and thought, *Oh, it can't be time to get up, already*, but she then rolled over in bed after realizing that the alarm had been set by her father, who would be going back to work.

After a quick shave, a cup of coffee and a cigarette, Vincenzo was out the door on his way to Luigi's Fresh Fish Market. He arrived at the fish market, which was located on the corner of Mott and Hester Streets in the heart of Little Italy, at about 5:30 a.m. to a very warm greeting by Luigi and his two other employees. Speaking in Sicilian, Vincenzo said with a warm glow on his face, "Luigi, I cannot thank you enough for allowing me to stay in Sicily for seven weeks."

"Think nothing of it. I know that when one makes a trip back to our wonderful birthplace, even for a sad occasion, he must spend a decent amount of time there to see the family and to enjoy the beauty of the island. After all, one never knows when, or if, he will ever return."

Vincenzo replied, "I'm so fortunate to be working for a *paisano*. If I worked for an *Americano*, he would have wanted me back at work in a week, or two."

Vincenzo then handed Luigi a shopping bag full of ceramics and Sicilian goodies—gifts from him and Rosaria, as well as Luigi's sister and husband, who had never left Capaci.

Rosaria arose at seven, still feeling the effects of jet lag. She figured that Maria would be very tired, so she decided to let her sleep until she woke up naturally. Maria got out of bed at around nine, still feeling somewhat exhausted. She moped into the kitchen and sat down at the table. Rosaria quickly poured her a cup of hot coffee and soon followed with two pieces of toasted Italian bread. Speaking in the Sicilian dialect, she started the morning conversation by suggesting, "Maria, I think you might want to take your hot bath, now, while I start a wash."

Responding in the Sicilian dialect, which had now improved to the point where she could, almost pass herself off as a native Sicilian, she replied, "Mama, why don't you take a bath first, and I'll do the laundry." Her offer was made out of fear—not kindness—since she still worried that her mother might, somehow, find some "unexplainable" stains on her black bikini panties.

"No Maria, I'll start your bath while you finish your breakfast."

Rosaria picked up the countertop that covered the bathtub and began filling the tub with water. After finishing her breakfast, Maria disrobed in the kitchen and hopped into the tub, which sat relatively high compared to modern-day tubs. She was used to bathing in the kitchen while her mother did some chores or cooking—something that would seem very strange to most people these days.

Rosaria took a close look at her naked daughter and said, "Maria, your body has changed a lot over these past couple of months. You've matured. You now look like a young woman, with curves in all the right places."

"Yes Mama, my body *has* changed…and I'm glad it finally has happened. Last year, I hardly had a figure, and I was very envious of my classmates who already had 'developed'…which was most of them."

As Maria was soaping up, Rosaria was going through the dirty clothes. Since she had washed clothes quite often during their stay in Capaci, the pile of dirty clothes was small, only consisting of clothes from the last couple of days of the trip. When she began to unravel Maria's black bikini panties, Maria tried to distract her by asking, "What are we doing today?"

"After the wash is done, I'll hang most of the clothes out on the clothesline…I'll hang your panties in the toilet because we don't want any of our neighbors getting any bad ideas about you," she added with a laugh. "I know there's nothing wrong with wearing sexy underwear. In fact, I would wear them myself if I had your figure."

"Oh, I suppose you did have a figure like mine when you were young."

"Yes, I did…I did…Anyway, later, after we dust the furniture, we'll go out to do some food shopping."

"Okay, Mama."

When the washing machine started filling up with water, Maria felt a sigh of relief. She was off the hook; one less thing to worry about. Now her only remaining worry—the biggest one of all—was when, or if, she would get her period.

At around ten, she went into the living room to make some telephone calls. She first dialed Judy's number, but no one was home. She then called Felicia, only to be told by Serafina that she should call back around 4 o'clock because Felicia was at work at the lingerie shop. She then called "Fat" Angie, who was more of a lunch mate then a close friend. She normally didn't telephone Angie, but she was dying to speak to anyone to catch-up on what had happened while she was in Sicily.

She started the conversation by telling Angie about the funeral, the beauty of Sicily and how much she had enjoyed meeting her family whom she had never met. The fact was that she had no close relatives in America. All of her aunts, uncles and first cousins lived in Capaci. The same held true for her second and third cousins. From the point of view of her Sicilian relatives, her father and mother were something like "pioneers" settling in the New World.

Angie related how she had met this nice, funny, heavy-set guy at Felicia's Sweet Sixteen Party. Everyone called him "Shortie," so she had taken to calling him by that name since he seemed to prefer it. She added that his real name was Eddie Rodriguez, and that he was a Puerto Rican.

"Angie, do you know if Judy is around?"

"No, I think she's up in the Poconos for the last two weeks of the summer…Part 2 of her family's summer vacation."

"Did you meet any nice guys in Sicily, Maria?"

"Well, I met this really handsome guy named Lorenzo, and we dated a bit."

At the point in the conversation, Rosaria yelled across the apartment, "Maria, I need you to help me clean the house!"

"Okay Mama, I'll be right there…Angie, I gotta hang up, now. I'll tell you more when I see you at school."

The rest of the week was a blur to Maria. Between the jet lag, the chores and going shopping for clothes with her mother, the time just seemed to evaporate. Of course, she constantly worried about whether or not she had gotten pregnant. Ironically, she would seek the help of God many times that week, begging, *Please God, don't let me be pregnant.*

On Saturday morning, her prayers were answered—she got her period just as Cousin Maria had said that she would. "Whew!" she said aloud in the privacy of the apartment's tiny toilet, feeling like a huge weight had been lifted from her shoulders.

At around four in the afternoon, she walked over to Nativity Church, which is located on Second Avenue, between Second and Third Streets. Within minutes, she was kneeling inside Father Sanfratello's confessional. Speaking softly, and with a "frog" in her throat, she confessed that she had had her first sexual experiences during a recent visit to Sicily and that these experiences included losing her virginity. Father Sanfratello, who was also of Sicilian heritage, seemed to be somewhat understanding and non-judgmental at first, and the tone of his voice was comforting and forgiving. He then proceeded to ask her probing questions relating to the details of her sexual activities. Her answers were repeatedly followed by, "What did he do next?" or "What did you do next?" It seemed to her that the good priest wanted to know far more than he needed to know to absolve her of her sins; but she dutifully complied, answering his questions and providing all the lurid details.

Once Father Sanfratello's prurient curiosity had been satisfied, he followed-up with a fusillade of reprimands, trying to instill the fear of God in her for her egregious sins. When Maria, almost in tears, convinced him that she was truly sorry for her sins, he absolved her, gave her a penance of twenty *Hail Marys* and twenty *Our Fathers*, and commanded, "Now, let me hear you say a good…and I mean a good, heartfelt, *Act of Contrition.*"

While reciting her prayers of penance, she could not help but think that she had gotten off relatively easy. The haunting question in the back of her mind was whether or not she would ever again engage in premarital sex. Her answer to her own question was that it would be very, very unlikely that she ever would; however, juxtaposed to that thought, she could hear the voice of her devilish cousin, Maria, in her head saying, *Have fun! Life is short! What do the priests know about love?*

The next week-and-a-half went by quickly for Maria. The Labor Day Weekend had been uneventful, and soon it was Wednesday, September 4th — the first day of school. That morning, when she slipped into her dowdy Basilica High School uniform, she was quite pleased with her image in the full-length mirror. In her eyes, she appeared more shapely; she filled-out her blouse better; her skirt fit looser; and her legs appeared to be thinner. Plus, her hair was far more stylish than it used to be.

At about 7:45 a.m., Maria, running a bit late, made her way to the nearest IRT Subway station, which was located on Bleecker and Lafayette Streets. She had hoped to meet Judy at the station, but she was nowhere to be seen. She reasoned that Judy, who had a reputation for always being early, had likely boarded the train well before Maria had arrived at the station.

She walked into her homeroom about three minutes before the start of the first period, leaving her no time to chat with her classmates. As she entered her first class, she reflected back on her very first day at Basilica High School, which seemed just like yesterday to her. Now she was starting her senior year and she would soon be meeting with her guidance counselors who would be preparing her for admission to college.

After her fourth period class had ended, she made her way to the lunchroom, eagerly anticipating the chance to talk to her girlfriends, whom she hadn't seen in more than two months. After buying lunch, she found her three usual lunch mates already seated at their favorite table, eating and gabbing away. At that point, "Fat" Angie was discussing her summer romance with Shortie.

"I wanna tell you, Felicia, I'm so glad I met Shortie at your Sweet Sixteen Party. I know he's a little stout, and he might not be what one would describe as handsome, but he's so much fun to be with. We laugh all the time. Plus, he's so warm, kind, and gentle. The only problem is that he's a Puerto Rican, and some people in my family don't like the idea of me datin' a Puerto Rican."

"Yeah," Judy blurted, "I know my parents wouldn't want me datin' a Puerto Rican."

Angie responded, "Well, my mother met Shortie the other day, and I think he may have won her over with his charm and sense of humor."

"How was the Poconos, Judy?"

"I had a great time in the Poconos, Maria. My family and I went there for the first two weeks of July. Then, in early August, my father told us that we would be goin' back to the Poconos for the last two weeks of the summer. We got home on Labor Day evenin'. Both times, we stayed at a hotel that caters to Polish people. In July, I became friendly with one of the waiters. We began datin' and we would spend as much time as we could together …although, he didn't have that much free time since he had to work about twelve hours a day with no days off. His name is Tommy Albinski…a good Polish name. He's nineteen years old and about six feet tall. He's thin but muscular, very good looking, and he has blonde wavy hair. He lives in Jersey City, but he says he can make it into lower Manhattan on the Hudson Tubes in about twenty minutes. I'm sure I'll be seein' him again real soon."

"Felicia, how are you doin' with John-John?" asked Angie.

"Well, I'm coolin' it a bit with him. He's the love of my life, but one time when we made-out in my hallway, he got a little too fresh with me…if you know what I mean?"

"No, I don't know what you mean. Details…Give us details!" Angie demanded.

Felicia responded, "He had his hands all over me, including under my skirt…and…"

"And what?" Angie further demanded.

"Never mind what!" Let's just say that when I told Father Montevecchio about that make-out session, he told me to stay away from John-John until I'm more mature…until after I'm at least seventeen."

Everyone was surprised when Maria blurted out, "Why listen to the priest? What do priests know about love?" To the girls, it seemed so out of character for Maria to say something like that, but she was just echoing the philosophy of Cousin Maria.

Maria continued, "If you cool it with John-John, he'll likely meet somebody else…maybe, a college girl."

Felicia replied, "That's a chance I gotta take. By the way, when I say that I'm coolin' things with him, I don't mean that I'm droppin' him. I still intend to date him occasionally…just enough to keep him interested in me. Anyway, once he starts his engineerin' studies, he'll hardly have any time for datin'."

"That's true," Judy interjected, "My cousin was studyin' engineering. It's so difficult that he almost had a nervous breakdown."

Felicia continued, "In my heart, I know that someday, John-John and I will get married. I think I've loved him from the first time I laid eyes on him standin' at Joe's Newsstand. My only real problem is to get my parents to like him, particularly, my mother. She always refers to him…excuse me, Maria…as that '*Siciliano bastardo,*' especially since she considers him to be the ringleader of the rowdy bunch of guys that hang out at the newsstand. Anyway, I plan to invite him up to my apartment durin' the holidays to have coffee and pastries with my family. I hope that once my parents really get to know him, they'll change their opinion of him. Plus, they should realize that he has a great future ahead of him and the girl that he marries will live quite well."

Changing the course of the conversation towards Maria, Judy commented, "Maria, you look fabulous! What a difference between June and now. Your body had changed for the better and your face looks great without those God-awful braces and those ugly, horn-rimmed glasses.

"Well, I still wear my eyeglasses in class and to watch TV."

Angie remarked, "Even your posture has improved…you no longer slouch."

Felicia added, "I love your new hairstyle, Maria. Where did you get it?"

I went to this great hairstylist in Capaci, about a month after we arrived in Sicily. The day before we returned to America, I stopped by his beauty salon for another one of his stylish haircuts."

"Enough about haircuts! Maria tell us about Lorenzo." Angie interjected.

Simultaneously, Judy and Felicia both said, "Who's Lorenzo?"

"I started to tell Angie about Lorenzo when I spoke to her on the telephone shortly after I returned to America…Lorenzo is this tall, handsome, nineteen-year-old Sicilian guy that I met in Capaci.

We hit it off really well and we began dating." "Where did he take you?" asked Judy.

Blushing, Maria responded, "To my uncle's orchard. Our dates were actually make-out sessions beneath an olive tree."

At that point, Angie, who always got to the heart of the matter without mincing words, said, "I hear those guys in Italy are really fast operators. How far did he get with you? Did you let him go 'all the way'?"

Maria stammered, "Um…well…no…no…we didn't go all the way."

To Felicia, Maria's response sounded a bit fishy—as if she were trying to hide something. *Did Maria actually go all the way with some Sicilian guy?* she wondered.

Maria wanted to get off the subject of Lorenzo, so she steered the conversation in another direction. "Guess what? I've taken up smoking."

"Welcome to the club," said Judy.

"Yeah, welcome to the club," seconded Angie.

"Felicia, that leaves you as the only non-smoker in our group,"

"I don't think I wanna take up smokin', Judy."

"I felt the same way, Felicia. But, after my cousin persuaded me to have a cigarette, I soon found that I liked smoking…that is, once I got past the choking and coughing, which didn't take very long. I find smoking to be very calming and relaxing…and it makes me feel like a sophisticated young woman. Why don't you give it a try, Felicia?"

"No, I think I'll wait."

"By the way, I haven't had a cigarette since I got back from Sicily. I'm really dying for a smoke. I'd love to have a cigarette when school lets out. Do either of you have any cigarettes?"

"I'm out of them," replied Angie.

"Yeah, I got two left, Maria. You can have one with me when we're a block away from the school," said Judy.

When 3 o'clock came, Maria found Judy waiting for her at the school entrance. They walked off together, chatting mostly about Sicily and Uncle Pino's funeral. About a block from the school, Judy stopped and reached into her handbag, pulling out a pack of Salem cigarettes. She handed Maria one of the two remaining cigarettes. Judy lit-up first. Maria soon followed. She savored every puff— inhaling deeply and exhaling slowly.

"Do you like the taste of the cigarette, Maria?"

"Yeah, it's pretty good."

"Why don't you buy a pack?"

"No, I don't want to buy my own pack because I'm afraid my mother will find it in my handbag, or wherever else I might try to hide it."

"Okay, I got an idea. You buy yourself a pack of cigarettes, today, and I'll hold them for you. It's no problem for me because my parents know I smoke. The way I figure it, you can have one cigarette before we get on the subway to school, and one up here after school…and maybe, another cigarette on our walk home from the subway. Also, on nights and weekends when we go out together, you'll be able to smoke *your* cigarettes…as many as you want. A pack should last you about five or six days."

"Sounds good to me, Judy."

After finishing their smokes, the girls went into a nearby drugstore and they each bought a pack of Salems for 35 cents.

Upon exiting the subway at the Bleecker Street stop, Maria asked Judy for *her* pack of cigarettes. She gingerly opened her very first pack, pulled out a cigarette and lit it up.

"Here, Judy, have one of my cigarettes."

"Thanks, Maria."

By the time the girls made it to the Bowery, there was almost nothing left of their cigarettes. So, they extinguished them against a building wall, and like typical New Yorkers of that time, threw the butts into the gutter.

"Perfect timing, Judy. I'm glad we were able to finish our cigarettes before we crossed the Bowery. You know, I don't want to take the chance of going past the Bowery with a cigarette in my hand. You never know who might see me."

Chapter 29: Joe's Just Desserts

There was a little more hustle and bustle in the neighborhood as its yearly street festival, the Feast of San Gennaro, was about to begin. The feast would extend along Mulberry Street for six blocks, beginning or ending—depending upon one's perspective—on Spring Street, directly across from John-John's building. The feast, which had become increasingly popular over the years, had made Mulberry Street synonymous with Little Italy.

"Good mornin', Joe. Did you see John-John this mornin'?"

"Yeah, Danny, he passed by when I was openin' the stand. He said he was goin' up to Columbia to meet with his advisors and to register…and that he should be back around three."

"You know that today is the first day of San Gennaro's Feast… Right?"

"Of course I know. The feast starts today at around noon… it always starts on a Thursday…and this year, it'll end on Sunday, September 22nd."

"Well, since I won't be startin' my job at Pan Am's flight control office until mid-October, I got myself a job workin' at Caffé Roma durin' the feast as a waiter workin' the outside tables…you know, servin' pastries, coffee, cappuccino, etc. Today and tomorrow, I'll be workin' from noon until six. I don't know my schedule for the rest of the feast, yet, but I suppose I'll be working some nights, too… depends on the manager."

"Good for you Danny. I'm sure you could use a few bucks until you start your full-time job. Will you be workin' at Idlewild Airport?"

"Yeah, I'll be workin' at Idlewild, but it's a little hard to get to. I'll have to take the subway and a bus, but I'll be workin' for one of the world's best airlines…Pan Am. When I save-up enough money, I'll buy myself a good used car to commute to the airport…and, of course, to drive around for fun."

"Was it hard to get a job at Caffé Roma?"

"Nah, they need a lot of help durin' the feast. In fact, Frankie will be workin' there too. He's startin' with me today, at noon."

"Won't he be in school until three?"

"He's supposed to be in school, but he's cuttin' out at eleven. He doesn't care. He's a 'super-senior.' Last night he said to me, "What the fuck are they gonna do to me, keep me for a sixth year?"

"You know Danny, the Feast of San Gennaro means a lot to me. First, because I'm a Neapolitan, and second, because my daughter, Clara, was born on San Gennaro's Feast Day."

Joe's feelings about San Gennaro were instilled in him by his parents who had been born in Naples. San Gennaro is the patron saint of Naples. He was martyred in the year 305. Over the years, the Neapolitans have sought the help of San Gennaro during times of war, earthquakes, famine, and pestilence, and to solve personal problems. In Naples, where a specimen of San Gennaro's dry blood is kept in a phial, the blood is said to liquefy every September 19th, which is the feast day of San Gennaro. The first Feast of San Gennaro in New York City was held on September 19, 1926. It was a one-day event sponsored by a group of Neapolitans living in Little Italy. The festival eventually evolved into an eleven-day event, which always includes two weekends and the September 19th feast day.

At that point, Frankie arrived at the newsstand. "Hi Joe. Yo, 'Plumber'."
"Hey Frankie, you're early."

"Yeah, I decided to skip school altogether, today, Danny. It would've been too much of a hassle to go there for two-and-a-half hours, so I slept until nine. I needed the rest."

"Why do you need to rest, Frankie? You don't do a fuckin' thing," Joe remarked.

"Well, I stood up until about one o'clock in the morning to watch the *Late Show* last night. I enjoy stayin' up late. You know, I think I'll do the same thing tonight."

"You'll never get anywhere in life if you don't get a high school diploma, Frankie."

"Don't worry, Joe, I'll get my diploma even if it takes me six fuckin' years."

"Hey, guys, I'd like you to do me a favor."

"What's the favor, Joe?" Danny quickly responded.

"I'd like you to get me a dozen Italian pastries from Caffé Roma 'on the arm'…you know…for free."

"This is our first day of work there, Joe. How the fuck do you expect us to get you a free dozen pastries? Why don't you just pay for them?" Frankie replied.

"'Cause free is much better…C'mon, I know you guys can do it. If you have a problem, just tell the manager that they're for the blind newsman on Spring and Lafayette."

"Okay, Joe," Danny remarked, "We'll give it a try, but no guarantees."

As Danny and Frankie made their way to Caffé Roma, which was (and still is) located on Mulberry and Broome Streets, they discussed what to do about Joe's request. After about five minutes, Danny suggested that they should play a nasty practical joke on Joe: Instead of trying to get him the free pastries, they would give him a pastry box filled with garbage. After all, they reasoned, wasn't it Joe who had instigated many of the crew's practical jokes, including the box of garbage given to Felicia on her fifteenth birthday?

After waitering for about three hours, Danny and Frankie left their posts for a few minutes and quickly collected various items that feast-goers had carelessly dropped or intentionally discarded in the street. These items included, a half-eaten jelly apple, a corncob, some cotton candy remnants, and one-third of a slimy sausage-and-peppers sandwich. They grabbed a pastry box from behind the front counter, brought it to the back room, and filled it with the refuse. Being well aware that Joe had an exceptional sense of smell, they sprinkled a lot of powdered sugar all over the contents of the box. They then closed the box, tied it with string and placed it in the refrigerator, figuring that the box should be cold; if not, Joe might get suspicious.

Shortly after six, Danny and Frankie approached the newsstand, grinning from ear to ear. John-John, Shortie, Charlie the "Ox" and Vinnie "Lemons" were hanging out at the newsstand talking to Joe, who was telling them that he always made more money during the feast because many more people passed by his stand.

"Hey, Joe," Danny blurted out, "We got you a dozen free pastries!"

"It wasn't easy," added Frankie, "But we managed to get you the pastries."

"Great, guys! You're the best. I can't wait to bring 'em home and eat 'em tonight with my wife and family."

As Joe grabbed the box from Danny and put it in a shopping bag, Danny and Frankie winked at the guys and motioned that they should join them behind the newsstand. Once safely out of Joe's hearing range, they let the guys in on the practical joke. Everyone thought it was funny. Joe, the practical joker, would get his "just desserts"—so to speak. No one thought of the embarrassment and anguish that Joe would feel when his wife would open the pastry box.

At around seven, Joe asked, "Hey, guys, would you keep the newsstand open for another hour? I wanna get an early start home, so me and my family can enjoy the pastries, tonight.... you know, when it's not too late."

"No problem, Joe," replied several of the guys in unison.

At that point, a bell rang in John-John's head. He suddenly thought that the practical joke might not be taken so lightly by Joe's wife. He considered telling Joe that the box contained garbage—not pastries. But, he knew if he did so, his good buddies would ostracize him. So, he kept silent.

Joe arrived at his apartment in the Bronx at around 8:30 p.m. He had made great time, spending just a few minutes waiting on the subway platforms for each of the three trains that comprised his commute. As he walked through the door of his apartment, he happily blurted out, "Hey, Virginia, I brought home some goodies...a dozen pastries from Caffé Roma...and they didn't cost me a dime. Danny and Frankie, two of the young guys who hang-out at the newsstand, got me the pastries for free. They're both workin' at Caffé Roma durin' the feast."

"Great! I could really go for some pastries right after you eat dinner."

Virginia served Joe some meatloaf and potatoes and then started brewing a pot of coffee. She told her unmarried daughter, Clara, to come into the kitchen in about ten minutes to join them for coffee and pastries. While the coffee was brewing, she went next door to her married daughter Anna's apartment and invited her and her husband, Paul, to come over.

Virginia poured the coffee a few minutes after Joe finished his dinner, She smiled as she placed the pastry box on the table and cut the string. When she lifted the cover of the box, she let out a loud scream, followed by, "Those bastards! Those dirty little bastards! How could they do this to you!"

Joe didn't know what to make of her sudden tirade. He couldn't figure out what the problem was until he heard his son-in-law yell, "Dad, the pastry box is filled with garbage, covered with powdered sugar!"

Virginia added, "I've got a good mind to go down to the newsstand with you tomorrow and throw the garbage in the faces of those snot-noses!"

"Do you know their telephone numbers, Dad?"

"Why, Anna?"

"I'd like to call up their mothers and tell 'em what their sons did to a poor, defenseless blind man."

"Maybe, their parents are a bunch of low-lifes," blurted Clara.

"I don't know their telephone numbers…but their parents are good people…not low-lifes," Joe responded with a sense of despair in his voice.

The following morning, Joe commuted to the newsstand by himself—as usual—glad that he had convinced Virginia not to come along to encounter Danny and Frankie. He was still seething, mostly due to the reaction of his wife and family. Yet, on another level, he actually appreciated the skillful execution of the practical joke—even though he had been the butt of it.

Danny and Frankie arrived at the newsstand at around eleven, dying to find out how their practical joke had gone down. They knew full well that Joe would be mad at them.

"Good mornin', Joe," they both said, almost simultaneously.

"Good mornin'," Joe replied softly and in a surprisingly friendly tone.

"How were the pastries?" Frankie inquired, holding back a laugh.

While reaching for his "pee jar"—his portable toilet—he replied, "Yeah, you guys really got me good."

Danny and Frankie let out a hearty laugh. Since the newsstand's window was relatively high above the sidewalk, it was not possible for them to see Joe reach for the jar, which was half-filled with Joe's urine; nor could they see him unscrew the lid.

"What did your wife do when she opened the pastry box?" Danny asked.

"Well, at first she got mad, but believe it or not, she soon began to laugh."

"Really?" questioned Frankie, somewhat relieved.

"Yeah, really."

Gaining Danny and Frankie's confidence—to the extent that they had dropped their guards—Joe quickly flung the contents of his infamous pickle jar out the window in the direction of the two, who were standing side-by-side. Fortunately for them, they each were hit with only a light spray of Joe's piss, but they had gotten wet enough to relearn a lesson: Don't mess with Joe!

"Hey, you don't know how lucky you are that my wife didn't come down here with me. She woulda given you guys a piece of her mind…and let me tell you, she can be nasty! She probably woulda found your mothers and told them what you did…and knowing your mothers the way I do, they probably woulda smacked ya around."

"Listen, Joe, we're sorry…we'll try to make it up to you," said Danny.

"Yeah, we'll try to make it up to you," seconded Frankie.

Chapter 30: The Feast

The "lunch mates" were at their usual table at Basilica High School gabbing away, mostly on their favorite subject—boys. Then, "Fat" Angie changed the subject. "Do you girls realize that today is Friday the Thirteenth?"

"No responded Maria, I hadn't noticed."

"Yeah, it's supposed to be a very unlucky day," added Felicia.

"I don't believe in that stuff," countered Judy.

"I do," said Angie, with a very convincing expression on her face. "My cousin Robert was hit by a car on a Friday the Thirteenth, and about ten years ago, my father was fired from his job as a butcher on Friday the Thirteenth."

"Do any of you girls know the fancy word for the fear of the number thirteen?" asked Maria.

Each girl nodded her head from side to side.

"Who cares if there is such a word," said Angie, "I'm sure I'll never use it in a sentence, Maria."

"Well, the word is 'triskaidekaphobia'…and believe it or not, there's an even bigger word specifically for the fear of *Friday* the Thirteenth. That word is 'friggatriskaidekaphobia.'"

"How do you know this crap?"

"I read Angie. I read. I borrow books from the library. Maybe, you should try it some time," replied Maria with a laugh.

Felicia joined in, "Look at Angie's textbooks. They look like they've never been opened! I doubt she would ever step in a library."

"Yeah that's true," but there's a lot more to life than buryin' your head in books like my studious friend Maria, here. Except for a little romance in Sicily, she has been leadin' a pretty dull life…socially, that is."

Maria responded, "Angie, that may be true, but reading is really a wonderful thing. It's both a form of learning and a form of escape. You can go all over the world, and back in time, without ever leaving the comfort of your living room sofa."

"You're really startin' to sound like a nerd, Maria," remarked Angie, while shaking her head disapprovingly.

"Felicia, did San Gennaro's Feast start yet?"

"Yeah, Judy, it started yesterday."

"I'd like to go to the feast, tonight. What about you, Maria?" asked Judy.

"Yeah, that sounds like a good idea. Why don't we all go?"

"Okay," replied Felicia.

"Okay with me." added Angie. "But you realize that I basically live in the feast since my apartment is on Mulberry Street, between Broome and Grand."

Maria suggested, "Felicia, suppose Judy and I come over to your apartment around seven. After we arrive, you can phone Angie to tell her that we're on our way. Then, the three of us will walk through the feast and meet her in front of her building about fifteen minutes later."

Felicia and Angie both agreed. Soon the lunch period was over, and the girls went off to their respective classes.

At about ten minutes to seven in the evening, Maria and Judy arrived at the corner of Spring and Lafayette. They were standing within ten feet of Joe's Newsstand looking perplexed because neither of them knew in which of the nearby buildings Felicia lived. Maria had assumed that Judy knew the address, while Judy had assumed that Maria—who seemed to know everything—surely knew where Felicia lived.

John-John, Danny, Frankie, Vinnie "Lemons" and Joey "Smiles," who were milling about the newsstand, couldn't help but notice the two attractive girls standing nearby. "Are you girls lost?" Danny inquired in a gentlemanly fashion.

"We're looking for Felicia Daniels. We know she lives somewhere around here, but we don't know which building she lives in," remarked Maria.

"Do you know her? Do you know where she lives?" asked Judy.

"Do we know her? Sure we do! Hey, John-John, tell these beautiful girls where Felicia lives…after all, you're her boyfriend."

At that point, Maria took a good look at the tall, handsome young man that Danny had addressed, and she realized that he was the cute guy in the photo that Felicia had shown her on several occasions in the cafeteria.

"Well, I wouldn't say that we're boyfriend and girlfriend. We're not going steady…but the answer to your question is that she lives over there…the third building from the corner, on the first floor."

Maria's eyes locked-in on John-John. She thought to herself that he was even better looking in person. She really felt drawn to him as if by magnetism. Then, the usually shy Maria did something out of character: She walked over to John-John and introduced herself and Judy to him.

"Hi John-John, my name is Maria…and this is Judy. We both go to school with Felicia. We're going to take a walk in the feast with her and then we'll meet our classmate, Angie, there."

John-John grasped Maria's hand and gazed into her eyes. "Nice to meet you, Maria." He suddenly felt a "certain something" that he couldn't describe. John-John continued, "Nice to meet you, Judy. Where are you girls from?"

"We both live off Second Avenue. I live on Second Street and Maria lives on First Street."

Maria thought, *Wow, what a great guy! I thought that Lorenzo was something special, but John-John is a dreamboat. Too bad he's dating Felicia.*

At that point, Danny made a beeline over to Judy, attracted by her blonde hair and fair Polish-Ukrainian looks, which were in sharp contrast to his dark Italian features. As he was making small talk with Judy, John-John did likewise with Maria, while continually eying her up and down. He was taken by her beauty, but as their conversation progressed, he was also taken by her apparent intelligence, which was reflected in the way she spoke. He noticed that she didn't have much of a Lower East Side accent; that she didn't drop her "g's" and that she didn't replace her "r's" with "w's"—pronouncing "New York" properly, as opposed to pronouncing it as "New Yawk."

"John-John, I hear that you will soon be studying engineering at Columbia University."

"You certainly know a lot about me."

"Well, Felicia told me that you were going to be a freshman at Columbia's School of Engineering."

"Are you interested in going to college?"

"Oh, yes. I plan to study marine biology…but I have a problem."

"Academics?"

"No, I have over a 90 average. My problem is that I can't swim… and I'm sure a marine biologist should be able to swim."

"Well, I'm sure you can learn. It's not hard once you overcome the fear of drowning."

"By the way, Felicia said that you're Sicilian, but she never mentioned what town your family is from."

"They're from Monreale, but they both came to America when they were young children. They were introduced to each other in America by some *paisani* when they were teenagers."

"My family comes from Capaci. Monreale is only about four or five miles from Capaci. Monreale is a beautiful town. I visited it in early August. It has a very impressive cathedral with gold mosaics… the most gold mosaics in all of Europe, they say."

At that point, Joey "Smiles" introduced himself to Maria. He was a newcomer to the newsstand crew. He used to hang-out on Hester Street, but his friend, Donny "Knobhead," had recently introduced him to the Sheiks and he found them—as well as Joe—to be much more fun than the guys on Hester Street. The nickname "Smiles" was an obvious choice because he appeared to be smiling all the time. His teeth were very white and prominent, and he looked like he had forty-two of them instead of the normal thirty-two.

Maria politely responded to Joey's introduction, "Hi, Joey. Nice to meet you." She then turned her head away and returned to her conversation with John-John.

"Maria, we better go up to Felicia's apartment, now."

"Okay, Judy…just a second."

With her head tilted, a broad smile on her face and a little bit of laughter in her voice, Maria continued, "John-John, it was really nice meeting you…I mean *really* nice."

As the girls walked towards Felicia's apartment, John-John took note of the back view, concluding that they looked as good from behind as they did from the front.

"Hey, John-John, I got Judy's phone number."

"Danny, you're one fast operator. None of the Sheiks would've been able to get a girl's phone number as fast as you…especially a pretty girl's phone number."

"I was thinking of asking Judy out for this Sunday. I guess I'll make it a lunch date because I gotta be at work at Caffé Roma at 6 o'clock on Sunday. Would you be interested in 'doubling' with Judy and me? I noticed that you were fixated on her friend, Maria…You couldn't take your eyes off her." Then he added with a chuckle, "I bet you didn't know I knew the word 'fixated.'"

"No, you surprised me with the use of that word, Danny. Let me tell you, that girl, Maria…Wow! She's beautiful, intelligent, well-spoken and she's even a Sicilian, but…"

"But what?"

"She's a very good friend of Felicia, and I still have feelings for Felicia even though, lately, I'm hardly ever alone with her."

"Look, you shouldn't pass up this opportunity. First of all, your romance with Felicia ain't what it used to be…and second of all, you're a Sheik …you're supposed to be a ladies man, and you can't be much of a ladies man if you just stick to Felicia."

"No, Danny, I just don't feel it's right to drop Felicia for one of her friends."

Then Joey "Smiles" interjected, "Hey, John-John, I overheard what you were just sayin' to Danny. If you're not interested, I'll gladly go on the double-date…You're not interested, right?"

"No, Joey, I guess I'm *not* interested."

"Good…Danny, see if you can arrange the double-date. I think Maria will remember me."

"Okay, I'll give Judy a call tomorrow and try to set it up. I was thinkin' of takin' the girls to lunch at Katz's Delicatessen."

"Fine with me, Danny."

About ten minutes later, Felicia, Judy and Maria passed by the newsstand en route to the feast. Surprisingly, Felicia gave John-John a hug, and a big kiss on the lips, seemingly unworried that word might get back to her parents. Her sudden display of affection was a way of marking her turf, for she had sensed that Maria had become infatuated with John-John. Up in the apartment, Maria had repeatedly told her how handsome and bright John-John was and how lucky she was to have him as her boyfriend.

As the three girls walked through the feast, Maria couldn't help but talk about John-John—reiterating his fine points when they met up with Angie. By then, Felicia had had enough. Yelling over the din of the festival, she exclaimed, "Listen Maria, don't you get no ideas about John-John! He's mine! You hear? He's mine!"

"Don't worry, I know he's yours. I was just saying how handsome and bright he is as a compliment to your taste. I'm sorry you took it the wrong way. Please forgive me. I'm not trying to step in."

"Yeah…okay, Maria…I forgive you."

Although Maria had sought Felicia's forgiveness, deep down inside she was hoping that, someday, Felicia and John-John would no longer be an item…and if that day ever came, she would certainly try to date him.

On Saturday morning, Danny telephoned Judy to set-up the double-date. She quickly agreed to the date, presuming that Maria would have no objections. Minutes later, Judy called Maria.

"Hi, Maria, Danny from the newsstand just called to ask us out for a lunch date, tomorrow, at Katz's."

"What do you mean, *us*?"

"Well, I'll be with Danny and you'll be with that guy, Joey 'Smiles.'"

"I don't think I want to go out with him. Why did you ever agree without asking me first?"

"Maria, if you don't wanna go, I'll call him back and tell him… but that would probably ruin my chance of seein' Danny…and I really like him."

"Oh, okay…being it's only for lunch, I guess I'll go, Judy…but don't ever do that to me again."

The lunch date was uneventful, but the food was great. The pastrami and the corn beef were lean, the pickles were very tasty, and the French fries were perfectly golden brown. The Dr. Brown's sodas only added to the experience. The sandwiches were so thick that Maria could only eat half. Joey "Smiles," who had a great appetite, wasn't embarrassed to eat the other half of her pastrami sandwich. Maria found Joey to be a nice guy—in the truest definition of the term "nice guy"—but she didn't find him physically appealing, and more important, she didn't feel the "sparks" that she had felt when she first met Lorenzo, or when she had spoken to John-John at the newsstand.

After leaving Katz's, they began walking west on Houston Street towards Greenwich Village. It was a very pleasant day for a walk, and the walk helped to promote the digestion of the fatty delicatessen food. During the walk, Maria would occasionally ask questions about John-John, including questions relating to his feelings for Felicia. Danny offered his opinion: "Look, I think he has a warm spot for her mainly because they shared their first kiss together. But, I think they'll eventually grow apart, especially when he gets to meet some college hotties this year…besides, they haven't had any real make-out sessions in a couple of months."

After walking through the arch in Washington Square Park and looking at some paintings that some artists were trying to sell along the perimeter of the park, they started heading towards Little Italy. When they reached the intersection of Prince and Mercer Streets, Danny "steered" the couples into a right turn onto Mercer. Although the others may have thought that they were just meandering their way to Little Italy, Danny had something else in mind: He knew that *that* block would be totally deserted on a Sunday since all the buildings—which were either factories or lofts—would be closed. He wanted to get "cozy" with Judy, and he figured that there were many good make-out spots on the block to choose from. He wasn't sure if Joey would follow his lead and make-out with Maria, but he really didn't care what they would do as long as they gave him and Judy some privacy.

Danny and Judy lingered a bit allowing Joey and Maria to go on ahead. About halfway down the block, Danny and Judy disappeared into a deep cubbyhole, which was actually the entrance to a factory. Joey and Maria soon sensed that they were alone on the sidewalk. When they instinctively glanced back, Danny and Judy were nowhere in sight. It was obvious that the two had slipped away to make-out. Not wanting to be out-done, Joey guided Maria into another cubbyhole. He grabbed her tightly and began to kiss her. She didn't resist because she was curious to see how his kisses would compare to Lorenzo's. She soon realized that while Lorenzo's kisses had been tender and passionate, Joey's kisses were stiff and somewhat harsh—the harshness exacerbated by his large, protruding teeth. She tried her best to get into the moment, but she just couldn't. She did let him feel her up a little, but when he tried to put his hand into her blouse, she stopped him, by firmly saying, "No!"

After about ten minutes with Joey, Maria said, "I think I need a cigarette." She reached into her handbag and found the pack of Salems that Judy had been holding for her all week. She lit-up and then offered a cigarette to Joey.

"Thanks, Maria. I like a girl who smokes. At least I won't have to explain my habit to her."

"I picked up smoking this summer when I was in Sicily. Have you ever been to Sicily?"

"No, but I would like to go to Italy, someday. I have some long-lost relatives in Naples."

When they finished their cigarettes, they noticed that Danny and Judy had made their way back onto the sidewalk, and that they were smiling and giggling while walking hand-in-hand. The couples continued their walk back to the neighborhood. When they reached Joe's Newsstand, Judy and Maria said good-bye and headed for home. While walking up Lafayette Street, Judy asked, "Whatta ya think of Joey?"

"He's a nice guy, but I don't think he's my type. What do you think of Danny?"

"Oh, he's a really great guy…and boy, can he make-out. He has soft lips and big hands. By the way, you know what they say about guys with big hands, don't you?"

"No, what do they say?"

"Well, they say guys with big hands are big somewhere else, if you know what I mean."

A giggling Maria responded, "Oh, I guess they haven't covered that in my biology class, yet."

"Guess what? Danny would like to set-up another double-date for next Sunday. Are you interested?"

"Not really. As I said, Joey's not my type."

"Would you do it for my sake? Danny seems to like the idea of double-datin'."

"I don't know Judy, I really didn't care for Joey very much."

"Give him a chance. Maybe, you'll like him more on the second date."

"Okay, okay…I'll go, Judy…I'll give it one more chance, but I'm doing it for you, not for me."

"Thanks, I owe you one."

Chapter 31: Back to Work

The telephone rang in the Daniels' apartment at around nine in the morning. Serafina, who was sipping her second cup of coffee, sashayed over to the telephone in the living room and picked-up the receiver on the fourth ring,

"Hello. Is this Serafina…Serafina Daniels?" asked the unidentified male voice, speaking with a slight Eastern European accent.

"*Sì*, this-ah Serafina."

"This is Izzie. I got good news for you. We just got two big contracts and we will soon be getting back into full production. The layoff is over! We need you to come back to work next Monday."

"Oh, thank God…Izzie, do you-ah mean-ah this-ah Monday or next-ah Monday?"

"Well Serafina, when I said next Monday I meant the Monday that is five days from today…Monday, September 23rd."

"Oh, you-ah mean-ah this-ah Monday."

"Call it whatever you like, but I expect to see you back at work on Monday morning, September 23rd."

"Very well-ah. I'll-ah be there-ah…*Ciao.*"

She had mixed feelings about going back to work. On one hand, she was happy because her family could certainly use more money, especially since she knew that Zeke's overtime wouldn't last forever; but, on the other hand, she had gotten used to not having to spend eight hours a day, five days a week behind a sweatshop sewing machine. She enjoyed having some time for herself. Of course, she still had much to do as a housewife: cooking; washing clothes; ironing; food shopping; house cleaning; and taking care of her children's needs. But, when she was working, she still was expected to do all those chores, anyway.

Her thoughts soon shifted to how her return to work would affect her trysts with Orazio. Since she would no longer be free on weekday mornings, her dalliances with him would have to come to an end within days. She wondered if he would then end Zeke's overtime. She thought back on how her relationship with Orazio had evolved from one in which she was simply "servicing" her husband's boss to keep her family afloat, to a relationship that had grown into something approaching love. In fact, over the last month, she had become so infatuated with him that she managed to visit his office two or three times a week. When she wasn't with him, she found herself thinking about him constantly—imagining the passion of their next rendezvous. She came to realize that Zeke could never make her feel truly happy in the way that Orazio could. It wasn't only Orazio's passion and sexual prowess; it was a cultural thing: Orazio's European ways were in sharp contrast to Zeke's Tennessee hillbilly mannerisms.

She decided to go to Orazio's office to tell him her "good news." Assuming that it might be her last lovemaking session with him, she would pull out all of the stops. She went into her lingerie drawer and found the sexiest undergarments she owned. She put on her recently bought black lace garter belt and sheer bikini panties. She then put on a pair of black silk stockings, carefully fastening them to her garter belt. After trying on a couple of black bras, she opted for a black lace teddy—another recent lingerie purchase. She then slipped on a pair of black stilettos. She was impressed by her sexy image in the full-length mirror. In her estimation, she looked more voluptuous than ever because her breast seemed to have gotten slightly bigger. *Maybe, I'm pregnant... My period is two weeks late. No, it's too early to worry about that. My periods often come late.*

She took off the stilettos and put on a pair of baggy brown pants and a plaid blouse. Since she didn't want to be seen walking through the neighborhood in stilettos, she donned a stretched-out pair of old flats and put the stilettos in a shopping bag. As usual, she made her way to Orazio's office via a circuitous route and entered it after a large a truck shielded her from the view of the ever-present Fasano sisters. Although she had successfully dodged the sisters this time, the sisters *had* spotted her going in or coming out of the office on several other occasions.

Orazio was pleased to see her. He gave her a wonderfully warm greeting, and soon—as was usually the case—they began speaking to each other in their dialect.

"Orazio, I've got good news and bad news for you."

"What do you mean? What's the good news and what's the bad news?"

"The good news is that my layoff has ended. I'll be going back to work on Monday."

"Oh...and?"

"The bad news is that with me working, I won't be able to visit you, anymore."

Orazio assessed the situation carefully, not saying a word for nearly a minute. Then, with a slight smile on his face he said, "All is not lost. I have an idea."

"What's your idea?"

"Well, suppose every two weeks on a Saturday morning, you tell your family that you're going shopping in downtown Brooklyn because prices are much cheaper there. You take the subway to Brooklyn and go into A&S Department Store, or Mays Department Store, to shop. After you do some shopping, you meet me outside at a certain time and we drive to my warehouse, which is on Hamilton Avenue, right next to the Brooklyn Battery Tunnel. The drive should take less than fifteen minutes."

"Does your warehouse have an office?"

"Yes, it has… and it's much larger and better than this one. Aside from having a much larger table, it has a long sofa, covered in fine Italian leather. The sofa used to be in my house, but my wife got tired of it…It's not worn out…it looks like new."

"For your plan to work without anyone getting suspicious, I'll have to buy something every time I go to Brooklyn."

"No problem, Serafina. I'll pay for whatever you buy."

"What about Zeke?"

"Don't worry about him. I'll make sure he'll be working all day on Saturdays…in Queens or up the Bronx."

"Orazio, you're so smart! I thought we would have to end this thing of ours, today, or maybe by Friday. I want you to know that you're special to me. You have captured my heart. When I'm having sex with Zeke, I close my eyes and make believe that he's you…but he doesn't thrill me like you do…he doesn't have your passion and your tenderness. I know it might sound a little crazy, but sometimes I fantasize that you and I are husband and wife."

Her words overwhelmed him. He realized that she was a perfect match for him, but given the circumstances, the best he could hope for would be a long, fulfilling love affair.

"Orazio, since I thought that today might be our last time together, I put on my sexiest outfit. Let me go into the back room first so I can get ready for you. Wait here until I call you."

She entered the back room and quickly took off her pants and blouse, and then replaced her flats with the stilettos.

"Orazio, I'm waiting for you," she called out in a sweet, sexy voice.

When he opened the back-room door, he gasped with delight at the sight before his eyes. Serafina looked like a goddess to him, especially in contrast to his frumpy wife. She smiled at him and then sat on the edge of the table. He knelt down and began making love to her by kissing the instep of her stocking-covered left foot, and working slowly upward and then downward, tenderly kissing and caressing nearly every part of her.

Their love-making session was their longest by far. Serafina had lost all track of time. She and her lover were deep in the moment. For the first time in her life she had had multiple orgasms; the last one occurred when Orazio finally "came" about twenty minutes after he had entered the back room. When he pulled out of her, she kissed his softening member, speaking directly to it, while giggling, "I'll see *you* this Saturday."

"Serafina, let's make our plan for Saturday."

"Okay, where shall we meet…and at what time?"

"Try to get to A&S by about eleven in the morning. Do some shopping …make sure you buy something nice for yourself, on me… I'll give you the money you spent when we meet. I'll be waiting for you in my car at noon. I'll probably be parked by a fire hydrant, or I might be double-parked."

"Sounds good to me, my love. I'll see you this Saturday…three days from today."

"I'll be there, *cara mia*."

The next three days passed rather quickly for Serafina. She had resigned herself to the idea of going back to work, recognizing that her lifestyle would soon become far more frenetic than it had been since the layoff. On Saturday morning, shortly after ten, she headed for the downtown IRT subway station. John-John caught a glimpse of her entering the subway kiosk across the street, while he was helping Joe stack the morning newspapers. About ten minutes later, Felicia strolled over to the newsstand.

"Good morning, John-John. Good morning, Joe."

"Good morning, Felicia, we certainly haven't seen much of each other, lately."

"Well, it's been difficult. Between my Italian relatives visiting us, your goin' away to Long Branch in August, and my mother constantly keeping tabs on me…"

"Oh, by the way, I saw your mother going down the subway across the street about ten minutes ago."

"Yeah, she's goin' to A&S Department Store on Fulton Street in downtown Brooklyn. She said that the prices are much better in Brooklyn than they are in Manhattan."

"Is you father workin' today?"

"Yeah, Joe, he's been workin' just about every Saturday since the beginning of the summer."

"Felicia, I'll be going up to Columbia tomorrow morning to start Freshmen Week. I'll be sleeping there for four nights, plus one night at Camp Columbia, in Litchfield, Connecticut. It's a very intensive orientation program for the new students…By the way, it will be the first time that I'll be away from home by myself."

"So, I guess I won't be seein' you for about a week."

"No… a little less. I'll be back on Friday afternoon."

Joe, forever the matchmaker, assessed the situation and said, "Why don't you two lovebirds go into Felicia's hallway now, while no one's around?"

Felicia blushed a bit, but her eyes revealed that she was amenable to Joe's suggestion.

"What about your brother and sister?" asked John-John.

"Oh, Little Zeke is still in his pajamas, sittin' in front of the television watching cartoons. Francesca is busy writing a book report on *The Red Badge of Courage*. The only problem is that she didn't read the book."

"C'mon, what are you two waitin' for?"

With Joe's encouragement, Felicia headed for the hallway; John-John followed about two minutes later. As the front door was closing behind him, he pulled her into his arms and said, "Felicia, oh how I've missed you!"

"Me too, John-John…me too!"

As he tried to heat things up, he detected a little stiffness in her body and a lack of passion in her kisses. Although she *did* allow his hands to roam a bit, she parried him every time he tried to put his hands under her blouse or inside her pants—occasionally making sure that he got the message by saying, "No, John-John, no!"

After a few minutes of being thwarted, John-John's frustrations came to an end when the sound of a slamming door, followed by the sound of footsteps, echoed throughout the hallway. The footsteps sounded as if they were coming from several flights above and getting closer. Things had to come to an end, so John-John left the building and Felicia made her way up to her apartment. When she reached the first floor, she encountered the elderly Mrs. Fanelli, who was descending the stairs.

"Good morning, Mrs. Fanelli."

"Good morning, Felicia. Did the mail come?"

"No, not yet."

When John-John got back to the newsstand, Joe's first words were, "Did you have a good time?"

"No, Joe, the best I can say is that it was okay…only okay."

"How far did you get?"

"She seemed to be holding back. She kept pushing my hands away every time I tried to make a move. The make-out session ended when one of the neighbors started coming down the stairs. To tell you the truth, I was glad to hear the neighbor's footsteps."

"Well, maybe next time she'll loosen up a bit. You know, women are funny that way. On certain days, they could be as hot as a brandin' iron, while on other days, they can be cold fish. Trust me, I know."

Meanwhile, Serafina's trip to downtown Brooklyn had gone as planned. Despite having to change from the IRT local to the express at the Brooklyn Bridge subway station, she had arrived at the Fulton Street station in downtown Brooklyn within twenty minutes. She was able to shop in A&S for a little more than an hour, in which time she bought a pair of corduroy pants for Little Zeke and a blouse for Francesca.

After the cashier rang-up her purchases, which totaled $9.48, she headed for the exit. The big clock above the revolving doors read 11:55. She was five minutes early, but she figured that it would be better if she were a little early, because Orazio might have difficulty finding a place to wait due to the traffic congestion in the area. As soon as she stepped outside, she spotted a black Cadillac approaching, with its headlights flashing. As the car got closer, she could see Orazio behind the wheel. He double-parked the Caddy right in front of her. She quickly got in and greeted him with a kiss on the cheek.

"Serafina, thanks for being a little early. It's like a madhouse around here…cars double-parked everywhere and people crossing in all directions."

"I see what you mean. I'll try to be early the next time, too. It's better if I have to wait instead of you."

They arrived at the warehouse in fifteen minutes. Orazio parked the Caddy in the small parking lot on the side of the warehouse—a large, one-story, tan brick building with two big garage doors. There were no other cars in the lot. On Saturdays, only one worker manned the warehouse, providing parts and equipment to Martucci's crews between 7:30 a.m. and 11:30 a.m.

The couple entered the warehouse through the side door and made their way to the office in the back. Since the office had glass panels on one of its walls, Serafina could see from afar that it was neat and well furnished—an oasis within a sterile industrial-type building that was filled with all kinds of parts and equipment.

Realizing that they would have at least two hours together, they proceeded at a slower pace than usual. They conversed for about a half-hour as they sipped espresso and munched on the Italian cookies that Orazio had brought along. When the serious lovemaking began, Serafina found the long leather couch to be far more comfortable than his Spring Street office table. As before, she had prepared for the liaison by wearing very sexy undergarments. Their lovemaking session proved to be as good as their last, leaving both of them totally satisfied and elated—and quite in love with each other.

While riding in the car back to Fulton Street, Serafina remarked, "I haven't gotten my period in about six weeks. I might be pregnant…and if I am pregnant, it's very likely that it's your baby I'm carrying."

"Don't worry, you will probably get your period soon. But, if you are pregnant, why do you think that I would be the father instead of Zeke?"

"Well, lately I've been avoiding Zeke in bed. I haven't been doing my wifely duties very much," she said with a slight laugh. "This may sound crazy, but when I *do* have sex with him, I feel guilty…I feel like I am cheating on you."

"It's not as crazy as it sounds, Serafina. Since our affair began, I've made love to my wife only two times, and each time it was all over in less than ten minutes…and both times I was fantasizing that she was you. Concetta is a wonderful woman and she has been a good wife, but she no longer has any sex appeal as far as I'm concerned."

"What should I do if it turns out that I'm pregnant?"

"You should do whatever your heart tells you to do."

"Well, I could have the baby and probably convince Zeke that it's his. He's not too bright, you know…and to help him forget that we have hardly made love lately, I'll make love to him tonight, even if he's totally exhausted from working too hard."

"That sounds like a good idea, but if you don't want to start all over again with raising a child, you could have…you could have… an abortion."

"No, I'm too afraid to have an abortion. I've heard that a lot of women have died because of complications."

"Well, that's because the abortions were done by people who were self-taught and not medically trained. If you should decide that you want an abortion, I know someone who could do it safely."

"Who?"

"*Dottore* Alphonse Lombardi."

"Is he really a doctor?"

"Yes…well, in Italy, but not in America. He studied medicine at the University of Pavia. He will probably get his license to practice here in about a year. He comes from the town of Caserta, so he's almost a *paisano*. He's a good man and an excellent doctor."

"Where would I have it done?"

"Right here on the table. I would bring in some blankets and pillows to make the table more comfortable for you."

"Do you really think that *Dottore* Lombardi can do the abortion right here on the table?"

"I'm quite sure he can, Serafina, and you probably won't feel a thing…as I said, he's an excellent doctor."

"Well, if I don't get my period within the next two weeks, I guess I should consider myself pregnant, and I will *then* decide whether to have the baby or have an abortion."

"Okay, *cara mia*, but in the meantime, I'll talk to *il Dottore* and tell him that we might need his services.

Orazio dropped Serafina off at the Fulton Street subway station at about 2:30 p.m. Before she got out of the car, he gave her a ten-dollar bill to cover her purchases at A&S. She was back in her apartment by three, wondering what her fate would be.

Chapter 32: Freshman Week

John-John exited the BMT Subway at Prince and Broadway at around 2 o'clock on Friday afternoon, lugging a small, beat-up blue suitcase. He was returning from Columbia University after spending five nights away from home for freshman orientation. Freshman Week had been a wonderful experience for him. He was introduced to a whole new world—the Ivy League—and he was enthusiastic about becoming a part of it. As he approached the newsstand, he could see Danny, Frankie and Shortie hanging-out in front, as usual. *Back to the real world*, he thought. When he arrived, they greeted him like a long-lost cousin.

"Hey, John-John, welcome back," shouted Shortie.

"How was it?" asked Danny.

"It was great! I had a wonderful time. They made us wear baby blue beanies with '67E' embroidered on them. The '67' is the year we are to graduate, and the 'E' stands for the Engineering School. Columbia has a fantastic campus, considering that it's in Manhattan. I met many professors and learned about the school's history and traditions. I got to visit Baker Field…Columbia's football stadium… and I spent a night up at Camp Columbia, in Litchfield, Connecticut. Last night, I went to a dance where I met this very hot Jewish girl who is a freshman at Barnard College, which is our sister school across the street…Now, let me tell you a little more about the school and Camp Columbia.

"Don't bore us about the school and that stupid camp. Just tell us about the hot Jewish girl you met," demanded Joe.

"Okay. Man, she showed me a really good time…and it could've been even better if we hadn't been interrupted."

"Interrupted? Tell us what happened...and don't leave nuttin out," ordered Danny.

"Well, most of the girls at the dance were Barnard freshmen. The guys were freshman from Columbia College and the Engineering School. Anyway, after about a half-hour, I spotted this nice-looking girl who had long, blonde hair and a very sexy body...you know...well stacked. We danced several times. I noticed that during the slow dances, she pulled me very close to her...so close, that just about every part of our bodies were touching each other."

"Then what happened?"

"Well Frankie, she said that the place was getting too hot, and she asked me to step outside with her for a while to get some fresh air. Of course, I agreed. We decided to walk towards Riverside Park and soon the wind blowing across the Hudson made the temperature seem about ten degrees cooler than it was on campus."

"C'mon, get to the point, John-John! I don't want no fuckin' weather report!"

"Okay, Joe, okay...Well, we sat down on a park bench in a dark area, deep within the park. Seconds later, she surprised the hell out of me. She whipped out a joint and lit it. She inhaled deeply and held the smoke in her lungs a long time before exhaling slowly. She offered me a drag several times, but I kept turning her down... telling her that I was an athlete. Finally, I took one shallow puff to satisfy her, because I expected we would soon be making-out, hot and heavy, if I played my cards right."

"Well...did you get to make-out hot and heavy?" asked Danny.

"Oh yeah, I had the best make-out session of my life. She had no inhibitions, whatsoever. I had my hands all over her. Instead of me trying to unbutton her blouse, she beat me to it...she unbuttoned it herself!

"Wow!" exclaimed Frankie.

"Get this...She was braless! Her big, beautiful tits were right there in front of me. While I was busy playing with them, she unzipped my pants, put her hands inside my underwear and began to play with me. She kept saying that she wished we had a bed."

"Man, those college girls really *are* hot," remarked Shortie.

"I suppose it wouldn't have taken much on my part to convince her to let me screw her right on the grass, but, unfortunately, just when I was about to suggest that we lay on the grass, I spotted a cop out of the corner of my eye. He was about 100 feet away and walking towards us. When I told her that the cop was coming, she quickly buttoned-up her blouse and I zipped-up my pants. The cop stopped at our bench and advised us…basically ordered us…to leave the park because he said it was a dangerous place at night."

"So, I guess you wound-up with 'blue balls,'" said Danny, shaking his head while chuckling.

"Yeah, I suppose you could say that."

"Will you be seein' her again?"

"I would like to, Joe, but I don't know how to get in touch with her. All I know is her name…Leslie Birnbaum."

"Well, I'm sure if you do some detective work, you'll probably find her," said Frankie in a confident tone.

"Probably…but once classes start on Monday, I don't think I'll have much free time for girls."

"C'mon, John-John, make time! You can't pass up an opportunity like this. Most Jewish girls are easier than Catholic girls when it comes to sex. I think it's because Catholic girls fear goin' to confession and havin' to tell the priests everythin' they did. Believe me, when it comes to Jewish girls, I know what I'm talkin' about. I went out with a couple of Jewish girls back in the day…and they were hot!"

"Maybe, I'll manage to find some free time to track her down, Joe."

"Yeah, you should do that, John-John. Listen, you're goin' nowhere fast with Felicia. I think it's time for you to dump her. Why waste your time with her when you have an opportunity like this fall right in your lap? And, I'm sure you'll have other opportunities comin' your way up at Columbia."

"You're probably right, Joe."

That said, John-John left for his apartment, promising to return soon. As he walked along Spring Street he ruminated on Joe's advice regarding Felicia: *Maybe, Joe is right…He usually is…Maybe, I should cool things with Felicia…at least for a while.*

After a warm greeting from his mother, he gave her a recap of Freshmen Week. Of course, he didn't tell her about his escapade with Leslie Birnbaum. Within fifteen minutes, he was out the door and back at the newsstand. A few minutes later, Felicia exited from the subway and walked over to the newsstand.

"Hi guys. Hi Joe."

"Hi Felicia," they all responded.

"How was school?"

"Same old thing…just a different year, Joe."

"Felicia, I think we should talk, in private…behind the newsstand."

"Okay, John-John. Excuse me fellas."

Once behind the newsstand, John-John began to speak softly: "Felicia, I've been trying to figure out where we stand with each other. Ever since our first kiss on Crosby Street, I've considered you to be my girlfriend."

"Well, *I've* considered you to be my boyfriend since then, too."

"You know I would love to date you…I mean, take you to the movies…to lunch or dinner…go uptown with you…but, your parents won't let you date anyone yet…especially me."

"I'm gonna work on my parents to try to get them to see that you're really a great guy. I'm hopin' to convince them to let you come up and visit us around Christmas. I think if I nag them enough, they'll probably allow you to come up to see the Christmas tree... and, maybe, sit down and have some coffee."

"I really doubt they'll let me come up. But, be that as it may, I would like to get to my point."

"What's your point?"

"Sneaking kisses in your hallway isn't enough for me. Since we can't date at this time, I want to be free to meet and date other girls. I'm entering a whole new world…a world totally different from this neighborhood. I'm sure I'll soon be meeting many mature and sophisticated college girls. In fact, last night at a dance I met a very pretty freshman from our sister school, Barnard College. We hit it off very well."

"So, you hit it off very well, did you?"

"Yeah, I think I would like to see her again."

"What about me!"

"Well…maybe…"

"Fine! Go have your fun with your college slut! I no longer consider you my boyfriend!" she yelled. That said, she angrily walked away and headed for her apartment. When John-John came around to the front of the stand, he briefed the guys and Joe on what had just happened, but it was basically unnecessary since they had clearly heard Felicia's parting words.

"I'm glad you took my advice, John-John. Don't worry, you made the right move," said Joe in a reassuring tone.

"I guess I won't ever need to use the *Wolverton Mountain* signal again," said Danny with a laugh."

"No, I guess you can put that signal to rest, Danny."

"I suppose you don't know…you've been away for five days… but Judy's beautiful friend, Maria, gave Joey "Smiles" the heave-ho after last Sunday's date. She told him that he was a nice guy, but there was no chemistry between them. She said that she didn't want to go on any more dates with him and that they should just remain friends."

"How did Joey take it?"

"He was disappointed…after all, she's a beautiful girl…but, he took it okay."

"You know, Danny, if I hadn't been involved with Felicia at the time, *I* would have gone on that double-date instead of Joey.

"Well, I'm sure that once Maria finds out that you're no longer Felicia's boyfriend, she'll jump at the chance of datin' you. Listen, every time I saw her, she would ask me a lot of questions about you… she's obviously very attracted to you."

"What about the Jewish girl…what's her name…Leslie?" Shortie inquired.

Joe jumped in, "Who's to say he can't go out with both of 'em?"

"Yeah, that's right," Frankie added, "A handsome guy like you should be entitled to havin' more than just one girlfriend at a time. Go for it!"

"Come in the stand, John-John, I wanna see for myself just how handsome you really are."

"How can you *see* how I look? You're blind."

"With my hands, college boy…with my hands. Come in. I'll show you."

John-John obliged and entered the newsstand.

"Face me, John-John, and stay still." Joe then proceeded to feel the contours of John-John's face with the fingertips of his right hand. After about twenty seconds, he announced, "You really *are* handsome! Now, I have a good mental picture of what you look like."

"Hey Joe, feel my face," Frankie demanded.

"Okay, Frankie, let me see what you look like." After only fifteen seconds, Joe blurted out, "Frankie, you got a face that could stop a fuckin' clock. If you ever find a girl who likes you, you better marry her quick! Ha, ha. ha."

All the guys joined in the laughter, as Joe added, "No, Frankie, I'm only kidding. You're okay, but you're no John-John."

"Who is?"

"Well, maybe Danny is in John-John's league when it comes to looks," Shortie responded.

"Yeah, that's true, I checked-out Danny's face last month with my fingertips…He seems to be a handsome devil."

"Thanks, Joe, I'm glad you said that. You know, when it comes to gettin' girls, I'm *the* sheik of the Sheiks."

"Ah, don't let it go to your head, Danny."

"So, John-John, do you want me to ask Judy for Maria's phone number?"

"No. Why don't you ask Judy to find out if Maria would like to go out with me. If she says 'yes,' you setup a double-date with you and Judy for next Friday night."

"What am I, your fuckin' manager? Why don't you ask Maria out, yourself?"

"Oh, do me this favor, Danny…you handle it for me."

"Okay. I'll setup the date…I'm sure it's gonna happen because I don't think there's any chance that Maria would say 'no.'

The weekend passed by quickly for John-John. On Monday morning, the last day of September, he was on the subway commuting up to Columbia for his first day of classes. After attending his calculus and English classes, he was off to lunch with a few of his new classmates. At about the same time, the Basilica High School "lunch mates" were sitting down at their usual table.

"What's new?" asked Judy, posing her question to no one in particular.

Maria responded first, "Nothing's new with me as far as guys are concerned. As you know, after my second date with Joey, I told him that he was a nice guy, but not quite my type. I actually said, 'there's no chemistry between us.' We agreed to remain friends…that's it. So, this weekend, I helped my mother with the chores and did my homework. I also did some reading."

"Sounds excitin'!" said "Fat" Angie, facetiously… "As for me, Shortie took me to the movies on Saturday night."

"What about you, Judy?"

"Well, Danny and I went up the Bronx Zoo, yesterday."

"Felicia, did you find some time to sneak around with John-John?" Angie already knew the answer to her question since Shortie had told her about "the break-up" while they were on the way to the movies.

"Angie, John-John told me that he wants to be free to date other girls since I'm not allowed to date him…or anybody else for that matter. He thinks he'll have a lot of college girls chasing after him. So, we parted ways for now, but I know in my heart that someday, perhaps, within a year, we'll be back together…and when that day comes, I won't lose him to no college girl!"

Maria tried to show empathy, but the best that she could come up with was, "Felicia, I'm sure that whatever happens, it will be for the best."

Chapter 33: First Date

It didn't take John-John very long to realize that Columbia was going to be difficult. By the end of his second day, he had attended all of the classes in his freshman program, which amounted to seventeen credits. His program consisted of calculus, physics, chemistry, graphics, English Composition and Contemporary Civilization. The latter course entailed reading and analyzing excerpts from the difficult writings of famous philosophers, such as Plato, Descartes and Locke; and both science courses were supplemented with weekly three-hour labs that required conducting experiments and presenting the results in extensive reports.

On Wednesday, he managed to track down Leslie. To his dismay, she told him that she was busy for the next few weekends, mostly with sorority and fraternity parties; but, she was able to find room for him on her busy calendar, agreeing to go out with him on Saturday, October 26th. The three-week delay didn't faze him because it would give him a chance to, possibly, date Maria in the interim.

When he returned from school on Wednesday, he met up with Danny at the newsstand. "Hi Danny, what's the story with Maria?"

"Oh, I spoke to Judy on Sunday while we were on our way to the Bronx Zoo. She was sure that Maria would want to date you, but she didn't want to ask her until Felicia had told the lunch table girls that you and she were no longer boyfriend and girlfriend."

"So, did Felicia tell the girls about our break-up?"

"Yeah, on Monday. Later on, Judy found out that Maria would *love* to date you."

"Oh boy! Sounds great, Danny!"

"The girls will meet us here on Friday night at around seven."

The next two days flew by quickly for John-John because he was absorbed in his studies. He found all of his courses to be very interesting, but the homework was very time consuming. Although he had a scientific bent, he really enjoyed reading the thoughts of some of the world's greatest thinkers in his Contemporary Civilization course, even though he often had to use a dictionary to understand the writing.

John-John arrived at the newsstand at about 6:30 p.m., anxiously anticipating his first date with Maria.

"Hey, John-John, are you ready for the double-date?"

"Sure am, Joe…sure am."

"Where are you gonna take 'em?"

"I think we'll head for Dave's Corner for some dessert…coffee and pie, or whatever. Then, hopefully, we will head back here via Crosby Street…if you catch my drift."

"Yeah, I know, if you spend some money on a girl, you certainly wanna make sure you at least get to kiss her and feel her up a bit…Right, John-John?"

"Right, Joe. That was one of the first things you taught me."

Danny arrived at the newsstand just before seven. Judy and Maria arrived shortly thereafter. John-John was immediately struck by Maria's appearance; she seemed even more beautiful than she had looked when they had first met three weeks earlier. After exchanging greetings with the girls, John-John, almost reflexively, glanced towards Felicia's bay window. He was surprised to see her standing at the side window panel taking in the scene. Although her face was somewhat distorted by the angle of the glass pane, he could easily tell that she was seething.

"How would you girls like to go over to Dave's Corner to have some dessert?" asked Danny.

"I've heard of Dave's Corner, but, I don't know where it is," remarked Judy.

"It's on the corner of Canal Street and Broadway," replied Danny, pointing south—in the opposite direction of Felicia's window.

"Okay, let's go," replied Judy, as Maria nodded affirmatively.

At that point, the squeaky sound of a window sash being lifted with great difficulty caught the attention of the two couples. They instinctively turned their heads towards the source of the sound. Felicia popped her head out of the window and yelled in a shrilly voice, "Maria, how could you do this to me? How could you? You couldn't wait to move right in…you poor excuse for a friend!"

"Pay no attention to her, Maria. She has no claims on me. Let's go!" With that, John-John grabbed Maria by the hand and the two couples began walking down Lafayette Street.

"I guess Felicia won't be talkin' to you anymore, Maria," remarked Judy.

"No, I suppose not."

"Listen girls, we shouldn't let Felicia spoil our evening."

"I agree, Danny Boy. We shouldn't."

"Let's forget about Felicia and have a good time," said Judy.

"Okay, but she's making me feel like a traitor."

As they walked hand-in-hand behind Danny and Judy, John-John and Maria talked to each other almost non-stop. Every time he would try to inject some humor into their conversation, she would laugh heartily, no matter how funny he *actually* was. As she squeezed his hand, she could feel the "electricity" between them—and so could he. Even if he had doubts about what he was feeling, her starry-eyed expression made it quite clear that she was infatuated with him.

As they got deeper into their conversation, John-John began to sense that Maria was much more than just a beautiful girl. He could tell that she was very intelligent—clearly, far more intelligent than Felicia—and she seemed to be exceptionally mature and sophisticated for a girl who was yet to turn seventeen.

"So, John-John, can you speak Sicilian?"

"Well, I understand it quite well, but I have a little trouble putting sentences together."

"Let me see if you can understand Sicilian?" With that she quickly rattled off two sentences in Sicilian. "Okay, what did I say?"

Blushing, John-John replied, "You said, 'I don't care what happens between Felicia and me. Whatever happens, it will be worth it as long as I can be with Giovanni.'"

"*Perfetto, Giovanni.*"

While the couples sat in a booth in Dave's Corner awaiting their orders, Maria just couldn't take her eyes off John-John, and he couldn't stop staring at her. Although, it was a double-date, there was very little cross-conversation with Danny and Judy. It was almost as if John-John and Maria were alone in the booth. As Maria cut into her piece of warm cherry pie—a Dave's Corner specialty— her brain was processing everything she had learned and felt about John-John during the past half-hour; and then, almost in a flash, she decided that he could possibly be *Mr. Right*—Felicia's ambitions notwithstanding.

Danny suggested, "Since next Saturday will be Maria's seventeenth birthday, why don't we all go out to dinner at Angelo's Restaurant on Mulberry Street. Being that her birthday falls on Columbus Day, I'm sure the food that night will be extra special."

"Um…I certainly would love to celebrate Maria's birthday with dinner, but why don't we go out for Chinese food instead…let's say we go to Yat Bun Sing's at 16 Mott."

"Since, it'll be Columbus Day, John-John, won't Italian food be more appropriate?" questioned Judy.

"I hate to say this…it's embarrassing…but I have very little pocket money left by the end of the week. Someday, I'll have plenty of money, but right now, I'm just a poor college student."

"Don't be embarrassed, John-John, I understand. I'll be happy to celebrate my birthday with all of you at…what's that restaurant's name…Sing Yat Sing?"

"No, Maria, it's Yat Bun Sing…but thanks for understanding my money situation."

"I'm actually looking forward to eating Chinese food. I've never had it. All of my life, it's been nothing but Italian food, Italian food…and more Italian food…specifically, southern Italian food. To my parents, any cuisine north of Naples is *foreign* food."

"Okay," said Danny, "It's decided, we'll go eat Chinks on your birthday, Maria."

Danny thoughtfully picked-up the Dave's Corner tab so that John-John would have some more money in his pocket for next week's dinner. The couples exited the coffee shop and headed north on Broadway. When they reached Broome Street, Danny "steered" the group into a right turn onto Broome, followed by a left turn onto Crosby. Each of them knew that Danny's chosen route had not been unintentional. Crosby Street was, as usual, dark and desolate. Maria squeezed John-John's hand very tightly, anticipating that they would soon be sharing their first kiss.

About halfway to Spring Street, Danny and Judy peeled-off into a cubbyhole leaving John-John and Maria on their own. John-John spotted a dark and deep loft entrance about twenty feet farther up the block, and he soon guided Maria into it. In an instant, their lips met and they were in a passionate embrace. The intensity and sensuality of Maria's kisses surpassed what he had experienced with both Felicia and Leslie. Even though Leslie had certainly excited him, he came to realize that what he had experienced with her was more akin to lust, while what he was now experiencing with Maria bordered on feelings of love—if, indeed, that's how "love" was supposed to feel, he wondered.

Their make-out session quickly progressed to the point where she allowed his hands to roam all over her clothed body. He was very surprised by the depth of her passion—especially, for a first date. Feeling brave, he unbuttoned the top two buttons of her blouse, and when she didn't object, he soon had his hand inside her bra. At that point, she could feel his aroused member pushing against her lower abdomen. Feeling adventuresome and curious, she shocked the hell out of him when she reached down over his pants zipper and gently patted his "package." She continued to do so for about ten seconds, concluding that he was "built"—so to speak—about the same as Lorenzo. She then lifted her arm and began to hug him as tightly as she could.

Judy's voice soon broke the silence of Crosby Street. "Maria …Maria…Where are you?"

"I'm over here, Judy."

"I think it's time to go."

With that, the two couples joined each other on a slow walk back to the newsstand. During the walk, Maria thought to herself how John-John was the "real deal." He was extremely handsome, tall, athletic, and obviously, intelligent. She found him to have a pleasant, easy-going disposition and she was impressed by the fact that aside from his being attracted by her appearance, he seemed to be genuinely interested in her intellect.

When they reached the intersection of Spring and Lafayette Streets, they all noticed that Felicia was stationed at the open bay window as if on guard duty. "You think she's been by the window since we left?" Danny asked, addressing his question to all of them.

"No, I doubt it," John-John replied, "but when we cross the street, let's stay on Spring Street and turn left on Mulberry."

As they were nearing the newsstand, they could hear Felicia yelling at them, but they couldn't quite make out the words—although, it was obvious that she was steaming. Rather than acknowledging her, they walked past the newsstand and out of her sight.

"We'll walk you all the way home, girls," said John-John.

"Yeah, it wouldn't be safe for you two to cross the Bowery by yourselves."

Upon reaching Houston Street, Maria turned to Judy and said, "I'm in the mood for a cigarette. Do you have my pack of Salems in your handbag?"

"Yeah, I forgot to give them to you." Reaching into her handbag, she quickly found Maria's pack of Salems and gave it to her along with a book of matches.

"Care for one, guys?"

"No, Maria, " Danny responded.

"What about you, John-John?"

"No, I don't smoke. I'm surprised that a bright girl like you smokes. Don't you realize that smoking is bad for your health?"

"I don't know if that's true. Sure, I've read some articles that say smoking is unhealthy, but I've also read other articles that say it isn't. Anyway, it makes me feel good…and it relaxes me. I only started smoking in August. My cousin Maria, in Sicily, goaded me into trying a cigarette, and about halfway into that first cigarette, I started to enjoy smoking. I had to stop smoking for a few weeks after I got back from Sicily, but I've been smoking about two or three cigarettes a day ever since school started."

"Aren't you gonna offer me a cigarette, Maria?" Judy asked somewhat sarcastically.

"Oh, I'm sorry, Judy…of course."

As they were walking along Houston Street, John-John noticed that Maria was truly enjoying her cigarette. She inhaled more deeply than Judy did and she seemed to savor every puff. The fact that Maria smoked really turned him off. He decided that if their relationship would ever blossom to a serious relationship—that is, true love—he would have to find a way to rid her of that "terrible habit."

The guys said "goodnight" to the girls in front of Maria's building and headed back to the neighborhood.

"How did you like Maria?"

"Wow, she great! She's beautiful…and she has brains!"

"How was your make-out session? Is Maria hot?"

"Oh yeah, she's hot all right, Danny."

"How far did you get?"

"Well, let's say I got a little past second base…She let me put my hand inside her bra."

"Congratulations, you did a lot better than Joey 'Smiles'."

"One more thing, Danny…she rubbed me through my pants."

"One date, and you almost caught up to me."

"What do you mean?"

"Well, Judy gave me a hand job…I "came" all over the sidewalk!"

While John-John and Danny were comparing notes, Judy and Maria were also comparing notes.

As they stood at the top of the metal stairway by the door to Maria's building, Judy asked, "Did you like John-John?"

"Oh yeah, he's wonderful…a dreamboat! I hope we'll be going steady, someday. I've never known anyone like him."

"Was he passionate, or does he make-out like a nerd?"

"He was *very* passionate…and I think we're quite compatible."

"How far did you let him get?"

"Why must you ask such personal questions?"

"Because, we're best friends, Maria. That's why."

"Okay, I'll tell you, if you first tell me how far you let Danny get?"

"Promise not to tell anyone, Maria?"

"I won't tell anybody anything…I promise."

"Tonight, I said to myself, 'why should he be the only one with roamin' hands?' So, while he had his hands all over me, including inside my panties, I reached down and unzipped his pants. Boy was he surprised!"

"What did you do next?"

"I reached inside and tried to pull-out his 'thing.' I was havin' trouble doin' it, so he took it out himself. I began strokin' it and he began to moan. Did you guys hear him?"

"No, I didn't. I don't know if John-John did."

"Well, he got so excited, that he 'came' all over the sidewalk."

"Oh, I suppose he might expect even more the next time."

"Maybe. But promise me, on your mother's life, that you'll never repeat what I just told you to anyone."

"I *already* told you that I wouldn't tell anybody anything, Judy. Don't worry, my lips are sealed."

"Now, what about you? You owe it to me to tell me everything."

Maria knew that what she had done with John-John was nothing in comparison to what she had done with Lorenzo; however, she had kept her Sicilian escapades to herself—even though Judy had probed her for details several times. So, feeling somewhat guilty that she hadn't been forthcoming to her best friend about Lorenzo, she reluctantly decided to tell Judy every detail of her make-out session with John-John. Upon hearing the details, Judy was surprised at how far John-John had gotten on the first date. She had figured Maria to be very reserved and somewhat nerdy. She was particularly surprised when Maria told her that she had felt-up John-John—albeit, over his pants.

Judy remarked, "So, I guess on your second date, you'll do to John-John what I just did to Danny…and at that rate, you'll probably be way ahead of me after your third date.

"Judy, you're making it sound like some sort of contest…a competition."

"No, Maria, I was only kiddin'."

"Well, to be honest, I'm not sure what I'll do on our next date…I guess I'll do what comes naturally."

Then, Maria in a serious tone said, "Judy, I know you'll never repeat this conversation to anyone. You're like a sister to me. So, I trust you…and you can trust me."

When Monday's lunch period began at Basilica High School, the "lunch mates" were down to three because Felicia wanted no part of Maria. As Felicia walked past their table, she looked Maria straight in the eyes and exclaimed, while distorting her face, almost to the point of ugliness, "Bitch! Traitor!"

She then walked off in a huff and sat down with some other girls at the other end of the lunchroom. Although the lunch mates couldn't hear what she was telling those girls, it was clear by her gestures that she was badmouthing Maria.

"What's that all about, Maria?" inquired Angie with a puzzled look on her face.

"Angie, on Friday night John-John and I went on a double-date with Danny and Judy.

"Oh…Shortie didn't mention it."

"Well, Felicia is mad at me. She feels that John-John should be off-limits to me because I'm her friend…or, at least, I *was* her friend."

"So, what's her problem? He's no longer her boyfriend…Right? He can go out with anybody he wants to…Right?" Then, she added with a smile, "Even me, if he wants to!"

"You're right, Angie. As I see it, Maria did nuttin wrong."

"Don't worry, Maria, when things cool off in a couple of weeks, I'll sit down with Felicia and have a good heart-to-heart talk with her," said Angie in an assuring manner. "She'll be friends with you, again, and back at this table where she belongs."

"I hope so," replied Maria.

Chapter 34: The Decision

The telephone rang in Orazio's office at 10 a.m. on Wednesday, October 9th.

"Good morning, Martucci and Sons Commercial Heating and Plumbing Company."

"*Buon giorno*, Orazio, this-ah Serafina."

Orazio responded in Neapolitan dialect, "Why are you calling, my dear? Is anything wrong?"

"Well…yes. I'm quite sure I'm pregnant. My periods is now about five weeks late and I've had morning sickness the last few weeks."

"What do you want to do, Serafina? Have the baby? Or…"

Before he could finish his sentence, she blurted, "I don't want to have the baby! I want *Dottore* Lombardi to take care of things."

"Are you sure?"

"Yes, I'm sure."

"Okay, I'll make the arrangements…and don't worry, *il Dottore* told me there won't be any problems since you're early in your pregnancy. Call me tomorrow morning. By then, I'll know when he can do it."

"Very well, Orazio, I'll call you tomorrow during my coffee break at around this time."

Over the next twenty-four hours, Serafina was a bundle of nerves. She kept second-guessing her decision, but every time she would analyze the situation, she would reach the same conclusion: to abort the pregnancy. This would not be her first abortion. She had had an abortion back in Naples during her days as a prostitute. That abortion, which had been performed by a so-called midwife, had been a painful experience.

At ten the following morning, Serafina made a beeline to one of the factory's pay phones and dialed Orazio's office.

"Good Morning, Martucci and Sons Commercial Heating and Plumbing Company."

"*Buon giorno*, Orazio, this-ah Serafina. She continued in dialect, "Have you made the arrangements with *il Dottore*?"

"Yes. Don't worry. The arrangements have been made. I'll meet you in front of the A&S Department Store at noon, this Saturday…Columbus Day."

"Do you want me to go shopping first?"

"No, skip the shopping. When you go back home, just say that you didn't find anything you liked."

"Okay, but how will I get back home?" I'm sure that riding the subway will be difficult for me after *il Dottore* does what he has to do."

"Don't worry, Serafina, I thought about that. I'll drive you back and drop you off close to home."

"You know that I can't be seen getting out of your car."

"Trust me, no one will see you…You will sit in the backseat and when we reach Manhattan, all you have to do is lie down on the seat until you're ready to get out of the car. I'll drive down Crosby Street and let you out there…Otherwise, I'll find some other deserted place. Don't worry. No one will see you getting out of my car."

The next two days passed very slowly for Serafina. She was tense and on edge, yelling at her children for what seemed to them to be no reason. *I can't wait for this to be over…I'm sorry I got myself into this mess. I hope il Dottore knows what he's doing.*

When Saturday morning "finally" arrived, she anxiously made her way to downtown Brooklyn, exiting the subway just before noon. She was glad to see the familiar Cadillac parked in front of a nearby fire hydrant with Orazio behind the wheel. She jumped into the car and greeted him with a perfunctory kiss.

Sensing Serafina's anxiety, he said, "Don't worry, *Dottore* Lombardi is the best. You won't feel a thing. Everything will be fine. I promise you."
When they arrived at the warehouse, they spotted a red car parked at the far end of the lot. "Oh, there's *il Dottore*, Serafina… right on schedule."

As they parked close to the side door of the warehouse, a tall, young man with Italian features came out of the red car and started walking towards them. Serafina noticed that he was carrying a black leather bag.

"*Buon giorno, Dottore.*"

"*Dottore* Lombardi, this is my very dear friend, Serafina."

"Pleased to meet you, *Dottore*," she replied, with a bit of nervousness in her voice.

"Don't be afraid, Serafina, all will go well. I am an experienced doctor."

As Orazio was fumbling with the keys to the side door, a dark blue 1960 Ford was just about to pull into the parking lot. Phil Di Chiaro, one of Orazio's employees, was behind the wheel. He had locked-up the warehouse and departed shortly before noon, but when he got close to the Brooklyn Bridge, he realized that he had left a large piece of provolone cheese in the office refrigerator—a gift to him from one of Orazio's truck drivers. So, he had decided to return to the office to get the cheese and bring it home.

None of the three noticed the dark blue Ford which had stopped just before the driveway. When Orazio finally opened the warehouse door, the three quickly entered—but not before Phil recognized the woman. *What's Zeke's wife doin' here? And why is she here with Martucci?*

He knew Serafina quite well. In fact, he and his wife had been guests at Felicia's Sweet Sixteen party. He didn't know who the tall young man was, but he had spotted the black leather bag, and it gave him cause to wonder about what was going on. His instincts told him that he had seen something he shouldn't have seen. So, he decided to forego the provolone, and he quickly pulled away. Seconds later, it registered in his mind: *There must be something goin' on between Orazio and Serafina.*

Orazio went back to his car and pulled-out a couple of old blankets and several pillows from the trunk. Upon re-entering the warehouse, he covered the office table with the blankets and put the pillows on top of them to make the "operating table" more comfortable for Serafina.

Serafina stripped from the waist down and laid down on the pillows. *Dottore* Lombardi then proceeded to administer a local anesthetic. Within fifteen minutes, the deed was done—she was no longer pregnant. *Dottore* Lombardi hung around for an hour while Serafina rested on the table. He then examined her and satisfied himself that there would likely be no complications. Orazio took *il Dottore* over to the side and handed him an envelope containing the cash for his services. Before departing, *Dottore* Lombardi instructed Serafina to relax on the leather couch for about an hour and then go home to rest. He added, "Don't do anything strenuous for the next few days…Don't worry, you will be fine."

During the next hour, the couple drank some espresso and chatted about all sorts of things, including "their future."

"Serafina, I hope you will continue to see me after all of this is behind us."

"Yes, I'll still go on seeing you. You have come to mean a great deal to me. But from now on, you must use protection."

"We'll talk about that, later, *cara mia.*"

Then, Orazio gathered the blankets and pillows and put them into two black plastic trash bags. Once outside, he threw the trash bags into the parking lot dumpster, and he and Serafina got into his Caddy. By force of habit, she had gotten into the front seat, but he quickly reminded her to get in the back.

The trip back to the neighborhood took about twenty-five minutes. Orazio made his way to the intersection of Houston and Crosby Streets and started heading south on Crosby. Shortly before reaching Spring Street, he pulled his Caddy into the empty, unattended, parking lot on his left. Although the parking lot did a thriving business on weekdays, it was usually totally empty on weekends because all of the factories and lofts were closed.

To ensure that no stray passerby might see Serafina getting out of his car, he pulled the car behind the parking lot attendant's booth. With the back door of the car shielded from the street by the booth, he told her that it was now safe to get out. After a quick good-bye kiss, he said, "Don't worry my dear, in a couple of days you will be feeling as good as new, and in two weeks, you can go shopping in downtown Brooklyn again…if you know what I mean."

"Yes, I know what you mean…but right now, the thought of having sex is the last thing on my mind!"

Serafina remained behind the booth until the Caddy was long gone. Then, she began her slow, two-block walk back home. When she arrived in her apartment, she was greeted by Felicia.

"Hi Mama, you look tired."

"Yeah, I feel-ah tired and-ah I have-ah big-ah headache. I think-ah I lie-ah down-ah."

"You didn't buy anything today?"

"No. I no find-ah anything-ah."

Serafina then stepped into the bathroom and removed a wad of bloody gauze. Following *Dottore* Lombardi's instructions, she replaced the gauze with a sanitary pad. She put the bloody gauze inside the sanitary pad box and left the bathroom with box in hand. While alone in the kitchen, she removed the bloody gauze from the box, put it in a brown paper bag and placed the bag deep within the kitchen garbage pail, under some vegetable scraps.

She felt fairly well after a two-hour nap. The only problem she would have to contend with would be to keep Zeke away from her in the bedroom, since *il Dottore* had recommended that she abstain from sexual intercourse for ten days or more. Her solution to that problem was simple: She would tell Zeke that she had just gotten her period and that it was extremely "heavy"; but she would keep him happy by servicing him orally every other night. She knew he wouldn't mind because he seemed to enjoy oral sex just as much as he enjoyed intercourse—perhaps, even more so.

When Phil arrived at his Mott Street tenement apartment, his wife, Tina, greeted him with an angry look on her face. "You're over a half-hour late for lunch, Phil!"

"I know…I know, dear…You see, when I was just about to go over the Brooklyn Bridge, I remembered that I hadn't double-locked the side door…so I went back to the warehouse."

He had wanted to tell her that he had gone back for the provolone, but then, he would have had to explain why he didn't bring it home. He figured it would be best if he kept what he had seen at the warehouse close to the vest—at least for a while—because Tina was quite a gossip.

"Well, now your pasta is cold…and it's kinda mushy."

"No problem, Tina. Just warm it up and I'll eat it."

During his drive home, Phil's initial thoughts had focused on his friend, Zeke. *That dumb hayseed...he probably has no idea his wife is screwin' around with Orazio.* But as he was driving across the Brooklyn Bridge, he tried to figure out how the "mystery man" with the black leather bag fit in. As he was squeezing his car into a tight parking space on Spring Street, bells went off in his head: *The young man with the black leather bag must be a doctor... and the only reason that Orazio, Serafina and a doctor would be at the warehouse, would be for the doctor to perform an abortion...Orazio must have gotten her pregnant...that bastard. Why else would he be involved?*

"So...anything new, Phil, besides forgettin' to double-lock the warehouse door?"

He was almost about to "spill the beans" to Tina, but he feared that should the word get back to Orazio that Tina had been the source of any neighborhood gossip about him and Serafina, he would surely be fired; and where would a man like Phil—a convicted felon—find such a good-paying, easy job? So, he decided not to tell her anything about what he had seen.

"Nah, it was a pretty dull mornin', Tina."

Chapter 35: The Phone Calls

Maria had a little hop in her step as she was going down the stairs of her apartment building. She was feeling exceptionally happy in anticipation of the start of a wonderful evening. It was Columbus Day, and more important, her seventeenth birthday. Her parents would not be acknowledging her birthday with a cake—let alone a party. It just wasn't their custom to celebrate birthdays with any sort of fanfare. However, they did give her a beautiful 18-carat gold bracelet and a birthstone ring for her birthday. They had bought the jewelry in Palermo without Maria's knowledge and, fortunately for them, had gotten it past Customs without it being discovered.

When Maria opened the building's front door, she saw Judy waiting on the sidewalk below at the foot of the exterior metal stairway.

"Happy birthday, Maria! You're five minutes late, but I won't complain since it's your birthday."

"What time do you have, Judy?"

"I have ten minutes to seven."

"Where are we supposed to meet the guys?"

"Well, Danny and John-John will be meeting us at the bus stop on Second Avenue and Third Street. Angie and Shortie will meet up with us at the restaurant. We'll take the bus to Park Row...the closest stop to Chinatown."

As they walked at a leisurely pace to the bus stop, Maria asked, "How was your date with Danny last night?"

"It was wonderful. I think I might be in love with him. Too bad you and John-John couldn't double-date with us."

"Well, he was up to his ears with homework. Did you and Danny go anywhere?"

"Yeah," Judy replied with laughter, "He took me to a garage on Mulberry Street."

"A garage?"

"Yeah, Danny just bought a used Chevy convertible and it's sittin' in the garage until he gets it registered."

"Great! I'm sure you'll be going all over the city now that Danny has a car…and, you'll be able to make-out in the privacy of his car instead of in a Crosby Street cubbyhole."

"Speaking of Crosby Street, after seein' his car, we walked over to Crosby Street. We had a wonderful time together…much passion. I played with him like I did the last time, but this time he pushed down on my neck…but I resisted."

"I guess you know what he was hoping you would do."

"Yeah, I know, but I'm not sure if I'm ready for that, yet."

"Listen, my cousin, Maria, back in Sicily, told me to think of it as just a form of advanced kissing…or a more intimate way of showing affection…nothing more, nothing less. She said that all a girl has to do is to put her lips around her boyfriend's *salsiccia* and do what comes naturally. She made it sound like it's no big deal."

"His *sal-zeek-ah?*" Judy laughed.

"Well, when you say it, it sounds Polish," replied Maria, while giggling. "*Salsiccia* is the Italian word for "sausage." Cousin Maria preferred to refer to it as a *salsiccia*, rather than use an anatomical or vulgar name for it…to make it sound more palatable…Pardon the pun."

Judy, who didn't catch the double entendre, replied, "So, did you show your affection for Lorenzo in the 'more intimate way'?"

Pausing a couple of seconds to think about her answer, Maria responded, "No, I didn't."

"Well, if I get up enough courage, I might do it. What about you?"

"I don't think so, Judy…Well, perhaps, depending on how things go and how I feel at the time."

"Maybe, we should both do it at the same time…maybe, tonight. It'll be our little secret plan. After all, you know that John-John is gonna meet many college girls, soon…and a lot of 'em are quite loose when it comes to sex. I think you should try to keep him extra-happy, so he doesn't look elsewhere."

"You realize that you have already been on at least a half-dozen dates with Danny, while this will only be my second date with John-John."

"Yeah, that's true, but if you're really as crazy about him as I think you are, you might consider doin' it, tonight."

John-John and Danny had been waiting at the bus stop for about ten minutes when the girls arrived. As they greeted each other with hugs and kisses, a bus pulled into the stop. The door opened and John-John yelled up to the driver, "Is Johnny Cara in front of you or behind you?"

"He's the next bus. Are you gettin' on?"

"No, we'll wait for *him*. He's my father."

John-John explained, "I hope you guys don't mind waiting another five minutes for the next bus. You see, my father is working tonight. It would be fun to have him drive us to Chinatown…plus, he'll get to meet Maria and Judy."

"I would love to meet your father."

"So would I," added Judy.

Five minutes later, an M-15 bus pulled into the bus stop with John-John's father behind the wheel. He had a surprised look on his face because he hadn't expected to see his son at the bus stop.

"Just put 20 cents into the fare box," he whispered to John-John. So, all four got on the bus for a nickel apiece.
"Hey, Pop, this is Maria…and this is Judy. Maria is with me and Judy is with Danny."

"Nice to meet you, girls…Wait a second while I cut-off this cabby. He cut me off on Fifth Street to pick up a fare…now, he's comin' up on my left. I'll show him who's the boss!"

After "teaching the cabby a lesson" by squeezing the cab almost onto the sidewalk as he steered the big bus way over to the left, he resumed the conversation, "Where are you youngsters goin'?"

"Today is Maria's seventeenth birthday, Pop. We're going to Yat Bun Sing's to celebrate it. Shortie and his girlfriend will meet us there."

"Happy birthday, Maria. I see that my son has good taste...You're beautiful."

Blushing, Maria replied, "Thank you, Mr. Cara."

"So, you're all gonna eat Chinks. That Yat Bun Sing gives you the best food for the buck in all of Chinatown."

After about fifteen minutes, the bus reached Park Row.

"Nice to meet you, Mr. Cara," the two girls said in unison before exiting.

"Nice to meet you. Have a good time, and once again, happy birthday, Maria."

When they arrived at 16 Mott Street, they walked down the steps leading to Yat Bun Sing's restaurant. They could see Shortie and Angie through the glass doors, waiting for them at a table for six. As the four were getting seated and greeting Shortie and Angie, menus were handed out; and in less than a minute the waiter was back, hovering over the table ready to take the orders. Of course, the guys couldn't order the food without joking and mimicking the waiter's Chinese accent—although most of their efforts at being funny seemed to go right over the waiter's head.

After the serving of soup was finished, six different main courses were quickly placed on the table to be shared by all. Maria soon discovered that Chinese food was very much to her liking. In fact, she liked it so much that she was stuffing herself—eating much more food than she normally would. The restaurant soon filled up and a line of customers was forming outside. So, in the tradition of Chinese restaurants of that era, Yat Bun Sing's goal was to get the customers out the door as quickly as possible. Therefore, as soon as a course was finished—or was close to being finished— the serving dish was quickly removed. In less than an hour, their table was cleared of everything except for the tea and teacups. The waiter promptly placed the check on the table and inquired, "Ev-ting aw-right?"

As they exited the restaurant, Angie asked, "Where to?"

"How would you like to see my car? It's in the garage on Mulberry and Kenmare. It's a '58 Chevy convertible with a 348 cubic inch engine. It's white...and the body's in great shape."

"Yeah, let's go see it," said Shortie.

"Three deuces, Danny?"

"Of course it has three, two-barrel carburetors, John-John! It's a hot car!"

"I thought you were gonna wait a while before you bought a car."

"I was, Shortie. As you know, I start my job on Monday. It's out at Idlewild Airport. I was gonna commute there by public transportation until I saved up enough money to get a car. But, my parents decided to lend me some money for a car. I paid $1,000 for it…a great buy. I bought it from Joey "the Sport." He needed money to pay-off some shylock. He's always borrowin' money when he's shootin' craps or playin' cards."

"When will you get the car on the road?" asked John-John.

"Probably, by Wednesday or Thursday…All the paperwork should be in my hands by the middle of the week and I'll have my mother go down to the Department of Motor Vehicles on Worth Street to get the license plates. So, I guess I'll only have to commute to work by subway and bus for a few days." The three couples started walking slowly up Mott Street. Within fifteen minutes, they arrived at the garage. No attendants were around. Danny led them to his car, which was parked at street level in the back corner of the garage.

"She's a beauty, Danny!"

"Let me start it up, John-John. I want you guys to hear the sound of the engine."

The Chevy started quickly and Danny began to "goose" the pedal. The engine had a deep, throaty sound that exuded a sense of power. After everyone wished him good luck with the car, the group started to head towards the street.

"Hold-on!" Danny commanded, "I've got a little surprise." That said, Danny went back to the trunk of the car and opened it. A few hours before the date, Danny had placed a small, ice-filled cooler containing a bottle of champagne in the trunk. He reached into the cooler and pulled-out a bottle of Andre Champagne, which had only cost him $2. But, everyone was impressed, since none of them was a champagne connoisseur.

"Wow, Danny, champagne!" Judy exclaimed.

"I figured that we should have a bit of the 'bubbly' to celebrate Maria's birthday. Don't worry about bein' too young to drink, girls. Nobody's gonna see us in here."

Danny opened the champagne in a stylish manner and poured it into six paper cups. "I'm sorry I couldn't provide real champagne glasses, but after all, this is a garage."

"Here's to Maria! Happy birthday!" John-John toasted.

Neither Maria nor Judy had ever drunk champagne, though Maria usually drank wine at home and Judy often had a bit of beer at family picnics. After Shortie and Angie had finished their champagne, Angie announced that she and Shortie would be going up to her apartment to have some coffee and cake with her parents. They hugged and kissed everyone good night and left the garage.

"Let's finish the bottle," said Danny as he proceeded to pour. Recognizing that it might be to the guys' advantage to get the girls a little tipsy, he filled their cups to the top and divided the remaining amount with John-John, which amounted to less than half a cup each.

"I've got an idea. See that beat-up old Plymouth in the other corner? Do you notice that all of its tires are flat?"

"Yeah, Danny, it looks like that car's been sitting there for months."

"Right. So, I'm gonna take off the plates and put 'em on my car. Then, we can take a quick ride to Crosby Street and make-out in comfort…you and Maria in the back and me and Judy in the front.
Whatta ya say, girls? Okay with you?"

"Won't you get in trouble if the cops stop us?"

"Maybe, Maria, but I *do* own the car. At worst, I'll get a ticket… but what are the odds that we'll get stopped in this neighborhood?"

"In that case, it okay with us," said Judy, deciding for both of them.

While Danny and John-John were trying to loosen the old Plymouth's license plate bolts, using the tools that the previous owner of the Chevy had left in the trunk, Judy and Maria were standing by the Chevy having a serious conversation.

"Maria, I'm thinkin' of gettin' more intimate with Danny, tonight…You know, to give him what he wants…right in the front seat. And I'm hopin' that you'll do the same for John-John in the back seat…After all, as your cousin says, it's only a more intimate way of showin' affection…Whatta ya say?"

After a moment of silence, Maria laughingly replied, "No promises, but if you hear John-John moaning, then you'll know I did it."

"Who would ever have thought that we'd be discussing such a thing? You, for one, have a reputation in school of being kind of a 'Goody Two-Shoes,' and I'm, by no means, considered wild."

"Are you sure you don't want John-John and me to get out of the car and find a cubbyhole so that you and Danny can have some privacy?"

"No, I want you and John-John in the back seat. Don't worry, you won't be able to see what's goin' on in the front seat."

"I guess not…But listen, I'm not sure I'm going to go through with it. As I said before, it's only my second date with John-John."

Judy, who was clearly feeling the effects of the champagne, responded, "It would certainly be memorable. You would never forget your seventeenth birthday…Well, are you gonna do it?"

"Let me just say that I *might* do it…but no guarantees."

"Okay, Maria."

"One thing Judy."

"What?"

"You should have some tissues ready?"

"Why?"

"Isn't it obvious? Unless you're gonna swallow that stuff, you'll need the tissues to discreetly get rid of it."

"Whatta ya mean 'discreetly'?"

"I mean, don't make it obvious that you're spitting it out…He might get insulted. Just turn your head away from him and quietly spit it into the tissues."

"Maria, you seem to know way much too much about this. Are you sure you didn't do it to Lorenzo?"

"Yeah, I'm sure…Listen, Judy, you know I would've told you if I did. You're my best friend. Right? You're like the sister I never had… Anyway, I learned all this stuff from Cousin Maria. She felt it was her duty to teach me all about sex."

As soon as the "borrowed" plates were fastened to the Chevy's bumpers, the two couples got in the car. Danny started the engine, put the top down and eased the car out of the garage. As he drove slowly up Mulberry, he occasionally revved-up the engine as a way of showing-off his car. He turned left onto Prince Street and then turned left again onto Lafayette.

"Hey, Danny, I thought we were headed for Crosby. Why did you turn on Lafayette?"

"I wanna have some fun with Felicia, John-John."

"No, let's not rile her up."

But, Danny ignored him. He pulled the car to the curb directly across the street from Felicia's apartment and he blasted the radio and honked his horn a few times.

"Danny," Maria shouted, "Don't tease Felicia!"

Within seconds, Felicia appeared at the bay window and started gesturing in an angry way. The sight of John-John and Maria cuddling in the back seat of the convertible most certainly added some fuel to the fire. To further anger her, Danny made a U-turn right in front of her window and yelled, "Hey, Felicia, beautiful night for a ride…ain't it?"

"Maria, I guess Felicia will *never* talk to you after this," said Judy while shaking her head.

Within a minute, Danny was driving down Crosby Street. Using the same logic that Martucci had employed only hours before while driving Serafina home, Danny pulled the Chevy into the parking lot on the left and parked it behind the attendant's booth in such a way that the car couldn't be seen from the street.

"We don't want any cops interrupting us, girls," said Danny while chuckling.

He then raised the convertible top, and moments later the couples were embracing in near darkness. Maria instantly realized that making-out in the back seat of a car was far more comfortable than making-out in a cubbyhole. Although she did feel a little apprehensive at first about having Danny and Judy so close—close enough to hear them breathing and sighing—within a minute, she was "in the moment" and completely oblivious to what was going on in the front seat.

John-John contorted his long body the best he could across the back seat, as Maria got on top of him—while kissing and hugging him without losing a beat.

"I think I love you," Maria whispered.

"I really…I really have strong feelings for you, too, Maria," was the best he could come up, stammering all the way.

As the level of passion rose, she allowed his hands to roam all over her. She even unzipped her pants and guided his hand inside her panties. *Maybe, it's the champagne,* he thought, pleased with the way things were going.

Soon, she was so hot that she wished they could "go all the way." Having once experienced intercourse, she wanted to experience it again. However, she knew that doing it would be out of the question; the combination of John-John's height and the smallness of the convertible's back seat would make it next to impossible—even if they could somehow overcome Danny and Judy's presence. So, she decided to pull a version of her "Lorenzo move." She slowly dropped her knees down to the floorboard while pulling down his zipper. He was totally surprised by her maneuver but said nothing—happily anticipating what was to come. Soon, she was pleasuring him orally, and as with Lorenzo, she found that she was getting pleasure out of performing the act.

John-John couldn't help but moan, "Oh, Maria…Oh! Oh Maria!"

At that point Judy *knew* what was going on in the back seat, and Danny had a pretty good idea of what was happening. So, Judy took John-John's moans as her cue to fulfill her part of "the secret plan"— to give Danny what she knew he wanted. Within seconds, she began to satisfy him orally, quickly overcoming her fears about performing the act, and blocking out the fact that John-John and Maria were in the back seat.

Wow, this is great! thought Danny. "Oh, Judy…Oh…Oh!"

After a couple of minutes of virtual silence, Danny popped his head up and asked, "Are you guys about ready to leave?"

"Yeah, Danny, I guess it's time to go," John-John replied.

Judy popped her head up as Maria and John-John wiggled themselves back to their upright seating positions. While John-John was looking to his left, Maria quickly threw her wad of gummy tissues out the car window—

forward enough for Judy to glimpse it whizzing by before it disappeared into the darkness to her right. A split second later, Maria saw Judy cast her tissues out the car window. Thus, at that moment, both girls knew for sure what they each had done.

As Danny was putting the convertible top back down, Judy turned around and offered Maria a cigarette. When Maria leaned over the front seat to get the cigarette and matches, Judy whispered, "Advanced kissing?"

Maria softly replied, "Ah-ha."

Maria quickly lit-up, took a couple of deep drags and said, "John-John, why don't you take a puff?"

"No, I'd rather not."

"Oh, c'mon, just one puff."

So, John-John reluctantly grabbed the cigarette from Maria's hand and took a shallow puff. She was surprised that he didn't cough or choke.

"John-John, you didn't inhale. You just blew on the cigarette… you didn't really smoke. At least, take a deep drag and let the smoke fill your lungs."

"Okay, Maria, I'll give it a real try."

Upon inhaling deeply, he let out a slight cough and said, "I'm not sure if smoking agrees with me."

"Look, you've come this far, why don't you finish the cigarette. That way, you'll know for sure whether or not you would want to become a smoker."

"Okay, I'll try to finish the cigarette."

After about five drags, he began to find smoking to be somewhat relaxing, but he wasn't sure he wanted to make a habit of it.

"You look good puffing that cigarette," said Maria with a smile.

When Judy turned around to look at John-John in action, she seconded Maria's opinion.

"Are you going back to the garage, Danny?"

"Yeah, but first I think we should drive the girls home."

"That's okay, Danny, we don't mind walking home," said Maria.

Danny would have none of it. When he reached the intersection of Spring and Lafayette Streets, he turned left onto Lafayette Street; but, instead of proceeding up Lafayette, he pulled over in front of Felicia's building and began revving-up the engine and tooting the horn. Within seconds, Felicia appeared at the bay window looking quite angry.

"Hey, Felicia, how do you like my car?"

"Get the hell outta here, Danny! You and my *former* friends, get the hell away from my buildin'!"

Always wanting to get the last word, Danny replied, "Stop making angry faces, Felicia…or you'll wind-up a wrinkled old prune before you know it."

Danny quickly accelerated the Chevy, leaving a lengthy patch of rubber on Lafayette Street's cobblestone pavement. Within five minutes, Maria was dropped off in front of her building—missing her 10 o'clock curfew by ten minutes—and three minutes later, Judy was dropped off in front of her building. On the way back to the garage, the guys were ecstatic about what had happened on the double-date—and as young guys do—they told each other every detail of their sexual escapades.

"Man that Judy is hot!"

"Yeah, Maria, too! She surprised the hell out of me tonight!"

"Yeah, who would've thought we'd both be gettin' our first blow jobs, tonight, in my car at the same time!"

Meanwhile, the neighborhood's big Columbus Day bash at the Knights of Columbus Hall on Grand Street was still going strong. Phil Di Chiaro and his wife were seated at the same table with Tessie Fasano, her two sisters and their husbands, and Lennie "Squirm's" parents, Dom, and Stella Muccio. By that time, Phil, who was quite a drinker, had drunk eight Dewars' and water. He was "feeling no pain," as it is often said about a person who is quite intoxicated, and he just couldn't help but spill the beans on what he had seen at the warehouse in the early afternoon.

Speaking to everyone at the table, Phil blurted out, "You'll never guess who I saw with Martucci at the warehouse this afternoon?"

"Who?" the always-nosy Tessie Fasano inquired.

"Serafina."

"You know," remarked Tessie, while pointing to her sisters, "We've been suspicious of her for a long time. We've seen her go into Martucci's office a lot, lately…and she's usually in there for about a half-hour, or more. We've been thinkin' there must be some hankypanky goin' on between 'em."

"Yeah, once a who-ah, always a who-ah," added Tessie's sister, Fannie.

"Well, I think you're right…and…I think he must've 'knocked her up' because I saw a man who looked like a doctor goin' into the warehouse with them. He must've been there to…"

"He must've been there to give her an abortion," Dom interjected. "Why else would the three of 'em be there…in a closed warehouse? I'm no genius, but it don't take no fuckin' genius to figure this thing out."

Everyone at the table nodded in agreement.

"It serves that rat bastard of her husband right that he should be a *cornuto*. He's been on my shit list ever since he called the cops on my son, Lennie…just because he was makin' a little noise with his car."

"Yeah, he's a real *cornuto*, alright." Then Phil added, "What's the English word for *cornuto*?"

Phil's wife, Tina, who liked to read and was far more intelligent than her husband, volunteered a translation: "I think *cornuto* is the Italian word for 'cuckold'…you know, a husband whose wife is cheatin' on him."

Phil replied, "Tina, the Italian word sounds so much better to my ear…'cuckold' reminds me of the sound a rooster makes."

Tina added, "You know, for a man in Italy, especially southern Italy, there's no bigger insult than to be called a *cornuto*. If someone in Italy dares to do so, he should be prepared to defend himself to the end because there's a good chance he'll be knifed by the insulted man…It's a matter of honor."

Phil, a pleasant drunk, then began to sing a song about Zeke and Serafina to the tune of *O Sole Mio*, improvising the lyrics as he went along:

"Zeke's a *cornuto*, a big *cornuto*

His wife's a who-ah, a great big who-ah

She screws Martucci, while Zeke is workin'

She is a who-ah, and Zeke's a *cornuto*"

After he sang the same verse two more times, Tessie and her sisters applauded while Dom yelled, "*Bravo, Phil! Bravo!*"

The party ended at about one in the morning. When Dom and his wife made it into their apartment, Dom, who had had a few too many drinks, got the "bright idea" of giving Zeke an obscene phone call. He grabbed the phone book and was happy to find that Zeke Daniels' phone number was listed. With some difficulty, he managed to dial, W-A-5-6…Zeke, who had been fast asleep, picked up the receiver on the fifth ring, only to have it drop out of his hand and onto the floor.

"Your wife's a who-ah, and you're a *cornuto*…a fuckin' *cornuto*, you rat bastard!" yelled Dom, and then he quickly hung-up the phone.

"Who was-ah that-ah, Zeke?"

"I don't know. It must've been one of those nasty kids that hangout at the newsstand. All I heard was, 'you rat bastard.'"

"I bet-ah it-ah was Danny."

"It didn't sound like him, but who knows…Well, Serafina, since we're both awake, how's about a quick roll in the hay?"

"No, I'm-ah too tired."

"C'mon honey, I need some lovin'!"

"No, I-ah gotta my period …very heavy…and I'm-ah too tired, anyways-ah…*Buona notte*, Zeke." With that said, she turned over and moved to the edge of the bed—as far from him as possible.

The ringing telephone had awakened Felicia. As she tossed and turned in her bed trying to go back to sleep, she suddenly got an idea. She turned on the table lamp, picked up the telephone receiver and dialed, A-L-4-0… By the sixth ring, Maria groggily made her way into the living room and answered the phone.

"Hello…Hello."

After a moment of silence, Maria heard an obviously disguised, muffled, female voice say, "Keep away from John-John! You hear me? Keep away from him!" Then, the caller hung-up.

"Who was that, Maria? Who woke us up in the middle of the night?"

"I don't know, Pappa, it must have been some drunk who dialed a wrong number."

After regaining her composure, Maria concluded that the person behind the disguised voice must have been Felicia. *Who else could it be?* she thought.

Chapter 36: Right Thing – Right Fist

John-John and Danny always stood in the back of Old Saint Patrick's during mass because they could talk to each other without getting any nasty looks from the other parishioners, and they could step outside for a few minutes if the homily was boring. As Father Montevecchio began the12:30 mass, the head of the Holy Name Society, who was also the chief usher, was frantic because two of his ushers hadn't shown up. Spotting John-John and Danny milling about in the back of the church, he decided to put them to work as replacement ushers. Their job would be to collect money from the parishioners twice during the mass. John-John was assigned the row of pews along the south wall and Danny was assigned the adjacent row.

After Father Montevecchio's homily, the ushers walked briskly down the long aisles, genuflected at the altar, turned around and began collecting donations. Danny soon came upon Serafina, Felicia and Francesca, who were seated in the fifth pew. He first put the straw collection basket, which was attached to the end of a wooden pole, in front of Francesca, who was seated the farthest from the aisle. She dropped fifteen cents into the basket. Felicia did likewise, while giving Danny a dirty look. Then, he placed the basket in front of Serafina who dropped in some loose change. Danny being a prankster at heart couldn't pass up the opportunity of having some fun—even during mass. As he was about to continue on to the sixth pew, he decided to irk Serafina by putting the collection basket in front of her once again. While doing so, he gestured to her with his right hand to put some more money in the basket—the unspoken, but clearly understood message to Serafina, was that she had not put enough money in the collection basket the first time.

Danny's action angered Serafina so much that she couldn't contain herself. While gritting her teeth, she blurted out a string of Neapolitan curse words in a voice loud enough to be heard by the parishioners within several pews of her. He responded by smiling and then by putting his index finger vertically across his lips while whispering, *"Silenzio."*

To really get Serafina's goat, Danny repeated his collection basket maneuver during the second collection; she responded as before, but this time adding some curse words in English while gesturing with both hands as she looked up to Jesus on the cross. After dumping his collected money into the burlap sack held by the chief usher, Danny gave John-John the "let's go" signal, not wanting to come face-to-face with Serafina when the mass ended. As they were walking back towards the newsstand, Danny couldn't stop talking and laughing about his collection basket stunt. After about five minutes of listening to Danny's "replays," John-John changed the subject to their previous night's escapades with Maria and Judy.

"Danny, Judy and Maria are both beautiful and hot…real hot! I can't believe how far we got with them last night."

"Yeah, that's true. But, I'm really surprised how far you got, especially since it was only your second date with Maria…After all, you're not known for your speed when it comes to girls."

"Danny, that Maria is something special. You know, my father has a saying: 'Every pot has its lid'…I think I found my lid. I realize she's only the third girl I've ever been with, but she meets all of my specifications for the perfect girl."

"Specifications? You're already startin' to talk like an engineer… but, don't you think there might be some other girl out there who might be even better for you than her?"

"I don't think so…but I guess it's possible. Anyway, I'm not gonna drop her to go looking for someone better, right now."

"Boy, I can't believe you have such strong feelings for Maria after only two dates…What about Felicia?"

"My feelings for Felicia aren't what they used to be now that I've been out with Maria."

At that point, they arrived in front of the East River Savings Bank and sat on one of the stoops. They knew that Serafina wouldn't spot them because she likely would be returning home via Prince and Lafayette—the shortest route back to her building.

As they basked in the sunshine of that unusually warm October day, Danny remarked, "You know, if we play our cards right, we both might get laid by Christmas!"

"Well, I really wouldn't wanna force myself on Maria. I'm sure she's a virgin."

"Well, if I get an opportunity, I'll screw Judy…virgin, or no virgin!"

"Do you feel as strongly about Judy as I do about Maria?"

"Nah, I don't think so…but, maybe, someday I will. You and I are great friends, but we're very different. You have no trouble deciding on what you want. A few years ago, you decided that you wanted to be an engineer, and now, you're in engineering school. As for me, I'm not sure what the fuck I wanna do with the rest of my life…I know if you *do* decide that Maria is the girl for you, I'll be dancing at the wedding of you two, someday."

"Danny, no matter who I marry, you'll be at the wedding…and you'll be the Best Man!"

Just then, two young black youths arrived at the corner dressed in their Sunday best. From their facial expressions and the way they were looking up at the street signs, it was apparent to John-John and Danny that they were lost. Why else would they be in the neighborhood? Most blacks were well aware that Little Italy (at that time) was a very dangerous place for them, especially after dark and on weekends.

Like sharks being attracted to blood in the ocean, the presence of the two black youths soon attracted four young neighborhood "toughs." The ringleader, Mickey "Black," was brandishing a three-foot-long 2 x 4; Jimmy "Beef" was carrying a stickball bat; and the other two sported clenched fists. These ruffians were each about sixteen years old, while the black youths appeared to be somewhat younger.

"Hey, what the fuck are *you* guys doin' in this neighborhood!" shouted Mickey.

"We don't mean to be here, man. We're lost. We don't know where we are," responded the chubby black youth, who could best be described as looking as NBC's Al Roker might have looked when he was fifteen years old.

"Listen, we don't allow no fuckin' coons in our neighborhood!" exclaimed Jimmy, while cocking his stickball bat as if ready to swing.

The wiry black youth shakingly replied, "We're not lookin' for no trouble. Just leave us alone and we'll be on our way."

"We're gonna teach you fuckin' spooks a lesson!" shouted Mickey as he and his friends encircled the two black youths.

I gotta do something, thought John-John. His sense of right-and-wrong simply wouldn't allow him to stand by. He knew that once the attack would begin, the group dynamic would take over and create a frenzy of punching and kicking, accompanied by blows with the 2 x 4 and the stickball bat— most likely, to the heads of the black youths.

"Hey, leave these guys alone! They ain't bothering anybody!" yelled John-John, as he approached the group.

"Mind your own fuckin' business, John-John!" snapped Mickey.

John-John pushed his way into the circle, putting himself directly between the black youths and Mickey "Black," who ironically was darker than both of the black youths.

Although John-John was much bigger and stronger than the four young toughs, Danny knew that he shouldn't let him try to handle the situation alone. So, he shoved his way behind John-John to cover his back, while yelling, "Get the fuck out of here, Mickey! Leave 'em alone, Jimmy! They're lost! They're not fuckin' troublemakers!"

"Fuck you, Danny!" yelled Mickey, as he and his three pals slowly started backing off.

"No, fuck you!"

With that, the four toughs turned around and walked away.

"Hey guys, where do you want to go?" asked John-John.

"We wanna go back home to Brooklyn," the chubby youth replied.

"Well, you need to go across the street and take the train to Brooklyn Bridge Station…then, go across to the other side of the platform and take the express."

"Thanks, man. Thanks for jumpin' in," said the wiry youth as he pointed to John-John…"And thank you, too, man," pointing to Danny.

The chubby youth couldn't thank John-John and Danny enough as all four of them crossed Lafayette Street and walked to the subway kiosk. After the youths went down the stairs to the subway station, John-John and Danny walked back across the street and resumed their conversation back on the stoop.

"Danny, I think we did a good deed, today. Who knows what could have happened to those guys? I'm glad we nipped it in the bud."

"Yeah, that Mickey is one crazy bastard…and his buddies are just as bad. If they started swingin' at us, I'm sure we would've won, but I bet our suits would've gotten messed up."

"I bet that within the next five-to-ten years, they'll all be spending some time up the river."

"Yeah, I'm sure they'll be doin' time in Sing-Sing or some other joint, John-John."

"Well, I'll be heading home, now, for some macaroni and meatballs. I'm not coming back down. I gotta catch-up on my reading assignments…Good luck on your first day of work."

"See you tomorrow, big guy."

John-John crossed Spring Street and headed towards Mulberry. The three Fasano sisters were sitting in front of their building, as usual.

"Hey, John-John, I saw what happened on the corner…You know, you should've minded your own business. We don't want no coloreds walkin' around this neighborhood. Let 'em stay up in Harlem where they belong!"

"Listen, Tessie, those young black guys just got off at the wrong subway stop. They weren't looking for trouble."

"You know, John-John, you may be goin' to some fancy college, but remember, you're still one of us…and we all stick together around here."

Fannie chimed in: "Next time, don't butt in. Mickey and his friends were just tryin' to protect the neighborhood…You know, if we don't keep them *mou-lin-yans* (southern Italian dialect for eggplants) outta here, the next thing you know is that they'll be tryin' to mess around with the neighborhood girls."

As the other sisters shook their heads in agreement, John-John realized that any further words on his part would be a waste of time. So, he just nodded his head and said, "Have a nice day, ladies."

Shortly after leaving the Fasano sisters, a bottle whizzed by his head and broke against the building wall. He instinctively covered his head and then turned to see where the bottle had come from. Standing opposite him on the other side of the street were Mickey "Black" and his three buddies.

"Who threw that bottle?"

"I did, you fuckin' scumbag!" yelled Mickey.

"Yeah, you should learn to mind your own fuckin' business!" added Jimmy.

John-John's blood began to boil. "You think you're so fuckin' tough Mickey…Come over here and let's see how tough you really are!"

To his surprise, Mickey, armed with his 2 x 4, crossed the street. Although he probably wouldn't have done so if he were by himself, he couldn't lose face in front of his pals. As he approached within 2 feet of John-John, he began to curse and grind his teeth. When Mickey raised the 3-foot long piece of lumber close to his right ear, as if in a batter's stance, John-John knew that he was about to take a swing at his head. As he started to swing, John-John blocked the 2 x 4 with his left forearm while simultaneously landing a quick right "roundhouse" punch squarely on Mickey's jaw. The punch was so powerful that it knocked the 150-pound Mickey down.

Mickey's friends, who had lagged a few feet behind him, arrived at the curb just as Mickey's limp body dropped onto the sidewalk.

"Mickey, are you okay!" John-John yelled as he stooped down next to Mickey.

Jimmy gently smacked Mickey's face a few times and shook him. To everyone's relief, Mickey opened his eyes about ten seconds later.

"Listen guys, you know I really didn't wanna let it come to this. I had no choice…I had to hit him."

They all shook their heads in agreement. Soon, Mickey was back on his feet, but he was obviously groggy and his eyes were glazed.

"Mickey, I'm sorry I hit you so hard…but I only threw one punch…and I didn't stomp on you when you were down. Your friends can back me up on this."

Mickey's reply was incomprehensible, but John-John sensed that he was grateful that he hadn't beaten the crap out of him while he was unconscious on the sidewalk. He knew that had Mickey successfully conked him on the head with the 2 x 4, he wouldn't have shown any mercy. He likely would have beaten John-John to a pulp.

With Mickey seemingly okay, John-John decided to head for home. His apartment at 214 Mulberry Street was less than 100 feet away. As he was ascending the steps leading to his third-floor apartment, he thought, *Boy, I'm glad Pop taught me how to throw a punch. Those lessons really came in handy, today!*

"John-John, the macaroni will be ready in about five minutes… you just made it! You know your father wouldn't have let me hold up dinner for you. Once the food is ready, he's ready to dig in."

"Yeah, I know, Ma."

"Next Sunday, try to get home about twenty minutes before dinner, so I won't have to listen to your father."

"Okay, Ma."

"Why are you late, John-John?"

"I just lost track of the time, Ma...I just lost track of the time."

He had decided not to mention the fight since he felt that parents shouldn't get involved in what happens on the street; that is, what happens on the street should stay on the street. Had his suit been ripped in the fight, then he would have been compelled to tell his parents what had happened; but, since his clothes were fine, there was no need to mention the fight.

After devouring a full dish of ziti, topped with his mother's great gravy— or as some say, "sauce"—John-John went on to eat two meatballs, a *braciola*, two sausages and a stuffed artichoke—eating the entire meal in less than ten minutes because his heart was still racing as an aftermath to the fight.

Shortly after dinner, he went into the living room and began reading from his *Contemporary Civilization* textbook. His homework assignment required reading a 40-page excerpt of Saint Augustine's *City of God* and answering four philosophical questions. It was difficult reading, especially in a noisy three-room apartment; but, his ability to concentrate was exceptional; he could tune-out the noise of his family and even the TV set.

After a restless night's sleep, he set off for school on Monday morning. While riding on the subway, his mind wandered back and forth to Sunday's incident. He knew that many neighborhood people would have agreed with Tessie: that he should have minded his own business. But, he concluded that he had done the right thing by stepping in and preventing the two black youths from getting beat-up just because they were black.

Upon exiting the Broadway Local at 116th Street, he took in the impressive panorama of the Columbia campus. As he walked along College Walk—a brick-paved extension of 116th Street, which is closed to traffic—it became obvious to him that this enclave of academia was so, so, very different from the tough streets of Little Italy that the two places might as well have been on two different planets.

He was hoping that he wouldn't bump into Leslie because he wasn't sure if he should go through with their planned date the week after next or come up with some lame excuse to postpone or cancel it. He had deep feelings for Maria, even though they had only been on two dates; however, he wondered if he should spend some time getting to know Leslie, so he could better gauge his feelings for Maria. He knew enough to understand that an eighteen-year-old probably wasn't mature enough to distinguish between love and lust. As it turned out, he didn't run into Leslie that day, and by 4 o'clock, he was back in front of the newsstand talking to Joe.

"C'mon inside, John-John."

"Okay, Joe."

Once inside the newsstand, Joe started talking in a serious tone of voice. "I heard you saved two colored kids from gettin' a beatin' from Mickey 'Black' and his buddies."

"Yeah, that's true. But, it wasn't only me. Danny also got involved."

"I heard, later, Mickey threw a bottle at you and he tried to hit you with a 2 x 4. They say you blocked the 2 x 4 and hit him with a 'haymaker' right on the chin."

"Boy, you know everything that goes on around here…Yeah, I hit him so hard that I knocked him out for a few seconds."

"You did good, John-John…you did good. That Mickey is a rotten, treacherous bastard. But, listen, you better watch your back. Mickey's the type of guy that'll sneak up behind you and whack you in the head with a pipe or somethin'."

"I know he's treacherous, but I think deep down inside he feels that I let him off the hook by not stomping on him while he was down…and he's grateful for that. Besides, he knows that he started everything by throwing the bottle and swinging the 2 x 4."

"Yeah, maybe, but be careful for the next couple of weeks, anyhow…and keep an eye on his friends, too."

"I guess if Mickey had cracked my head with that 2 x 4, I might have gotten brain damage."

Joe laughed, "Yeah, instead of bein' an engineer, you would have to make a livin' by sellin' fuckin' pencils in the subway, or somethin' like that…By the way, that knock-out punch of yours did a lot for your reputation in the neighborhood. I don't think nobody's gonna try to mess with you from now on."

"Well, I hope you're right. I hate to fight, but I'm glad I'm able to handle myself. If Mickey 'Black' was built like me, I'm sure he would be beating up someone new every day."

"You know, I really can't understand all this hatred towards the coloreds. They're human bein's just like us…only with darker skin. People around here often call them animals and apes."

"Yeah, Joe, that's not all they call them."

"Well, ever since I went blind and opened this newsstand, I got to know a lot of colored customers who mostly work in the factories on Crosby Street or Broadway. Most of 'em are really nice people… nicer than some low-lifes around here. Since I can't see 'em, my opinion of them is based on their characters…You know, the way they talk to me…the way they treat me…the way some of 'em offer to help me out."

"Joe, I have a stupid question."

"What?"

"Since you can't see them, how do you know they're colored?"

"Well, usually, their voice gives 'em away. Most of 'em speak like southerners. Also, they use some different words and expressions, like 'hey, man'…Too bad there's so much hatred in this world. Why can't we all just get along?"

"You're right, Joe. We should all try to get along with each other."

"You know Tony 'Gallons,' the old bachelor who's always bettin' the numbers with me?"

"Of course. How could I not know him?"

"That really wasn't a question, John-John…Anyway, you wouldn't believe what he did the other day."

"What? What did he do?"

"He told me that he got a new refrigerator last week. It was delivered to his apartment by two colored guys. Well, one of 'em asked Tony for a glass of water. Tony gave him a glass of water, but when the guys left, he threw the glass away. He said, 'I'm ain't never gonna drink from a glass that a spade drunk from.' How prejudiced can a person be?"

"Oh boy, that man is a fuckin' idiot. I've heard about being prejudiced, but that really tops the cake. Couldn't he just wash the glass like a normal person would?"

"No, he said that washing it wouldn't be good enough."

"Joe, it's good he never married."

"Why? I don't get it?"

"Because, he hasn't reproduced…His prejudices will die with him."

"Hey, John-John, let's change the subject…I wanna hear the details of what you and Danny did with your Lower Eastside gals in his convertible Saturday night."

"How do know about that? I'm sure Danny hasn't stopped by the stand, today…It's his first day of work."

"Well, Frankie told me about it…but, he didn't know all the details."

"How did Frankie find out?"

"Danny hung-out with Frankie on Sunday while you were doin' your homework." Joe added with a laugh, "Anyway, I wanna blowby-blow description, if you catch my drift."

"Okay, Joe, since you've taught me so much about the facts of life, I owe it to you to tell you everything…but, please don't spread it around. I might marry Maria, someday."

"Don't worry, my lips are sealed."

Given Joe's assurance, John-John gave him a play-by-play description of what had happened in Danny's convertible on Saturday night; and Joe enjoyed every minute of it. Then, John-John switched gears: "Should I go on that date with that Barnard girl, Leslie, I told you about?"

"That's a no-brainer…of course you should go. You need to date many girls to be sure you really know what you want. You shouldn't decide so soon that Maria is the girl for you. Listen, not long ago you thought Felicia was the right girl for you…and now, she's history. My advice is to go on that date with Leslie. But, make up some excuse so that Maria doesn't go out with somebody else."

"I hate to lie to her."

"Trust me. Lie to her! If things don't work out with Leslie, you can drop her like a dead fish and go back to Maria without her bein' any the wiser. If you're not sure about Leslie, try to keep both of 'em on a line while you make up your mind."

"I guess I'll follow your advice, Joe. You haven't steered me wrong yet."

"That's right, John-John, when it comes to dealin' with women, I'm smarter than any of your Columbia *perfessers!*"

Chapter 37: Blessing the Car

"**Hey, Joe**, gimme 6-4-2 and 9-6-9, combination…and gimme 2-1-5, straight. Here's \$3…put a buck on each."

"Okay, Tony, you got it," replied Joe to the elderly Tony "Gallons."

"I hope your luck changes. You ain't won in a long time. I never make nuttin on your fuckin' bets."

Shortie, who just then got the bug to play a number, asked Danny, "What's the first three numbers of your new license plates?"

"7-3-2."

"Okay, Joe, here's half-a-buck. I want 7-3-2, combination."

"Joe, here's another fifty cents. Put me down for the same number," said Danny.

"Danny, what you up to tonight?" asked Shortie.

"Well, me and Judy, and John-John and Maria are going up to Radio City to see that new Elizabeth Taylor-Richard Burton movie, *The V.I.P.s*. We're aimin' to be there at around 7 o'clock. The movie starts at 7:20 and the stage show with the Rockettes starts about two hours later…Do you and Angie wanna join us?"

"Nah, I don't think so…By the way, are you drivin' up to Radio City?"

"No, we're gonna take the subway. Parkin' uptown is a pain in the ass… especially on a Saturday night…too many fuckin' tourists."

"Yeah, I know what ya mean…You know, Danny, it's a shame to keep a car like yours parked on a Saturday night. It should be put to good use."

"Oh man, I certainly put it to good use last night. I drove John-John and the girls out to Plum Beach to watch the 'submarine races'…if ya know what I mean."

"Yeah, Murray 'The K,' the disk jockey, mentions submarine race watchin' all the time on his radio show on WINS."

Plum Beach was a popular make-out spot just off Brooklyn's Belt Parkway. It wasn't much of a beach. The water was polluted, the stretch of sand was quite narrow and filled with litter and debris, and there were "No Swimming" signs posted everywhere. Still, many young people found Plum Beach to be a romantic setting, and many a girl was lured to the site on the pretext of watching the so-called "submarine races," although just about every girl knew that there was no such thing as submarine races.

"Say, Danny, since you're not using your car tonight, can I borrow it?"

"Oh, I don't know…I really don't like the idea of lending out my car."

"Listen, I won't go very far…only to Pier 40…you know…off Houston Street. I never get a chance to be alone with Angie. This would be a great opportunity for me."

"Okay but drive carefully…No accidents!"

"Don't worry, man, I'll be very, very careful."

The Saturday evening double date was an enjoyable experience for all. Maria, who had never been to the Radio City Music Hall, was totally awed by the magnificence and grandeur of the place. The movie was good, but the stage show was superb—its theme being the Far East and the Far West. After the show, the two couples strolled down Sixth Avenue to 42nd Street and then to the Horn and Hardart's Automat on 42nd and Third for dessert.

For many people—especially "first-timers"—eating at the Automat was a fun experience. The Automat was a self-service restaurant chain with a unique twist: Food items were displayed behind tiered 5"x 8" windows which would spring open once the customer inserted the appropriate number of nickels into the adjacent slot, and turned the knob. The Automat was known for its cups of baked beans, its dishes of macaroni and cheese, and its warm pies. It's equally famous coffee, which was dispensed from a gold-colored lions head, could be had for just two nickels.

Danny, always the clown, decided to have some fun by annoying the staff behind the little windows. He tapped his ring against a pie window until a middle-aged man dressed in white slid open the metal back closure and peered out from behind the window.

"Do you have any dinkleberry pie?" yelled Danny through the closed mini-window.

"No. We don't have no dinkleberry pie…I never even heard of dinkleberries."

"Well, scratch your asshole and you'll find some!"

The girls chuckled while the angry employee slid the metal backing sheet closed with so much force that one of the little windows sprung open, thereby allowing Danny to grab a *free* piece of huckleberry pie.

Meanwhile, Shortie and Angie were going at it hot and heavy in the back seat of Danny's convertible, which Shortie had parked at the foot of Pier 40, facing the Hudson River. Pier 40 was a secluded and dimly lit spot where one could gaze across the river to the lights of Jersey City while making out. The only drawback to this location was that it was immediately adjacent to the Westside Highway. The old, elevated steel structure detracted from the ambiance of the make-out spot, not so much by its appearance, but by the din of the vehicles whizzing by about 20 feet above.

On Monday, the three "lunch mates" were seated at their usual table in Basilica High School when Maria asked Angie about her weekend.

"Saturday was a big day in my life…Shh, keep it quiet"…Lowering her voice, Angie continued, "I finally went 'all the way.' Me and Shortie did it in the back seat of Danny's convertible on Saturday night at Pier 40."

"Oh my God!" Judy exclaimed, louder than she should have.

"You did it? You did it?"

"Shh…yeah, I did it."

Oh, my…How was it?" Judy continued.

"It was great! A little painful at first, but then, it was very enjoyable."

"You were able to do it in the back seat?" asked Maria.

"Yeah, no problem. Both of us ain't very tall…By the way, Judy, I think you'll be the next one to lose your 'cherry' in the back seat of Danny's convertible."

"Why do ya say that?" gasped Judy.

"Well, guys will be guys…I bumped into Frankie on Sunday night. You know, he doesn't hold anythin' back. He told me that Shortie couldn't wait to tell Danny about…" With her voice trailing to a whisper, she continued, "about him screwing me in the back seat. Shortie had started off the conversation by saying, 'Danny, I blessed your car last night.'"

"Oh, that's a strange way of expressing it," remarked Maria.

"Well, Frankie said that Danny was really pissed off because he felt he should've been the first one to score in his car. So, my guess is that Danny will try to make up for lost time by gettin' into your pants as soon as he can." Angie added with a smile, "Don't worry, you'll enjoy it."

"Oh, no wonder Danny called me last night and asked me to go out with him, tonight."

"Did you say 'yes,'" asked Maria?

"Yeah, I figured why not. I'll do my homework as soon as I get home and I'll meet him around seven. As long as I'm home by ten, my parents won't make a big deal out of my bein' out on a weekday night."

"Well, Judy are you gonna let Danny have his way with you, tonight?" asked Angie, getting right to the point, as usual.

"I don't know. I'll cross that bridge when I come to it."

"Trust me," said Angie, reassuringly, "It'll be great…I was a bit nervous, but now that it's all behind me, I feel like I've entered a whole new world. Last week, I was a girl, now, I'm a woman!"

When the school day ended, Judy and Maria made their way back home, together. Upon exiting the Bleecker Street Station, they lit-up their cigarettes and began their leisurely walk to Second Avenue.

"Judy, about how many days ago did you get your last period?"

"About three weeks ago…say, twenty or twenty-one days ago. Why?"

"Well, if you decide to go all the way, tonight, it would be almost impossible for you to get pregnant."

"Says who?"

"Says Cousin Maria. She taught me all about the Rhythm Method…you know, what time of the month you could have sex without getting pregnant and what time of the month you could get pregnant."

"Oh yeah, good ole Cousin Maria. She's the one who told you about 'advanced kissing'…right?"

"Yeah, she's the one."

"Maria, I really don't know what I'll do tonight, but I'll call you after the date and let you know what happened…that's if your parents won't mind me callin' you between nine and ten."

"No, they won't mind. Anyway, I'll tell them you need some help with your homework."

"Okay, I'll definitely call you, tonight."

Judy sat in her living room for about an hour after dinner, contemplating her coming date. She was experiencing anxiety because she wasn't sure if she should fend off Danny or just let things happen. When she heard a horn beep outside, she looked out the window and spotted Danny in his convertible with the top down. Judy, who loved punctuality, was happy that he was right on time. She put her anxiety behind her and headed for the door, after first donning a jacket. As soon as she was comfortably seated in the convertible, Danny floored the gas pedal, leaving a long patch of rubber on Second Street, as a way of highlighting their departure. Within ten minutes, they were parked by Pier 40.

"Let's go to the back seat, Judy."

"Not yet," she responded, with a tinge of nervousness in her voice. "Let's look at the river and listen to *Murray 'The K's' Swingin' Soiree* for a little while."

"Okay…Boy, you really get a nice view of Jersey City's lights from here."

"Yeah, you sure do."

After about ten minutes, Judy overcame her nervousness, and unbeknown to Danny, she had decided to 'go all the way'—assuming Danny would attempt to do so.

"Danny, I'm ready to go to the back seat with you, now."

"Sure, but let me put the top up, first."

After about twenty minutes of steamy passion in the back seat, Judy was no longer a virgin.

Danny dropped her off at her building at a few minutes after nine. She immediately picked up the phone and dialed Maria, who was sitting next to the phone anticipating her call.

"Hi, Maria,

"Hi Judy. How did it go?"

"Let's just say that I joined Angie's club…and that I'm glad I did."

"Judy, I guess your parents can hear what you are saying to me."

"Ah-ha."

"Okay. I understand, but let's see if you can tell me a little more in a way that your parents won't understand…By the way, I'm free to talk because my parents are in the kitchen and I'm sitting here in the living room."

"Okay. It was wonderful. Maybe, you should join the club."

"Do it with John-John?"

"Who else?"

"Sure, if I would decide to join the club, John-John would be the one…Did it hurt…Did you bleed, Judy?"

"The answer to both of your questions is 'yes,' but not much in either case."

"Are you feeling any guilt?"

"Yeah, but only a little...and I think I'll get over it."

"Are you gonna have sex with Danny, again?"

"Yeah, maybe on the weekend…if we're alone."

"John-John told me that this coming Saturday he might have to spend most of the day and night up at Columbia working with some classmates on a project. If that's the case, we'll double-date with you and Danny on Friday night, and you'll be alone with Danny on Saturday night...Don't worry, you can screw all you want on Saturday night without getting pregnant."

"You sure?"

"Yeah. Next time I see you, I'll teach you the fine points of the Rhythm Method."

"Okay, have a good night, Maria. See you in the mornin'."

"Goodnight, Judy, I'm sure we'll have plenty to talk about tomorrow."

Chapter 38: Electricity

"Hey, Joe, how's it goin'?

"Okay, I guess."

"You don't seem to be your usual happy self, today."

"Ah, I'm pissed off, John-John. That miserable bastard, Seymour, told me he'll shut-off my electric if I don't start payin' him twenty bucks a month for it in November…I been payin' him $10 a month. Now he wants to double my electric bill…*and*, he wants me to give him a two-month security deposit because I'm late payin' him, sometimes."

"Joe, I never realized that the newsstand's electricity came from Seymour and Elaine's luncheonette."

"Yeah, the electric cable goes from their luncheonette under the sidewalk and up into the newsstand."

"Is there a separate electric meter for the newsstand?"

"Nah, my electric is included in the electric bill for the luncheonette."

"How did Seymour come up with the $20 figure?"

"He just decided, out of thin air, that I should pay him $20 a month…that greedy bastard!"

"You hardly use any electricity. Between May and September, the only electricity you use is for the radio. The rest of the year, you have the radio, plus the electric heater, and in the evening, two, 40-watt light bulbs. Even ten bucks a month is too much."

"He wants all the money by November 1st. Today is Thursday, October 24th. So, if I don't come up with $60 for him by next Friday, he'll shut-off my electric."

"That Seymour really has no compassion for you, Joe…no compassion."

"I'll say. To make matters worse, he said if I don't pay, he won't allow me to use his terlit anymore. As you know, I use it whenever I gotta take a dump."

"Do you use it every day?"

"Nah, about two or three times a week. Pissin' is no problem as long as I got my pickle jar, but taking a dump is somethin' else… when you gotta go, you gotta go!"

"Where else can you use a toilet around here?"

"I used to use the terlit in Jake's Luncheonette, but as you know, he went out of business in September…I can't use Luigi the barber's terlit. We recently had an argument 'cause I took too many of his numbers players away from him…I didn't try to steal 'em from him…they just like me better than him."

"Yeah, I can understand that. That Luigi is plain nasty."

"In an emergency, I could go across the street to Piccolo's Bakery or Anthony's Liquor Store. They're nice people. I'm sure they would gladly let me use their terlits, but, I hate to cross the street, especially if I can't get someone to help me cross."

"Seymour certainly has you over a barrel."

"Well, enough about that fuckin' rat bastard for now…did you hear that Shortie and Danny both scored…Shortie on Saturday night, and Danny on Monday night?"

"Of course I heard. That kind of news travels fast among the Sheiks…we are like brothers, you know."

"How are you doin' with Maria…and what about that Jewish girl you met up at Columbia?"

"Joe, I really have deep feelings for Maria, but I'm going to take your advice and see Leslie."

"When are you goin' to see her?"

"Saturday. We confirmed our date, today. I was looking for her all week on campus, but I couldn't find her. Then, surprisingly, she was waiting for me outside Pupin Hall at 2 o'clock, today. It seems she did some detective work and found out that I would be coming out of my Physics class at around that time.

"How did she greet you?"

"She gave me a hug and a kiss on the cheek."

"Where are you goin' on your date?"

"She told me that she had picked-up two tickets for the Columbia-Lehigh football game. So, I thought our date would just be the football game followed by dinner…Well, as it turns out, she has more in mind than dinner. She told me that she wants to drive us to the football game, which is up at Baker Field…and after the game, we're going up to her parents' home in Scarsdale."

"Scarsdale? Her family must be fuckin' loaded."

"I guess so…Here's the kicker. She wants me to bring a change of clothes because she want me to spend the night at her parents' house."

"Sounds like you're gonna score with her."

"Maybe…we'll see, Joe. It's going to be a busy weekend for me. Friday night, I have a date with Maria, and then for the rest of the weekend, I'll be with Leslie. I don't know when I'll be able to do my homework."

"Screw the homework!"

"That's easy for you to say, Joe."

"Does Maria know that you'll be away for the weekend?"

"Well, last week, I told her that I might be working on a project up at Columbia…and I said the project could go on well into the night."

"Good, I taught you well. You know, you didn't actually lie to Maria."

"I didn't?"

"No, your project is Leslie…ha, ha, ha."

"I actually feel a little guilty about lying to Maria, but dating Leslie will help me figure out if my feelings for Maria are really as deep as I think they are."

"Hey, John-John, do you wanna have some fun and do me a favor at the same time?"

"What do you have in mind?"

"Why don't you call-up Seymour and give him a phony delivery order."

"Okay, Joe, I'll do it. He deserves it…and much more…because of the way he's trying to put the screws to you."

That said, John-John crossed the street and "squeezed" into the phone booth in front of the East River Savings Bank. He deposited ten cents and began to dial the luncheonette's phone number, which was posted in large letters on a sign in its window. Affecting a slight Yiddish accent, he began his phony order.

"Hello, this is Milton of the J & S Hat Company, 85 Spring Street, 4th Floor. I'd like six cups of coffee with milk and sugar; two prune Danishes; three jelly donuts, two 7-Up floats; one vanilla malted; and two hamburgers with tomatoes and pickles."

"Anything else, Milton?"

"Let me see…hang on…Oh yes, a ham-and-cheese sandwich."

"Okay, your order will be delivered in about fifteen minutes."

John-John then crossed the street and told Joe that the phony order had been placed. Then, he proceeded to give Joe a play-by-play description of what was going on inside the luncheonette.

"Joe, the cook just put two hamburgers on the grill. Elaine is making a malted and Seymour is pouring the coffee into paper cups."

"You did real good, John-John. You did real good," said Joe while chuckling.

"Now, Kelly the waitress is helping out with the order."

"Wow, this is fun! I can picture it all in my mind."

"Joe, it looks like the order is ready to go."

Soon, the delivery boy left the luncheonette carrying the order in a cardboard box. John-John could see him as he made his way to 85 Spring, which was less than a block away. Within five minutes, the delivery boy was back at the luncheonette.

"Joe, Seymour looks very mad. He's making a lot of gestures. Too bad, I can't read lips."

"Great! Fuck him! Hey, why don't you call Seymour again and complain that you didn't get your order."

"Joe, you're a ball-buster from the old school." John-John then put Joe's idea into effect.

"Hello, this is Milton. Where's my order? My employees are yelling at me!"

"We tried to deliver your order, sir. The delivery boy came back and told me he couldn't find your factory."

"Listen, it's J & S Hats at 89 Spring Street, 4th Floor."

"Oh, I see what's the problem. We tried to deliver your order to *85 Spring*...There must've been some kind of mix-up on our part."

"Well, sounds like an honest mistake...Oh, by the way, why don't you add two pieces of apple pie to the order...and please hurry up!"

"Okay...and because of our mistake, the apple pies are on the house."

Ten minutes later, John-John gave Joe the results of the second wild-goose chase. Joe was particularly pleased to learn that all of the beverages were thrown in the garbage pail and that Seymour and Elaine were eating the hamburgers, while apparently arguing with each other.

"Now that we've given Seymour some grief, I think I'll head home and start on my homework."

"Okay, John-John...If I don't see you, good luck on Saturday with Leslie."

As John-John approached his apartment building, he noticed Big Sal and Gappy standing near the entrance. This was not unusual, for it seemed that as long as John-John could remember, Big Sal and his cronies could almost always be found standing near John-John's building in the afternoon.

Salvatore "Big Sal" Tusa was a *Capo* in one of New York City's Five Families. The 65-year–old Mafioso was always impeccably dressed in a finely tailored Italian suit. He usually wore a tie and a white-on-white, cuff-linked shirt with a heavily starched collar. When the weather was cold he would don a wool topcoat and a fedora with a wide brim. His deportment was that of a "man of respect"—and he was accorded great respect by everyone in the neighborhood. Big Sal was very congenial and he displayed Old World manners. He was particularly respectful to the older ladies of the neighbor-hood, always tipping his hat to them as they walked by, and occasionally exchanging pleasantries. In short, Big Sal was the prototypical *Don*—right out of Hollywood's central casting.

Everyone knew that there was a dark side to Big Sal; one doesn't become a *Capo* by being an altar boy. Big Sal's rap sheet was quite long. He had "made his bones" in the Roaring Twenties but he had apparently continued his rise to the top by committing various crimes in the 30's and 40's. The latest entry on his rap sheet was an acquittal on a homicide charge in 1946.

Big Sal got a great deal of gratification out of doing favors for neighborhood people. If somebody's son needed a job, Big Sal, who had much influence on the waterfront and in the construction industry, would usually find a decent job for that son; some were even given "no-show jobs." Big Sal asked for nothing in return, although it was tacitly understood that should he ever need a favor in return, it had better be done with alacrity.

When John-John reached the two men he said, "Good afternoon, gentlemen."

"Good afternoon, John-John," they both replied in unison. Then, Big Sal added, "How ya doin' up at Columbia…you know I'm really proud of you. Imagine, Gappy, an Ivy Leaguer comin' out of this neighborhood."

"Thanks, I'm doing good, so far…By the way, there's something going on that I think you should know about."

"What's that?" Big Sal responded.

"Well, you know Joe, the blind newsman on Lafayette…"

"Of course we know him," replied Big Sal. "What's the problem?"

"Well, Seymour, the owner of the luncheonette next to the newsstand, wants to raise Joe's electric bill from $10 a month to $20 a month. Also, he wants Joe to give him $40 as a security deposit. Seymour says that if Joe doesn't pay him the security plus the twenty bucks by November 1st, he'll shut off his electricity…plus he won't allow him to use the luncheonette's toilet if he doesn't pay him the entire $60 by November 1st."

"That's really low…shakin' down a blind man. First of all, I'm sure Joe uses very little electric, especially durin' the summer."

"There's nuttin I hate more than a connivin' chiseler," added Gappy in an angry tone.

"What kinda miserable low-life prick withholds a terlit from anyone, especially a blind man?" questioned Big Sal in an even angrier tone.

"I hope I wasn't out of line by telling you about Joe's problem."

"What, are you kiddin'? You did the right thing by tellin' us," reassured Big Sal.

As John-John entered his building, Big Sal and his loyal underboss, Gaspare "Gappy" Serra started walking to the luncheonette. By the time they reached it, they had fire in their eyes and their blood was boiling. They simply couldn't fathom how Seymour could be so heartless to a poor blind man.

Once inside the luncheonette, Big Sal and Gappy "nudged" Seymour into the back room and had a "very meaningful conversation" with him. For sure, they put the fear of God in him. When the two men exited the luncheonette, they told Joe that the newsstand's monthly electric bill had actually been reduced—from $10 to $5—and that he didn't have to give Seymour a security deposit; plus, he could use the toilet whenever he needed to.

"I'm so grateful to the both of yous. By the way, who told you about my problem?"

Big Sal replied, "John-John told us about it a few minutes ago… He's a great kid, that John-John. I know him ever since he was a baby. He's smart, respectful…and I hear he's got a great right!"

"Listen, Joe," Gappy added, "Let us know if that scumbag gives you any more problems. If he does, we'll fuckin' shut him down!"

"Thanks, gents. If he gives me a problem, again, I'll definitely let you know."

Chapter 39: Scarsdale

"Good mornin', Joe."

"Hey, John-John, you sound like you're in a hurry."

"Yeah, I'm running a little late. I'm on my way up to Columbia for my weekend date with Leslie. I'm supposed to be at the 116th Street Station at 11 o'clock, and it's already 10:20."

"Okay, you better get goin'. You don't wanna be late for *that* date. I have a feelin' that she'll show you a real good time this weekend."

As John-John headed north on Lafayette Street, carrying his little maroon satchel, containing pajamas and a change of clothes, he came face-to-face with Serafina, who was heading for downtown Brooklyn for her rendezvous with Orazio Martucci.. Two weeks had passed since she had had her abortion, and she felt she could now safely resume her relationship with Orazio. Her plan was to tell him to be gentle with her; but if she were to experience any pain, she would satisfy him in other ways.

When John-John and Serafina's eyes met, they both instinctively looked down at the sidewalk. Once past Serafina, he began to jog to the Prince Street Station, not wanting to risk being late for his date. Fortunately, he made good connections and he reached the 116th Station at a few minutes before eleven. Leslie was waiting for him right in front of the station kiosk. She looked very attractive and collegiate, wearing plaid pants, a dark green turtleneck sweater and a tan jacket.

"Hi Johnny. You're right on time. I like punctuality in a guy… except during sex," she added with a laugh.

"Please, Leslie, call me John-John."

"I like Johnny…I think it suits you better, but I'll call you John-John if you absolutely insist…Do you insist, Johnny?"

"Okay…you can call me Johnny."

"My car is parked on 114th Street."

After a three-minute walk, they arrived at the car—a late model Jaguar sedan; British Racing Green with a tan leather interior.

"Is this *your* car?"

"Well, actually it's my father's car, but I keep it here at school… so, in essence, it is *my* car."

"Gee, I never rode in a Jaguar."

He enjoyed the ride up to Baker Field, and he enjoyed the football game even more because Columbia trounced Lehigh 42-21. Plus, every time Columbia had scored, Leslie had given her "Johnny" a big hug and a kiss.

Archie Roberts, No. 20, Columbia's outstanding quarterback, had treated the fans to a tremendous performance, throwing two touchdown passes and scoring two touchdowns on runs. In addition, he had played defense and also punted. As the happy home team crowd filed out of the stadium, the Columbia Band could be heard over the din, playing *Who Owns New York* and *Roar Lion Roar*.

"Well, Johnny, let's head for Scarsdale. Hopefully, you'll get to meet my parents. At a minimum, you will see my wonderful home and the town where I was raised."

Riding in the Jaguar on the open road was a thrill for John-John, especially since Leslie had a "lead foot." When she pulled into her family's driveway, he was instantly overwhelmed by the grandeur of her house. It was huge and the landscaping was exquisite. Although the house technically might not have been classified as a mansion, to John-John, it was every bit a mansion. He wondered what Leslie would think of his three-room Mulberry Street apartment. *She probably has no idea how the "other people" live.*

Upon entering the house, Leslie was greeted by her parents, less warmly than John-John might have expected.

"Mom, Dad, this is Johnny. He's studying engineering at Columbia."

As John-John shook hands with Leslie's father, her mother announced that she and her husband were going to a dinner-dance at the nearby country club.

"Muffin, there are plenty of leftovers in the fridge. I recommend the Chinese. We had it delivered for lunch," advised Mrs. Birnbaum.

"Tell me Johnny, what is your full name?" Mr. Birnbaum inquired.

"My name is John Cara."

"That's Italian, isn't it?"

"Yes. Sicilian to be exact."

"Where do you live?"

"On Mulberry Street in Little Italy."

"Oh, don't tell me that your family's in the Mafia!"

"No. Not everyone in Little Italy is in the Mafia."

"Um…okay, young man," he nodded, "You don't look like the Mafia type…By the way, I guess Leslie told you that we are Jewish."

"Well, actually, she didn't, but I kind of figured she was Jewish based on her last name."

After about twenty minutes of small talk during which John-John learned that Mr. Birnbaum was a partner in a big Park Avenue law firm, Leslie's parents headed off to the country club.

"Well, Johnny, let me see what you have in your little bag."

She unzipped the bag, sifted through the contents, and started laughing. "Pajamas? You're certainly not going to have any need for PJ's!"

"By the way, Leslie, where's my room?"

"Johnny, you'll be spending the night in *my* room…in *my* bed."

"You're kidding me. What about your parents? I'm sure your father would kill me if he caught me in bed with you."

"Don't worry, my father and mother are very, very liberal. When I turned eighteen, they told me that from that point on they considered me to be a grownup and that my bedroom was my private domain. They allow me to have overnight guests…in fact, they encourage it…and, not to disappoint them," Leslie continued with a laugh, "I've had many guys spend the night with me in my bed…so don't worry about it."

"What a difference between your parents and mine. If my father ever caught some guy with my sister, even after she turned eighteen, he would most likely bash his head in with a baseball bat or a pipe."

"Really?"

"Yeah, really…I'm not kidding. We definitely come from two different worlds, Leslie."

"Well, my parents are extremely liberal when it comes to sex. In fact, I've heard rumors that there is a great deal of hanky panky going on at their country club. There is much gossip…you know…about who is sleeping with whom, or who wants to sleep with whom, etc. Actually, there are rumors that some of the members even participate in a 'key club.'"

"What's a key club?"

"It's a wife-swapping game played among several or more couples. The way the game works is that each wife throws her house keys into a bag. Then, the husbands in the game reach into the bag, without looking, and grab a set of keys. They are then paired with the respective owners of the keys. Each husband winds up with another player's wife, and all of the newly formed couples go off and have sex in the women's houses. There are only two rules: Rule No. 1 is that if a husband inadvertently winds up with his wife's keys, he must throw them back into the bag; Rule No. 2 is that after the game is over, the spouses are not allowed to ask each other questions about what happened that night."

"Do you think your parents are into this key club thing?"

"Well, first of all, the existence of the key club is *only* a rumor… but usually, there is some basis for a rumor. Anyway, I really don't know if my parents would participate in such a thing, but I wouldn't put it past them."

"One thing I know for sure, there's absolutely no way on earth… no way on earth…that my parents would ever play such a game… and frankly, if I were married, there's no way that my wife and I would play that game. The people who play it, definitely, cannot be in love with their spouses."

"No, Johnny, I actually think that most of those couples *do* love each other, but they are just looking to spice-up their sex lives. They're bored and are looking for something different."

"How can their lives be so boring when they are living like this?"

"Let's forget about the country club set, Johnny. Are you hungry?"

"Yeah. Let's eat the Chinese leftovers that your mother left in the refrigerator for us."

After eating the leftovers and watching the news, Leslie suggested that they go upstairs.

"Each bedroom has its own bathroom and shower. Why don't you take a shower in the bathroom of the bedroom next to mine, while I shower in my bathroom."

"Okay."

He showered for about five minutes and put his clothes back on, although he had a strong feeling that he would soon be taking them off, again. When he entered her bedroom, he found the curtains drawn and the lights turned down low—almost to the intensity of a night-light. Once his eyes got used to the dim lighting, he could see Leslie sprawled on the bed, wearing only a pair of light-colored bikini panties.

"What are you doing all dressed up? Take off your clothes and jump into bed with me, silly!" she ordered, with a slight chuckle.

He dutifully complied, stripping off all of his clothes except for his jockey shorts, and he gingerly joined her on the bed. She could sense that he was a bit apprehensive.

"Tell me, Johnny, have you ever screwed a girl?"

He wanted to lie but decided to tell the truth. "No, this will be my first…presuming you want me to screw you."

"Oh, you may presume so, Sweetums. In fact, you're coming here a virgin, but I guarantee you that after I'm through with you, you'll be almost an expert in the art of lovemaking."

John-John was soon aroused. Leslie pulled off his jockey shorts and was pleased with what she saw.

"Johnny, just do what I say." adding with a laugh, "Consider me your teacher…your professor."

Leslie was very adept at sex. After a few minutes of foreplay, she guided his swollen member deep inside her. At that point, John-John felt that he had truly become a man. He knew enough about sex— particularly, from his discussions with Joe—that it was important for a man to try to hold back until the woman had achieved an orgasm. Surprisingly—and to Leslie's great satisfaction—he managed to do so for about seven or eight minutes.

"Johnny, you were great! Are you sure you never did it before?"

"Yeah, I'm sure. You're my first, Leslie."

She turned on the table lamp, giving John-John a good view of his "first conquest."

"Oh my, you look so beautiful and sexy in the glow of this light."

"Thank you, Johnny…And you look so handsome and sexy."

As she slipped her panties back on, John-John remarked, "Hey, they're Columbia Blue!"

"Yeah, I'm a Columbia fan all the way."

"So am I, but I only wear *white* jockey shorts."

"Johnny, tell me about Little Italy and what it's like to live there."

"Well, Little Italy is a place like no other…"

Doing most of the talking during the next two hours, he told her all about Joe and the newsstand crew; the illegal activities that were carried on right in the open; the mob guys; police corruption; and he told her about his family and his tiny apartment. She was fascinated because what he told her was so far out of the realm of her own life experience.

"You've rested long enough, Johnny. Now, I'm going to teach you some different positions."

She started off by showing him the female superior position, and then followed-up with several "athletic" positions. She nearly exhausted him, but after they had finished watching the eleven o'clock news, she was ready to give him another lesson.

"Now, let me teach you how to play '69', or as the French would say, *Soixante-Neuf.* I guess you've never played that game, right?"

"Well, I have been on the receiving end, but never on the giving end."

"You know, the Bible says that it is better to give than to receive. Don't worry, I'll teach you how to be a great *giver*," she added with a laugh. "Once you know how, you'll always be able to keep a woman happy."

By morning, they had had sex several times. He had learned a lot about sex from Leslie, and she seemed to be proud of her "star pupil." At around nine, they made their way to the kitchen. He was hoping that her parents were still sleeping-off their evening gala. However, to his dismay, they were already seated in the kitchen drinking coffee and eating bagels.

"Good…good…good morning Mr. and Mrs. Birnbaum," stammered John-John with guilt written all over his face.

"Good morning, Johnny," Mr. Birnbaum replied in a surprisingly warm tone.

"Did you sleep well?" Mrs. Birnbaum inquired with a slight smile.

He just nodded. After a very long moment of silence, he said, "By the way, your house…it's so beautiful…it should be in a magazine like *Architectural Record*."

"Thank you, Johnny, it actually *has* been featured in *Architectural Record*."

Leslie and John-John joined in on the breakfast. Mrs. Birnbaum encouraged him to try a bagel with lox—and he liked it. Still hungry, he followed up with a second bagel—this time, with a *shmear* of cream cheese. The breakfast conversation was quite cordial, but superficial. John-John had trouble looking Mr. Birnbaum in the eyes because he felt guilt-ridden; plus, he just couldn't fathom how Leslie's father could let a guy spend the night in bed with his daughter. *What kind of man would permit such a thing going on under his roof?* he wondered. *Certainly, no neighborhood guy would let it happen.*

Shortly after breakfast, Leslie and John-John headed back to Manhattan, but not before she had given him a tour of Scarsdale and the surrounding area.

"Leslie, I'll never forget last night. I had a great time…and you're a great teacher!"

"You were a great student. Maybe, we should do it again some time. Perhaps, around the Christmas break. But, there's one thing you should know: I'm not interested in going steady with anyone. I want to explore before I settle down. I want to live life! My goal is to experience many, many guys before I get married."

"I bet you've experienced quite a few already."

"True. From the time I lost my virginity at the age of fifteen, I must have been with over twenty guys…I've lost count of the actual number."

"Do you think that too much sexual experience could be bad for you?"

"No. Why would it?"

"Well, if one has sex with dozens of different partners, it seems to me that sex becomes superficial; whereas, sex should be something special

…something that ensures a deep emotional bond between two people…a way of connecting to each other's innermost feelings."

"Johnny, perhaps, you have the wrong major! Maybe, you should be studying psychology instead of engineering."

"Sorry, I don't mean to be playing amateur psychologist, Leslie… Anyway, suppose after you've been with thirty guys, you come to realize that Number 24 was *Mr. Right?* What would you do?"

"Has he found someone else?"

"Yes, let's assume he's found someone else."

"Well, I would simply move on…I wouldn't even try to get him back."

"So, true love isn't very important to you?"

"Oh, it would be nice to be deeply in love with my future husband, but when I do marry, in all likelihood, it will *not* be for true love. I'll probably marry an up-and-coming lawyer from father's firm, or perhaps, a Wall Street–type. My parents will see to it that I'm matched with someone who can support me in the manner in which I am accustomed. One more thing…I'm quite sure that my parents would disown me if I didn't marry within my religion."

"Well, that leaves me out."

"Most likely, but that doesn't mean we can't see each other, occasionally, and have some fun. As I said, let's try to get together around the Christmas break. In the meantime, as a homework assignment, I want you to read and study *The Kama Sutra.*"

"What's *The Kama Sutra?*"

"It's a great ancient Hindu sex manual from which one can learn just about every sexual position known to mankind."

"Oh, it sounds interesting. I'll see if I can find it in the Butler Library."

On the subway ride back from Columbia to Little Italy, John-John came to realize that his relationship with Leslie would certainly lead nowhere. In fact, even if he were to see her during the Christmas break, it would only be to satisfy each other's sexual needs—nothing more. Maria, on the other hand, fulfilled him on an emotional level, an intellectual level, and on a cultural level. Plus, although Leslie was certainly attractive, in his eyes, she couldn't match Maria's classic Italian beauty.

Before hitting the books at home, he telephoned Maria.

"How did your project turn out?"

"Oh…oh, quite well," he responded, fighting off his feelings of guilt. He justified his wild weekend to himself by concluding that he had gained some valuable sexual experience…and that a man *should* have some experience so he will know what to do with a woman when the time comes.

As they continued their conversation, he felt so happy that Maria had come into his life—and it was his goal to keep her in his life; there would be no further need to "sample" other girls—regardless of Joe's advice.

After school on Monday, John-John stopped by the newsstand to give Joe his "mandatory briefing" about his wild weekend with Leslie. Before he could get started, Junior Lizzano stopped by. Junior, who never used his given name, Federico, was a fifty-something, low-level ex-con who ran a small social club on Mott Street. He was one of the biggest sports gamblers in the neighborhood.

"Hey, Joe, is this *Journal* the latest edition?"

"Yeah, Junior."

"John-John, I hear you go to Columbia."

"Yeah, I just started my first year."

"You know, you would be doin' me a really big favor if you could find out certain things about the Columbia football team."

"What kinds of things?"

"I'm lookin' for a bettin' edge. I wanna know who's injured… how serious the injuries are…who might be sick…whatever. I'm lookin' for things that ain't in the newspapers…you know, inside information."

"I don't think I can help you out this season, since I'm only a freshman and I don't know anybody on the team, yet…but, I'll keep my ears open."

"Whatta bout next season?"

"Yeah, I'll probably be able to get you some inside information next season."

"Good. You're not gonna let me down, are you?"

"No, don't worry, I'll do my best, Junior…But, it all depends on if I can make some friends on the football team."

"I hear you're a pretty good football player, yourself. Are you gonna try out for the team?"

"No. Even if I could make the team, engineering is so difficult and time consuming, that I think I would flunk out of engineering school if I played on the football team."

"Okay, John-John, I'll be on my way back to the club. See ya, tomorrow, Joe."

"Yeah, see ya Junior."

A few seconds later, Joe asked John-John, "Are you really gonna help him out?"

"Well, I'll try to. It's no skin off my back. If I can help out someone from the neighborhood, I will. Anyway, I wouldn't be doing anything illegal… right?"

"Right…But, what if he asks you to help try to fix a game?"

"No way! That's where I'd draw the line. Inside info is one thing. Fixing a game is a whole other story."

"Listen. My advice is not to get involved with him. You're better off. Next year, all you gotta do is tell him you didn't make any friends on the football team, yet. To keep him happy, tell him you'll keep tryin'."

"Yeah, Joe, I guess you're right."

"I'm always right. Haven't you learned that by now? Now, come inside and tell me how everything turned out this weekend."

Chapter 40: The Burglary

John-John and Maria's relationship was blossoming and gaining momentum during the month of November. He was able to manage his time effectively, completing all his homework assignments while still making time for Friday and Saturday evening dates with her. Besides making time for her, he still squeezed in some time for Saturday afternoon activities with the guys, such as touch football, pool or bowling. Sometimes he and Maria would date with Danny and Judy, and/or Shortie and Angie, and sometimes they would be by themselves.

Their date on Friday, November 22nd was shrouded with sadness as a result of the assassination of President John F. Kennedy. They had both been caught up in the Camelot mystique and had been particularly proud of the fact that JFK had been the first Roman Catholic president of the United States. To them, as well as to many of the young people throughout America, the change from Ike and Mamie to Jack and Jackie had in effect changed the stewardship of the nation from the aged to the young; old Ike had, indeed, been a great man, and the nation was particularly indebted to him for his expert military leadership in World War II, but he undoubtedly lacked the exuberance and playful wit that Jack Kennedy projected.

John-John was in a physics laboratory in Pupin Hall working on an experiment dealing with kinetic energy while Maria was in her English class, when they each learned that President Kennedy had been shot. By the time they each had gotten home from school, the news of the young president's death had spread throughout the country. Maria had actually shed some tears when she watched the TV news. John-John, who just couldn't believe the assassination had actually happened, read the front-page story of every paper at the newsstand—reading aloud for Joe's benefit—as a way of coming to terms with Kennedy's death.

That evening, neither John-John nor Maria was in the mood to make-out. They both felt, without expressing it, that it would be disrespectful to enjoy themselves in a passionate way in light of the tragic events of the day. So, they spent the evening just walking around the neighborhood rehashing what had happened in Dallas and wondering how the nation would fare under Lyndon Johnson.

On Saturday evening, rather than spending another evening just walking around aimlessly, they decided to have dinner at their favorite Chinatown haunt—Yat Bun Sing's—with Danny and Judy, and Shortie and Angie. The conversation at the table, understandably, focused on the assassination. Danny expressed his theory that Johnson had been behind the assassination —especially since it had happened in Texas. John-John, who was particularly interested in the accused assassin and his possible motives, questioned the others, seeking to find out what they had learned about Lee Harvey Oswald.

The following afternoon, Maria telephoned John-John.

"Hi, John-John. Did you see it?"

"See what?"

"I was watching Oswald being transferred from a Dallas police station… I don't know where they were taking him…Anyway, all of a sudden, this man appeared with a gun and shot him. I couldn't believe what I saw!"

"You're kidding!"

"No, he was shot while the TV cameras were rolling…It was a live broadcast. I was watching Channel 4…NBC."

"Oh my! I didn't see it. I was busy doing my calculus homework."

"Why would someone shoot him?"

"Maria, there can be only two reasons…Number One would be to get revenge…Number Two would be to silence him if he was a part of a big conspiracy to kill the president."

"Well, I suppose it's got to be either one or the other."

"Maria, I'll say good-bye, now. I'm going to turn on the TV and see what I can find out about this."

Two weeks later, just before noon on Saturday, December 7th, John-John was getting ready for a touch football game with some guys from Hester Street. He had just donned his Sheiks shirt and was admiring his physique in the mirror when the telephone rang. He had a feeling that it might be Maria, so he raced to the living room, just beating his sister, Vivian, to the phone.

"Hi, John-John."

"Hi, Maria."

"I've got good news. Tonight, my parents are going up to White Plains for an early Christmas Season gathering with their *paisani*. They'll be spending the night up there, so I can stay out as late as I want."

"How come you're not going?"

"I'd rather be with you than a bunch of old *paisani*…so I told my parents that I was loaded with homework."

"You lied to your parents?"

"Well, it wasn't a total lie. I do have a lot of homework, but I'll be able to finish it all by Sunday night, even if I stay out late with you, tonight."

"Great! At least I won't have to worry about your curfew."

"What do you want to do tonight, John-John?"

"Why don't we go up to Radio City to see that new movie *Charade*?"

"Wonderful idea. I just love Cary Grant and Audrey Hepburn."

"Maybe, Danny and Judy will be interested in joining us."

"I'll check with Judy while you check with Danny…Good luck on your football game."

"See you later, Maria."

When John-John arrived at the newsstand, he found Lennie "Squirm," Tommy "Yeah-Yeah" and Frankie in the middle of a lively discussion.

"Hey, Joe, what's going on?"

"Lennie is talkin' about breakin' into the hardware store across the street. He already convinced Tommy to join him and now he's tryin' to convince Frankie."

"C'mon Frankie, it'll be a piece a cake. All you have to do is watch out for the cops while me and Tommy are inside."

"No, Lennie, I don't wanna be a part of it."

John-John approached the three as Lennie repeated his burglary plan. Lennie knew that John-John wouldn't want to participate, but he also knew that he wasn't a squealer, so he had no qualms about detailing his plans in front of him.

"Listen, this'll be an easy score. All we gotta do is hacksaw the padlock on the cellar door on the sidewalk in front of the store. Within three minutes, we can fill-up four bags with expensive tools…you know, ratchet sets, power saws and drills. We can also empty-out the cash register while we're in there."

"Yeah-yeah," said Tommy living up to his nickname. "It's less than three weeks to Christmas. I could sure use some extra dough."

"I'm sure my cousins can fence the goods for us in no time…We'll make a good buck for just five minutes work…Whatta ya say, Frankie? Whatta ya say?"

"Nah, count me out, Lennie. I don't wanna take no chance of getting pinched…it would be just my fuckin' luck to get pinched."

As Lennie and Tommy headed towards Mulberry Street, Joe remarked, "Frankie, you did the right thing. Those knuckleheads might get away with the heist this time, but eventually they'll get caught…and they'll do some hard time."

"Frankie, Joe's right. You made the right decision. Now, let's get ready to make a few bucks on today's football game. It's me, you, Danny and Donny "Knobhead" against Joe Clorio and his Hester Street guys…$3 a man."

"Let's convince them to play for $5 a man 'cause there's no fuckin' way those guys are gonna beat us."

"Okay, Frankie, I'm sure they'll go for five bucks a man because they think they're really good."

"Hey, Joe, give us the new football we left inside the stand on Wednesday," demanded John-John.

Joe reached down and grabbed the new football from the shelf, and then put it under his nose. "Boy it smells like good leather."

"Well," said Frankie, "it was originally $12.95, but we only paid $3.95 for it."

"So, I guess you pulled the old 'price-tag switch-er-oo' that I taught you guys."

"Yeah, replied Donny. John-John and I went down to Modell's on Chambers Street at around four on Wednesday."

John-John added, "I found a good, expensive Wilson football and removed the price tag. Then, Donny got the price tag off a cheap Wilson ball and put it on the expensive one. It's a college-level football. I was thinking of trying to pull the 'switch-er-oo' to get 'The Duke'…Wilson's pro football…but I figured that the cashier would spot the switch."

Frankie added, "They told me where they had hid the football, so I went into Modell's about ten minutes later, found it and bought it for $3.95, plus tax…Done deal!"

"Well, I guess I taught you guys real good."

"Now, let's go show those Hester Street guys how to play football!" yelled John-John.

They did, indeed, show the Hester Street team how the game should be played. John-John threw five touchdown passes and Frankie intercepted an errant Joe Clorio pass and ran it in for a touchdown. The final score was Sheiks 36, Hester Street 12. It was a nice and legal way of making $5 each. For John-John, the five bucks would go a long way in paying for his evening date with Maria.

Danny and Judy had agreed to the double-date. At around seven, they all rendezvoused in front of the Broadway-Lafayette Street Subway Station. While on the train, John-John took a good look at Maria's outfit and was very impressed. She looked like a model ready to do a photo shoot. She was wearing a tan pleated skirt, high-heeled brown leather boots, a matching leather jacket, which was unbuttoned at the top, revealing an off-white knit blouse. This was the first time Maria had worn a skirt on a date with him, and he found the skirt, in combination with the boots, to be very sexy—especially when she was sitting down.

They all enjoyed the movie and the stage show. Both Judy and Maria fawned over Cary Grant, leading Danny to remark, "Someday, I'm gonna learn to speak like Cary Grant."

"That'll be the day!" replied Judy.

Realizing that Maria had a free pass to stay out as late as she wanted, and with Judy not having to abide by any curfew, the guys suggested that they should continue the night with a walk down Fifth Avenue followed by a taxi ride down to Caffé Roma.

They were greeted warmly by the manager at Caffé Roma due to Danny's brief stint there during San Gennaro's Feast. Within minutes, the two couples were sharing assorted pastries and sipping cappuccinos. They all were enjoying the evening, especially Maria, who felt a new sense of freedom in not having to watch the clock.

"Oh my, it's gettin' close to midnight, Maria. Are you gonna turn into a pumpkin?" teased Danny.

"I don't know. Let's wait and see."

"I bet you'd be a very cute pumpkin."

"You never know, John-John…Excuse me, I need to use the Ladies Room."

As she was freshening up her makeup, she decided to follow through with what she had been contemplating all day: to "go all the way" with John-John. Her make-out sessions with him had been very passionate and enjoyable, but having once experienced intercourse, she knew there was much more to lovemaking than just making out. Given her lack of a curfew and the fact that she was expecting her period in a little more than a week, she decided that later in the evening would be the perfect time to seduce him. She recalled Cousin Maria's advice about not telling her true love in America that she had already lost her virginity. In fact, she remembered her words verbatim: *When you meet your true love later on in America, simply tell him that you are a virgin. Men believe what they want to believe. He will respect you and he will never know the difference.* So, she decided to see if she could pull it off.

She had seriously considered sneaking John-John up to her apartment, but had decided against it because she knew that he couldn't make it in and out of her building without being seen by one of her neighbors. Then, her parents would surely hear about it the next morning and she would be branded a *puttana*. It would break her parents' hearts and devastate them to the core. There was absolutely no way that she could take such a risk. Of course, there was always good old Crosby Street, but making love in a cubbyhole wouldn't be very easy, especially given their height difference. The only viable alternative was to use the newsstand. She knew that John-John, like many of the newsstand crew, had a key to the stand, so he could open or close-up for Joe when necessary.

Given the tight confines of the newsstand, she decided to make things easier when the big moment would arrive. She slipped off her bikini panties and placed them in her handbag. Thus, when the time was right, she would just lift up her skirt.

Walking out of the Ladies Room *sans* panties felt a little strange to her. When she sat down at the table, she was very careful to keep her knees locked together to avoid anyone getting a "free show."

"Gee, it's midnight Maria and you haven't turned into a pumpkin," joked John-John. "How late do you want to stay out?"

"At least a couple more hours. Who knows when I'll get another chance like this."

"Maria, I think I'll have Danny take me home, soon."

"Judy, my car is parked on Lafayette Street right in front of Felicia's building. Let's walk there and I'll drive you home."

"Let's join them John-John," suggested Maria, spurred on by the fact that Danny's car was parked within 50 feet of the newsstand.

"Okay with me. The walk will help me digest the three pastries I ate."

As they walked the three blocks to Danny's parked car, Maria could feel the cold draft of air rising up her skirt. "It's a good thing that tonight's temperature is in the low 40's and not the 20's," she remarked.

"Yeah, it's not bad for early December," replied John-John, not knowing the real reason behind Maria's comment.

Maria considered telling Judy what she had in mind, since Judy had confided in her every time, she and Danny had made love—a total of four times to date. But, she decided to keep her cards close to the vest.

The couples stopped in front of Danny's Chevy and continued chitchatting. Danny was being boisterous and extra-loud—loud enough to cause Zeke to get out of bed to see what was going on. When he peered out the kitchen window and saw who was making the racket, he opened the window and yelled, "Go hang out somewhere else!"

"Ah, go back to bed, Zeke!" yelled Danny.

"Show some respect, Danny! Don't let me come on down there and teach y'all some respect!"

"Hey, look who's standing by the bay window," remarked Judy. I guess Zeke's yellin' must've woken Felicia."

"Maybe, we woke her up, Danny."

"Who cares, John-John…Let's go, Judy. We don't want that hillbilly rebel to get too riled up."

As Danny and Judy sped away, John-John asked, "Where do you want to go now?"

"Well, since it's after midnight, I don't think we should go to Crosby Street. You never know what creeps might be lurking about at this time of night. How's about going into the newsstand to make out?"

"Okay. The newsstand will be a nice private and cozy place… and it'll be much warmer in there than in our favorite Crosby Street spot."

Just before turning the corner, John-John glanced over his shoulder and spotted Felicia still standing at the bay window. When they turned the corner, they were no longer in her view. John-John reached into his pocket, found the newsstand key, and quickly opened the padlock. He went inside first and sat himself down on Joe's stool. Maria followed and closed the door behind her.

"There's a hook-lock on the door, Maria. See if you can find it and hook the door closed."

Although it was almost pitch black in the newsstand, she managed to find the hook and lock the door from the inside. Soon they were embracing and kissing passionately. When his right hand roamed under her skirt up her thigh to where her panties would normally be, he was surprised to encounter bare flesh.

Maria pulled back and softly said, "I have a surprise for you."

"What's the surprise?"

"Tonight, I want to give myself to you…I want you to be my 'first.'"

John-John was stunned. He had thought that Maria was the type of girl who would save her virginity for her husband. After a couple of seconds of silence, he remarked, "Are you sure you want to 'go all the way,' tonight?"

"Yeah, I'm sure. I really want to do it, tonight...with you, sweetheart. There would be no better way of proving my love for you."

"Maria, I know you love me. You don't have to prove it."

Without uttering another word, she pulled down his zipper, reached inside, and skillfully managed to guide his swollen member through the fly of his jockey shorts. As if she were reading his mind, she whispered, "Don't worry about getting me pregnant, tonight. I'm not fertile right now because I'll be getting my period in about a week."

Maria did her best to get on top of John-John, as he balanced himself on the edge of the stool. After about ten seconds of twisting, turning and gyrating within the tight confines, they found what seemed to be the optimum position. But, as he tried to penetrate her, she intentionally stiffened herself and moved her thighs close together to thwart his efforts.

Then, as he forcefully pushed forward once again, she feigned pain and moaned, "Ow! Ouch!"

"Oh, am I in the right spot, now?"

"Yeah, I think so…push a little harder."

A few seconds later, figuring that she had made it difficult enough for him, she relaxed and spread her thighs farther apart, enabling his member to slide right in. He was somewhat surprised by how relatively easy it had been, but his thoughts on this matter were quickly cast aside by the pleasure he was experiencing, which was heightened by Maria's sighs and moans of delight to his rhythmic movements and her counter-movements.

After about five minutes, she had a powerful orgasm—a more intense orgasm than she had experienced under the olive tree. John-John, who was doing everything in his power to hold himself back, finally let himself go about five seconds after she had climaxed.

"Oh, John-John, I love you with all of my heart."

"I love you, too, Maria."

At that moment, he realized that although Leslie may have been a "sexual athlete," sex with her was based only on lust, while sex with Maria was founded on love.

Maria then reached into her jacket pocket, pulled out a couple of tissues and wiped herself. "Let's get out. It's warm and stuffy in here."

John-John laughed, "What do you expect? We certainly generated a lot of heat."

Once outside, a draft of chilly night air blew under Maria's skirt causing her to decide to go back inside to put her panties on. While she was doing so, John-John asked, "Any blood?"

"Well, I feel what I think is some blood on my thighs…and I'm very moist and sore down below, if you know what I mean…but of course, I can't tell if it's blood since it's still very dark in here, even with the door partly open. I'll let you know when I get home. I put some tissues inside my panties to catch any blood that might drip out while we're walking."

"Good idea."

"By the way, why are you so concerned about blood?"

"Oh…Joe told me that women bleed a lot the first time they have sex."

"Well, I think the amount of bleeding varies from woman to woman… Judy told me that she hardly had any blood when she did it with Danny the first time."

While John-John was putting the padlock back on the door, Maria was feeling a little guilty about faking the loss of her virginity. But, her guilt feelings vanished once she concluded that her ruse had been a smart move. *Why complicate things by telling him about Lorenzo?* she thought. *Why take a chance on ruining things? Guys are funny that way…especially Italian-American guys.* She knew full well that someone like John-John would want his future wife to have had no other sexual partners. She figured that her convincing bit of subterfuge would certainly cause him to believe that before this evening, she had been "as pure as the driven snow," and now *he* was her one and only "driver." Then, the pragmatic, and somewhat devious side of her brain kicked in: *If for whatever reason things don't work out with John-John, I might be able to fool some other guy into thinking I've given him my virginity…and I'd probably be even more convincing.*

"Hey, Maria, do you see those guys up the street?" remarked John-John as he pointed to two shadowy figures on the other side of Lafayette Street about halfway up the block from them. "Do you know who they are?"

"Oh…yeah…now, I see them…but I can't make them out."

"Well, they're Lennie 'Squirm' and Tommy 'Yeah-Yeah'…and they're getting ready to break into that hardware store."

"Boy, you must have great eyesight…Wait a minute. How do you know what they're about to do?"

"Well, my eyesight isn't that good. I know it's Lennie and Tommy, and I know what they're up to because I heard them talking about their plan earlier today at the newsstand…Let's watch and see what happens."

At that point, Lennie knelt down and began hacksawing the padlock on the steel cellar door, which was flush with the surface of the sidewalk and located close to the hardware store's entrance. John-John and Maria could faintly hear the sound of the hacksaw blade as it rhythmically ripped through the padlock's steel shackle. The padlock didn't offer much resistance to Lennie's efforts, and after about two minutes it was history.

As Lennie removed the padlock from the door's hasp, he remarked, "I told ya it would be a breeze, Tommy."

"Yeah, yeah, let's hurry up and get inside."

When Lennie lifted up the right door leaf with his right hand, a totally improbable thing happened: The door's hinges broke, and the door—with Lennie still hanging on—went tumbling down the cellar steps. The sound of the steel plate door banging against the concrete steps was quite loud, producing a discordant bell-like clanging that could be heard a block away. Fortunately for the agile Lennie, he wasn't injured in the fall; however, as luck would have it, a patrol car had just turned left from Prince Street onto Lafayette as the door and Lennie were falling down the steps. Alerted by the loud sounds breaking the silence of the night, the police officers sped towards the middle of the block with the patrol car's red-light flashing.

"Cheeze-it, the cops!" yelled Tommy, as Lennie quickly scurried up the steps.

"You run that way!" exclaimed a shaken Lennie, pointing towards Prince Street.

The two cops jumped out of the patrol car right in front of the hardware store and while drawing their revolvers, they each yelled, "Stop or I'll shoot!"

Neither Lennie nor Tommy heeded the warnings. Lennie darted towards Spring Street, while Tommy ran as fast as he could towards Prince.

Both cops were quite overweight. They no longer were the fine physical specimens they had been when they had graduated from the Police Academy; they had obviously consumed far too many donuts since that day. The "Squirm," who was one of the fastest guys in the neighborhood, was way ahead of the pursuing cop.

"Wow, look at Lennie go!" exclaimed John-John.

When Lennie reached the corner directly across the street from the newsstand, he made a snap decision to run down into the subway station. So, he made a quick right turn, ran a few more steps and turned into the subway kiosk—all of this occurring out of the sight of the pursuing officer. Lennie whizzed past the token booth without being seen by the token clerk, who had dozed off due to late-night boredom. He vaulted over the turnstiles with the ease of an Olympic gymnast, while hoping that Lady Luck would intervene and provide him with an incoming train. But Lady Luck let him down; there was no incoming train, and no train headlights were visible in the downtown tunnel as far as he could see. The subway station was eerily quiet. Instinctively, Lennie headed towards the front of the station and hid behind a tile-covered column as he contemplated his next move. His hope was that the cop had assumed he had run into the hallway of 65 Spring Street, or that he was hiding behind some parked cars on Spring.

Meanwhile, "Yeah-Yeah" was running as fast as he could up Lafayette Street towards Prince. The cop who was chasing him ran back to the patrol car after realizing he was no match for the fleet-footed youth. He quickly put the car in reverse and backed-up as fast as the car could go. When he caught up to Tommy, the street-smart youth dashed over to the other side of Lafayette. The officer tried to make a u-turn, but two cars heading uptown failed to yield the right-of-way, allowing Tommy enough time to make it into the hallway of the corner building—265 Lafayette Street—known throughout the neighborhood as the Monroe Building.

The unusual thing about the Monroe Building is that it has four stairways in the hallway, each leading to different wings of the building. Tommy lived in a third-floor apartment in the "B"-wing. However, he raced up the "A"-wing stairway. The cop could hear Tommy's footsteps when he entered the hallway, so he followed Tommy up the "A"-wing stairway as fast as he could;

but after climbing two flights, he began to huff and puff, and his rate of climb slowed appreciably. By the time the cop had reached the third floor, Tommy had reached the roof of the five-story building. He quickly exited the "A" -wing roof door and ran over to the "B"-wing stairway. Once inside the stairwell, he gently closed the door behind him and raced down to his apartment. He opened the apartment door with his house key and quietly closed it behind him, while exhaling with a sigh of relief. *There's no fuckin' way that cop's gonna catch me now!* he thought—and he was right.

Meanwhile, Lennie felt like a cornered rat. If the police began to search the subway station, they would surely find him hiding behind the column. He knew he must act quickly. The prospect of running between the rails down to the Canal Street Station was simply too scary and dangerous. Although there was no train in sight, one could catch up to him when he was deep within the tunnel and squash him. *What a way to go!* he thought, as he began to perspire profusely.

Soon, Lennie heard some muffled voices coming from the vicinity of the token booth. He figured it was the police questioning the token booth clerk. He knew he had to make a move. So, he quietly jumped down to the tracks. Then, after checking that no express train was coming, he carefully hurdled over the "deadly" third rail. Once on the downtown express tracks, he leaned over and looked to his right, and was glad to see that there was no uptown express train in sight. He repeated this maneuver until he reached the opposite platform. The "Squirm" had lived up to his name. Within a matter of thirty seconds, he had crossed all four tracks, safely hopping over four third-rails. He boosted himself onto the platform of the uptown station and stealthily made his way to the exit, hiding behind every column on the way for a second or two.

Just before he reached the turnstiles, he heard the unmistakable rumbling of a subway train. He hoped it was an uptown local with passengers getting off at Spring Street, figuring that he could mingle with them as they exited to confuse any police who might be lurking about. But, the train turned out to be an uptown express, which zoomed right past the station. However, the passing express train did temporarily shield him from the view of anyone on the downtown platform—especially any police that might be searching for him across the way.

The token clerk was somewhat surprised to see Lennie exiting through the turnstile since the last train had stopped at the station about ten minutes earlier. But, he paid Lennie no mind and went back to doing the *Daily News* crossword puzzle. Lennie went to the left of the booth and up the stairway. When his head reached the level of the sidewalk, he could see the rear fender of a police car parked on Mulberry Street, blocking the crosswalk. He didn't know if those cops were looking for him or if they were just making the rounds. Deciding that heading towards Mulberry would be too chancy, he carefully peeked around the kiosk wall towards Lafayette Street. He couldn't believe his eyes when he spotted John-John and Maria standing by the newsstand. *I might get away, yet,* he thought, as he whistled towards John-John the two-note "secret" signal that the Sheiks often used to get one another's attention. Upon hearing the whistle, John-John turned towards the source and quickly spotted Lennie's face hovering about a foot above sidewalk level.

"John-John, come here…and bring Maria. I need yous for cover," demanded Lennie as loudly as he dared.

John-John knew that by helping Lennie, he would be aiding and abetting a criminal, but he put that thought in the back of his mind. Lennie was a Sheik, and John-John was a Sheik who really believed in the Sheiks' credo: All for one and one for all.

Maria walked with John-John over to the kiosk without any concerns that she would be helping Lennie to try to get away from the police.

"Listen, Lennie, I think your best bet would be to walk behind Maria and me towards the newsstand. I'll open the door and lock you inside. The cops will never figure out that you're inside the newsstand because they'll see the locked padlock. Then, I'll come back an hour later and let you out."

"Where's the cops?"

"The cop who was chasing you just came out of the subway across Lafayette and he's walking slowly towards Crosby. The other cop has the car and he's down by the Monroe Building."

"Okay…Sounds like a good idea. Lock me in the stand!"

A few minutes later, the patrol car turned from Crosby onto Spring with its red light flashing. The car pulled up alongside the newsstand and stopped with both officers inside. It was obvious to both John-John and Maria that the driver had given up on catching Tommy and had picked up the other cop on Crosby Street after his search for Lennie had proved fruitless.

The cop behind the wheel blurted out, "Hey, did you two happen to see a young skinny guy, dressed in black, run by here?"

"No, officer," replied John-John, with that lie quickly echoed by Maria.

Lennie thought that it was rather funny that he could hear every word being said and that the cops had no idea he was hiding within five feet of them. Then, just as Lennie believed that he was free and clear, Zeke Daniels approached the newsstand wearing only a pair of khakis, a white t-shirt and sandals.

"Good evenin', officers. I done witnessed the whole thing from my window."

"Do you know the two guys we're lookin' for?"

"Well, I only got a good look at the one who was running towards Spring Street. I'm quite sure it was that young fella they call Lennie 'Squirm.'"

"Do you know his last name?"

"I'm not rightly sure, but I think his last name is Muccio. I reckon that it is spelled M-U-C-C-I-O."

Lennie gritted his teeth and exclaimed, almost loud enough to be heard outside, "That rat bastard! That dirty rat bastard!" John-John was surprised that Zeke had broken the Cardinal Rule of the neighborhood: Thou shalt not squeal. The common responses to police questioning were imprinted on the brains of neighborhood people almost from the time they learned to speak; and the responses were usually made in neighborhood vernacular, for effect. The canned responses were: "I don't know nuttin"; "I didn't see nuttin"; and "I didn't hear nuttin." However, Zeke was essentially an "outsider," although he had lived in the neighborhood for many years. In neighborhood lingo, a person such as Zeke would be referred to as "a citizen"—a pejorative term for someone who cooperates with the authorities. Although a distrust for the government, and lawmen in particular, had been inculcated in Zeke while growing up dirt-poor in the hills of Tennessee, his years in the Army had transformed him into a person who respected the government and its authority figures. In his mind, helping the *po-lice* was the right thing to do.

"Do you know where he lives?"

"Well, I'm not rightly a hundred percent sure, but I think he lives down that a way," pointing across to the other side of Lafayette, in the direction of Kenmare Street.

"Thanks, sir, you've been a great help," replied the driver.

"Yeah," added the other officer, "We usually don't get much cooperation around here."

"Glad to help y'all out."

"Will you be willing to be a witness, sir?"

"I sure enough will!"

That said, Zeke provided the police officers with his full name, address and telephone number, thereby angering the eavesdropping Lennie almost to the point where he couldn't contain himself: "That fuckin' rat bastard! That fuckin' rat bastard!" said Lennie repeatedly, in a muffled voice, while gritting his teeth.

John-John looked and listened to what was going on and shook his head with Zeke's every word of cooperation.

"Goodnight, Mr. Daniels. We're gonna look for him a little bit more and then turn the case over to the detectives if we can't find him. You'll probably be hearing from a detective sometime tomorrow."

Shortly thereafter, another patrol car arrived on scene, and after the police officers conversed for a few minutes, both cars headed to the hardware store to secure the property.

"Lennie, both cars are parked in front of the hardware store. Sit tight, I'll be back in about an hour, or so."

"Okay."

John-John and Maria then started walking, arm-in-arm, towards Mulberry. When they reached the corner, Maria paused to reach into her handbag and pull out her pack of Salems.

"What are you doing, Maria?"

"What does it look like I'm doing? I'm having a cigarette. I know you don't want me to smoke, but I really need a cigarette, now. Between losing my virginity and helping a thief all within the same hour, I feel a little nervous. The cigarette will calm me down."

"I understand, but please try to quit."

"Suppose I make it my New Year's Resolution to quit smoking?"

"Fair enough, but try to keep it."

"Don't worry, I won't go back on my resolution," replied Maria in a sincere voice, as she lit-up her cigarette.

After three deep drags, she began to experience the calming effects of the smoke. She wondered if she actually would be able to keep her New Year's Resolution, but concluded, *I'll worry about it next year… although next year is only a few weeks away.*

"Where to now?" asked Maria.

"Let's walk over to Chinatown to kill some time."

As they walked, all they could talk about was the attempted burglary and Zeke's "fingering" of Lennie. When they reached Chinatown, they found it to be relatively dark because all the restaurants had closed. As they walked down Mott Street, a closed Chinese curio shop caught their attention. Its lighted fronted windows displayed an intriguing assortment of Chinese knickknacks, crockery and statues of Buddha.

"Hey, Maria, doesn't that Buddha remind you of Shortie?"

"Oh, c'mon, he's not that fat."

"Well, not yet, but if he doesn't stop eating those *cuchifritos*, he'll look like that in about ten years."

Using that bit of levity as a point to "switch gears," John-John turned the conversation to their lovemaking session in the newsstand.

"Maria, I feel so close to you…closer than I've ever felt with anyone."

She laughingly replied, "Of course that's true…not only were you close to me, you were deep inside me." Then she added, in a seemingly sincere tone, "I gave you my virginity, tonight, because I've never loved someone as much as I love you, and because I know that no one could ever take your place in my heart…I hope you won't think less of me now…like I'm some kind of a tramp."

"Oh no, Maria, I know you did what you did out of your love for me. I'll never forget tonight. On every anniversary of the Pearl Harbor attack,

I'll remember our special night in the newsstand… although, technically, we did it on December 8th, since it was after midnight."

"You're such a stickler for details, John-John. That's why you're gonna be a great engineer."

"I hope so…I hope so. Okay, let's go back to the newsstand to see if we can let Lennie out."

When they arrived at the newsstand, they spotted one patrol car parked in front of the hardware store.

"Lennie…Lennie. It's John-John."

"Is the coast clear?"

"No, not yet. There's one patrol car parked in front of the hardware store. Sit tight. I'll be back in a half hour. I'm gonna take Maria home."

"Okay…but it's gettin' fuckin' boring in here."

John-John and Maria walked over to Mulberry and proceeded down to Broome Street—a good location for hailing a cab. After about ten minutes, John-John spotted the unmistakable outline of a Checker Cab heading towards them. He stepped into the street with his right arm raised as the cab began to stop for the red traffic light. He quickly opened the door for Maria and followed her into the commodious backseat.

"First Street, between First and Second Avenues, please."

When the cab reached Maria's apartment building, he told the driver to wait while he escorted her up the metal stairway and into the hallway of her building.

"I'll wait here until you're safely inside your apartment."

"Okay."

After a deep kiss, she ran up the stairs, and in less than thirty seconds, she opened the door to her apartment, three flights above the hallway.

"I'm in my apartment. Goodnight, John-John."

"Goodnight, Maria."

The taxi made it back to the neighborhood in about five minutes. John-John directed the driver to pass right in front of the hardware store. *Oh, good, the cops are gone.*

"Driver, let me off on the corner."

Once out of the cab, he crossed over to the newsstand.

"Lennie, the coast is clear. I'm opening the lock."

Lennie was happy to breathe fresh air, again. "John-John, you're a great pal...a stand-up guy. I won't never forget how you helped me out, tonight...Never!"

"Hey, Lennie, you're a Sheik...All for one and one for all... Right?"

"Yeah, right...I can't believe that fuckin' Zeke fingered me... that dirty rat bastard. I'm sure by tomorrow mornin' the detectives will be knockin' on my door. What the fuck should I do?"

"Zeke has to, somehow, get amnesia. Talk to your father first thing in the morning...and I mean the first thing. He, or somebody else, has to convince Zeke not to be a witness against you."

"My father probably shouldn't be the one to talk to Zeke. He's got some temper and I'm sure this thing with Zeke will really get him goin'. He might wanna put a bullet in him."

"No, no, Zeke doesn't deserve to be shot for something like this...he only needs to be intimidated...you know, made scared enough *not* to talk to the detectives."

"Yeah, I guess you're right. I know that without Zeke, there's no case against me...but even with Zeke, the cops ain't got much of a case since I wasn't caught and it was very dark...Plus, if the detectives question me, I'll just say I was home sleepin'...My mother and father will back me up on that."

"Yeah, it would be tough to prove it was you, but without Zeke as a witness, you'd have no worries, whatsoever. Now, go home...and good luck."

Chapter 41: Didn't See Nuttin

Zeke was startled by three pounding knocks on the door as he was sipping his second cup of coffee at around eleven on Sunday morning.

"You spectin' anybody, Serafina?"

"No."

"Oh, maybe it's the *po-lice* detectives followin' up on last night."

Upon opening the door, he instantly realized that the big guy staring him in the eye was *not* a detective. Far from it! He was a neighborhood wise guy, known as "Gappy"—his real name being Gaspare Serra. Zeke could tell by the scowl on his face that he wasn't making a social visit. Standing right behind Gappy was his trusted henchman, Tony "Green"—the nickname "Green" being derived from the fact that he always flashed a wad of cash that was big enough to choke a horse. Although Zeke knew quite well who these wise guys were, he had never spoken to them.

"Good mornin'."

"What can I do for you fellas?" asked Zeke, with a stern face.

"Listen, we'll get right to the point. Last night you think you saw somethin', but you didn't see nuttin. You understand…you didn't see a fuckin' thing last night! I know you weren't brought up in this neighborhood, so maybe you just don't get it. Around here, we don't cooperate with the cops…And if you want to still live around here, you won't tell the detectives nuttin about what you think you might have seen last night."

"Well…"

"Well, what? Just don't tell the detectives nuttin! If you do, somebody's gonna get fuckin' hurt! *Capisci?* Also, if you squeal, you could forget about workin' for Martucci because he don't like rats, and he definitely won't have no fuckin' rat workin' for him!"

After thinking about his predicament for about ten seconds, Zeke decided to capitulate, mostly because he feared losing his job.

"Okay, I didn't see nuttin last night. It was all a dream, I reckon."

"Good. That's better. You made the right choice. You doin' the right thing."

When Lennie's father, Dom, got the good news from his old buddy Gappy, he was very pleased and said, "Thanks, Gappy, I owe you big time!"

"No problem, Dom…my pleasure. You helped me out a lot over the years, and I'll always remember that you took good care of my kid brother when both of yous were in the can together."

Although Zeke "did the right thing"—according to neighborhood standards—his reputation had been sullied by the Saturday night incident. The word would quickly spread around the neighborhood that he was a "rat"—and everyone in the neighborhood despised a rat; with the exception of a rapist or a child molester, the lowest thing that one could be was a rat.

When two detectives stopped by to question Zeke in the early afternoon, they were only half-surprised to learn that he had changed his tune about what he had seen the night before. They quickly concluded that someone from the neighborhood had gotten to him. So, they decided that it would be a waste of time to proceed any further with the investigation, especially since the case was only for attempted burglary, not an actual burglary.

John-John finished his Sunday dinner shortly after three, and decided to go out for a couple of hours before hitting the books. To his surprise, none of the guys were at the newsstand corner, so he decided to phone Maria to kill some time until they arrived. He crossed over to the telephone booth in front of the bank. After depositing a dime, he dialed her phone number.

"Hi Maria, how do you feel today?"

"I feel fine."

"You don't feel guilty about last night, do you?"

"No. I have no guilt feelings. Actually, I feel more like a woman today…thanks to you."

"Maria, last night meant a lot to me."

"It meant a lot to me, too."

"By the way, did you find any blood in your tissues?"

"Yeah, there were some blood stains."

"You're not in any pain, are you?"

"No…But, enough about blood and pain…Everything worked out well, and I couldn't be happier."

"Me, too. I couldn't be happier."

"By the way, how did Lennie make out last night?"

"By the time the taxi got back to the neighborhood, the cops had gone. So, I let Lennie out of the stand, and he went home. Hopefully, the police won't track him down."

"Yeah, hopefully, they won't."

"Well, I'll speak to you tomorrow. I love you. Take care."

"I love you, too, John-John. Goodbye."

When he hung-up the phone, he was happy to see Danny and Shortie standing right outside the phone booth. The three pals were soon engaged in a conversation about the bungled burglary attempt. Danny and Shortie were totally absorbed by John-John's play-byplay account of the incident, including the details of how he and Maria had helped hide Lennie from the cops.

"You did real good," said Shortie, with a tone of admiration in his voice.

"Yeah, seconded Danny. It was a great idea to lock him in the newsstand. Not only are you book-smart, you're street-smart!"

Then, Danny focused in on Zeke. "Boy, I always knew that Zeke was the type of guy who would rat-out someone…Look at how many times he's called the cops on us just for makin' some noise or bein' a pain in the ass in some way. But, this was different. Fingerin' Lennie could've put him behind bars!"

"Yeah," added Shortie, "Zeke is one rat bastard!"

At that point, John-John shifted the conversation to his "conquest" of Maria. Although he had thought about keeping it private, he just couldn't contain himself. Most guys his age couldn't help but tell their buddies all the intimate details of their sexual escapades—especially one that involves "taking" a girl's virginity. Besides, both Shortie and Danny had shared the details of their conquests with him.

Shortie playfully remarked, "Man, if those newsstand walls could talk… ha-ha-ha."

About an hour later, John-John returned home to finish his homework and to prepare for a calculus exam. At about the same time, Maria's parents returned from White Plains, totally unaware that their daughter had had quite a wild evening in their absence.

Maria awoke about a half-hour later than usual on Monday morning. Her mother, who had taken Monday off to do some Christmas shopping, was still asleep when Maria finally got out of bed. Despite making every effort to eat and dress quickly, she couldn't get herself out of the house in time to travel up to school with Judy— and she really wanted to, because just before falling asleep on Sunday night, she had decided to tell Judy that she had "lost her virginity" in the newsstand on Saturday night. But, that conversation would have to wait.

At lunchtime, Maria joined Judy and Angie who were already seated at their usual table. As soon as she plopped her lunch tray down on the table and sat down, Angie greeted her with a Cheshire Cat-like grin and asked, "So, how was it?"

Maria quickly realized that Angie already knew about Saturday night, and she deduced that Judy had also gotten the word. "Well, I suppose that Shortie told you what happened, Angie."

"Yeah, he called me last night and told me."

Judy quickly added, "Danny, also told me last night."

"No problem. I was gonna tell both of you at lunch, today, anyway."

"Tell us the details," demanded Angie.

After she gave the girls a very descriptive account of her Saturday night escapade, Angie smiled and said, "Welcome to the club."

Maria resisted the temptation of telling them that she had actually been the first of the three to "join the club." So, she simply replied, "Thanks. I feel like a woman, now."

"Yeah," remarked Judy, "Right now, it seems like we're three women alone on an island in a sea of girls."

"That's a very poetic way of putting it, Judy."

"Well, Maria, I always did like poetry…By the way, look at Felicia sittin' at that corner table all by herself…What a mope!"

Maria resisted the temptation to glance at Felicia, but when Felicia noticed Angie staring at her, she gave her half a smile; and Angie did likewise.

At around 3 o'clock, John-John exited the subway at the Prince Street Station. He was in a good mood because he felt he had done quite well on his calculus exam. Within five minutes, he was at the newsstand. None of the guys were there. The only person hanging around was old Tony "Gallons," who was waiting for the last digit of the daily number.

"Good afternoon, Joe. How's it going, Tony?"

"I'm hopin' for a three, kid!" exclaimed Tony. "I've got the first two numbers…all I need is the fuckin' three."

"Forgetta about it, Tony! You know you're a born loser!" yelled Joe in a sarcastic tone.

"Hey, Joe, open the door and let me in. I've got some things I wanna tell you."

Upon entering, he blurted out, "Joe, I 'blessed' the newsstand on Saturday night."

"Ah-ha! I figured that somethin' sexual had happened in here. When I opened up the stand this mornin', I could smell a faint aroma that was either rottin' fish or pussy…I didn't find any fish in here, so…"

"You're kidding me. Right? You didn't really smell something?"

"Yeah. You know that we blind people have a great sense of smell."

"I still don't believe you, Joe."

"Okay, I'll come clean. Shortie stopped by this mornin' and told me about you and Maria…and he also told me about Lennie using the newsstand to hide from the cops."

"Joe, nothing gets by you. You know everything that goes on in the neighborhood."

"True…Anyway, I wanna congratulate you, John-John. You're the first guy to get laid in my newsstand…and with a virgin, no less. Now, give me the details, and don't leave nuttin out."

"Okay, Joe, I'll tell you everything. After all, I owe it to you since you did teach me the facts of life…plus, I know you really enjoy a good sex story."

Chapter 42: Chili Today?

"Fat" Angie was in her dingy Mulberry Street kitchen drying the dishes after Monday's evening meal. Feeling bored and a little catty, she suddenly got an urge to get under Felicia's skin—to pull her chain about Maria's Saturday night romp with John-John in the newsstand. After finishing the dishes, she decided to act upon her urge, knowing that she would get some perverse pleasure out of rattling Felicia, especially since she never really liked her, despite being lunch mates for quite some time. So, she went into the living room to make the call.

"Hi, Felicia."

"Who is it?"

"It's me, Angie. Don't you recognize my voice?"

"Oh, I forgot what you sound like…You haven't spoken to me since I stopped eatin' lunch with you and Judy…and that bitch, Maria."

"So, how are ya?"

"I'm fine. Why are you callin' me?"

"Well, I got a hot flash for you, Felicia."

"What is it?"

"Guess who had sex in the newsstand on Saturday night."

Instantly, an image of John-John and Maria flashed before her eyes, but she simply responded, "Who?"

"John-John and Maria…that's who."

Before Felicia could get a word in, Angie continued in a smug tone, "She gave John-John her 'cherry' right inside the newsstand! She told me it wasn't easy to do it in the newsstand because it was dark and tight…but, somehow, they managed."

"That slut! That who-ah!" screamed Felicia, with such intensity that Angie had to pull the receiver off her ear. "In school, she acts like the holy and innocent one, yet she's really a no-good slut!"

"I'm sorry I had to tell you this, but I felt you should know."

"Well, I'm glad you let me know."

"Listen, you probably should forget about John-John for good. Find yourself another guy...there's plenty of guys out there."

"Angie, do you know what the difference between me and Maria is?"

"No. What?"

"The difference is that John-John would have to *marry* me before I would let him screw me!"

Straining to sound sincere, Angie remarked, "Yeah, I feel the same way ...but not all girls are like us...Well, goodbye. See ya in school, tomorrow."

On Tuesday, Maria was sitting alongside Judy at the usual lunch table. Angie, who was sitting directly across from them, was leading an animated conversation about sex.

"You know, I think I love Shortie, but I can't help but wonder how sex would be with another guy."

"Well, that thought has also crossed my mind, but right now, I'm not ready to cross that bridge...but who knows what'll happen in the future," remarked Judy.

Maria dipped her spoon into her bowl of chili, as she was about to "put her two cents in." She didn't notice Felicia walking right behind her until Felicia caught her foot on the leg of Judy's chair, and in one well-choreographed move, "tripped," causing her lunch tray to flip and much of her lunch to land on the back of Maria's head. The chili spilled all over Maria's beautiful auburn hair and down her back. Her uniform also took quite a beating—too many stains to count. In addition to the chili stains, her uniform sported spinach and carrot stains from the vegetable side dishes. Since the serving temperature of the chili was nearly as hot as soup, Maria received a minor burn on the nape of her neck.

"Oh, I'm so, so sorry, Maria...I tripped. It was an accident."

"Accident, my ass!" yelled Maria, using language that she normally wouldn't use.

"Listen, I tripped."

"Yeah…right. You're a liar! You did it on purpose!"

"Look, it was an accident. Don't call me a liar…you slut!"

Felicia's last words stunned Maria. She didn't know how to respond to being called a "slut."

"Get the hell out of here, Felicia!" yelled Judy, who was angry because she had been in the splash zone. "You're gonna pay the cleaning bills for Maria's uniform and my uniform!"

"Oh, yeah, who's gonna make me pay?"

Clenching her fist, Judy replied, "I'll make you pay…you'll see!"

"Felicia, why don't you just get the hell outta here!" ordered Angie, acting as if her instigating the night before had nothing to do with the incident.

Just then, the two nuns who were monitoring the cafeteria ran over to try to defuse the situation. Felicia told her side of the story to the nuns, insisting that she had accidentally tripped on the leg of Judy's chair.

Angie interjected, "I saw the whole thing, Sisters. It looked to me like Felicia did it on purpose."

"No, I didn't!"

Judy chimed in: "Oh, I think you *did* do it on purpose. First of all, why did you have to walk behind Maria and me to get to your table when you could easily have used the main aisle?"

When questioned, Maria said that from her angle, she couldn't tell if Felicia had done it on purpose or if it was an accident; but she did tell the nuns that there had recently been some "bad blood" between Felicia and herself over a guy.

Initially, the nuns didn't know how to handle the situation. But, after discussing the matter off to the side, they told Felicia to stay away from the three other girls, and that should she be involved in another such "accident," she would be suspended or, possibly, expelled. Then, they advised Maria to avoid Felicia whenever possible.

Angie and Judy did their best to cleanup Maria in the bathroom, but their efforts didn't help much.. Maria walked over to the nuns looking like a terrible mess. Before she could utter a word, the older nun, Sister Margaret, said, "Maria, get home as quickly as you can and hop into the shower. Shampoo your hair at least twice and you'll be back to your beautiful self."

The other nun, Sister Regina, added, "Don't worry, I'll inform the Principal's Office that you're excused for the rest of the day."

"Okay, I'll go home…I wonder what the people on the subway will think when they see me."

"Don't worry about the people on the subway," replied a sympathetic Sister Regina.

As Maria exited the school, she knew that she couldn't follow Sister Margaret's advice to the tee because there was no shower in her apartment—only the bathtub in the kitchen. She, instead, would have to wash her hair in the kitchen sink and then bathe in the kitchen tub.

As she lay in the tub after twice washing her hair, she let out a sigh and said, "What a horrible day…What a horrible day!"

Chapter 43: Cornuto!

Several days had passed since the bungled burglary attempt and Lennie hadn't been arrested. In fact, not one detective had as yet knocked on his apartment door. He figured that he was home free, thanks to the intimidating efforts of Gappy and Tony "Green"—and he was right. However, he still couldn't get over the fact that Zeke had "fingered" him. The very sight of Zeke, or even the mention of his name, turned his stomach and caused him to go into a curse-filled tirade. His hatred for Zeke had become visceral. He wanted to exact some form of revenge, but what? He certainly didn't want to confront Zeke; Zeke was as strong as an ox and could easily tear him apart if he got in his face. Lennie had to find another way to get even with Zeke, and he wasn't going to rest until he did.

Playing the role of peacemaker, Joe had tried on several occasions to convince Lennie to forget about getting even with Zeke; but Joe's words went in one of Lennie's ears and out the other. Not even Joe's reassurance, "Don't worry, I'm gonna talk to that dumb fuckin' hillbilly and teach him the rules of the neighborhood," could quell Lennie's anger.

On Saturday night, a week after the attempted burglary, John-John was free to hang-out with the guys because Maria couldn't get out of going with her parents to visit some *paisani* up in the Washington Heights section of Manhattan, not far from the George Washington Bridge. At around eight, John-John was standing in front of the closed newsstand along with Lennie, Shortie and Donny "Knobhead," when Frankie and Danny arrived, each packing a pint of Jack Daniels in their jacket pockets. They generously began sharing the booze with their buddies.

"Boy, this Jack is really helpin' to take the nip out of the air."

"Yeah, Shortie, I can sure feel the heat in my stomach," said "Knobhead."

The six guys finished the two pints in no time, and they wanted some more. So, they reached in their pockets and chipped-in enough loose change to cover the cost of one more pint. Danny then raced over to Anthony's Liquor Store, which was on the other side of Spring Street, near Martucci's office, and bought a pint of Jack Daniels minutes before the 9 p.m. closing time.

As the guys were sharing the next pint of Jack Daniels, Danny remarked, "I wonder if Zeke Daniels is related to Jack Daniels."

"You had to ruin the night by bringing up that fuckin' rat's name, Danny! What the fuck's the matter with you!"

"Sorry about that, Lennie."

Lennie sucked on his cigarette trying to get every ounce of nicotine. Then, he exhaled with lips curled. "You know, not only is Zeke a fuckin' rat, but he's also a fuckin' *cornuto*!"

"What's a *cornuto*?" asked Shortie.

John-John decided to enlighten Shortie: "I don't know if you Puerto Ricans have a word for it, but in Italian, a *cornuto* is a man whose wife is being screwed by another man, and the husband finds out what's going on, but does nothing about it. In southern Italy and especially Sicily, the husband of a cheating wife is *expected* to kill, or at least, stab the guy who is fooling around with his wife. If he doesn't, he'll be branded a '*cornuto*.' He'll lose the respect of all the people in the town...Many will actually shun him, and some of the nervy people will shout '*Cornuto!*' whenever he walks by."

"Oh, man, they say we Puerto Ricans are bad, but your Italian *paisans* are worse," remarked Shortie, with a hint of laughter in his voice.

"So, Lennie, you think Zeke's a *cornuto*?" asked Frankie.

"Oh yeah, I hear Serafina is being laid and 'par-laid' by Martucci. They say that he even got her pregnant...and that she had an abortion."

"Who's they?" asked Danny.

"A lot a people around here."

"You think Zeke knows what's going on?" asked John-John.

"Yeah, I think so…Get this…a couple of months ago, my father gave Zeke a crank phone call in the middle of the night. He called him a *cornuto* and hung up. He was mad at Zeke for siccin' the cops on me back in July…just for revvin' up my engine and playin' the radio loud in front of his buildin'…Remember?"

"Of course we remember," replied John-John, answering for the group.

"Hey, why don't we make sure that Zeke knows that Martucci is screwin' his wife," suggested Danny, with a sly grin on his face.

"Yeah," said Frankie, followed by Donny saying, "Yeah, let's make sure that rat bastard knows what his wife's been up to!"

"Listen," said Shortie, "I got a great idea on how to do it."

"What's your idea?" asked Lennie, anticipating that Shortie had something good up his sleeve.

"Well, we go down to Broome Street and hail a cab…We get the cabbie to stop in front of Zeke's building, and then, we yell '*Cornuto!*' out the windows as loud as we can. Maybe, we can even get the cabbie to blow the horn."

"Great idea, Shortie!"

"Well, Lennie, John-John ain't the only one with brains around here."

Danny interjected, "All of us won't be able to fit in a cab."

"You're right, said "Knobhead." So, we better hail a Checker cab…at least it fits five with the two jump seats. But even then, one of us can't be in on this. Any volunteers?"

"Yeah, me," said John-John, "I really don't want to be a part of it. Things could get out of hand. Zeke could wind-up killing Serafina."

"Ah, John-John, you fuckin' think too much," remarked Danny. "Do us a favor. At least, stay here and watch what happens. Then, meet us at Dave's Corner and tell us what you saw."

"Okay, but I still think that you guys should reconsider…"

"Ah, reconsider, my ass!" blurted Lennie, before John-John could finish his sentence.

About ten minutes after the guys had gone off to hail a cab, John-John saw the unmistakable silhouette of a Checker cab in the distance, slowly heading up Cleveland Place. As the cab drove past him, he could see Danny and Lennie waving at him from the passenger-side rear window. The cab soon stopped in front of the Daniels' building. The driver honked the horn three times, apparently following the directions of his drunk and rowdy passengers. John-John would later learn that the guys had promised the driver a big tip if he would follow their instructions to a tee. The guys then lowered the rear windows of the cab and let loose with a barrage of insults and nasty words directed at Zeke.

"Hey Zeke, you're a fuckin' *cornuto!*"

"Martucci is screwin' your wife while you're workin' for him! Ha-ha-ha."

"Your wife's a fuckin' who-ah!"

Zeke ran to the window and opened it. The sight of the cab at the curb below perplexed him; and even though his apartment was only one flight above street level, he couldn't see who was yelling those nasty words at him from the cab.

"Who's down there in that cab?"

"Your friends!" yelled Lennie in a disguised voice. "Listen, Zeke, you're a *cornuto.* Your wife is getting laid by Martucci!"

"I'm comin' down! Talk to me man to man!"

"Driver, let's get outta here!" ordered Shortie.

The driver hit the accelerator and the cab sped away a few seconds before Zeke reached the sidewalk. John-John could see that Zeke was fuming. *Good thing the cab pulled away before Zeke caught them*, thought John-John.

The guys were "laughing their asses off" as the cab headed up Lafayette Street. It didn't seem to register with them that they were playing around with people's lives. Of course, Lennie was really relishing the whole thing because it was a great way of getting even with Zeke. The other guys should have known better, but under the influence of alcohol, what they had just done seemed hilarious— and they were ready to perform an encore. When the cab reached Bleecker Street, the driver was directed to turn right and then again, to turn right onto the Bowery. After right turns on Kenmare Street and Cleveland Place, the cab was in position for another sortie. As the cab passed the newsstand, Frankie yelled, "Yo, John-John!"

Zeke had just returned to his apartment when he again heard the honking of a horn. The cab was back and venom was being spewed up at him again.

As before, he couldn't see who was in the cab—although he had a pretty good idea of who they might be.

"Serafina's a big who-ah! She loves Martucci's..."

"Zeke, you're a *cornuto*!"

"Ask your wife about her abortion! Yeah, ask your wife about her abortion!"

Zeke ran down just in time to view the back window of the cab as it was pulling away. He could see that the cab was full, but he still couldn't make out any of the passengers. Rather than going back upstairs, he decided to wait in the hallway just in case the cab would return a third time.

The cab returned about five minutes later, but this time it had traveled south on Lafayette and stopped directly across the street from Zeke's building. As the driver began honking the horn, Zeke jolted out of the hallway and raced across the street towards the cab.

"Gun it!" yelled Danny, having spotted Zeke just in the nick of time.

As all the guys ducked below the cab's windows, the cabbie, who actually found the whole thing to be rather amusing, quickly responded to Danny's command, even passing the red traffic light on the corner to ensure their getaway. It was a near-miss. Zeke had gotten within 10 feet of the cab, but he hadn't been able to get a glimpse of anyone but the driver. As the cab crossed Spring Street, Danny popped up his head and yelled out to John-John, "Dave's! Dave's!"

Zeke glanced over at John-John and then kicked one of the building's metal garbage cans in frustration. When he entered his apartment, he confronted Serafina who had heard most of the inflammatory words and insults.

"Serafina, what's goin' on between you and Orazio?"

"Nothin-ah."

"Nuttin! You were nuttin but a whore when I met you in Naples. Maybe, you're still a whore! I know enough Italian to know what *cornuto* means!"

"No. No. You-ah no *cornuto*."

"Well, why are those guys sayin' those nasty things? And, what's this about you done havin' an abortion?"

"I don-nah know. I don-nah know. They-ah lie-ah! They ah wanna make-ah trouble!"

"I see the way you cozy up to Martucci. You seem to be way more friendly to him than I reckon you oughtta."

"That-sah caus-ah he come-ah from-ah Napoli…like-ah me."

"Well, on Monday I'm gonna look him in the eyes, man to man, and ask him straight out if he's been messin' around with you."

"Okay. But-ah if-ah you-ah get-ah him mad-ah, he might-ah fire you-ah…and then what-ah?"

That said, things simmered down and they went to bed— leaving a big gap between them. Felicia had heard everything—the hail of insults directed at her father, and her parents arguing. She tossed and turned in bed for about an hour before her tiredness overcame her angst. Francesca and Little Zeke, on the other hand, had, fortunately, slept through the whole incident.

John-John's walk to Dave's Corner took about ten minutes. When he stepped inside the coffee shop, he found the guys occupying two adjacent booths, drinking coffee and eating pieces of Dave's famous deep-dish pies. John-John was greeted warmly by all his buddies as he joined Danny and Frankie in one of the booths.

"What took you so long?" asked Frankie, with a broad grin on his face.

"Well, not like you guys, I had to *walk* here…and it's a seven-block walk."

"Ah, you take everything too fuckin' serious."

"Well, how did Zeke take it?" asked Danny.

With the full attention of the five instigators, John-John replied, "He took it hard. Even though it was dark, I could see he was mad as hell. He even kicked one of the garbage cans in front of his building. If he would've caught up to the cab, he would've beaten the shit out of at least two of you…You know, he's one strong son-of-a-bitch."

"You mean one strong *cornuto*," remarked Lennie, with a sly smile.

After replaying the incident five times, punctuated by progressively increasing crescendos of laughter, the guys decided to call it a night. Only John-John had any sympathetic feelings about the damage that the guys had probably done to Zeke and Scrafina's marriage.

At Sunday afternoon's dinner table, it was obvious to the Daniels children that their parents weren't speaking to each other and that there was a lot of tension between them. Only Felicia knew what the problem was, and she thought it would be best if her younger siblings were spared the details of what had happened the night before. She felt that everything might get back to normal in a couple of days. She recalled the terrible words yelled from the cab and she wondered: *Was Mama really a who-ah back in Naples? Is she screwin' around with Martucci? Did she really have an abortion?*

From various tidbits of information that Felicia had gleaned over the years, she had come to suspect that her mother *might* have engaged in a bit of prostitution to survive during World War II. However, she had given her mother the benefit of the doubt, putting her suspicions in the back of her mind. As far as Martucci was concerned, she had noticed that her mother seemed to be extra-friendly towards him, but she had dismissed any thoughts of impropriety, concluding that her mother and Martucci were simply Neapolitan *paisani* whose friendliness was based on having a common upbringing.

Chapter 44: The Showdown!

I gotta talk to that man, *first thing, and ask him straight out if he's been a messin' with Serafina. I gotta get to the bottom of this.* Those and similar thoughts raced through Zeke's angry mind as he went off to work on Monday morning, hoping to confront Martucci in private, man to man; but, when he arrived at the office, four workers and one of Martucci's sons were already there. So, he kept his anger to himself and went outside for a smoke. Ten minutes later, he was in one of Martucci's trucks en route to the Bronx to work on a boiler replacement job. While he worked, he couldn't help getting more and more riled up as he pictured Serafina having sex with Martucci.

He figured that his best chance to be alone with Martucci would be to go to the office about an hour after all the crews had returned from their jobs. So, when his workday was done, rather than going home, he decided to kill some time by taking a walk around the neighborhood. After walking for about an hour, he made his way into Martucci's office like a man on a mission.

"*Buona sera,* Zeke. Did you forget something? Do you need something?"

"Yeah…I need to talk to you." Zeke was pretty sure that they were alone, but he had to ask, "Is there anyone in the back room?"

"No, I'm the only one here," replied Martucci as he tensed up, reacting to the obvious anger in Zeke's voice and facial expression.

"Listen, Orazio, people are sayin' that you been a messin' with my wife! Is that true?"

"What do you mean 'a messin' with your wife?"

"I mean people are sayin' that you been screwin' her and that you even done got her pregnant! That's what I mean!"

"Don't mind the people in this neighborhood. They have nothing to do, so they gossip…they make things up."

Zeke could sense from the way that Martucci was speaking and from his body language, that he was lying. So, he pressed on, trying to get him to admit to his affair with Serafina.

"People are calling me a *cornuto*. They say that Serafina had an abortion 'cause you done got her pregnant!"

"Who are these people? Who are these no-good liars?"

"I don't know…On Saturday night, a cab done stopped in front of my buildin' and the guys inside yelled out nasty things about you and Serafina… and they called me a *cornuto*!"

"Did you see who they were?"

"No, I couldn't get a look at them…though I tried."

"Ah, it was probably some kind a joke."

"No, I don't think it was a joke. I been seein' the way you look at Serafina. I notice the way the both of you done talk to each other."

"Ah, it's all in your head, Zeke. Why don't you just go home."

"No, not until I get to the bottom of this!"

"I told you the truth!"

Unconvinced, Zeke yelled, "No, you're lyin'!"

"Oh, get the hell out of here, Zeke, before I lose my temper!"

Upon hearing those words, Zeke moved forward, grabbed Martucci by the collar, and said, "Lose your temper! Lose your temper! You done been screwin' my wife right under my nose and you're gonna lose *your* temper!"

Martucci managed to push Zeke's hand off his collar, and as he did so he yelled, "You're fired! You're fired! Now, get the hell out of here!"

As Zeke started to back off, he yelled, "You done been foolin' around with my wife and I get fired!"

"That's right! That's right!" replied Martucci, not realizing that he had inadvertently admitted to the affair in the heat of the argument…"And about your job…you should've thought about it before you put your hands on me."

"So, it's true about you and Serafina!"

"No, it's not true!"

"You just admitted it, you no good rottin' snake!"

"Ah, get the hell out of here!"

Zeke didn't budge. "I'm not leavin' 'til you come clean!"

"Ah, get the fuck outta here…and don't come back!

Zeke leaned over the desk and exclaimed, "Listen, I'm not goin' 'til I get to the bottom of this!"

"I said, get the fuck outta here! You…you *cornuto!*" yelled Martucci, waving his index finger within inches of Zeke's face.

Those last words drove a stake in Zeke's heart. Martucci hadn't meant to call Zeke a *cornuto*, but his Neapolitan temper had taken over.

Hearing the word, "*cornuto,*" being yelled at him by his wife's lover was simply too much to take. He pounced on Martucci and grabbed him by the neck. As his powerful hands applied more and more pressure, the airflow into Martucci's lungs was being cut off. He squirmed in his chair and tried to push Zeke away, but his efforts were fruitless. Zeke's hands felt like an ever-tightening vise. Gasping for air and close to passing out, as the flushness in his face was fading to blue, he reached into his desk's top drawer and found his loaded 38-caliber revolver. With the little strength he had left, he barely managed to put the gun barrel against Zeke's ribs and squeeze the trigger. Zeke's upper body instantly became limp and dropped onto the desk. Martucci was totally frazzled. He was hoping against all hope that he hadn't killed Zeke, but it was soon obvious to him that he had. He pushed Zeke's hands off his neck and they slowly fell away, with the fingers still curled. There was blood splattered everywhere, including some on Martucci. After about five minutes, he regained his composure—although he was far from being calm.

He pondered the situation: he was absolutely sure that no one outside had witnessed the shooting since the storefront glass and the small pane of glass on the front door were painted black; and he was reasonably sure that no one outside had heard the gunshot over the din of the rush-hour traffic. *He* knew that he had killed Zeke in self-defense, but he also knew that he would have a tough time proving it. Even if he were to be acquitted of murder, he would certainly lose respect in the neighborhood because his affair with Serafina would surely come out in the trial.

He had to find some way out of his predicament that didn't involve the law. But, what should he do? He slowly got up from his chair, and operating purely on instincts, tugged at Zeke's lifeless body, managing to get it off the desk and onto the floor. Then, with all the strength he could muster, he dragged the heavy corpse into the back room. While mopping his brow with his handkerchief, he thought, *How am I going to get rid of this body? Who can I get to help me?*

He didn't want to get his sons involved because if things went wrong, they could be prosecuted as "accessories after the fact." He didn't want to get his two most loyal workers involved because he figured they might ultimately blackmail him—loyalty notwithstanding. After some soul-searching, he concluded that his only viable alternative would be to get Big Sal Tusa involved. Like most business owners in the neighborhood, Martucci paid Big Sal a monthly payment—in his case, $150 a month—to ensure that he would have "no problems." It was protection money—although that term was never used—but it also gave the business owners access to Big Sal. Since Big Sal had a reputation of being able to take care of just about any situation, Martucci hoped that he would "take care" of the messy situation in his office.

Chapter 45: He Was Mugged!

Martucci paced back and forth in the back room of his office, being careful not to look down at the still body on the floor. He was puffing on his cigarette almost in sync with his rapid heartbeat as he nervously readied himself to meet with Big Sal. He took off his bloodstained shirt and threw it on the floor. He then pulled a clean shirt out of the metal closet and put it on. He took a close look at his pants and was glad to see that they weren't stained with blood. He donned his black leather coat, shut-off the lights, and headed for the corner of Spring and Mulberry. He had expected to find Big Sal standing on the corner "holding court" with some of his associates; however, Big Sal wasn't there. So, he walked over to the social club across from John-John's building to see if Big Sal might be there.

When he entered the club, he was quite relieved to see Big Sal playing cards at a table just to the right of the front door. He had no qualms about interrupting the game because he was friends with all the other card players: Gappy; Tony "Green"; and Joey "Jumps."

Resorting to his native tongue, out of nervousness, he said, "Excuse me, gentlemen. Salvatore, I need to talk to you in private about an urgent matter."

Big Sal put down his cards and said, "Time out for a few minutes, boys...and don't get no fuckin' ideas about lookin' at my cards!"

Martucci followed Big Sal to the back of the club near the toilet—a spot that was out of earshot from everyone else. He told Big Sal his version of what had happened. Pulling his gold watch out of his vest pocket, Big Sal flipped it open and calmly remarked, in dialect, "It's 6 o'clock. We should wait until one or two in the morning to get the body out of your place...you know, when the neighborhood quiets down."

Martucci breathed a sigh of relief. Big Sal was going to help him—and he had full confidence in Big Sal when it came to such a matter as getting rid of a body.

"Do you have any boxes in your place that are big enough to fit a body?" After pausing a couple of seconds to take mental inventory, he replied, "Yes, I do. I have three big crates in the backroom that contain equipment for a big job that will start next week. I had the equipment shipped to my office instead of my warehouse because the job is less than a mile away from here, up on 14th Street."

"Good, that makes things easier…Let me ask you one thing…Were you fooling around with his wife?"

Martucci was smart enough to know that Big Sal wouldn't like the true answer. Although Big Sal had plenty of women on the side—"hot tomatoes," *commare*, and an occasional call girl—he truly believed in the sanctity of marriage; that is, he would never "fool around" with a married woman and he had no respect for anyone who would. Knowing this, Martucci replied, "I never fooled around with his wife. We were just good friends…*paisani*. He was a jealous man…a very jealous man who accused his wife, all the time, of being unfaithful."

"Good. Too bad things had to work out the way they did. Now, let me figure out what to do. Have a drink while I finish my hand. I'll talk it over with the boys because they will be involved in one way or another."

After playing out his hand, which turned out to be a winner, Big Sal approached Martucci as he was gulping down his second shot of Sambuca and began speaking to him in English.

"Well, the way I figure it, there's two choices…Number One… Bring the body to a junkyard that one of my friends runs out in Canarsie…bury the body and cover the spot with a pile of junked cars. Number Two…Drop the body on Crosby Street in the parking lot near Spring…put it behind the attendant's booth, so it ain't noticed right away…and take his wallet and rings, so it looks like he was mugged."

"I guess the first choice is better, right?"

"Nah, not really. If the cops don't find the body, the case will remain open. But if they find the body and it looks like the guy was mugged, there ain't gonna be much of an investigation…*Capisci?*"

"Yeah, I understand. So, you're gonna drop the body off on Crosby Street, tonight?"

"Yeah, that's the plan. But, to make sure the police investigation ends right away and that no detectives question you, I'll need to 'grease' one of the police sergeants in the 5th Precinct who will see to it that the dough gets spread around to the right people in the Precinct."

"How much money will you need to give him?"

"I think a grand will do."

"I'll give you $1,000, tomorrow…Is that okay?"

"No problem. You can pay me when you get a chance. I know you're good for the dough…and I know where you live!" he added with a forced laugh. "Now, give me the keys to the place and go home and relax. When you come to work in the mornin', you'll find the body gone and the place cleaned-up real good...better than it ever was. There won't be no evidence of the killin'…and I'm sure no 'dicks' are ever gonna come to your office to question you. That grand will be money well spent."

Serafina and her children were puzzled that Zeke hadn't returned home in time for dinner. At around six, Serafina sent Felicia over to Martucci's office to find out if Zeke was working overtime; but she found the office closed. At nine, a worried Serafina called the police to inform them that her husband was missing, but she was told that they couldn't take any action unless he was missing for at least twenty-four hours.

At about 6:30 a.m. on Tuesday morning, Leroy Chisholm arrived at the Crosby Street parking lot, toting a brown paper bag containing a strong cup of coffee and a cheese Danish. While fumbling in his pocket for the keys to the attendant's booth, he looked down and got the shock of his life. The sight of the lifeless body on the pavement so stunned him that he dropped the brown paper bag, spilling his coffee all over the place. He remained transfixed with his eyes and mouth wide open. Just then, the first customer of the day pulled into the parking lot. The white '62 Buick Electra 225 was driven by Seymour, the owner of the coffee shop next to Joe's Newsstand. Seated at his side was his wife, Elaine.

"Seymour!" screamed Elaine, pointing to the body on the ground. "There's a man on the ground and he looks dead!"

Seymour couldn't see the body from the driver's seat, but he *could* see Leroy, who appeared to be in a state of shock. When Leroy walked over to the driver's side of the Buick, he stammered, "Mr. Seymour…I can't believe what I just found…what I just found near the door of the booth…the body of a dead man!"

"Are you sure he's dead?"

"Oh yeah, I'm quite sure he's dead all right…the poor soul… but, why don't you come over and take a look for yourself."

"Seymour, stay in the car!"

Ignoring his wife, he got out of the car and slowly walked over to the body, which was lying on its back. He reached down and gingerly touched the man's forehead. He instantly felt the chill of death, causing his stomach to become a bit queasy.

"Is he dead?" yelled Elaine, after cracking open the car window a couple of inches.

"Oh, yeah…definitely. He's ice cold…and I'm pretty sure I know who he is."

"Who?"

"Zeke…you know, the hillbilly that lives right up the street from our coffee shop."

"Oh my God! Are you sure?"

"Well, I'm about 90 percent certain that it's him…Is there a phone in the booth, Leroy?"

"Yeah, there sure is Mr. Seymour."

"Well, we better get the police here right away. You go in the booth and make the call. Elaine and I will stay here with you until they come."

It took about ten minutes for the patrol car to arrive on the scene. Seymour quickly introduced himself to the police and then told them whom he thought the victim was and where he had lived.

"Sir, do you know his last name?"

"No, all I know is that everyone calls him Zeke. I don't even know if that is his real first name…Are you going to send someone to his house to contact his family?"

"No, not yet. That would be too premature. I'll pass on the information that you gave me to the detectives when they arrive here, shortly. They'll conduct the investigation. Thanks for your assistance."

"No problem."

"Mr. Seymour, I guess you best be heading to your coffee shop, now."

"Yeah, Leroy, we already are about twenty-five minutes late in opening up the place…C'mon, Elaine, let's walk as fast as we can. We don't wanna lose too many customers."

"Mr. Seymour, when the delivery boy comes in, could you send me a coffee and a cheese Danish?"

"Sure will. In fact, I'll send over a few cups of coffee and a half-dozen Danishes…on the house…so you and the police can have something to *nosh* on."

"Thank ya, Mr. Seymour, thank ya."

"No problem. That's the least I can do."

Chapter 46: O Dio!

"Elaine, I think we should find Serafina and ask her if Zeke is missing," suggested Seymour as the couple walked briskly towards their coffee shop.

"No, I don't think we should get involved. Let the police do their job."

"Yeah, but…"

"No buts! I learned one thing about this neighborhood…mind your own damn business!"

Margie and Kelly, two of the coffee shop's waitresses, and Leo, the short-order cook, had been waiting in front of the shop's locked door for over a half-hour, when they spotted Seymour and Elaine on the other side of Lafayette Street. Their concerned looks quickly turned to smiles of relief. While Seymour was unlocking the door's three heavy-duty locks, Elaine nervously began to tell the workers about the dead body in the Crosby Street parking lot. With her voice quivering, she continued to fill in the details about what she and Seymour had just seen, as all five of them rushed to get the coffee shop ready for business. Seymour would occasionally add a word or two, but he let Elaine do most of the talking—as she usually did.

Twenty minutes after the late opening, the coffee shop was running normally. As Seymour was serving a customer at the counter, he happened to notice Serafina walking her dog past the coffee shop. She looked disheveled and tired. Ignoring his wife's admonitions, he ran out to talk to her.

"Good morning, Serafina."

"Good-ah morning, Seymour," she replied, with her eyes looking down at the sidewalk.

"How's Zeke?"

"I don-nah know where he is-ah. He no com-ah home-ah."

"Listen, Serafina, I think you should walk over to the parking lot on Crosby Street."

"Why-ah?"

"Something bad might have happened to Zeke."

"What-ah?"

"Something bad."

"Tell-ah me what-ah you mean-ah, something-ah bad-ah."

"Well, a man was found dead in the parking lot and he looks like Zeke...but maybe it's not him."

"*O Dio*! Oh my God-ah! It can't-ah be true!"

"Listen, Serafina, as I said, *maybe* it's not Zeke...maybe it's somebody else. Compose yourself. Wait, I'll walk over there with you."

When they arrived in front of the parking lot, a burly, plainclothes detective raised both palms, signaling them to stop. "Sorry folks, you can't come beyond this point. This is a crime scene."

"Sir, I was here about an hour ago with my wife and Leroy, the parking attendant. I saw the victim and I believe he might be this woman's husband."

"Well, right now we are in the middle of our investigation, and..."

Not waiting for the detective to finish his sentence, Serafina bolted right past him. When she reached the rear of the attendant's booth, she looked down and stopped dead in her tracks. Her whole body began to tremble when she immediately recognized the man lying on the pavement. She knelt down and touched his face. The cold and clammy feeling on her fingertips confirmed what her eyes had already told her: Zeke was dead! She screamed, "Zeke! Zeke! *O Dio!* Oh my God-ah!" as tears poured out of her eyes.

Seymour and the detective tried to comfort her. She could hear their voices but couldn't make out their words. In her shocked state of mind, their utterances sounded like mumbo-jumbo. After several minutes, she regained her composure and responded to the detective.

"Ma'am, you know this man?"

"*Si*, he-sah my husband-ah...Zeke-ah Daniels."

"Are you sure, Ma'am?"

"Yeah, I'm-ah sure-ah," she responded, as she again began to cry.

"I'm so sorry, Ma'am…We think he was mugged. He had no wallet or jewelry on him."

"*O Dio! O Dio mio!*"

I will need some information from you, Ma'am. Come and sit in my car. It's too cold out here. You can help me complete my report inside the warm car."

"What about-ah my dog-ah?"

"You can bring your dog in the car."

Just before Serafina stepped into the unmarked police car, Seymour went over to her and gave her a big hug. "Serafina I'm sorry for your loss…so sorry."

She responded tearfully, the dryness in her mouth making her voice nearly inaudible, "Thanks-ah. Seymour…and thanks-ah for your-ah help-ah."

After about fifteen minutes of answering the detective's numerous, and sometimes redundant, questions, his report was completed. Rather than letting her walk back to her apartment building, he did the right thing and drove her home. She found her apartment totally quiet since her children had already gone off to school. After pacing up and down the living room floor for about five minutes, she decided to pick up the telephone to call her brother, Paolo. By the end of her tearful ten-minute conversation with her brother and his wife, she felt a bit more composed. As soon as she hung-up, she dialed her brother, Pietro. After ten rings, she reluctantly hung up. She was disappointed because if anyone could have lifted her spirits in her time of need, it would have been her warm and lively younger brother, Pietro, whose personality sharply contrasted that of the sullen and dour Paolo.

She turned on the TV and flipped through all the channels, twice, before settling on *The Today Show*. She couldn't concentrate on the program, but she left the TV on to fill the emptiness. She was fidgety. She needed to talk to someone. She decided that "that someone" would be Orazio. *I'll go see Orazio. He will comfort me… plus, he must be wondering why Zeke didn't show up for work, today.* So, she headed for his office. She didn't bump into any of her friends on her walk to his office. It was 8:45. Even the "ever-present" Fasano sisters didn't leave their cozy little apartments until about 9:30 during the winter.

Orazio proved to be a great actor. He pretended to be totally astonished when she told him what had happened to Zeke and how she had viewed his lifeless body lying on the parking lot pavement about an hour before. He gave her a shot of Sambuca and then proceeded to make a pot of espresso. As they were waiting for the coffee to brew, he tried to console her by hugging her and gently kissing her on the cheek. He was acting more like a very dear friend and less like her lover.

"I suppose you should begin making the funeral arrangement. Do you know when the body will be released?"

"No."

"Well, I'll call Guidetti's Funeral Home and tell them the situation. They are good people. They will take care of everything and I'm sure they won't overcharge you."

"Thanks."

After about an hour, she left Orazio's office and headed back to her apartment. On the way, she met Tessie Fasano, who had just stepped out of her building. Still visibly shaken, she told Tessie that Zeke had been murdered, apparently during a mugging. She related how shocking it was to have seen Zeke lying dead in the Crosby Street parking lot. Tessie was empathetic. She could feel Serafina's pain and she did her best to comfort her.

"Serafina, let me walk you up to your apartment."

"Okay-ah."

When Serafina opened her apartment door, Tessie said, "Take care and rest...rest in bed. I'll stop by with my sisters at lunchtime. We'll bring you a nice potatoes-and-eggs hero."

"I no feel-ah hungry."

"Listen, you gotta eat. You gonna need your strength to get through this."

As Tessie was going down the stairs, a "light bulb" suddenly turned on in her head; she quickly put two-and-two together, making sense of what she had seen in the wee hours of the morning: At about 2 a.m., she had gotten the urge to go to the bathroom—being a middle-aged woman, her bladder wasn't what it used to be. It was a rare night when she could sleep straight through to the morning without having to get up to pee. After relieving herself, being nosy by nature, she had walked over to the kitchen window and looked down at the street, three stories below, just to see what might be going on. She was surprised to see three men carrying a large crate out of Martucci's office and loading it, with some difficulty, into a black van. She was quite sure that one of the men was Tony "Green," but she wasn't able to determine who the other men were. She had found it rather strange that Tony "Green" and two of his associates would be removing an apparently heavy crate from Martucci's place in the middle of the night. Still partly asleep, and feeling chilly because the heat in the building had been turned off during the night, she decided not to burden her brain with trying to figure out what was going on; so, she went back to bed and covered herself with her heavy chenille bedspread.

Now everything gelled in her mind; the pieces fell into place. *Zeke wasn't mugged on Crosby Street,* she thought. *Martucci must've killed him in his office, probably because Zeke had figured out that Serafina was having an affair with him. That crate I saw last night was as big as a coffin. Martucci must've gotten Tony "Green" and his crew to carry the body out in the crate and dump it on Crosby Street. Big Sal must've given his 'okay' to get rid of the body, or Tony "Green" wouldn't have been involved.*

Tessie told everyone she met during the day about Zeke's mugging and murder. She kept her theory of what *really* had happened to Zeke to herself—although she did share it with her sisters. By about three in the afternoon, just about everyone in the neighborhood had heard the shocking news about Zeke.

John-John returned from Columbia at four and stopped by the newsstand. He was stunned when Joe told him the bad news about Zeke. Shaking his head back-and-forth, he remarked, "I can't believe it. I just can't believe it, Joe."

"Well, it's true. Zeke's as dead as a doornail."

"What was he doing on Crosby Street? And, who would have the balls to mug a 'moose' like him? Usually, muggers go after weaklings or old people."

"Well, whoever did it had a gun…and that's a great equalizer."

"Have you seen Felicia?"

"No. Not yet."

"She must have taken it really hard. She was very close to her father …much closer to him than to her mother. I know that with Maria in the picture, our relationship hasn't been very friendly, lately, but I would like to give her my condolences…Do you know when and where the wake will be?"

"The wake will probably be at least several days from now 'cause I'm sure there's gonna be an autopsy…and that's gonna take some time."

"Oh, God, it's going to be a very sad Christmas for Felicia and the rest of her family."

"It sure will…it sure will."

"Well, I've got to hit the books. See you tomorrow, Joe."

Tessie's urge to gossip far exceeded her ability to rationalize the effects of her gossip. By Thursday afternoon, she just couldn't contain herself. She started telling her friends about the crate she had seen being removed from Martucci's office in the middle of the night. Her sisters, who hadn't seen anything, would usually chime-in, adding a few tidbits of gossip about Serafina's purported affair with Martucci. By Friday morning, the gossip had been spread throughout the neighborhood, typically in this manner: "Don't say nuttin, but I heard that Zeke was killed in Martucci's office…probably by Martucci himself…Zeke was arguing with Martucci 'cause Martucci was foolin' around with Serafina…Big Sal's boys dumped the body in the middle of the night as a favor to Martucci and made it look like a muggin'."

When the word on the street got to Big Sal's ear, he was furious. "If I find out who started this talk, I'll break that person's fuckin' legs…or worse…Tony, you go try and find out who the fuck it was!"

"Okay, Boss."

About two hours later, Tony returned and said, "It didn't take too much detective work for me to zero-in on who's responsible. I'm almost one-hundred-percent sure that Tessie Fasano…the mouth of Spring Street …started spreadin' the story."

"Ah-ha! I should have known! That ugly douche bag has a fuckin' big mouth!"

"Yeah, and a fuckin' face that could stop an eight-day clock! Whatta ya wanna do with her, Sal?"

"Nuttin."

"Nuttin, Sal?"

"Yeah, I thought about it a little bit while you were doin' your detective work and I figured out that the talk is good for business."

"Good for business? How?"

"Well, when the other store owners find out how I took care of Martucci's problem…how I got him out of his mess…they won't mind as much when they fork over their dough to me every month."

"Hey, Sally Boy, you're a fuckin' genius. If you had gone straight, who knows…you could've been a big company exec."

"Yeah, maybe…but workin' in a fuckin' office ain't for me."

Chapter 47: Vengeance

Zeke's body was released to the undertaker late Friday afternoon. The wake, which would be held at Guidetti's Funeral Home, would begin on Saturday evening at seven. There would be afternoon and evening viewings on the following two days. The funeral mass and burial would be held on Christmas Eve—of all days.

At around eleven on Saturday morning, John-John arrived at the newsstand as Danny, Frankie, Lennie and Shortie were in the middle of a lively conversation with Joe about Zeke's murder. The guys were dressed in their warmest clothing because the temperature was a bone-rattling 15 degrees. By then, everyone had heard the rumor of how Zeke had "actually" been murdered, and they all agreed that the rumor made much more sense than the police version.

Soon, Tony "Gallons" stopped by to bet his daily numbers. After five minutes of hemming and hawing over his picks—sometimes changing his numbers several times, much to Joe's annoyance—he handed Joe three bucks.

"Good luck, Tony."

"Thanks, I need it…I wanna buy my nephew's kids some nice Christmas presents, but I'm low on dough."

"Yeah, I hope you hit. It'll be good for me, too…but you ain't been lucky in a fuckin' long time."

I know, but my luck's gotta change…By the way, did you hear about the killin' on Grand Street, last night?"

"No, who got killed?"

"A young fella they call 'Fat' Carlo."

"Fat Carlo?"

"Hey, I know him," interjected John–John. "We graduated from P.S. 130 the same year. He's from around Hester Street."

"Yeah, must be the same kid…Anyway, my brother Pete, who lives on Hester Street, just told me the whole story…The kid was stabbed to death…He was stabbed about fifteen times by two of his friends durin' an argument over somethin'…It happened about two in the mornin' right across the street from Police Headquarters…on Grand and Centre Street."

"Do they know who killed him?" asked Joe.

"Sure. Almost everyone around there knows who did it, but nobody's talkin' to the cops. I don't know the guys that killed that kid, but maybe some of yous might know 'em." "Who are they?" asked Shortie.

"One guy is Mike…they call him 'Crazy' Mike…the other guy is called Sonny 'Splits.'"

"Oh shit!" said Frankie, "Me and John-John threw those assholes a beatin' a few years ago."

"Do you think they'll be nabbed by the cops, Tony?"

"Nah, Lennie, I hear they're already on the lam, and there ain't gonna be no witnesses…even though there were a few."

"Well, I hope they get caught…but like everyone else in the neighbor-hood, I won't rat them out," said John-John.

"Yeah," added Danny, "That's the way it is around here."

Tony remarked, "You know Joe, they say these things come in threes. First Zeke…now this kid…I wonder who's gonna be next."

"I hope there ain't gonna be a 'next,' Tony, especially with Christmas just around the corner."

Tony left just as Felicia arrived at the newsstand. She had a very sad look on her face, and her eyes were bloodshot. She was wearing a black dress, which was partially covered by a black woolen jacket. Her head was protected from the unusually cold air by a black felt hat, which she appeared to have borrowed from her mother. It was obvious that she was already dressed for the evening wake since she was wearing black high-heeled shoes and black nylon stockings. When she reached the newsstand, the guys expressed their condolences.

Rather than graciously accepting their condolences, she yelled, "You're sorry? You're sorry?" Then, exhaling with tense lips, her breath forming a smoky puff of vapor, she continued her rant: "You phony no-good bastards! You aggravated my father for years…and now you expect me to believe that you're sorry he was mugged and murdered!"

Danny just couldn't let her last comment go by. He countered, "So, you think your father was killed in a mugging? Well, the rumor on the street is that Martucci killed your father!"

"Martucci? Martucci? Why, Martucci?"

Lennie, who couldn't resist spewing out some venom, replied, "Because your mother…the who-ah that she is…was gettin' laid by Martucci…he even knocked her up…and Martucci shot your father durin' an argument over your mother."

At that point, John-John pushed Lennie up against the window of the coffee shop and yelled, "C'mon, Lennie, cool it! Watch your mouth!"

"How dare you say those things about my mother, Lennie! My mother is not a who-ah, you squirmy little bastard!…And she never cheated on my father!"

Lennie and Danny both responded with sarcastic laughs—which only made her angrier.

"You know, I bet it was you guys who were yellin' all those nasty things up at our window last Saturday night."

Then, turning her attention to John-John, she yelled, "And I bet *you* were behind it!"

"Me? Not me, Felicia."

"Sure, you always act like the innocent good guy, but I know you're the one who pulls the strings of these low-lifes! You're the one who calls the shots!"

"You're wrong…Anyway, you shouldn't be mad at me, or any of the guys. You should be focusing your anger at Martucci!"

Rather than responding, she just turned her head slowly from side to side, looking into the eyes of all of the guys while mentally processing what John-John had said.

"Hey, Joe, won't Martucci be comin' by in a few minutes to buy his 'scratch sheets'?"

Joe, who had just gotten up from his stool to stand for a while, replied, "Yeah, Shortie, he's due. He buys two every day at about this time. He loves bettin' on the ponies."

"Felicia, why don't you wait until Martucci comes here and ask him yourself about what happened to your father," said John-John, adding, "You know, rumors in this neighborhood are usually true about ninety-eight percent of the time."

Felicia stared at John-John without saying a word, turned around and headed back to her building. As she was walking up the stairs, all she could hear were John-John's words echoing and echoing loudly in her head: *You know, rumors in this neighborhood are usually true about ninety-eight percent of the time…You know, rumors in this neighborhood are usually true about ninety-eight percent of the time…*

When she entered her apartment, she breezed right past her brother and sister. Her mother wasn't home; she was at the funeral home finalizing arrangements. She made her way into her parents' bedroom and headed for the Seven Seas Chest in the corner of the room. After searching through two of the chest's drawers, she found what she was looking for: her father's pistol—a 25-caliber Beretta that he had brought home at the end of World War II as a souvenir.

Not thinking clearly, she decided that the only way to find out if the rumors were true would be to threaten Martucci when he stopped by the newsstand. She was too agitated to think about what she would do beyond threatening him. Her focus was simply on finding out the truth. She knew that the gun was loaded because her father had always said, "What's the dang use of havin' a gun with no bullets in it?" Without deliberation, she slipped the pistol into her handbag and headed out to confront Martucci. Rather than walking right up to the stand, she stopped by the trashcan, 10 feet away.

Martucci showed up at the newsstand about five minutes later for his scratch sheets: *The National Program* and *The Armstrong Daily*—both excellent horseracing guides for serious bettors. Felicia confronted him just as he was handing Joe a $5 bill: "Orazio, the rumor around the neighborhood is that *you* killed my father!"

Orazio, who spoke English with only a slight accent, nervously replied, "Who is spreading that lie? That's crazy! Why would I kill my best worker?"

"They say it was over my mother."

As Martucci's face began to redden and stiffen, the only word he could utter was, "What?"

Felicia could sense from his body language and tone of voice that he wasn't being truthful. As he was about to walk away, she reached into her handbag and whipped out the Beretta. "Don't move!" she ordered, as she waved the gun within 2 feet of his face.

"Hey! Put that gun away! Whatta ya crazy, or what!"

The guys remained literally and figuratively frozen in place and speechless, as two pedestrians hurried past the newsstand with their heads down, either not wanting to get involved, or too cold to get involved. As the two passersby disappeared into the subway kiosk, Felicia yelled, "Listen, Orazio, I want the truth. Did you kill my father?"

He was too stunned to reply, so she repeated herself in a deliberate manner: "Did…you…kill…my…father?"

He remained silent, causing her blood to come to a boil. She stepped closer to him, pointing the gun within 12 inches of his face. When John-John calmly said, "Felicia, put that gun away," Martucci grabbed her wrist with his left hand and tried to wrestle the gun away from her. As they struggled, the silence was broken with a loud "boom" as one shot rang out, barely missing Martucci's face; but Joe wasn't as fortunate. The errant bullet had penetrated the right side of his head. The force of the bullet caused his head to slam against the back wall of the newsstand. A split-second later, he collapsed like a ton of bricks, falling to his right upon his nearby stool.

When Felicia realized what she had done, she dropped the gun on the newspaper counter and cried out, "Joe! Joe! Are you all right?

Are you okay? I'm sorry! I'm so sorry!"

Realizing that he had an opening to leave the scene, Martucci hurried away without bothering to check if Joe was dead or alive.

Danny raced into the newsstand and yelled out, "He's alive… but his forehead is bleedin' and there's blood all over his face!"

Danny quickly spotted the bullet entry wound, which was just behind Joe's right ear, and he noticed that it wasn't bleeding very much. It soon became obvious to him that the blood oozing from Joe's forehead was due to the nasty gash he had received when he collapsed upon his stool's curved metal seat back. Danny propped up Joe's limp body and tried to stop the bleeding with his handkerchief.

Then, John-John took command of the situation, barking out orders like a brigadier general: "Shortie, you call for an ambulance… and tell 'em to hurry! Frankie, hide the gun under your jacket and drop it down a sewer on Mercer Street…and make sure that no one sees you! Lennie, your job is to tell any nosy outsiders who might come by that Joe was shot by some guy who tried to rob him just before we got here…Got it?"

At that point, Felicia, who was crying uncontrollably and feeling as guilt-ridden as one could possibly feel, started walking slowly back towards her building. John-John followed her and caught up to her in the hallway.

"Felicia, don't worry. Everything is going to be all right."

"What about Joe?" she replied, with tears rolling down her cheeks.

"I think he'll be okay."

"Really? You *really* think he'll be okay?"

"Yeah, I do…I do, Felicia."

"Do you think I'll get arrested?"

"No, I don't think so."

John-John then gave her a bear hug and kissed her cheek in a consoling manner. Shifting into neighborhood vernacular—perhaps out of nervousness or, perhaps, for effect—he said, "Don't worry, there ain't gonna be no witnesses. In this neighborhood, no one cooperates with the cops…as your father once had to learn. Also, Martucci ain't gonna say nuttin. He doesn't wanna get involved. Joe can't be a witness…He can't see…and even if he could, he wouldn't squeal on you. He wouldn't want you to go to jail. He knows you didn't mean to shoot him…that it was an accident."

"John-John, you're such a great guy. I'm so sorry I said those bad things about you, before, and I wish we hadn't broken-up. I really do. Too bad I let you slip away from me and into Maria's arms."

That said, she surprised him by turning and tilting her head and putting her lips on his. She then gave him a tearful but passionate kiss, which he didn't resist, for he still had some feelings for his first love. Their kiss lasted quite a long time, considering the circumstances. As she pulled back she said, "John-John, in my heart I know that someday we'll wind up together."

He didn't know how to respond, so he changed the subject, saying, "Listen, Felicia, you better get ready to tell your mother the truth about what you did before she finds it out for herself…probably from Tessie Fasano, who always seems to know everything that happens around here. Now, go upstairs and try to compose yourself."

As he walked out of the hallway, he could hear the siren of an ambulance getting increasingly louder. The ambulance, with red lights flashing, came into view as it sped south on Lafayette Street. It soon turned sharply left onto Spring Street and came to a screeching stop alongside the newsstand. Two paramedics bolted out of the red-and-white, hearse-like Cadillac to attend to Joe. The ambulance was from St. Vincent's Hospital—the best hospital in lower Manhattan—located in nearby Greenwich Village.

The paramedics did their best to usher away the teenagers crowding the newsstand, but they weren't too successful. They quickly bandaged Joe's head and carefully placed him on a wheel-supported stretcher as more and more people gathered around the newsstand. In addition to the newsstand crew, the onlookers included curious passersby, Seymour and Elaine, and various neighborhood people, including the Fasano sisters, and Serafina, who was on her way back from Guidetti's Funeral Home.

Joe was lapsing in and out of consciousness, barely aware of the words of encouragement offered by several of the onlookers: "Don't worry Joe, you'll be okay," or words to that effect. The stretcher was wheeled over to the ambulance. The rear door was swung open by one of the paramedics. As the stretcher was pushed into the ambulance, the wheels automatically sprung up under the stretcher, thereby providing about 3 feet of clearance between Joe's head and the roof of the ambulance. Once the stretcher was secured, the rear door was slammed shut and the ambulance quickly sped away with its siren blaring and red lights flashing. Several women, including Serafina and Tessie Fasano, made the Sign of the Cross as the ambulance headed down Spring Street.

A patrol car arrived at the scene just in time to see the ambulance speeding away. When the two cops got out of the car, they began to ask questions. Danny immediately volunteered that just before losing consciousness, the newspaper dealer, Joe, had told him that he had been shot during an attempted robbery. Lennie then added, "Listen, the man who got shot was blind, so he didn't know who shot him...and nobody saw nuttin...nobody was hangin' around at the time...it was freezin'!"

"Let's get a cab and go to St. Vincent's," said John-John, with a crack in his voice and a worried look on his face.

"Yeah, let's do it," said Danny, adding, "We'll need a Checker, since there are five of us."

The cops didn't stop the guys from leaving the scene. They knew they wouldn't get any more information from them.

After about five minutes, the guys managed to hail a Checker cab. Ten minutes later, they were at the hospital's front desk where they were told that there was no information regarding the condition of "the Lafayette Street shooting victim." The woman at the front desk didn't even know Joe's name at that time.

"Ma'am, if you want, I can give you some personal information about the shooting victim," said John-John.

"Okay...Please do, young man."

John-John quickly rattled off Joe's full name, address and telephone number, and he added that Joe's wife was named Virginia.

Back at the Daniels' residence, Felicia approached Serafina who was tidying up the kitchen, mostly as a way of relieving some of her anxiety over the upcoming wake. Felicia got right to the point, quickly telling her that she had accidentally shot Joe as she was confronting Martucci with a gun to find out if he had killed her father.

"But-ah, why would-ah Orazio kill-ah Zeke-ah?"

After freezing for a few seconds, Felicia blurted out, "The rumor in the neighborhood is that Papa got into an argument with Orazio over *you!*…Because you were having an affair with him!" With tears streaming down her cheeks, she screamed, "Is it true? Is it true?"

"Disgraziata! How-ah dare-ah you-ah ask-ah me that-ah!"

Serafina was steaming. She was furious that Felicia had the *audacity* to ask her such a question, even though she was, indeed, having an affair with Martucci. In southern Italy during Serafina's day, a child would never dare question his or her parent about anything—let alone sexual matters. So, Serafina decided to teach her daughter some respect. She picked-up the wooden gravy spoon from the counter and swung it violently towards Felicia's face. Fortunately, she managed to turn her face away just in time; otherwise, the spoon would have hit squarely on her nose instead of on the side of her head. Serafina continued to hit Felicia, mercilessly, with the wooden spoon, as she kept yelling, *"Disgraziata! Disgraziata!"*

Though cornered, Felicia did her best to cover up her head with her arms. So, Serafina changed her target to Felicia's back. After the third blow across her back, Felicia managed to spin away. As she headed towards the living room, Serafina hit her with a parting blow squarely on her right breast. Felicia screamed in reaction to the unbelievable pain. She knew she had to get away from her mother, so she ran downstairs and remained in the hallway for about a half-hour, spending most of that time in tears. When she mustered up enough courage to return to the apartment, she was relieved to see that her mother had cooled off, somewhat.

Chapter 48: What do Doctors Know?

The guys were fidgety—nervously milling about in the hospital's lobby, hoping to hear some news about Joe. There wasn't much to do to kill time except to recount the details of the shooting, ad nauseam. After hearing the story retold at least a half-dozen times, John-John decided he had heard enough. He reached into his pants pocket, found a dime, and headed for a nearby phone booth to call Maria. She answered the phone on the third ring. He was comforted by her warm and friendly voice, and although he felt a little guilty about having shared a somewhat passionate kiss with Felicia a couple of hours earlier, he quickly put that in the back of his mind.

After they exchanged pleasantries, he nervously blurted out a recap of the shooting incident and the aftermath, only omitting the part about kissing Felicia. Initially, Maria thought he was kidding, but she quickly gathered from the tone of his voice that he was dead serious. Ironically, although he had been tired of hearing the guys rehashing the shooting incident, he didn't seem to mind telling Maria the story in great detail.

"Is she going to be arrested?"

"No, I don't think so. There won't be any witnesses."

"But there were witnesses...right?"

"Sure, there were many witnesses, including me, but the bottom line is that there ain't gonna be no witnesses…it's the neighborhood way. Besides, it was an accident."

"Well, there wouldn't have been any *accident* if Felicia hadn't decided to threaten Martucci with a gun."

"That's true, but she really didn't mean to shoot anyone…let alone Joe. She was just trying to scare Martucci into telling the truth."

"Do you think Martucci killed Zeke?"

"I would bet the family farm that he did," adding with a chuckle, "But my family doesn't have a farm…we barely have an apartment."

Maria then broached the subject of attending Zeke's wake. John-John suggested that he should go alone in the evening, and that she should go with Judy and Angie on Sunday afternoon. Although he didn't explain why he wanted to go to the wake without her, she knew the reason: he didn't want to get Felicia all riled up by the sight of the two of them as a couple.

"Okay, John-John, you go tonight and I'll go tomorrow with the girls."

"I'll pick you up at 8:30, after my visit to Guidetti's. How's about dinner at Yat Bun Sing's with Danny and Judy?"

"Sounds good. By the way, is Danny going to the wake?"

"No. He figures that he wouldn't be welcome, considering his terrible relationship with Zeke and Serafina."

Maria changed the subject: "John-John, today my father told me something that broke my heart."

"Broke your heart? I thought you were the apple of his eye."

"Yeah, that's true, but he's so set in his old Sicilian ways. He doesn't want me to go to college."

"Oh my. You're so intelligent…too intelligent to limit your education to only high school."

"I've tried hard to change his mind. I've cried; I've stomped my feet; I've slammed a few doors…but nothing worked. He wants me to go to work right after graduation…and that's it!"

"What a waste of brains! You know, besides your great looks and gentle ways, the thing that attracted me to you was your intelligence…an intelligence that Felicia could never come close to matching."

"Well, my father is like an immovable rock. Once he makes up his mind, he won't change it. My mother tried to convince him to let me go on to college, but she had no luck."

"Maybe, you can go to college in the evening…you, know, after work. Even if you take one course every semester, it's better than nothing."

"Yeah, maybe I'll try to take evening classes."

"Well, I'll see you at 8:30, Maria."

"*Ciao*, sweetheart."

When he returned to the guys in the lobby, he learned that there still was no word regarding Joe's condition. He noticed that three more of the guys had joined the group: Charlie "the Ox," Vinnie "Lemons" and Joey "Limp."

"Why don't we hang-out in the front of the hospital for a while…it's getting stuffy in here," suggested John-John.

At around three, the guys immediately recognized the middle-aged woman who was approaching the hospital entrance to be Joe's wife, Virginia. She knew most of the guys because she usually stopped by the newsstand about every two weeks to visit her sister who lived on Elizabeth Street.

"Any news, John-John?"

"Well, Mrs. Sorrentino, all we know is that he's still alive."

"Oh, thank God he's still alive. When I was on the train, I was hopin' against hope that he wouldn't die before I could get here…the train just couldn't go fast enough for me. It seemed like it was taking forever to get here."

"Where are your two daughters and your son-in-law?"

"None of them were home when I got the call. I'll try to get in touch with them after I see Joe."

"I'm sure they'll let you see him right away, since you're his wife," Danny interjected.

"When you find out how Joe's doin', would you please come down and tell us?"

"I will, Shortie. I appreciate you guys being here. I know how fond Joe is of all of yous, even though you sometimes play some awful tricks on him."

"That's true, Mrs. Sorrentino, but we love him like an uncle… we all do," said Frankie, doing his best to hold back a tear.

"We'll be in the lobby, waiting to hear from you," said John-John in a muffled tone.

About a half-hour later, Virginia returned with some somber news. She told the guys that Joe was in a coma and that the doctors were waiting for a specialist—a neurologist—to determine the amount of brain damage and whether or not to remove the bullet from his head. She also indicated that the doctors had told her that Joe had received a deep gash on his brow, which had likely occurred when he had fallen down after being shot.

"Is he stable?" asked John-John.

"Yeah, he's stable. He's on oxygen and he's got a lot of wires connected to him. The doctors have no idea how long he'll be in a coma. One doctor told me that he could come out of the coma within minutes, or that he might never come out of it."

"Is that the best they can say?" asked Danny.

"Yeah, that's the best they can say." She looked down and slowly shook her head from side to side. "Ah, Doctors…what do doctors know? I guess they don't know as much as we think they do…Anyway, you guys should go home, now. There's nuttin you can do here."

Realizing that she was making sense, they reluctantly agreed to go home.

"We'll call the hospital every hour to see if we can get some new information on his condition," promised John-John, adding, "We'll all be here tomorrow."

Chapter 49: The Wake

Martucci was nervously pacing back and forth in his small office. It was Monday, December 23rd. He was alone and trying to decide whether or not he should pay his respects to the Daniels family at Guidetti's Funeral Home. The radio announcer's voice provided the only sounds in the quiet office. Although he was oblivious to the radio, he did note the two-second beep and the announcement that the time was exactly 2 p.m. At that moment, he decided that as difficult as it would be for him to look at Zeke in the casket and to face the Daniels family, he had to do it; and he had to do it, today, since tomorrow would be the mass and the burial. Although he had acted in self-defense, he was haunted by what he had done and was plagued by nightmares ever since the shooting. Even when awake, the vision of Zeke's face at the moment of his death would occasionally flash before his eyes.

As Zeke's boss, it was expected that he attend the wake. Not doing so would only reinforce the rumors that were circulating throughout the neighborhood. He figured that his presence at the wake might put doubt in some people's minds about the truth of the rumors, and he hoped that with the passage of time, the rumors would fade away and that he would regain the respect of most of the neighborhood people.

He went into the back room and changed his clothes, putting on a dark blue suit that he always kept handy in the metal closet. He returned to the front office, reached into his desk drawer, and found a business envelope, which had the name of his company embossed on it. He pulled out a wad of cash from his pocket and found four, crispy, fifty-dollar bills. He put the $200 in the envelope, sealed it, and put the envelope in his jacket pocket. He then walked over to Guidetti's, which was only a block away from his office. He climbed up the tight stairway to the second-floor chapel. The room was about half-full with friends and relatives. John-John, who was paying his second visit, was seated next to Felicia in the second row. As Martucci made his way to the casket, he spotted the large floral wreath that his sons—who had paid their respects on Sunday—had sent on behalf of the Martucci family.

He shut his eyes as he knelt down in front of the casket. He didn't want a close-up view of Zeke's face. His feelings of guilt caused him to tremble inside, but he was able to mask his feelings, maintaining a strong and rigid appearance on the outside. After some perfunctory prayers, culminating with the Sign of the Cross, he got up and approached Serafina, who was seated in an armchair in the first row.

She stood up to greet him. He gave her a hug and kissed her on both cheeks. He expressed his condolences in Neapolitan dialect and then went over to Francesca and Little Zeke, expressing his condolences to them in English. He then approached Felicia, not knowing how he would be received. Before he could say a word, Felicia lashed out, loudly, "Get the hell out of here, you murderer!"

As his face began to redden, she spat at him, spraying both of his eyes. John-John grabbed her as she tried to get up from her chair, believing that she was about to hit Martucci. He had to use quite a bit of strength to hold her down. As he did his best to calm her, Martucci went over to Serafina and gave her the envelope containing the $200. Without saying a word, he sheepishly walked out with his head down.

A few minutes later, John-John and Felicia went downstairs for a change of scenery. She steered him into the hidden corner of the dimly lit vacant chapel on the ground floor. She was still clearly angry. After several minutes of conversation, she surprised him by wrapping her arms around him and kissing him on the lips.

John-John, I need you…I need you," she whispered as she pulled her head back slightly. "I feel so alone."

When she tried to follow with another kiss, John-John gently nudged her away, saying, "This is not the right time or place for this. Come, let's go have a seat in the lobby."

Once seated in the lobby, he told her about his morning visit to St. Vincent's. He related how Joe was no longer in the Intensive Care Unit; he was still in a coma, but the doctors had concluded that his life was no longer in danger.

"Did you see him, John-John?"

"Yeah, I was with him for a couple of hours. He's in a room with three other patients. He's resting comfortably. The doctors didn't remove the bullet, yet, but they might remove it soon…maybe, tomorrow or the next day. Joe's wife told me that the doctors say that the bullet wound up behind the top of his right ear. It went into his head on an angle, but, fortunately, it didn't go into his brain."

"Oh, I feel so bad about what I did. Too bad the bullet hit Joe instead of that lousy bastard, Martucci!"

"Well, if Martucci *did* murder your father, God will be his judge, someday."

"I hope he burns in hell, that no-good rotten bastard!"

"I gotta go now. I'm going back to the hospital to see how Joe's doing. I have no classes for the next ten days, so I'll be able to spend a lot of time at the hospital. Every one of the guys has spent many hours at the hospital, but I think I might've spent the most time there. I actually feel closer to Joe than any of my uncles…and I'm sure most of the guys feel the same way."

Chapter 50: Christmas Eve

John-John was having a leisurely breakfast with his mother and sister on the morning of Christmas Eve while his father was driving his bus through the rush hour Second Avenue traffic.

"How's Joe?" asked Vivian.

"Ah, he's still in the coma, but last night he looked a lot better to me."

"Are you goin' to the funeral mass at St. Patrick's?"

"Yeah, Ma. What about you?"

"No, I never was close to that family and I'm glad you're no longer seeing that Felicia."

"Okay, Ma, okay…So, what's the plan for Christmas Eve?"

"Well, we'll have the Feast of the Seven Fishes at around six… Make sure you don't eat any meat, today…You hear me?"

"Yeah, don't worry, I won't."

"We'll open our Christmas presents at around seven and head over to Grandma's at eight."

"Why do we eat seven fishes on Christmas Eve? Is it in the Gospels?"

"No, I don't think it's written in the Gospels. It's just a tradition. Most southern Italians do it."

"What happens if you only eat five or six fishes?" asked Vivian.

"Well, I don't think you'll go to Hell for that…but we like to follow tradition because it makes us remember who we are and where we came from."

Shortly before 9:30, John-John walked into St. Patrick's from the Mulberry Street entrance, along with the entire newsstand crew, with the exception for Lennie "Squirm," who felt that "the fuckin' rat bastard" had gotten what he deserved. All the guys, but Danny, seated themselves along the center aisle on the left side, about ten rows back from the altar. Danny, who was sure he was *persona non grata*, walked down the left aisle and sat in a pew about twenty rows back from the altar, right next to a beautiful stained-glass window—far enough away not to upset the grieving family.

Ten minutes later, Zeke's flag-draped casket was wheeled towards the altar from the main church entrance on Mott Street. Father Montevecchio and the family walked slowly behind the casket in sync with the lugubrious sounds from the church's antique organ. Since Zeke wasn't a practicing Roman Catholic—although he had ostensibly converted when he married Serafina back in Naples—the service was a brief one, lasting all of fifteen minutes. It was basically a blessing, not a mass.

As Father Montevecchio was incensing Zeke's casket as a way of honoring the body of the deceased, Danny came to realize that he would miss Zeke. He had enjoyed breaking his balls and taunting him over the past few years, but he never truly hated him. Only Lennie "Squirm" had developed a visceral hatred for him.

At the end of the service, Zeke's casket was wheeled up the aisle to the church entrance and then carried outside by six pallbearers and into the black Cadillac hearse. Before heading for the limousine, the grieving family gathered at the door of the church receiving hugs and kisses from friends, including the three Fasano sisters and Seymour. Martucci was conspicuously absent. All the guys, with the exception of Danny, expressed their condolences to the family.

Felicia, who was sobbing, hugged John-John and whispered in his ear, "Oh, John-John, my heart is so broken."

Within five minutes, the funeral cortege was on its way for its hour-long drive to the Veterans Cemetery in Farmingdale, Long Island.

"Are any of you guys coming with me to St. Vincent's?" asked John-John.

"Yeah, I'll go with you," said Frankie, while the rest of the guys indicated that they had other things to do.

When John-John and Frankie reached the corner of Prince and Mulberry, they met up with Danny, who had exited from the back of the church, not wanting to come face-to-face with Serafina.

"Hey Danny, Frankie and I are going up to St. Vincent's. Do you want to come with us?"

"I would, but I gotta buy a Christmas tree, and then help my mother decorate it."

After a brief stop at Buffa's Coffee Shop on Prince Street, John-John and Frankie headed to the hospital, arriving at St. Vincent's at eleven. When the elevator door opened at the 6th floor, their noses were greeted by that unmistakable odor which seems to be present in all hospitals, regardless of their degree of cleanliness: a combination of disinfectants, medicines, and bodily wastes.

Once inside Joe's room, it was apparent to them that Joe's condition hadn't changed. He still looked like he was in a deep sleep.

"Hey, Joe, how you doin'?" asked Frankie.

There was no answer, even when John-John repeated the same question. So they pulled up two chairs and sat down next to his bed in the rather cramped room. The two began to talk about Zeke's church service and they wondered how the burial was going.

"It's about 11:30. Zeke must be in the ground by now."

"I guess so, Frankie. They must've played *Taps* over his casket since he was a World War II vet."

Just then, Joe began to make some sounds that were unintelligible—but sounds nonetheless.

"Oh my God, Frankie, did you hear that. Maybe, Joe's coming out of his coma!"

They jumped up from their chairs and got within inches of Joe's face.

"Joe…Joe," they repeated, as if in a chorus.

"What?" Joe, softly replied, in a tone indicating that they were somehow disturbing him.

"Frankie, go get a nurse. Joe's back! He's out of his coma!"

As Frankie went to the floor desk to find a nurse, Joe slowly opened his eyelids, which were sticky and gummy. He was shocked and awestruck by what happened next: He was seeing color and light—not dark shadows—for the first time in more than two decades.

"I can see! I can see!"

"What?"

"I can see! Things are blurry, but I can see that the wall in front of me is green."

"I can't believe it, Joe! It's a miracle! It's a miracle!"

Frankie and a nurse entered the room just as Joe repeated, "I can see!"

"Really?"

"Yeah, really, nurse. I can see that the wall in front of me is green."

Not knowing if Joe's sudden exposure to light might be harmful, the nurse quickly covered his eyes with a folded white washcloth, forming a makeshift blindfold. She then told him to remain still and keep his eyes shut while she went to get a doctor. She was smiling from ear to ear, caught up in this "Christmas Eve miracle."

Soon, a rather young doctor, with a stethoscope dangling from his neck, entered the room along with the nurse.

"Mr. Sorrentino, I'm glad to see that you've come out of your coma. Nurse Reynolds, here, told me that me that when you opened your eyes, you were able to tell that the color of the wall in front of your bed is green, despite your having been blind for over twenty years. Is that true?"

"Yeah, Doc," replied Joe, breathing heavily from excitement, "I could see that the color of the wall is green…hospital green… and then, I could sorta see the nurse's hands when she was coverin' my eyes."

"Oh my!…Were you blind from birth?"

"No, Doc."

"What caused your blindness?"

"When I was eighteen, I got hit in the head with a baseball and knocked unconscious."

"Did you go blind right after that?"

"No, it took four years before I realized I had somethin' wrong with my eyes…It's a long story, Doc…I need to rest right now," replied Joe in a groggy tone.

"Okay, I'm going to leave the blindfold on…and please keep your eyes shut until I return."

About a half-hour later, the young doctor returned and gently shook Joe. "I'm not ready to remove the blindfold, yet, but open your eyes and tell me if you can see some light coming through the blindfold."

"Yeah, I can see some light…but not as much as I could without the blindfold."

"Wonderful! We are going to take you down to the ophthalmologist, and then we will have a neurologist examine you."

John-John and Frankie headed for the lobby as the nurse and orderly were transferring Joe to the gurney.

"Frankie, let's call Danny. He's probably at home decorating his Christmas tree. We should tell him to round up as many of the guys as he can and get over here, quick."

After making the telephone call in a booth in the lobby, they crossed paths with Joe's wife and daughters, who were making their way to the elevators. When they told them the good news, Virginia said, "Ya wouldn't be jokin' about somethin' like this, would ya?"

John-John assured, "No, no, it's true! Joe came out of the coma and he can see! At this time, the doctors don't know how well he can see, but I guess they'll find out soon."

"Yeah, he's bein' examined by some specialists right now," added Frankie.

Joe's wife and daughters began crying tears of joy. The last few days had been an emotional roller coaster for them, and now they might soon be receiving the greatest Christmas present they could ever have imagined. Occasionally, Virginia would fantasize about what it would be like if Joe were to regain his sight. She would wonder what his reaction would be upon seeing her again after so many years—especially since she was far from being the beautiful young girl he had married.

"Why don't we all go up to the 6th floor to see what's going on," suggested John-John.

The nurse at the floor desk told them that there was no news because the doctors were still examining Joe. The nurse directed them to the waiting room at the end of the hallway. After about an hour-and-a-half, during which time John-John and Frankie thumbed through a slew of outdated magazines and Joe's family prayed for the news that would make this their best Christmas ever, Nurse Reynolds entered the room with a broad smile on her face.

"I've got great news for you! Mr. Sorrentino seems to have regained the sight in his right eye! He will be temporarily moved into a private room on this floor because the doctors want him to be in a quiet, dimly lit room until his right eye can slowly readjust itself to focusing. She added, "You, the family, will be able to see him in about two hours."

"When can we see him?" asked Frankie.

"Maybe, a little later."

A little more than two hours later, Virginia and her two daughters were escorted to Joe's room. Virginia, who couldn't contain her tears, bent over the bed and kissed Joe, who was no longer blindfolded.

With his eyes partially open, he softly said, "Virginia, you're even prettier than I remember."

"You can really see me?"

"Well, my vision's a little blurry, but I can see that it's you."

"Oh my, Joe, God has made this the very best Christmas of my life!"

As his daughters drew close to him, he remarked, "You must be Clara…and you must be Anna."

"You're right, Dad…But how did you know? You didn't hear our voices."

"You know that I've felt your faces for many years. Right? So, by doin' that, I was able to get pictures in my mind of what yous looked like…and I guess my mental pictures of both of yous were pretty good."

While John-John and Frankie were hanging out in front of Joe's room, they spotted the head nurse walking towards them. Close behind her, walking with an air of authority, was a distinguished looking man in a white coat, who appeared to be about sixty years old.

"Hey Frankie, that guy must be one of the specialists who recently examined Joe."

"Yeah, or maybe he's the big cheese around here…you know, the chief doctor of the hospital…He looks kinda important."

John-John sidled over to his right and blocked the door to Joe's room. When the nurse and doctor were within 5 feet of him, he raised his right hand in the universally understood gesture indicating, "stop," and said, "Doctor, Joe Sorrentino is my uncle. Would you please explain to me how he got his vision back in his right eye… and is it permanent?"

"Well…okay young man, I'll try to explain it to you in layman's terms…By the way, I am Doctor Morris Goldman. My specialty is ophthalmology. As you probably know, your uncle likely went blind from trauma-caused cataracts. It is my understanding, based on what your uncle told me, that during an operation to remove a cataract from his left eye, he suffered a hemorrhage in that eye…in medical terms, a massive expulsive choroidal hemorrhage. That hemorrhage caused your uncle to permanently lose the vision in his left eye. Well, at that time…back in the late 1930s…his ophthalmologist must have concluded that it would be best not to remove the cataract from his right eye, fearing that the odds were that the operation might cause *it* to hemorrhage, too."

John-John nodded, acting as though he knew all of the details of his "uncle's" cataract operation.

"Well, his ophthalmologist likely figured…or at least hoped… that years down the road, medical science and ophthalmology would progress to the point where the cataract could be removed from his right eye with very little risk of it hemorrhaging."

"How did the bullet to the head cause my uncle to get his sight back in his right eye?"

"Well, in my opinion, the bullet, in itself, did *not* cause him to regain his vision in that eye. I didn't see the bullet wound because it's covered with a bandage, but I was told that it's not a deep wound… so, the bullet, likely, did not affect his brain at all."

"Gee, I had figured that the bullet must have hit some spot in his brain that controls vision, and that's how he got the sight back in his right eye."

"No, I'm quite sure that your uncle's regaining of his vision is not a brain-related phenomenon."

"So, how come he can see now, Doc?" interjected Frankie.

"I believe that it was the impacts to his head right after being shot that caused him to regain his sight. Dr. Tucker told me that it took some thirty-odd stitches to sew-up the nasty gash on his brow, and that there was a big bump on the back of his head, indicating that he probably banged his head hard against something as he recoiled from the shot."

"Doctor, I heard that my uncle was standing up in his newsstand when he was shot. So, his head must have hit the back wall of the newsstand, hard enough to cause the bump…The gash in his forehead must've happened when he fell…probably on the metal stool."

"You said that you 'heard.' Did anybody witness the shooting?"

"No, there were no witnesses. I meant to say, 'I *guess* my uncle was standing up.' Be that as it may, I really don't understand how the blows to his head could have caused him to regain his vision."

"Well, the impacts to his head, probably, were so forceful that they caused the cataract in his right eye to become dislodged. The fact that the cataract was quite mature…about twenty-five years old…may have made it easier to dislodge it. When I examined the eye, I could see that the cataractous lens had slid down within the eyeball…into the vitreous humor, in medical terms…leaving an unobstructed path to the retina, thereby allowing him to see again."

"Do you mean that the impacts did what an operation would've done?"

"In a manner of speaking, yes."

"How is it that he can see without a lens?"

"It seems that you know something about the functioning of the eye, young man."

"Well, I did enjoy my biology classes in high school, Doctor."

"As far as his being able to see without a lens, that's due to the fact that he had been severely nearsighted before his blindness…It's complicated to explain to a layman. You would really need to have an in-depth understanding of the eye and of optics. Suffice it to say that his severe nearsightedness proved to be a blessing in the long run. Had he once had normal vision, he would now need an extremely thick eyeglass lens to see with his right eye…but the thickness of such a lens would create a tunnel vision effect, impairing his visual field…I am quite certain that in his case, which is rather rare, he may actually be able to see normally with his right eye…and I mean without any eyeglass lens, whatsoever."

"Has anything like this ever happened before?"

"I recall reading about something like this in one of my medical journals several years ago. The facts were somewhat different. Unfortunately, I don't remember the details."

"Doctor, what will happen to the dislodged cataract?"

"We will probably leave it where it is for now, but we will surely monitor it. It could turn out that the dislodged cataract can remain where it is, indefinitely."

"Doctor Goldman, thank you so much for taking the time to explain everything to me."

"Oh, you're quite welcome."

"Now, I can tell the rest of the family how this miracle came about."

"Miracle?"

"Yes, miracle. It certainly seems like a miracle to me."

"Well, strictly speaking, it really wasn't a miracle, but…well, how's about we call it 'a miracle with a medical explanation'?"

"Okay, Doctor, that works for me."

After the doctor and nurse entered Joe's room, Frankie averred, "To me, it's a fuckin' miracle, plain and simple. Screw the medical explanation part! It's a Christmas miracle…a Christmas miracle!"

Meanwhile, Danny, accompanied by six of the newsstand crew, was in the lobby at the front desk trying to get visitor passes.

"Sorry, you're too many," said the surly middle-aged woman sitting at the front desk.

"C'mon, it's Christmas Eve!" yelled Charlie "the Ox." Have a heart!" yelled Joey "Limp."

Each of the guys smiled and said, "Merry Christmas," to the woman, who broke into a grin and reluctantly waved them through.

John-John and Frankie entered Joe's room at about the same time that the guys stepped into the elevator. Squinting at John-John, Joe remarked,

"You gotta be John-John. Even though my vision is fuzzy, I can tell it's you just by your height…and that little squirt behind you has gotta be Frankie."

Joe now had five visitors, plus Dr. Goldman and the nurse at his bedside. When Danny and the rest of the crew soon crowded into the room, the nurse yelled, "You guys can't stay! There are way too many people in here! This man needs his rest. I want everyone of you, including you two," pointing to John-John and Frankie, "to get out."

"Ah, go call a cop…we're stayin'!" shouted Donny "Knobhead."

John-John tried to calm the situation by saying, "Listen, Ma'am, we'll all get out and then go in, one at a time, for no more than a minute…Would that be okay?"

"Yeah, that would be okay. But, if you guys don't keep your word, I *will* get a cop…and the first guy that he'll throw out of here will be that goofy lookin' wise guy!" wagging her finger at Donny "Knobhead."

Surprisingly—or maybe not surprisingly—Joe was able to recognize each and every one of the newsstand crew. Over the years he had felt each of their faces, plus he had heard numerous comments about their appearances, as they "ranked" each other out, mocking each other with such comments as: "Danny, your nose is so big that if it was filled with quarters, you'd be as rich as Rockefeller!" or, "Frankie, you're so short, you could play handball against a curb!" The guys made it back to the neighborhood at around five. They were totally elated and truly in the spirit of Christmas. As they noisily neared the Daniels' bay window, Felicia scurried over to the window and peered down. She then tapped on the glass while yelling, "How's Joe?"

John-John looked up and saw Felicia looking dour, with her nose pressed against the cold windowpane in the dimly lit room: "Felicia. Felicia. Open the window."

As she popped her head out the window, he yelled. "Joe's out of his coma, and, somehow, the bullet…your bullet…has caused him to regain his sight."

"You're not kiddin' me, are you?"

"No, of course not."

"It's the truth, Felicia! It's the truth!" yelled Shortie.

"Meet me downstairs in your hallway. I'll fill you in on the details."

"Okay, John-John, I'll be right down."

While he was waiting, he suddenly thought of Charles Dickens' classic, *A Tale of Two Cities*, and paraphrased its well-known opening lines in his mind: *It was the best of times for Joe and his family, and it was the worst of times for Serafina and her family.*

When she opened the hallway's inner door, he noticed tears running down her cheeks; but he gathered that unlike the tears she had been shedding all week, these were tears of joy.

"Oh, Felicia, God works in strange ways. Your accidental shooting of Joe turns out to have been a blessing in disguise."

"Oh, I'm so relieved…I'm so relieved. I still can't believe it. This news makes me feel so much better…It's been a very rough day for me."

"Yeah, I know. I know."

"At least this great news about Joe gives me somethin' to be happy about, today."

As they continued to talk, John-John couldn't help but notice that she was wearing a light-colored, semi-sheer nightgown, which was hardly covered by the black woolen jacket draped over her shoulders. He surmised that she had taken a bath after returning from the burial and had decided to put on her nightclothes because she certainly wasn't going anywhere on Christmas Eve; nor would her family be expecting any visitors that night, given that everyone would be celebrating the holiday with their families and friends.

The hallway was cold—only slightly warmer than the 35-degree outdoor temperature. Even though the hallway was dimly lit by only a 40-watt light bulb, he could clearly see the form of her breasts through her nightgown. It was quite apparent to him that she wasn't wearing a bra, and it was only natural that he would stare down at her breasts instead of looking into her eyes. She interpreted his leering as a signal that he was attracted to her. She lunged forward and kissed him passionately. He didn't resist. Her sudden move surprised and excited him. His feelings for Maria were cast to the inner recesses of his mind as he got into the moment, hugging and kissing Felicia with equal passion. But after about a minute, she forcefully shoved him away while taking two steps back. In a move that he could never have imagined—

and would never forget—she dropped her jacket to the floor and lifted her nightgown up to her chin, exposing her totally nude body.

"John-John, this could be yours…all yours. You can have me. All you have to do is dump Maria."

"What are you doing, Felicia? Have you gone crazy?"

"No, I'm not crazy."

The dim glow of light upon her naked flesh created an alluring and sexy vision—with her sexiness being accentuated by the way her breasts perked up in reaction to the coldness of the hallway. As he gazed at her naked body, he concluded that it rivaled Maria's, although he had never actually seen Maria in the nude.

When she let her nightgown fall back down, she said, "Well, whatta ya say? Me or Maria?"

Her titillating offer had stunned him. He couldn't bring himself to answering her question, although his gut feeling was that Maria was the right girl for him because she was the whole package: a girl with beauty; brains; and a pleasant disposition; while Felicia, though good-looking and shapely, wasn't very intelligent, and more detracting, had a volatile and uneven disposition.

"Well, John-John, me or Maria?"

As her words: *This could be yours…all yours. You can have me…* reverberated in his head, he asked, "Felicia, do you mean you're ready to have sex? Lose your virginity?"

"Yeah, that's what I mean. I'm ready. I'm ready to go all the way…as long as it's with you."

"I thought you were a good Catholic girl who was going to save her virginity for her wedding night."

"Well, I was gonna save myself 'til my wedding night, but ever since this whole thing with my mother and Martucci, I feel like I was raised by a hypocrite…a phony fuckin' hypocrite who watched me like a hawk while Martucci was fucking her behind my father's back!"

"Felicia, I never heard you use the F-word!"

"Well, I'm so mad at my mother that I could just scream!"

He nervously stammered, "So…so…you believe the rumors?"

"Yeah, I believe 'em…The pieces seem to fit. I've seen the way my mother acts when she's around Martucci, and there's a lot of other things, too…Anyway, I know what all you guys want, and I'm sure you're gettin' it from Maria." She then raised her voice, "You've screwed her, haven't you? Haven't you?" John-John remained silent.

"The fact that you're not answering tells me that you *did* screw her…that bitch…that conniving little who-ah! I heard you screwed her right in the newsstand. Is it true! Is it true!"

After about fifteen long seconds, he broke his silence: "Don't dwell on Maria. Don't get yourself so riled up."

"I can't help it. Picturing you with my former good friend doin' it in the newsstand…"

"Felicia, it's time for me to go. We'll talk some more about this when you're calmer. In the meantime, forget about Maria." He then gave her a quick peck on the lips, and said, "Goodnight, Felicia."

As he closed the door behind him, he realized that his words and actions might have unwittingly left her with the impression that the renewal of their relationship might still be possible. *I should've told her flat out that Maria is the girl for me, as hard as that might've been for her to take.*

When he walked past the closed newsstand and turned onto Spring Street, he took note of the many tenement windows with colorful Christmas lights and other decorations. Surely, these lights and decorations were no match for those in such neighborhoods as Bensonhurst, Brooklyn, where the homeowners would try to outdo each other with countless lights, and such eye-catchers as moving reindeer and talking Santas; but the lights shining brightly from the tenement windows were still very uplifting, and they added to the Christmas cheer and joy felt by most people in the neighborhood.

As he neared his apartment building, his thoughts flashed back to the hallway incident. *I can't believe what Felicia just did.* Then, shifting gears, he thought about what kind of advice Joe would give him, if he were around: *I know Joe would tell me not to pass up this chance with Felicia…to strike while the iron is hot…and lie to Maria if she should find out about it.*

As he ran up the three flights of stairs to Apartment 4E, he decided to put the Felicia episode in the back of his mind and focus on the holiday. His appetite for his mother's Feast of the Seven Fishes was heightened by the wonderful aromas of garlic, oil, tomatoes, and fried fish wafting throughout the hallway from the many open apartment doors.

Dinner was almost ready. Angie was busily stirring the linguine and readying the colander, which was always referred to as the "*sculapasta.*"

"Vivian, did you wrap-up Maria's Christmas gift?"

"Yeah, I did, John-John."

"Great! I'll give it to her tomorrow after church."

"You got good taste. It's a pretty silk blouse. I hope you got me a blouse like that for Christmas."

"Don't get your hopes too high, Vivian."

"Yeah, you probably got me the cheapest thing you could find."

Chapter 51: The Truth

Serafina and her children were moping around the apartment, still dressed in their nightclothes, despite the fact that it was well past ten in the morning. Three days had passed since the burial and the reality of the situation was starting to sink in. Occasionally, Serafina would scream out, "Why-ah? Why-ah?" or "You-ah were-ah too young-ah!" Even though she had never been head-over-heels in love with Zeke, their eighteen-year marriage had, on balance, been a good one. He had been a good father to their three children and a hard worker, always providing the basic necessities of life, but not much more. She did love him, but not in the heart-fluttering way she had come to love Orazio.

She decided that she had to visit Orazio to hear what he had to say about Zeke's murder and the rumors that were running rampant around the neighborhood. It was the Friday after Christmas—a day, she believed, would not be a busy workday for his business. She figured he would be alone in his office until the early afternoon.

She walked into her bedroom, took off her nightgown, put on clean underwear and slipped into a black dress. She then spent more than five minutes in front of a mirror applying makeup and lipstick. When she was satisfied with her appearance, she sprayed herself liberally with Chanel No. 5. Despite being in mourning, she still wanted her paramour, Orazio, to find her attractive.

She found Orazio alone in his office and not at all busy. He was a little surprised to see her when she walked in. He had mixed emotions. On one hand, he was madly in love with her, so he longed to be with her. On the other hand, he was burdened by the guilt of having killed her husband, so he wanted to avoid her for as long as he could. He didn't know if he should tell her the truth or if he should continue his charade.

They greeted each other cordially—more like friends than lovers—kissing each other on the cheeks. Slipping seamlessly into their Neapolitan dialect, they soon began to talk about the obvious: Zeke's death.

"This is a very sad time for you, Serafina."

"Yes, it is, and even more so for my children. Plus, I don't know how we will ever get along without Zeke's paycheck."

"Did he have any life insurance?"

"Very little…$750."

"Well, you won't have to worry about money for a while."

"Why?"

"Because I'm going to pay you Zeke's salary every week for the next two years."

"Really?"

"Yes, really."

"Oh, You're most generous Orazio. *Grazie, Grazie.*"

"You know I wouldn't do this for anyone else. I'm only doing this for you because I truly love you and I don't want to see you and your children suffer."

Serafina began to show signs of nervousness—so much so that Orazio could sense that something was bothering her. So, he took the initiative and asked, "What's wrong?"

"Orazio, I have to ask you something…Believe me, it pains me to ask you this."

"Go ahead. What is it?"

"Did you kill Zeke?"

"What! Why would you ask me such a question!"

"Because the rumor all over the neighborhood is that you killed him while the two of you were arguing over me."

Taking a deep breath and exhaling slowly, he replied, "Okay, here's the truth." Following with another deep breath and exhaling even more slowly, he continued, "Zeke came here on that Monday evening with fire in his eyes. He had learned about our affair and was trying to choke me to death. While

I was gasping for air and close to passing out, I reached into this desk drawer, pulled out my gun and shot him."

"So, the rumors are true!" she screamed, somewhat in disbelief.

"Yes, I'm sorry, but the rumors are true…but…but…I shot him in self-defense. Believe me, I wasn't trying to kill him. I was just trying to wound him, so I could stop him from choking me to death. You know how strong Zeke was. I could never have fought him off. If I hadn't pulled the trigger, I would have been the dead one." Tears rolled down his cheeks as he continued, "Listen, Serafina, I am constantly haunted by what I have done. I didn't want things to work out this way. Besides, I really liked him…and he was my best worker."

"You know, none of this would have happened if we hadn't fallen in love with each other, Orazio."

"Yes, that's true, but it was fate…it was the force of destiny… *la forza del destino*. I love you now even more than I ever have. Just being near you sets my heart on fire with a burning passion for you. In fact, if it weren't so totally disrespectful to the memory of your late husband, I would want to take you in my arms and make love to you right now. You own my heart, Serafina…you own my heart."

Serafina put her left hand on her cheek and stared at him with her mouth wide open. His romantic words had gotten to her, as they had on many other occasions.

Orazio continued, "Now you know the truth. My fate is in your hands. You can go to the police and have me arrested, or you can learn to live with what I just told you…and maybe, someday, we can be together again."

She continued to stare at him without saying a word for nearly a minute. Then, she said in a warm tone, "Orazio, I *do* believe that you shot Zeke in self-defense. I really do. It's too bad that things had to work out the way they did, but I understand and I forgive you. Don't worry. I won't have you arrested. I couldn't do that to you."

"*Grazie*, Serafina. You have taken a huge weight off my shoulders."

"Orazio, I too share some of the blame because none of this would have happened if I hadn't become your lover…your *innamorata*."

"Well, as I said before, our falling in love was *la forza del destino*…and, you know we can't control our destinies."

"Maybe, in a few weeks, if I'm feeling better, we can meet in Brooklyn."

"That would be so wonderful, Serafina…so wonderful."

"Yes, it would be."

"Wait a minute. Don't leave yet."

Reaching into the top drawer of his desk, he pulled out a sealed manila envelope and handed it to her. "Here's Zeke's salary. It's in cash and it's even $20 more than he usually took home. Come here every Friday after you come home from work to pick up his salary. As I promised, I will keep paying his salary for the next two years, no matter what happens between us."

"*Grazie*, Orazio." Then, she kissed him on the lips, holding the kiss for several seconds. At that point, Orazio knew that they would soon be resuming their romance.

As the cold December wind bit Serafina's face on the way back to her apartment, she wrestled with what she had just done. *Should I have forgiven him for killing Zeke? Was it right not to have him arrested?* She concluded that she had done the right thing. She truly believed that Orazio had acted in self-defense, and she couldn't bear the thought of him—her *innamorato*—going on trial and possibly to prison; plus, if she were to have him arrested, she certainly wouldn't be receiving Zeke's salary for the next two years—money she surely would need.

The days passed rather slowly for Serafina and her children, even though their monotony would be broken up to some degree when family or friends would occasionally stop by to console them. The visitors would bring fruit, candy, pastries or Italian cookies— or combinations thereof—since they would never dream of coming empty handed; it was the Italian way and the neighborhood way. Espresso and regular coffee would be served to the visitors to go along with the sweets; it was expected that the grieving family would do so. During the week following the funeral, Felicia would brew three-to-four pots of espresso and coffee every day. Thus, Serafina and Felicia, and to a lesser extent, Francesca and Little Zeke, were basically living on sugar and caffeine. Sleeping became difficult for Serafina and Felicia, in particular, because the large amounts of sugar and caffeine exacerbated the adverse effects that depression and melancholy would normally have on one's ability to sleep.

On the morning of New Year's Eve, John-John, Danny, Frankie and Shortie went to St. Vincent's to see Joe, who was scheduled to be released around noon. When they entered his room they found him dressed in street clothes, sitting on a chair next to his bed. He had a bandage wrapped around his head, which was extra-thick behind his right ear where the bullet had been removed the day before.

"How you doin'?" asked Shortie.

"I feel a little weak, but I'm real happy to get the hell outta here. The last couple of days in here, I couldn't get any rest. Every time I was sleepin', some nurse would come by and wake me up for one reason or another. It's true what they say… 'you can't get any rest in a fuckin' hospital.'"

"Hey, Joe," asked John-John, "How long before you're back at the newsstand?"

"I don't know. The doctors want me to take it easy for a few months. They wanna see me next week and every week or two for the next three months. They're gonna check my vision and they're eventually gonna decide if they should remove the dislodged cataract. Also, they're gonna make sure the bullet wound is healin' good…You know, I was very lucky that the bullet didn't damage my brain."

"Oh, your brain was already damaged," joked Frankie. "If the bullet had gone into your brain, it might've done you some good."

"Ah, kiss my ass, you little shrimp," replied Joe, as he broke into a smile.

"Well, Joe, at least you'll be home tonight to watch Guy Lombardo bring in the new year."

"Yeah, Shortie…if I manage to keep myself awake."

"Oh, just tell your wife to put on a nurse's outfit and wake you up just like they do in this place," quipped Danny.

Joe smiled then added, "You know, I've never seen television. It was invented long after I went blind. I'm really looking forward to seein' a television show."

At that point, Joe's wife and two daughters arrived to take him home. Joe's son-in-law, Paul, was waiting in his car, double-parked in front of the hospital. After about five minutes of chitchat, the guys bade Joe farewell.

"Remember, I expect you guys to come up to the Bronx and visit me."

"Don't worry," responded Frankie, "We'll be comin' every week to break your balls."

"Yeah, we don't want you to get bored," added John-John.

At around four, John-John telephoned Maria to wish her Happy New Year. She surprised him when she invited him to stop by to meet her parents during the New Year's Eve party that her family was hosting for some friends and *paisani.*

"Thanks, Maria, but I can't make it. We're going to my grandmother's apartment on Broome Street, tonight. All my aunts, uncles and cousins will be there."

"Oh, can't you come up for even a few minutes?"

"No, I really don't think I'll have the time."

Actually, he could have found some time to break away from the gathering at his grandmother's apartment, but he was apprehensive about meeting her parents. *If I meet them, they'll think that Maria and I will soon be heading to the altar. I know the way those real Sicilians think.*

"Oh, c'mon, John-John."

"No, I really won't be able to make it. But, please wish your parents Happy New Year…*Buon Capo D'Anno*…from me."

"Oh, very well…Happy New Year, John-John. I love you."

"Happy New year, Maria. I love you, too."

Within seconds of hanging up the phone, he dialed Felicia to try to cheer her up the best he could. He was hoping that anyone but Serafina would answer the phone. He was happy to hear Little Zeke pick up after the third ring.

"Hold on, John-John, I'll get my sister."

"Hi Felicia, it's John-John."

"Don't you think I know your voice by now. You don't have to tell me who you are."

"Yeah, I guess you should recognize my voice by now…Felicia, I just want to say that I hope 1964 will be a much better year for you than this year was."

"Yeah, I hope so…By the way, I'm alone in the living room, now, so I can talk…Listen, I want you to know that the offer I made to you in my hallway on Christmas Eve still stands. I meant what I said. I'll give myself to you as long as you dump Maria…I want *you* to be the one. I've been dreamin' about it every night. In my dreams, I can actually feel you inside me…like we are one. John-John, I love you. Do you love me? Tell me you love me."

He didn't know what to say. She seemed so fragile; so depressed. In a way, he did love her, but not in the same way he loved Maria. After an interminably long pause, he reluctantly replied, "Yeah…I love you, Felicia."

He didn't want to mislead her, but he knew that his words would help her get through the last difficult days of the holiday period; but then what? He didn't know; he would cross that bridge when he would come to it.

Chapter 52: Auld Lang Syne

New Year's Eve at John-John's grandmother's apartment could best be described as a warm, loving, fun-filled commotion. It was amazing how the tiny four-room apartment could somehow accommodate over two-dozen family members, many of whom were milling about in the cramped spaces, talking to each other while others played in a penny-ante poker game in the living room. John-John was happy to get into the card game—which was usually reserved for the older folks—and he managed to win a hand for his father, who had taken a fifteen-minute break. The pot didn't amount to much because they were only playing for pennies and nickels; but winning it caused him to smile from ear-to-ear.

Just before eleven, the poker game was interrupted to clear the table for the traditional New Year's Eve sweets: pastries, cookies and Italian candies, which would be served along with coffee and espresso. The old 19"-Dumont TV was then turned on to CBS's *New Year's Eve with Guy Lombardo and his Royal Canadians,* which was being telecast from New York's Waldorf Astoria. Everyone, even the youngsters, seemed to enjoy the big band sounds of Guy Lombardo's orchestra.

"Someday, I wanna be at the Waldorf on New Year's Eve dancing to Guy Lombardo and wearin' one of those funny hats," said John-John's Aunt Connie.

"Yeah, so would I," added John-John's mom, "But I hear it costs an arm and a leg."

Several minutes before midnight, the broadcast switched from the Waldorf's ballroom to Times Square. As usual, there was an amazingly large crowd gathered at Times Square—mostly, out-of-towners. Everyone in the apartment gathered close together, which wasn't very hard to do in the tiny flat. All joined the announcer in the countdown: "Ten, nine, eight…three, two, one…Happy New Year!" Guy Lombardo's signature song, *Auld Lang Syne*, could be faintly heard in the background as everyone hugged and kissed and blew horns to usher in 1964.

While most of the family was still wishing each other Happy New Year, John-John's oldest cousin, Sonny, motioned to him and cousins Johnny and Dominick to follow him. He led them into the bedroom and opened the window. He then turned around and grabbed a broken, 25-year-old Philco radio from the night table and flung it right out the window, while yelling, "Happy New Year!" at the top of his lungs. When the radio, which was about the size of a breadbox, hit the sidewalk three stories below, it broke into a hundred pieces. Soon, one could hear the sounds of other "stuff" crashing onto the sidewalks, punctuated by intermittent firework blasts.

It was an old neighborhood tradition to throw broken items, or things one no longer wanted, out the window at midnight to symbolically welcome in the new year. Those in the know usually avoided being out on the streets between midnight and 12:15 a.m. out of a fear of being hit by a flying object. The undisputed neighborhood record for the biggest and heaviest object ever thrown out a window as the new year rang-in was an old-style washing machine—one with a round tub and a mechanical wringer on top.

John-John returned to the living room in a pensive mood, thinking about what the new year might have in store for him. He wondered if he should take the bull by the horns and tell Felicia that Maria is the girl for him; or if he should take the easier path: letting things work out by themselves. Yet, the more he thought about the two girls in his life, the more confused and fickle he became. Felicia's surprising and enticing offer had struck a chord in him, causing him to try to assess and re-assess his true feelings for both girls. Uncertainty reigned in his mind as black and white shifted to gray. *Maria is a great girl. But who knows, Felicia might be the right girl for me…but…*

"Hey, John-John, use your long arms and grab me a cannoli," demanded Cousin Annette.

When he didn't react, she poked him in the ribs and loudly repeated her demand, adding, "Are you goin' deaf?"

"Oh, I'm sorry, Annette, I guess I didn't hear you, before, with all this noise."

He reached over his Uncle Mario, who was seated at the table, and picked up two cannolis from the platter. *I might as well get one for myself*, he thought.

While munching on his cannoli, alternating visions flashed before his eyes: Felicia with her nightgown raised to her chin seeking to rebel against her mother, and Maria, "losing her virginity" to him in the newsstand. *Who loves me more?* he wondered, thinking, as the immature youth that he was, that he could somehow quantify love and, maybe, use that as a yardstick for deciding between the two girls. Bottom line: he was one mixed-up young man.

Meanwhile, up in the Bronx, Joe was totally enjoying the New Year's broadcast. He had heard Guy Lombardo many, many times, but this was the first time that he was seeing him and his famous orchestra in action; and it was the first time that he had seen the Times Square New Year's celebration. As Guy Lombardo's orchestra accompanied the vocalists to the tune of *Happy Days Are Here Again*, a tear rolled down Joe's right cheek. He fervently hoped the song was the harbinger of brighter and happier days to come.

The End

Made in United States
North Haven, CT
27 January 2023